THE GATE
OF HEAVEN

BOOKS BY GILBERT MORRIS

THE HOUSE OF WINSLOW SERIES

1. *The Honorable Imposter*
2. *The Captive Bride*
3. *The Indentured Heart*
4. *The Gentle Rebel*
5. *The Saintly Buccaneer*
6. *The Holy Warrior*
7. *The Reluctant Bridegroom*
8. *The Last Confederate*
9. *The Dixie Widow*
10. *The Wounded Yankee*
11. *The Union Belle*
12. *The Final Adversary*
13. *The Crossed Sabres*
14. *The Valiant Gunman*
15. *The Gallant Outlaw*
16. *The Jeweled Spur*
17. *The Yukon Queen*
18. *The Rough Rider*
19. *The Iron Lady*
20. *The Silver Star*
21. *The Shadow Portrait*
22. *The White Hunter*
23. *The Flying Cavalier*
24. *The Glorious Prodigal*
25. *The Amazon Quest*
26. *The Golden Angel*
27. *The Heavenly Fugitive*
28. *The Fiery Ring*
29. *The Pilgrim Song*
30. *The Beloved Enemy*
31. *The Shining Badge*

CHENEY DUVALL, M.D.[1]

1. *The Stars for a Light*
2. *Shadow of the Mountains*
3. *A City Not Forsaken*
4. *Toward the Sunrising*
5. *Secret Place of Thunder*
6. *In the Twilight, in the Evening*
7. *Island of the Innocent*
8. *Driven With the Wind*

CHENEY AND SHILOH: THE INHERITANCE[1]

1. *Where Two Seas Met*
2. *The Moon by Night*

THE SPIRIT OF APPALACHIA[2]

1. *Over the Misty Mountains*
2. *Beyond the Quiet Hills*
3. *Among the King's Soldiers*
4. *Beneath the Mockingbird's Wing*
5. *Around the River's Bend*

LIONS OF JUDAH

1. *Heart of a Lion*
2. *No Woman So Fair*
3. *The Gate of Heaven*

[1]with Lynn Morris   [2]with Aaron McCarver

GILBERT MORRIS

LIONS OF JUDAH

THE GATE OF HEAVEN

BETHANYHOUSE

MINNEAPOLIS, MINNESOTA

The Gate of Heaven
Copyright © 2004
Gilbert Morris

Cover design by Lookout Design Group, Inc.

Unless otherwise identified, Scripture quotations are from the HOLY BIBLE, NEW
INTERNATIONAL VERSION®. Copyright © 1973, 1978, 1984 by International Bible Society.
Used by permission of Zondervan Publishing House. All rights reserved.

All rights reserved. No part of this publication may be reproduced, stored in a retrieval system, or
transmitted in any form or by any means—electronic, mechanical, photocopying, recording, or
otherwise—without the prior written permission of the publisher and copyright owners.

Published by Bethany House Publishers
11400 Hampshire Avenue South
Bloomington, Minnesota 55438
www.bethanyhouse.com

Bethany House Publishers is a Division of
Baker Book House Company, Grand Rapids, Michigan.

Printed in the United States of America

Library of Congress Cataloging-in-Publication Data

Morris, Gilbert.
    The gate of heaven / by Gilbert Morris.
        p.   cm. — (Lions of Judah ; Bk. 3)
    ISBN 0-7642-2683-5 (pbk.)
    1. Jacob (Biblical patriarch)—Fiction.   2. Bible. O.T. Genesis—History of Biblical events—
Fiction.   I. Title.
    PS3563.O8742G32   2004
    813'.54—dc22   2003022372

To Moody Adams, Evangelist

In one of his lyrics Shakespeare asked the question: "Tell me, where is fancy bred, or in the heart or in the head?"

In other words, does genius come from the intellect or from the emotions?

We all know the penalty of a sermon that is all "head," for all of us have been bored to tears by sterile intellectualism untouched by passion, just as we have been exposed to teachings that are totally emotional, devoid of serious thought.

Moody Adams is one of those rare servants of God who is blessed with both a burning heart and a penetrating intellect. Whether on the printed page or by means of the spoken word, this man speaks the truths we desperately need to hear with compassion, zeal, and bare-handed honesty.

In a day when some have lost their integrity and set their sails to catch the prevailing wind of popular opinion, Evangelist Moody Adams proclaims fearlessly the Good News that our world is starving to hear.

Our poor world needs men and woman who sound the trumpet with the courage of the Old Testament prophet and with the burning heart and clear vision of the New Testament apostle.

Brother Moody, you are an evangelist in the richest and purest sense of that word. May God continue to use you in the work He has given you to do.

GILBERT MORRIS spent ten years as a pastor before becoming Professor of English at Ouachita Baptist University in Arkansas and earning a Ph.D. at the University of Arkansas. During the summers of 1984 and 1985, he did postgraduate work at the University of London. A prolific writer, he has had over 25 scholarly articles and 200 poems published in various periodicals, and over the past years he has had more than 180 books published. His family includes three grown children, and he and his wife live in Alabama.

PART ONE

THE BROTHERS

CHAPTER

I

A war chariot cut a path between low-lying hills, its wheels swirling up a pillar of dust and crushing the delicate wild flowers that dotted the land. The horses' hooves thundered across the valley, breaking the silence of late afternoon. With reins in one hand, a whip in the other, and a fierce-looking sword dangling from his belt, a dark-skinned man wearing a bronze helmet drove the animals without mercy. Beside him lay a double-convex war bow, flanked by newly sharpened arrows, their bronze tips gleaming in the sunshine.

The driver yanked the horses to a halt and turned to the two men behind him who were clinging to the sides of the chariot.

"Magon, what's that camp up ahead?" he demanded as he sliced the air with his whip, indicating the tents and flocks they were approaching.

"I don't know, sir, but I hope they've got food. My stomach thinks I've been dead for hours!" The speaker was the shorter and stockier of the two men in the back of the chariot. A scar distorted his features, dragging his right eye downward into a squint and pulling the right side of his mouth up into a perpetual sneer. He shielded his eyes from the sunlight and peered toward the camp. "Oh, they're nothing but a bunch of Hebrews, Captain Ahad. They won't have any food fit for real men."

"Magon, you'd eat a dead buzzard," Ahad snorted.

The soldier shook his head. "They eat lentils and milk, sir. A man needs meat." He laughed. "We'll take one of those fat sheep over there— and the best wine they've got, eh, Remez?"

The third man in the chariot was tall and lean, with sharp, hawklike features. He wore a bronze helmet like his two companions, but his face was not as marked by cruelty. He gave the camp a quick examination and shook his head slowly. "I know this tribe," he said. "This is the camp I tried to tell you about, Captain Ahad. From what I hear, their leader is a man with strange powers."

Ahad stared disdainfully at Remez. "You told me, but it made no sense."

"Of course it didn't," Magon retorted. "The Hebrews are all crazy!"

"These Hebrews are a strange people," Remez said thoughtfully, ignoring his companion. "I know a little something about them."

"What do you need to know?" Ahad shrugged. "They're like those stupid sheep out there. Which gods do they worship?"

"Well," Remez said slowly, "they say there's only one god."

The two men stared at Remez and then Ahad guffawed. "They probably can't afford more than one."

Magon joined in with the joke, but Remez made no reply; he simply shrugged as the three men surveyed the scene again. Black tents sprawled across the landscape, and a line of donkeys waited patiently for their masters to finish loading them for a trip. Farther on, a boy drove six white goats into a shed built of saplings. Nearby, a woman was churning cream in a goatskin suspended over a wooden frame. As she rocked it back and forth her eyes turned toward the strangers, as did the eyes of others throughout the busy camp, until gradually everyone was staring at the war chariot.

"We'll take whatever goods we want," Ahad sneered, winking lewdly and adding, "We may even borrow some of their women for a while."

Magon smiled broadly. "I'll take that one over there." He indicated a young woman with glossy black hair who was grinding grain with a round stone. "Come on," he said. "Let's go take what we want. If they don't like it, we'll cut their throats." He pulled a wicked-looking dagger from his belt, licked the blade, and laughed.

A troubled look crossed Remez's face. "I don't know how wise that would be. As I told you, their leader is an unusual man—and one not to be trifled with. I've heard my grandfather tell about him."

"Humph!" Ahad snorted. "I'd fight their chief any day." Then as if doubting his own hubris, he asked Remez, "What else do you know about this chief of theirs?"

"Well, I know his name is Abraham and that he's very old now, but my grandfather told me he came up against him in a war once."

"What kind of a war?" Ahad grunted with disdain, gesturing toward the Hebrew men who stood watching, armed only with shepherds' staves. "They're obviously not fighters."

"My grandfather said the army he was with thought that too. They captured one of Abraham's relatives—some fellow named Lot. Abraham came tearing after them with a small army of Hebrews and rescued him."

"Your grandfather must not have had much of an army, then." Ahad shrugged.

"On the contrary, sir. My grandfather said the fighters he was with were the best. But this Hebrew leader—this Abraham—he's got some magical powers, or so my grandfather believed."

Ahad slapped the backs of the horses with his whip and laughed coarsely. "A magician, eh? Well, we'll make him do some tricks for us, then!" His white teeth gleamed as he grinned. "Mind you, the prettiest woman belongs to me!"

"Isaac, look! A war chariot with three soldiers in it."

Isaac turned to look in the direction Rebekah indicated. "Those are Hittite warriors," he said uneasily. "They're always causing trouble."

"Don't worry about them. We'll feed them and they won't bother us."

Isaac looked carefully at Rebekah, who was sitting on a wooden chest, holding her belly. He noticed the pained expression on her face and asked, concerned, "Are you hurting, dear?"

Even this late in her pregnancy, Rebekah was a beautiful woman, with skin like alabaster, dark, lustrous eyes, and coal black hair. But the pain she felt now was clearly etched in the lines of her face. "It's like a . . . a *war* going on inside me, Isaac," she whispered. "Feel."

Isaac leaned forward and put his hand on Rebekah's swollen abdomen. His eyes opened with astonishment as he felt the movement. "That's not natural, Rebekah!"

"I know it. I don't know what's wrong."

"Have you talked with the midwife?"

"Bethez insists that having twins is just harder," Rebekah said, shaking her head.

"But even so, they shouldn't be giving you such pain already." Isaac would have said more, but he saw that the chariot had drawn up to the center of the camp. The three warriors got out, and one of them pulled the horses and chariot to a nearby scrub tree to tie up the animals. "I wish they had gone on," Isaac murmured.

The trio wandered brazenly around the camp, making crude comments about the women. Isaac kept his eyes on the largest soldier, taking him for the leader. The shortest of the three grabbed a girl, who kicked and screamed for help. Isaac stepped forward and spoke to the leader. "Sir, my name is Isaac. Tell your man to release the girl."

"My name is Ahad," the captain announced boldly, ignoring Isaac's demand. "We require food and wine."

Isaac kept his eye on the big man but was most concerned about the girl. The short, swarthy soldier was laughing at her attempts to escape. "Have him turn the young woman loose," Isaac implored. "Then we'll sell you some food."

"Sell! Nothing was said about selling! We're your guests." Ahad put his hand on the hilt of his sword, his eyes mocking the smaller man. "I advise you to keep us happy. It'll be safer for you, shepherd!"

Unarmed, Isaac hesitated. He knew the soldiers would take whatever they wanted, and he feared for the safety of the women. "You must not molest our young women," he said firmly but quietly. "Tell your man to release the girl, and I'll have a meal prepared."

Ahad paid no attention to Isaac's words or the young woman's cries. "Where is this magician I've been told about?"

"Magician? We have no magician."

"Oh no? What about the old man called Abraham? Bring him out."

"That is my father, but he is no magician."

Ahad marched forward and stared down at Rebekah, who was wearing a dark blue dress and a scarf over her head. The warrior put his hand under her chin. "Well, now, she's a pretty one! Is this your wife?"

"Yes," Isaac said, his heart racing. He wanted to lash out and knock the man backward, but he hesitated.

"Well, you've been doing your duty, I see. I don't blame you with such a pretty bauble as this."

Isaac stepped forward despite his fear. "Take your hands off of her!" he ordered, but his voice sounded thin.

Ahad easily pushed him backward. "Why, you puny little shepherd! Keep your mouth shut or I'll slit your throat!"

The short man laughed and drew the girl he was holding closer. Her eyes were large with fear, and she begged, "Sir, don't let him do this to me!"

"That's right, shepherd." Ahad grinned cruelly. "Don't let him do that. Get yourself a sword. Do some magic for us. Maybe you can beat him."

"That'll be enough!"

Ahad turned quickly to see a figure that seemed to have materialized from nowhere. The speaker was a tall man wearing a simple shepherd's costume, a staff in his hand, his silver hair tied back with a leather thong. Though he was quite old, there was still strength to be seen in the cords of his arms and the depth of his chest. His lean and rugged face reminded Ahad of a predatory bird—especially the dark eyes that were now fixed on him.

"Well, is this Abraham, the famous magician?" Ahad laughed and winked at Magon. "Let's see some magic, sorcerer! Make our swords turn to dust!"

Abraham was unperturbed by the man's arrogance.

His calmness angered Ahad, who swaggered over to stand before him. "So you're the big warrior I've heard about, are you? Old man, get out of my sight or I'll gut you like a fish!"

"Take your men and leave," Abraham ordered quietly. "Your manners are bad."

"Teach him about manners, Captain!" Magon shouted, waving one of his fists at Abraham.

The captured girl took advantage of the moment and yanked herself free. The burly soldier shouted and took a few steps after her, but she was too fleet. Spewing a stream of expletives, Magon returned to stand beside his captain. Remez stood apart from the others, carefully watching Abraham.

"I don't think you're a magician, old man, or a warrior either!" Ahad snapped, drawing his sword.

Abraham did not move.

Then Magon yanked a curved dagger from his belt and waved it at Abraham. "He's as ancient as the hills, Captain. I'm not afraid of this old man."

Ahad felt rattled by the old man's calm yet bold demeanor, but being a captain he could not lose face before his men. He cut the air with his sword and laughed roughly. "I think I'll just cut off your beard!" As he moved forward, Rebekah uttered a cry of distress.

Ahad reached out to grab Abraham's beard, raising his sword with the other hand. But Abraham's staff shot out, catching the Hittite in the pit of the stomach and bringing him to an abrupt halt. The breath gushed out of his mouth as Abraham circled his staff in the air. He struck again, this time catching Ahad on the side of the head. The bronze helmet prevented the warrior's skull from being crushed, but the force of the blow drove him to the ground.

Magon stared blankly at his captain, who lay motionless, blood seeping out from under the bronze helmet and spreading into the dust. The warrior threw himself forward with a wild yell, his dagger raised, but once again the staff in Abraham's hands moved swiftly. The butt of it took the soldier right under his chin, striking him in the throat. Magon gagged, dropping his dagger and grabbing wildly at his throat, his eyes rolling upward as he staggered back.

Then Abraham faced the third soldier. "What about you?"

"I'm not in this!" Remez's voice was high and unsteady, for he could scarcely believe his eyes. His companions were tough, hardened warriors, but Abraham had swept them aside as a man sweeps away troublesome flies. Remez recalled his grandfather's tales about this fierce old fighter. The sight of his two companions—the one lying lifeless on the ground, the other staggering, clutching his throat—kept Remez utterly still.

"You Hittites are a wearisome bunch," Abraham commented, as untroubled and calm as a man could be. He studied Remez thoughtfully. "I bought a burial cave from a Hittite named Ephron for my wife Sarah after she died. Do you know him?"

"Yes, sir. He . . . he was a distant relation of mine." This was a lie, but Remez thought it might pacify the tall man, who held him with a steady gaze.

"You need to learn some manners from your forefathers."

"Yes, master, that is probably true."

Abraham signaled to some young men who had gathered. "Put the captain in his chariot and help these fellows get on their way."

Remez quickly helped the young Hebrews pick up Ahad, who still did not move. They carried him to the chariot and unceremoniously dumped him in. Magon put up no argument as Remez grabbed his arm and piloted him to the chariot. His face was pale, and he could not speak because of the damage to his throat from the fierce blow. Still making gagging noises, he slumped down in the back next to the unconscious captain.

Remez untied the horses and took the helm. He slapped the animals with the reins, and they surged forward. Remez took one backward look and saw Abraham staring at him with a mild expression on his face. Sweat popped out on the soldier's forehead. "That old man could have killed all three of us!" He glanced at Ahad's bloody head and grimaced. "I don't think the captain will want anything more to do with those Hebrews!"

Abraham watched the dust from the chariot grow smaller in the distance. He turned and smiled at his son, who was pale and shaken. "Those Hittites are arrogant at times."

"I-I'm glad you came along, Father."

Abraham did not answer, turning his attention toward Rebekah instead. She was trembling and swaying back and forth, her mouth open and a distressed look in her eyes. "Here, Isaac. Let's get your wife inside the tent where she can lie down."

"Yes, of course, Father."

The two got on either side of Rebekah, lifting her by the arms. They half carried her into Isaac's tent and lowered her gently onto the mat. She lay on her back, holding her stomach and gasping.

Abraham knelt beside her, compassion in his eyes. "Are you all right, daughter?"

"Oh, Father . . . it's like a battle going on inside me."

"Maybe two babies together are hard for a woman, but you'll be fine." Abraham rose and stood back while Isaac sat down beside Rebekah and took her hand. He comforted her, rubbing her belly and muttering consoling sounds. Finally, after she began to breathe more easily, he rose and stepped outside with his father.

"You're going to be a proud man, my son," Abraham said, putting his hand on his son's shoulder. "There's nothing like being a father. I've told you many times how long I waited for you, and how proud and happy I was when God Most High sent you to me and your mother."

Isaac had heard the story all of his life, how his mother had been childless until well past childbearing age. But God had appeared to his parents and told them that Sarah would have a child. Abraham and Sarah had never let their son forget that he was a very special gift from the Lord.

Right now, however, Isaac was not feeling particularly special. His mind was troubled over the scene with the Hittites. He stared at the ground, tracing a pattern in the dust with the toe of his sandal. "I should have fought those men."

"No, that would not have been wise," Abraham countered.

Isaac looked up, misery in his mild face. "Ishmael would have fought them."

"I suppose he would have."

At one time Abraham had fervently hoped that his firstborn son, Ishmael, would be the chosen of God to carry on the family line. But Ishmael was the son of Hagar, a mere bondservant, and God had made it clear that Isaac was the true son, the one chosen to carry on that line.

Abraham noticed the troubled look on his son's face. "You are the promised son, Isaac. There is no other like you, and I thank God for you every day of my life."

Isaac's heart grew warm at his father's praises, for he loved him dearly. He had always felt inadequate, however, compared to his stronger half brother, wondering if his father did not favor Ishmael over him. Isaac had never been a violent man and was not given to fighting, so he could not compete with Ishmael in battle. But Isaac was an excellent herdsman and took good care of his father's flocks, helping the family to prosper. Still, even after all these years, he sometimes wondered if that was enough.

"Go in and sit beside Rebekah, son," Abraham said, breaking into his thoughts. "She needs you at this time."

"Yes, Father."

Going back in the tent, Isaac sat down beside Rebekah. She reached out her hand, and he caught it and held it next to his cheek.

"Stay with me, husband. I'm so afraid!"

"Of course I will." He held her hand in both of his and then kissed it. He reached out and caressed her cheek and saw that this pleased her.

"You're such a gentle man," she said, smiling up at him. "You always were."

"I wish I were tougher like my father—or like Ishmael."

"No! Don't ever wish that," Rebekah responded. "You're just the husband I need."

"I don't know, Rebekah. I didn't even court you. My father arranged our marriage."

"That doesn't matter."

Isaac smiled at her but wondered if she really meant her words. After all, it had been his father who had sent his friend and the steward of his house, Eliezer, to find a bride for him.

For Rebekah's part, perhaps she did, at times, wish that Isaac were more forceful. But she had spoken the truth. He was a gentle man, exactly the kind of husband she needed.

"I've thought so much lately of how I was unable to have children and how you prayed for me, Isaac." She squeezed his hand and elicited a smile, despite his discomfort. "You prayed, and God Most High answered your prayer. I think that's more important than being able to fight."

Her words pleased him, and he leaned over and kissed her cheek. "I hope our son is just like you. Or better still, since we're going to have two babies, I hope one of them will be a beautiful *girl* just like you."

Rebekah gripped Isaac's hand. She would not have been so frightened if she carried only one baby in her womb, but she feared that the birth of twins would be more difficult than she could bear. She lay still as Isaac began to sing to her in his soothing voice. He was the best singer in the tribe, and he often made up love songs just for her that no one else ever heard. Rebekah clung to his hand and then whispered, "Sing to me some more, husband!"

Rebekah awoke in the darkness, the babies within her stirring as if they were fighting to find their exit. Isaac was gone, for he sometimes went to check on the flocks at night. Fearful at being alone, she began to pray, remembering her father-in-law's many encouragements to call on God often. *"Keep praying, daughter, and one day God Most High will speak to you."*

Rebekah did pray often, but she had never experienced the presence of God—at least not like the personal encounters Abraham described. "Oh, God, why do I feel like this? Something terrible is happening, and I am afraid! Please, God Most High, give me peace!"

Even as she prayed Rebekah became aware of a presence in her tent. It was so strong she thought at first Isaac had returned, but then she knew that could not be. The tent was no longer dark; a light was glowing directly in front of her. Unlike the light of a candle or of an oil lamp, it was pure, strong, and steady. Intense fear paralyzed her. She lay absolutely still as the light grew stronger, and finally she whispered, "O God Most High, is it you?"

Then a voice spoke to her—so gentle she could not be sure whether she heard it with her ears or discerned it in her heart. It was tender, yet strong. Powerful words filled her, words she knew she would never forget:

"Two nations are in your womb, and two peoples from within you will be separated; one people will be stronger than the other, and the older will serve the younger."

Then the voice grew fainter and repeated the last part of the prophecy: *"The older will serve the younger. Do not forget. . . ."*

Rebekah's vision blurred as her eyes filled with tears. She wiped them away and stared into the darkness. The strange light had dimmed, leaving her alone once again. She lay perfectly still, hardly daring to breathe, repeating what she had heard word for word, over and over, until the message was burned in her heart forever. Even though she did not understand the prophecy, she was filled with joy, for now she had met the God of

Abraham, the One who was all-powerful!

She laid her hands on her stomach and smiled. The children in her womb were peaceful and still. When her husband returned and lay down beside her, she whispered, "Isaac?"

"Yes."

"I . . . a strange thing has happened."

"What is it, wife?" Isaac listened as she spoke, and finally, when she fell silent, he said, "It must have been a dream, Rebekah."

Rebekah did not argue, but she *knew* it was no dream! She had been wide awake, and the words were etched on her spirit and her mind. She put out her hand, and Isaac held it. Firmly she said, "It was no dream, husband—and the older will serve the younger."

———————

Old Bethez was the best midwife in the tribe and had witnessed hundreds of births. But she had never seen anything like this one! They had called her in the middle of the night, but she was used to that. It was often the time that little ones chose to make their entrance into the world. She did not hurry on her way to Isaac and Rebekah's tent. After all, this was the woman's first birth, and it would be long and difficult, especially as she was having twins. When Bethez and her assistant, Naomi, arrived at Rebekah's tent, they were shocked to find that the labor had progressed so rapidly that the first infant was already emerging. The midwives rushed to assist, ushering the panicked father out of the tent as quickly as possible. Bethez soothed the mother, encouraging her to push and help the baby make its way out. As Rebekah strained with the effort, Bethez grabbed ahold of the baby's shoulders and expertly guided the baby out fully. Both midwives gasped at the strange sight. The boy infant was covered with reddish hair! As they started to remove the child, they noticed something even stranger.

As the second baby emerged, Naomi whispered, "Why, the second is holding on to his brother's heel!"

"I have never seen the like!" Bethez exclaimed, breathless. "It must mean something, but I surely do not know what."

After the two women had cleaned and swaddled the babies and tended to Rebekah, Bethez said to Naomi, "Go bring the master in."

At the midwife's invitation, Isaac rushed to his wife's side, taking her limp hand in his own and kissing it tenderly. Even though the birth had been quick, he had suffered through his own fear of the midwives not showing up in time and the heart-wrenching helplessness of hearing his wife's cries of pain. Now Isaac gently smoothed back her hair, damp and matted from the agonizing ordeal, and whispered, "Are you all right, my love?"

Rebekah tried to raise her head to see what the midwives were doing but did not have the strength. "My babies ... my babies ..." she answered weakly. "Where are my babies?"

Bethez turned and came to her side, holding a baby in each arm and smiling broadly. "You have two fine sons." She helped Rebekah cradle the infants in her own arms, and the new mother's eyes shone with joy and wonder at the tiny miracles snuggled against her. Bethez laid a hand on one infant and turned to Isaac. "This one with red hair was the firstborn, master."

Bethez watched as Rebekah held them gently, and then she added, "I don't know what it means, but the second baby, the smaller one, held the heel of his brother as he came from the womb."

Rebekah stared at the old woman. Then she looked down at the two babies, the one red-faced, his body already covered with hair, the other smaller and paler. "You name the firstborn, husband."

"We will call him Esau."

Rebekah smiled and nodded. The name, meaning "hairy," was appropriate.

Isaac stroked Rebekah's hair and said, "Now you name his brother."

"We will call him Jacob."

"Jacob!?" Isaac started. "'Usurper'? What a strange name to put on a baby!"

Despite Isaac's objections, Rebekah was sure of the choice. "His name is Jacob," she whispered sleepily, pulling the two infants closer and shutting her eyes. "His name is Jacob."

CHAPTER

2

Ten-year-old Jacob's most prized possession was an ancient game from Egypt called Hounds and Jackals. His brother had one called Senet. They had been gifts from their grandfather Abraham, who had acquired both games during his sojourn in Egypt decades earlier. Jacob had paid close attention to his grandfather's instructions on how to play and, as a result, had become adept at both games. They were intricate and required intense concentration, but Jacob had an inherent ability to work puzzles and loved any game that required skill and cleverness.

Esau, on the other hand, cared not a whit for either game, and he had finally traded his to Jacob for a bronze knife. Jacob cared little for weapons, so both boys were content with the bargain. Esau proudly carried the knife in a soft leather sheath, keeping the blade sharp enough to shave a man.

On one particularly hot morning, Jacob had persuaded Esau to play Hounds and Jackals with him and had handily beaten him three times in a row. Unfortunately, Jacob was too preoccupied with his own success to notice that his brother was getting angry. "There, I win again!" Jacob crowed, whereupon Esau leaped to his feet.

Esau was a head taller than Jacob and considerably stronger. He had defeated every other boy their age at games involving physical strength or agility. In a rage over losing, he kicked the board, shattering it and sending game pieces high into the air. Tiny sticks carved with jackal heads rained down around them. "I hate this stupid game!" Esau screamed.

"You've broken my board!" Jacob wailed. Ordinarily he would not have dared to fight Esau, but the game from his grandfather was irreplaceable. Now the polished wood with delicate ivory-and-gold insets lay splintered in pieces around them. Without thinking, Jacob threw himself at the larger boy and began pummeling him.

Esau was taken off guard by Jacob's unexpected ferocity and fell backward under the assault. He quickly recovered, however, jumping up and shoving his brother to the ground. "Your stupid old games aren't anything!" he yelled. "I'll tear up both of them!"

Pinned under Esau, Jacob was helpless to fend off the blows.

Rebekah heard Jacob's shrieks and came running. She grabbed Esau's hair and one arm and dragged him off, shouting, "What are you doing, Esau? Shame on you for hurting your brother!"

Esau jerked his arm out of his mother's grasp, ignoring the pain as she still held tight to his hair. "You always take his side, Mother!"

"Because you're always taking advantage of him. What's this all about?"

"He smashed my game!" Jacob cried out, struggling to his feet. With tears running down his cheeks, he picked up several of the pieces and held them out. "Look, it's all broken."

"We'll get it fixed, son. Don't worry about it. Now, aren't you ashamed, Esau?"

"No, I'm not!"

"Well, you should be!" Rebekah said, anger scoring her face. "You know how much he loves both of his games."

"Well, he cheated me out of one of them!"

"I did not!" Jacob shouted. "We traded. You wanted the knife, and I wanted the game!"

"That's right," Rebekah said, nodded and releasing her hold on Esau's hair. "Now you'll have to be punished, Esau."

"Me! What about him? He hit me first!"

"But you broke his game, and he didn't break anything of yours," Rebekah said. "Now leave us. I'll have your father deal with you later."

Esau gave his mother a wounded glance, then glared at Jacob before whirling and running away, his back rigid with anger.

"Don't worry about your game, Jacob," Rebekah said, putting her arms out to the boy. "Your father can fix it. He's clever with things like that."

Jacob collapsed against his mother's breast and whined, "I don't see why Esau has to be so mean."

Rebekah bit her lip as she enfolded the boy in her arms. She tried not to favor Jacob, but her heart was soft toward her younger son. Finding the courage to hold him away from her, she looked him in the eye and said firmly, "Your brother is not as smart as you are, Jacob. He can't win at mind games as easily as you do."

"Well, I can't run as fast as he can, but I don't hit him because of it."

"Your father will have to speak to him. Now, come along and I'll give you something you like."

Jacob and his mother picked up the broken game, then went inside the family tent. Jacob carefully tucked the pieces away in his wooden chest, hoping his father or grandfather would be able to put them together again, then went to his mother, who was holding out a dish. "Here, Jacob, have some of these fresh dates."

"Can I have some honey to dip them in, Mother?"

"Yes, but we're almost out."

Jacob greedily grabbed the dish and began to dip the dates in what was left of the honey. While he was eating his favorite treat, he listened to his mother. In a way, she was Jacob's best friend. He did at times play with other children his age, but he preferred his mother's quiet company. He spent little time with his father, who was more taken up with Esau. Perhaps it was natural for his mother to favor Jacob, for he was like her in so many ways.

Esau, on the other hand, was so unlike either of his parents that he seemed like a stranger in the family. His skin was tanned a deep bronze from staying outdoors constantly. Neither heat nor cold would keep him in their tent. His hair was bright red, and his young body was hairy, with forearms already covered with a furlike mat. It was difficult for those who met the boys for the first time to believe that they were brothers—they were so different physically and in every other way.

Finally Rebekah looked up and said, "Here comes your grandfather."

"Good. Maybe he'll play a game with me," Jacob said, brightening. When his grandfather stepped inside the tent, the boy ran to him and hugged his legs. "Grandfather, will you play with me?"

Abraham patted him on the back and said kindly, "Perhaps later, Jacob. I am busy with the flock just now." At Jacob's disappointed sigh, he stooped down and put his arm around him. "Actually, I came home just now to take you to see the new lambs."

"Oh, I'd like that, Grandfather!" Jacob said, running to his sleeping corner to grab his staff.

"Will you have something to eat before you go?" Rebekah asked Abraham quickly. "I'm fixing your favorite stew."

"Later, daughter. This young man and I have a lot to do just now. Come along, Jacob."

Giving his mother a kiss, Jacob happily left with his grandfather. Skipping alongside the old man and kicking pebbles out of the way as they made their way out of the camp, Jacob told Abraham about his fight with Esau. "I wasn't doing anything, Grandfather, and he just got up and smashed the board all to pieces!"

"Did you beat him at the game?" Abraham raised a knowing eyebrow at his grandson.

"Yes—three times!" Jacob crowed proudly.

"Well, then, you made him feel bad, Jacob."

"But he makes *me* feel bad all the time! He beats me at everything else. He's stronger and faster and wrestles better than any boy in the camp."

"Yes, I know. But I think your brother feels bad because you're so much cleverer than he is."

"Why, I can't help that!"

"I know, but you don't have to beat him so badly at games like that."

"You mean I should *let* him win?"

"What would it hurt to let him win a game now and then? It might make him feel better."

Jacob had stopped skipping and was now walking alongside the tall man, trying to keep pace with his steps as he pondered his grandfather's suggestion. He finally sighed and said, "I suppose I could do that."

"Good," Abraham smiled and put his hand on the boy's head. "There's my good grandson. Now let's go find Esau. I want him to see the new lambs too."

Jacob's heart sank. He liked having his grandfather all to himself, but he also knew that the old man was very careful not to favor either grandson.

"Oh, all right," Jacob said, wanting to please his grandfather. "He's probably with the other boys."

When they found Esau, the boy came willingly, as he too enjoyed his grandfather's company above that of his companions. The boys walked on either side of Abraham, each one stealing glances at the other. Esau seemed rather stiff to Jacob, who was uncomfortable that his brother kept glaring at him. *I suppose he's wondering if I told Grandfather on him,* Jacob thought.

When the three reached the flock, they were met by Hezbod, the master shepherd of all the flocks and herds. A tall, bronzed man with odd-looking yellowish eyes, he was tough as leather and could walk the legs off of any other man in the tribe. Now he greeted them with a friendly smile.

"Good morning, Hezbod," Abraham called out.

"Good morning, sir. You've brought the boys to see the lambs?"

"Yes, indeed. I understand we have some healthy ones."

"The best ever." Hezbod winked at Jacob. "I'll venture you have a lot of questions."

"I like to know things," Jacob replied, grinning up at the man. He looked around at the grazing animals with fondness. Every type of animal fascinated him, and he had shown an uncanny ability to handle them. Young as he was, he had even successfully trained a dog to help herd the sheep.

"This young fellow is going to be a great herdsman, master."

Abraham smiled. "Both of them will be, I hope."

"No, I want to be a warrior," Esau protested. "I get tired of these smelly old sheep."

Abraham stared at Esau in dismay. "Our people have always been shepherds," he said. "When I was your age, I was already learning to tend to the animals."

Esau did not argue, but the look on his face made it clear he was not thrilled with the idea of becoming a shepherd.

"All right, Hezbod, show us the lambs," Abraham said, putting his hands on the boys' shoulders. He studied his grandsons as they walked along, listening to Hezbod. *These boys are so different! I can't imagine how they'll get along when they grow up.*

Isaac was busy watching over the new lambs and their mothers when he looked up and saw the trio approaching. His heart raced with delight. Nothing pleased him more than to see the boys out with their grandfather, soaking up his wisdom and learning of the wonderful stories he had to tell. He hastily gathered up a special gift he had for each of them.

Seeing their father, both boys broke into a run, and Esau cried out, "Look, Father's got us each a bow and arrows!"

"Yes," Isaac said, nodding and holding out two bows, each with a quiver of arrows. "I bought them from a traveling merchant. I've been saving them for a present. Do you think you deserve them?"

"Yes, indeed!" Esau cried, his eyes bright at the pleasure of owning a new weapon. "Which one is mine?"

"You're the firstborn, so you have the first choice," Isaac said, smiling, "but they are about the same as far as I can tell."

Esau carefully chose his bow, and Isaac gave the remaining one to Jacob. Esau set about stringing his, which he did easily, but Jacob struggled, not having the strength to pull the string taut.

"Here, I'll help you with that, son," Isaac said. But seeing the dejection in Jacob's face, he was quick to add, "Don't worry. You'll be able to string it when you get a little older and stronger."

"*I* can do it now!" Esau crowed. He picked up an arrow, nocked it on the string, and aiming, drew it back easily.

"Don't shoot that goat!" Abraham cried out sharply.

"I wasn't going to shoot it, Grandfather. I was just aiming at it."

"Well, come along. We'll get away from the animals before you kill one of them."

Moments later the boys were shooting at an acceptable target—a rag on a bush. With little practice, Esau was able to pierce the rag with his arrows on almost every shot, but Jacob could not fully draw back the bow, and his arrows continued to fall far short of the target. He quickly tired of being bested and threw down his bow, while Esau grinned at him. "A bit harder than playing that dumb game, isn't it?" With that, he sent another arrow clean through the rag and shouted, "I did it again! You see, Father?"

"Yes, I saw. You're a fine shot, son."

Abraham stood back, watching Jacob, who was now sitting on the ground nursing his sore fingers. "That's enough archery for the day," he announced. Esau protested, but Abraham shook his head.

"Come on over here," Isaac said to the boys. "I brought something to drink." He gave them each a drink from his water flask, which was filled with a sweet herbal concoction he liked to make by brewing wild flowers and honey. In the heat of the day, it tasted cool and refreshing. He turned to Abraham and said, "Now, Father, why don't you tell us more about our family."

The four sat down under the sparse shade of a scrub tree and shared the drink from the goat-skin flask. Abraham looked down at the two boys seated at his feet. "What do you want to hear?" he asked.

"Tell us about Noah and the flood," Jacob piped up. He never tired of hearing the old stories of his family, even though he had memorized most of them.

"All right. I'll tell you about Noah," Abraham began.

Jacob sat in rapt attention while his grandfather related the story— Abraham having learned it from his own grandfather Nahor—of the godly patriarch whose family had been spared from the worldwide destruction. The boy was full of questions. "How did they get all the animals on the ark? Did they go out and catch them?"

"No," Abraham patiently explained. "God himself brought them."

"Why didn't the larger animals eat the smaller ones?"

"I never asked my grandfather about that," Abraham said, smiling. "I expect they kept them separated."

While Jacob and Isaac listened with interest, Esau fidgeted and drew in the dirt with a stick. He liked to hear stories of battles, not family genealogies—unlike Jacob, who could recite the family tree all the way back to Adam.

When Abraham had finished, Jacob said, "Show us the lion again, Grandfather."

Abraham smiled and pulled out the gold medallion he wore on a leather cord around his neck. He held it out for the boys to see, and Jacob ran his fingers over the carved surface. "What does the lion mean?"

"I don't know, my boy."

Jacob turned the medallion over and studied the other side. "This lamb looks so real! What does it mean?"

"I don't know that either, Jacob."

Isaac and his sons had heard the story of the medallion many times before, but they listened again as Abraham explained. "When my grandfather gave this to me, he said it had been passed down from our ancestors, possibly all the way from Adam."

"Who will get it when you die?" Esau asked bluntly.

"I don't know, Esau. My father told me that someday God himself will reveal the next person I'm to give this to—and that it will be someone in our family."

Esau frowned. "I don't like things I don't understand."

Jacob, however, was anxious to hear more. "Tell us what you *think* it might mean, Grandfather."

Abraham fell silent, then said thoughtfully, "I think it means that God is doing something wonderful for the whole world through our family."

"Like what?" Jacob demanded, his eyes bright with anticipation.

Abraham studied the faces of his son and grandsons before answering. "I believe that God is going to send a man into the world who will bring peace and joy to every person on earth."

"I don't see how one man could do that," Esau muttered, his lower lip protruding.

"He won't be just any man, Esau. He will be very special. Even our first ancestor, Adam, had a word from God about this man. Do you remember how God told him that the seed of a woman would crush the serpent's head?"

"Yes, but I don't get it," Esau grumbled.

Jacob turned to his brother and explained. "The serpent is the enemy, Esau. Don't you remember?"

Esau shrugged, tired of a discussion that centered on unexplained mysteries and riddles. What did he care what would happen in the future anyway? He was anxious to get back to his new bow and arrow.

"But what's the lion for, Grandfather—and the lamb?" Jacob persisted.

Abraham shook his head. "I don't think that's for us to know right now. In due time God will reveal what they mean." He leaned against the tree and slipped the medallion back under his garment, his eyes unfocused, staring off into the distance. "Someday God will send One who will make all things right."

A silence fell over the group as they waited for him to say more. Then Abraham slapped his thigh and stood up. "Well, that's enough for today. Let's go home and have some of that stew your mother's been preparing!"

CHAPTER
3

"I wonder how many times we've moved," Jacob grunted, lowering the heavy basket he was carrying and setting it on the floor of the tent. Noticing how tired his mother looked, the young man went to her and put his arms around her. "Why don't you sit down and let me move the rest of the things in, Mother?"

Rebekah shook her head, but Jacob insisted until she relented, allowing him to help her sit down on a pile of sleeping mats. She smiled gratefully and shook her head. "I wish everyone were as thoughtful as you, son."

Jacob shrugged his shoulders, then began to unload the baskets he had brought in. He too was exhausted by the move, made more so because of his disappointment at having to leave Beersheba. He had loved it there and had many fond memories, having grown to manhood in the pleasant hills and valleys. But with the drought encroaching on their pasturelands, the family had had no choice but to travel deeper into Philistine territory, where the grass was greener and the water more abundant.

Jacob removed items and set them in piles around the tent, then stopped and held something in his hands. "Why, this goes in *my* tent."

"What is it, son?"

"Oh, nothing."

Rebekah stretched up to see what Jacob was holding. "Why, it's your old game of Hounds and Jackals. Here you are thirty years old and still hanging on to your toys!"

Jacob ran his hand over the beautifully fashioned board. "I could never get rid of this. It reminds me of Grandfather. I remember we played a game the day before he died."

Rebekah's eyes grew tender. She rose and put her arm around Jacob.

"You still miss him a great deal, don't you?"

"Yes, I do. I've never known anybody like him."

Jacob grew quiet, remembering his grandfather's final days and the time they had spent together. Jacob had stayed by the dying man's bedside, hanging on every precious word Abraham spoke to him.

He smiled as he thought of the medallion his grandfather had given him the day before he died. He could feel its weight on his chest as it hung under his tunic. He fingered it under the coarse cloth but did not pull it out, for Abraham had made him promise that he would keep the gift a secret. It was to be between him and God. Jacob did not understand the meaning of the medallion—the carved lion with the jeweled eyes on one side and the lamb on the other—but he knew he would always cherish it. That his grandfather had chosen to give it to him, the younger brother, was a mystery. It was hard for him to understand, but it made him proud. In the distant future, God would reveal the person whom Jacob should pass the medallion on to.

"We all miss him." Rebekah's words brought Jacob back to the present, and he looked into her eyes, seeing the tenderness and love there that she had for him.

Rebekah had been watching Jacob while he remained deep in thought, his hand over his heart, his eyes watering with the memories. She kept her arm around him, proudly noting her son's attractive features. He was of medium height and build, still a head shorter than his brother but well-knit and strong. His brown hair had a hint of reddish gold in it that caught the sun at times, and his beard was neatly trimmed along a strong jawline. He could boast of perfect vision from his deep-set eyes and was able to see farther than anyone else among their people. His hands were delicately fashioned, with long, tapered fingers, well-suited for skillfully playing the harp. Even though he still enjoyed solitary pursuits, he had also become a fine herdsman. No other man in the tribe knew more than Jacob about protecting, breeding, and raising livestock. Rebekah had never been able to conceal her favoritism for Jacob over Esau. It made her feel better to tell herself that Isaac had made a favorite of Esau, so it was only right that she should favor Jacob.

"Why isn't Esau here?" Jacob asked suddenly. "He should be helping us unpack."

"Oh, he's out hunting."

"He's *always* hunting." Jacob scowled and continued with his task. "I wish we hadn't had to come to the land of the Philistines."

"So do I, but your father insists that God warned him not to go to Egypt."

"To Egypt?! I didn't know Father was even thinking of going there."

"Yes, he was. Water is plentiful along the Nile, but the Lord said we were to come here."

"I don't know why. The Egyptians are more civilized than these Philistines," Jacob argued. His eyes narrowed as he added, "They're a violent people."

"I said the same thing to your father, but he was so certain that God told him to come here he wouldn't listen to me."

Jacob faced his mother. "You know, Grandfather talked so much about the many times God spoke to him out in the desert. And God has spoken to Father too. Has He ever spoken to you?"

"Why do you ask, son?"

"Because He never speaks to me," Jacob said petulantly, "even though I ask Him to." Seeing that his mother was upset, he asked, "What's wrong?"

"Well ... I've never told you this, my son, but God *did* speak to me once."

Jacob's eyes lit up, and he gave Rebekah his full attention, firing questions at her. "Tell me about it. When was it? How old were you? What did He say?"

"I shouldn't have even mentioned it."

"Well, you did, so now you'll have to tell me."

Ever since the birth of her twin sons, Rebekah had kept God's prophetic words about them to herself. She had told Isaac of the vision immediately afterward, but he had been so disturbed by it that she had never mentioned it again. Now she hesitated at first, then relented and nodded. "All right. I think maybe you should know—but you must promise never to tell anyone else."

"Of course I promise. Now, what happened, Mother?"

"I still remember God's visit to me so clearly! It was the night before you were born—a very hard time for me, son. In those final months of my pregnancy, when I was carrying you and your brother, there seemed to be a war going on inside of me, and that night was particularly bad. I remember lying alone in the darkness. Your father had gone out to check the flocks, and I was afraid. So I cried to the Lord and asked Him for help, and ... and then He came to me."

"What did He look like?" Jacob's eyes were intent, and he leaned forward breathlessly, awaiting her answer.

"Why, I didn't *see* Him, Jacob. There was a strange light—stranger than anything I'd ever seen before—but no form of a man or any other created being."

"Well, what did He say?"

"I've never forgotten His words. 'Two nations are in your womb, and two peoples from within you will be separated; one people will be stronger than the other, and the older will serve the younger.'"

Jacob stared at his mother, his lips parted in wonder. "The older will serve the younger? Are you *certain* God said that?"

"I couldn't mistake it. I've thought about it for thirty years now, son."

"But that—that's *impossible*! Esau should have the first place."

"Yes, that's normally true, but God's word to me was very clear." Rebekah suddenly gave a great sigh and looked at Jacob with a strange expression in her dark eyes. "Somehow God is going to make it happen. Now, remember, you must never tell anyone what I've just told you."

"I won't, Mother." Jacob got to his feet, leaned over and kissed his mother, then left the tent.

Rebekah sat for a long time, thinking about him. *He's so different from Esau, and Isaac can't see it. Now he'll go out and think about this—like he always thinks about things. When he gets something in his mind, he just can't get it out. But I'm glad I told him!*

Jacob was stunned by this revelation from his mother. He quickly left the camp and made his way out into the hills, where he could sit and think about his mother's prophetic vision. He could not imagine how such a thing could come about. Now that he was alone, he pulled the medallion out from under his tunic and stared at it. Did this have something to do with his mother's vision? Why would God choose him? And how would such a vision be fulfilled? His father, Isaac, would never give him the blessing over his brother, who was the firstborn and legitimate heir of the birthright. With despair in his heart, he lifted his voice toward heaven and cried to the wind, "Oh, God, what would you have me to do?"

The only answer that returned to him was the distant echo of his own words.

The sun was settling down over the western horizon, melting into a formless blaze of gold as it touched the faraway mountains. Jacob had returned to camp wanting to talk with his father. After the burning heat of the day, this was ordinarily Jacob's favorite time. But now as he sat beside his aging father, his heart was heavy with the memories and revelations of this day. The smoke of the evening cook fires rose into the still air, and the aroma of roasting meat wafted over the camp. Jacob listened as Isaac related tales of his forebears, most of which he had learned from Abraham. There was still enough light to see the outlines of men on camels approaching. Jacob interrupted his father to say, "Look. There's a party coming."

Isaac's vision had dimmed in recent years, and he squinted but shook his head. "Who are they? I can't make them out."

"They're strangers. Philistines, I think. I can tell you that much." Jacob got to his feet and helped Isaac stand. It saddened him to see his father wince as he put pressure on his weak and painful knees. "We'd better go out and greet them," Jacob said, shaking his head. "I hope they're friendly. Most Philistines are not." Jacob counted six men on camels. "I think they're soldiers or officials of some kind."

When the men dismounted, Isaac advanced and bowed slightly. "Welcome to our camp, sirs. My name is Isaac. I am the chief of my people, and this is my son Jacob."

The leader approached them. He was a short, broad man with strange yellow-brown eyes and a scar running down the side of his face. He wore a dark green robe with a wicked-looking sword by his side. The others were dressed much the same, as if they wore uniforms.

"My name is Hazor. I am the captain of King Abimelech's army."

Both Isaac and Jacob bowed low to the Philistine king's officer. "We are strangers to this place, but we respect and honor the king," Isaac said.

Hazor stared at the two men. "Where are you bound?" he demanded, his yellowish eyes taking in everything.

"We are shepherds, sir, as you see," Isaac said, pointing toward their flocks. "The drought has driven us to find better pastures, and we intend to stay only until the rains return to our home country."

"We will have to inspect your camp," Hazor said.

"You're very welcome. The evening meal is almost ready. Would you care to dine with us?"

Hazor stared at the old man, then nodded. "Yes, I'm hungry—and have my men fed too."

"Of course, Captain," Jacob spoke up. "I will tend to your men, and my father will take you to his tent for a fine meal."

Jacob left promptly and organized a meal for Hazor's men. As soon as the soldiers were settled with plenty of food and drink, he hurried back to his parents' tent. Finding Hazor already seated and his mother serving, he sat down too and listened as his father spoke with the captain. The Philistine's manners left much to be desired, Jacob thought, as they ate the freshly roasted kid with mint, olives, and *kemach*—a special bread his mother often baked. As was their custom, Rebekah was careful to remain out of sight while the men ate, returning only to bring the next course and fill their cups with fine Syrian wine, of which Hazor consumed a great deal. They exchanged pleasantries throughout the meal until after the final course—a compote of plums and raisins served in copper bowls. Rebekah refilled the captain's cup as the men got down to business.

"We wish to have good relations with the king and your people, Captain," Isaac began.

Jacob could see that Hazor was only half listening to Isaac. Instead, the captain's eyes were fastened steadily on Rebekah as she moved in and out of the tent. Jacob was accustomed to this, for even in her later years, his mother was still an unusual beauty, and men of all ages enjoyed watching her.

"The king is a reasonable man." Hazor finished the wine and wiped his lips with the back of his arm. "We will expect you to pay taxes, of course, like our own people."

"Certainly, Captain. We will not abuse your hospitality."

After carefully questioning Isaac, Hazor took his leave, bowing to his host and saying, "Thank you for an excellent meal. I will be back from time to time. You will need to be told about our laws. Every region differs, you know."

"I would be most happy to hear them, sir."

Darkness had fallen, and taking oil lamps, Isaac and Jacob escorted Hazor back to his men and the waiting animals. Hazor shouted for his men to move out, then turned again to Isaac, his yellowish eyes gleaming in the lamplight. "King Abimelech is a fair man, but he does like his women."

Isaac nodded. "Well, that's as it should be, Captain."

"Yes, it is. I wish I had my choice like he does! Any woman he fancies, he just takes!"

Isaac felt almost faint, and Hazor laughed. "Sometimes men object when the king takes their wives, but that's what he has me for. Poor fellows! I have no choice but to cut off their heads." Hazor's brow knit tightly as he glanced back toward Isaac's tent. "That woman who served us—is she your wife?"

Isaac's breath caught in his throat, knowing he was in grave danger. Almost without thinking, he blurted out, "Oh, no indeed! That is my sister, Rebekah."

"Your sister, eh? Well, it's a good thing she's not your wife. If Abimelech were to take a liking to her, you'd have to fight for her. And"—he grinned wickedly—"I don't lose fights with men who have good-looking wives." He stared at Isaac to be certain that his meaning was clear, then turned away, saying, "You'll probably be seeing me again very soon."

Isaac and Jacob watched the troop ride off; then Isaac's shoulders sagged. Jacob followed his father back to the tent.

When they stepped inside, Rebekah took one look at them and asked, "What's wrong?"

Isaac responded. "He said that the king likes women. That he takes whatever woman he wants, and if she is married, he kills her husband. I . . . I told them you were my sister."

Rebekah took in a sharp breath. "That was the wise thing to do, but we must get away from this place at once."

"We can't go back to Beersheba," Isaac said. "The cattle were starving there."

"Well, we can't stay here!" Jacob exclaimed. "That fellow will be sure to return for Mother."

"Maybe not. There are lots of women here, and we're far out in the hills, away from the city. We'll probably never see him again."

In the days that followed Hazor's visit, Jacob was continually watchful. He was nervous, as were his parents, but as the days passed and the Philistine did not return, they all grew more confident that they would not be troubled.

The grass was green, and the cattle were doing well. Jacob, however, was disappointed by his father's lie about Rebekah. In his mind, he went over and over what had happened. He had always revered his father. He knew Isaac was not the man his grandfather Abraham had been, but he had at least always been truthful—or so Jacob believed.

Why did he have to lie to Hazor? Jacob often asked himself. It troubled him so much that one day, while he was with Rebekah, he brought up the subject. This was not unusual for him, for he was very close to his mother and told her most things that were on his heart. His mother was preparing supper, and as usual, Jacob was helping her.

"Mother," he said, "I've been thinking about what Father said to Hazor."

"What about it, son?"

"Well, he lied. That's wrong, isn't it?"

Rebekah turned quickly and studied Jacob. He was a man who thought a great deal about what went on around him. He was highly intelligent and had a mind and temperament that would not allow him to put anything aside.

"It was something your father had to do, son."

"But Grandfather wouldn't have done it, would he?"

"As a matter of fact, he did *exactly* that—two times!"

Jacob stared at his mother. "He did what?"

"When he was in Egypt, the pharaoh took your grandmother into his harem. Your grandfather had no choice but to lie. He was a stranger in a strange land, and the pharaoh would have killed him instantly had he told the truth. So he told the pharaoh that Sarah was his sister, not his wife. Then he did the same thing again with King Abimelech."

Jacob fell silent, and tears welled up in Rebekah's eyes. She loved this son with all of her heart and hated to see him hurt. Putting her arm around him, she said quietly, "Son, sometimes a person has to do *wrong* things in order to make other things go *right*. If your grandfather hadn't lied, he would have been killed, and that would have been the end of our tribe. And your father had the same choice to make. I don't like it, but it's the way the world is."

"So you're saying it's all right to do wrong if it's good for us?" Jacob's tone betrayed the bitterness and confusion he felt. He shook his head. "I wish I didn't have to know these things."

"You have to know them because that's the way life is. Now, put it out of your mind and help me with these beans."

———

Despite his mother's viewpoint on the matter, Jacob worried constantly over his father's lie to Hazor, especially when Hazor summoned his father to the palace. On Isaac's return to camp, he told his family that the king had asked about his lie, and he was so shaken he had confessed his duplicity.

Esau demanded to know what the king was going to do, but their father only looked dazed and said, "Nothing. He said I shouldn't have lied—and he's right."

Esau laughed. "Well, it all came out all right, so what's one little lie? I tell more than that every day!"

The seasons changed several times, and spring was upon them again. The new crops were springing up almost like magic, and the animals continued to bear and increase in a manner that none of them had ever witnessed before. It was a time of untold prosperity.

Jacob watched all this with a mixture of gratitude and doubt. He was not able to shake off his worries over his father's lie and his concern over how God would fulfill his mother's prophetic vision. As the family continued to prosper, he counted the livestock and watched the grain pile up so high that there was even plenty to sell to the neighboring Philistines. It was as if God had drawn a circle around the camp and prospered Isaac and his people beyond any others. *But for what reason?* Jacob wondered.

Unlike Jacob, Esau never questioned any of it. He reveled in the wealth that was rolling in, and well he might, for as the firstborn, it would all be his one day. He spent little time with the flocks, but he was a skillful hunter and brought in enough game that they never needed to kill any of the livestock for food.

Many times Jacob wished he could look at the matter as Esau did. He prayed fervently, but God never spoke to him. Finally he whispered in despair, "I guess it doesn't matter what a man does. God just blesses whomever He pleases."

His conclusion did not satisfy him, however, and he continued to carefully watch the growth of the flocks—waiting, perhaps, for God to strike down Isaac because of the lie he had told. But nothing ever happened, and Jacob finally succeeded in shoving it to the back of his mind, where he rarely had to think of it.

One day, as he frequently did, Jacob set about preparing the evening meal. His mother was feeling poorly, but he was so used to helping her that he had become almost as good a cook as she was. He had put several handfuls of wild lentils from a nearby field into a large clay pot, adding wild onions, water, and spices, and had built a fine fire of dry wood. When the embers were hot, he had placed the pot on them, and the stew had by now cooked slowly for many hours. Aware that his father was approaching, he dipped in a wooden spoon and tasted it.

"Come taste the stew, Father," he said. "I think you'll like it."

Isaac groped his way forward, allowing Jacob to guide him to sit by the fire, and Jacob dipped out a spoonful, saying, "Be careful. It's bubbling hot."

Jacob smiled as his father blew on the stew, then carefully tasted it. "It's good," he said. "What's the meat in there?"

"It's part of the venison Esau brought in day before yesterday."

"Well, it makes a fine stew."

Isaac listened as Jacob reported on the state of the herds. He couldn't see very well now and could not help with the cattle, but he loved to hear all that was going on.

Jacob's thoughts turned again to the matter of the birthright. He knew that tribal custom dictated that the oldest son should inherit everything, and—although an exception had been made in the case of his grandfather Abraham—Isaac had told Jacob many times that he would keep to the family custom unless God himself told him otherwise.

As he considered the tradition, great bitterness rose in Jacob, and he clamped his lips together. He wanted to say to his father "But Esau doesn't care about these things. All he cares about is hunting. I'm the one who's interested in the family and the tribe and in God." He wanted desperately to tell his father of God's promise to Rebekah, of Abraham's gift to him of the medallion . . . but he had promised to keep silent. How could his father know that God was choosing him if he could not tell him? He felt a great agony of spirit, feeling that he was caught in an impossible situation. There was no sense in arguing with Isaac when he wasn't able to reveal what he knew. All such argument would be useless, and wearily he put his hopes away. But he could not keep them from festering inside him.

Some days later, while fixing a meal, Jacob noticed that Esau had returned to camp. His bitterness against his brother seized his innards as he watched Esau stop long enough to grab one of the young unmarried women of the tribe and kiss her. She shoved him away but was laughing.

Jacob heard her say, "You have no manners, Esau. Why can't you be more like Jacob?"

"That baby!" Esau bellowed. "He's not a real man. He can't even *sneeze* without asking our mother!"

At that moment, as mild-mannered as Jacob was, white rage welled up in him. He would have thrown himself against Esau, but he knew it would be senseless. No man could stand against his brother in one-on-one combat! He managed to keep his face straight and watched as Esau strolled up. Esau was indeed a massive man. His red hair caught the sunlight, and over his back he wore the powerful double-convex bow that no other man in the tribe could draw. The quiver full of wooden-shafted arrows with heads chipped from flint poked up at the sky, and Esau's massive power seemed to flow out of him despite his weariness.

"Oh, brother, am I ever exhausted!" he said, dumping his bow and arrows at the doorway of the tent.

"Hello, Esau."

"I'm starving to death. What have you got in there?"

"It's a stew. I'm making it for Father."

"Give me some of it before I starve!"

Ordinarily Jacob would have complied with Esau's demand, but his anger was now deep and burning. How could he be left out of the inheritance—the wealth that he had almost single-handedly acquired for the family—and watch it be given to this crude hunter who had no concept of life other than hunting and women and living for himself? "You can't have any of it," Jacob muttered.

Esau's expression was almost comical. He blinked with shock, for never before had Jacob refused him anything. "What's that you say?" he demanded.

Jacob faced him. "I said you can't have any of this stew. Is something wrong with your hearing?"

"Oh, little brother, you're in a mean mood today!" Esau was more amused than angered. He towered over Jacob, and the humor of the situation struck him. "You know, I could just take it if I wanted to."

"Well, take it, then. If you're willing to kill your brother over stew, that shows what kind of a man you are."

Then, seeing the look in Jacob's eyes, Esau sobered. Deep down he had an affection, of sorts, for his brother. He felt Jacob was a weak man and had determined that when he became head of the tribe he would see to it that Jacob was provided for. He had told his friends, "Jacob would never be able to make it in the world if he didn't have a strong man to look out for him, but I'll never let him down." Now Esau was puzzled. "I'm really hungry," he said.

"I can't help that. How hungry are you?"

Esau was indeed famished. He had eaten nothing for two days, for surprisingly, the hunt had been unsuccessful. He swallowed as the aroma of the stew enticed him. "I'd give anything for all I could eat of that soup."

"All right, then. Sell me your birthright."

Esau laughed at his brother. "I can't sell you something that comes to me because I'm the firstborn, little brother! Now, be serious." But the gleam in Jacob's eye said that he was clearly serious.

Esau slapped his brother on the back and shook his head. What was the harm of playing along with this little game? he thought. It was worth a bowl of that hearty soup just now! He actually had no concept of the importance of the birthright. As far as he was concerned, he was the first-born and that settled it. He knew there were some rules governing this sort of thing, but he had utter confidence that what was his was his and no word spoken in private could change that. "All right. You can have the birthright if that's what you want, but give me something to eat before I die."

"Good!" Jacob said, as he served up a bowl of stew. "Sit down and I'll serve you. But you must swear I have the birthright."

"Yes, yes," Esau muttered as he took the steaming bowl. "It won't do me any good if I'm dead!"

Jacob's heart sprang up. He knew the value of the birthright—God's blessing—even if Esau did not. He filled the bowl four times for his brother, who devoured the food like an animal. Esau finally arose, saying, "That was good. You—"

Jacob interrupted him. "Don't forget. The birthright is now mine."

"All right, little brother, you can have the silly thing. I'll take everything else." Esau laughed and turned away. He stopped long enough to flirt with another young woman and then shuffled off to his tent to sleep, sated as he was with his brother's cooking.

Jacob stared down into the stew pot. "The fool!" he said triumphantly. "He doesn't even know what he's given away. Now I have something that's of great value—and I know that God himself wants me to have it!"

Isaac was furious with Esau when Jacob told him what had happened. He immediately demanded that Esau come see him. "What's this I hear about you selling your birthright for a bowl of soup?"

Esau shrugged. "Four bowls—I was hungry, Father." Esau's bulk towered over the old man, yet somehow he was intimidated. "What's the big deal? A few words . . . it didn't mean anything."

"For all your size you're like a child—a simpleton! The birthright— the *birthright!* You sold God's blessing for a simple meal?"

Esau listened as his father berated him but could not understand why he was so upset. "I'll buy it back from him. It's just a word anyhow. I'm the firstborn. He can't change that."

"Yes, you're the firstborn, but Jacob now has the birthright. Because you gave it away! Son, son, how foolish you are!"

Isaac drew close to his son in order to see his face. He had to look up, and he searched Esau's eyes and features. Whatever it was he was looking for, he did not seem to find it. He shook his head and murmured, "Go away, son. You've been very foolish."

Esau stared at his father, then whirled and left the tent. Anger seethed inside of him, for he realized now that he had been outwitted. He still did not understand the import of his action, but if nothing else, he had lost his father's respect. "That Jacob! That usurper! He has indeed lived up to his name! I'll beat him until he gives it back!" Violence was the only response Esau could think of. In matters of cunning, he knew he was no match for Jacob. "I'll never let him trick me again!" He spat out a stream of expletives, then stopped himself and shrugged. "But what does that old man know? It doesn't mean anything. It's just a word."

Isaac buried his face in his hands and wept. He could not believe that his favorite son would despise his own birthright and give up God's blessing for a bowl of soup! In his anger, he pleaded with God to intervene, but he didn't know that God would even hear such prayers. Then in the midst of his anguish, Isaac had a startling thought. He slowly raised his head, his weak eyes staring into the murky darkness of the tent.

"I do not have to accept this," he murmured slowly. His confusion cleared like so many cobwebs breaking apart in the wind. "This matter is too important for two foolish sons to decide." Tradition declared that the father's blessing was needed before the birthright was actually passed on— nothing happened without that final seal of God's approval. *Who says I must give my blessing to the wrong son because of this impulsive transaction.*

Isaac struggled to his feet and began to pace as hope rose in him that all was not lost. "I am the father," he said. "I will say who receives my blessing and who doesn't. And I say that Esau will still receive my blessing when I am ready to give it."

With his decision made, he stepped out of the tent with a lighter heart, shielding his eyes from the painful sunlight, and made his way to find Rebekah. He would tell her first. He was certain she somehow had a hand in this mess. The family needed to know that he was still in charge— he was still the head of the family, and *he* would pass the blessing on to the son of *his* choice.

CHAPTER

4

Hezbod gnawed at the last shreds of meat on a sheep bone, licked it thoroughly, and then tossed it aside. "That was good," he grunted. "Now, how about some wine, woman?"

Bethez stared at him with disgust. "You're going to get drunk again, old man."

Hezbod belched loudly and held out the cup. "A man's got a right to a little pleasure after runnin' with those sheep and goats all day long. Now, fill my cup and hush."

Bethez snorted with disgust but obeyed her husband's command. They had lived together for so long there were no surprises left for either of them, and lifelong habits were deeply ingrained. True enough Hezbod did drink too much, but by the same token, Bethez was prone to nagging. Many a time Hezbod had said, "You give up nagging, I'll give up drinking." But both of them knew they would never relinquish their chief preoccupations and pleasures.

The camp was quiet now except for the loud argument going on in Esau's tent. Hezbod turned and shook his head with disgust. "Esau should have never married them two Hittite women. He should have known better."

"Well, for once you're right."

"For once? I'm *always* right! Isaac should have told him to lay off them Canaanite women. They ain't nothin' but trouble." He grinned slyly and added, "But then all women is trouble, I expect."

Bethez sniffed, then lifted her head at the screams now issuing from Esau's tent. "Both of those women deserve a good beatin'. But you're wrong about one thing, husband. The master did try to talk sense to Esau. He just didn't have any luck."

"Nobody ever had any luck trying to talk sense to that man. I'm glad he's out huntin' most of the time. Jacob's a much easier master. Works hard, just like the rest of us. Quiet, soft-spoken. But that Esau—he's always fighting or shouting or causing trouble."

Bethez picked up one of her husband's robes and began to mend a tear in it. Even though her old fingers were stiff now, she worked steadily. Finally the screaming and shouting reached a crescendo and then was cut off as if with a sword. "I wonder if he killed 'em," she remarked. "Wouldn't surprise me none if he did."

"Me neither. He's got a bad streak in him."

Bethez pulled the needle through the cloth, then looked over at her husband. "I remember the night those two boys were born. They were no sooner out of the womb than Esau began actin' like he does now. He was big and shouted and kicked just like he's been doing ever since."

"What about Jacob?"

"Oh, he was a quiet one. I told you how he came out holding on to his brother's heel."

"Not more than a hundred times, I guess."

"Well, he *did*. Now those boys are forty years old, and poor Jacob has to put up with everything Esau hands him. I don't know what'll become of him when the master dies."

"That won't be too long, I wouldn't think. He's doin' poorly, ain't he?"

"Yes, he is. Almost blind now, but Jacob's got his mama. They've always been close."

"It'd be better if Jacob and Isaac were close, I'm thinkin'. We'd all be better off if he was the one to inherit," Hezbod grunted.

Bethez shook her head. "Will never happen, though. That silly old man still thinks the world of Esau. He's always been fooled by that boy—expecting great things, but he's the only one who does."

"Give me some more of that wine," Hezbod said moodily. "I ain't drunk enough yet. . . ."

———

Jacob had been sitting with his parents when Esau's wives burst in. Basemath was shouting so loudly that Jacob leaned back. She was a short, chunky woman with brown hair tied up by a thong, and her nose was bleeding.

"What happened, Basemath?" Rebekah asked.

"You know what happened. That son of yours hit me. Why didn't you raise him right?"

Judith, Esau's first wife, spoke up. She was a tall woman, strongly built, and with an arrogant look on her face. "I told you to leave him alone, Basemath. You knew what would happen when you started picking at him."

"I'll wait until he's asleep, and then I'll pour boiling water on him, that's what I'll do!" Basemath screamed.

"Now, just a minute. You can't do that," Rebekah said. "What brought the argument on?"

"I asked him to take me to town, and he said he wouldn't do it. Look at these clothes. He could buy me something decent to wear, but he won't. And it's all your fault, Rebekah."

Jacob reached over and put his hand on his father's shoulder. Isaac had dropped his head in anguish, and Jacob knew that he was a sick man and wanted nothing but peace and quiet. Jacob squeezed his shoulder and whispered, "I'll get rid of them."

Getting to his feet, Jacob said, "Father's not feeling well. Come along. I'll listen to your complaints."

"You!" Basemath snorted. "What can *you* do?"

Jacob's voice flared in anger. "I can explain to you what good manners are! Evidently your parents forgot that part of your upbringing." He dragged her out of the tent as she screamed and clawed at him. Jacob was not the powerful man his brother was, but he was still stronger than most. He clamped his hand down onto Basemath's arm until she began to whimper. "Now, stop this! There's nothing my mother can do, and certainly nothing my father can do. Go back to your tent and behave yourself."

Judith was following beside them. "You ought to know better than to cross him, Basemath. Come on. I told you it wouldn't do any good to come here."

Jacob was glad to see the two stalk off, and he went back into the tent. For some time he spoke with his father, who was shaking badly from the uproar. Jacob finally got him calmed down, and Rebekah led him off to help him into bed. When she had him settled, she came back and shook her head. With misery in every line of her face, she said, "Your father and I told Esau he shouldn't marry those Hittite girls."

"Everybody told him, but you know Esau. He won't listen to anyone."

Rebekah reached up and pushed a lock of Jacob's hair back from his forehead. "I want you to marry a Hebrew girl, son. Not one of the wicked women from this country."

"Mother, I'm not likely to marry anyone. I can't afford it."

"What are you talking about?"

"You know what I'm talking about. Esau will have control of everything, and he doesn't have any affection for me." Jacob wanted to scream in frustration. "What about your vision, Mother. What about—" Jacob put his hand to his chest. *No, I must not say anything about the medallion.*

"I do not know. Maybe your father will change his mind." Rebekah placed her hand on Jacob's shoulder. "If he weren't so ill, he'd see that you were treated better."

Jacob felt a pang of compassion for his mother, for Isaac was very stubborn where Esau was concerned. "Don't worry about it," he said. "We'll work something out."

―――――――

The next day Jacob tried to speak with Esau concerning the behavior of his wives. The two were standing out looking over the flocks where Esau, for once, had come to help with the shearing. He was a good hand at this when he wanted to be, but his interest usually tapered off after a hard day's work, and he would go off hunting again. He had listened impatiently while Jacob explained that their father was feeble and didn't need to listen to his wives complain.

"Just let me know if they give Father any more trouble. I'll give them both a beating."

That's his answer for everything, Jacob thought with disgust, and he changed the subject to the flock. "It's time to move from here, Esau."

"No, it's not time yet."

"But the grass is nearly gone, and our herds have grown. We've got to move up north."

Esau stared at Jacob and merely clamped his lips together and shook his head. Jacob continued to explain the need for the move, but Esau finally waved his hand and said, "I'm not ready to move yet."

"But the herds—"

"Look—Father's illness has put me in charge of this clan. Despite your trickery, Father knows I am the better leader. And I'll tell you something else, Jacob—when Father dies, I'll be the master. Then you'll have to work instead of being a woman. Mother spoils you, but I'll take care of that."

"That's not fair, Esau. I work very hard."

But Esau just shook his head and shouted, "We're not moving and that's final! Now, don't talk to me about this again."

"But, Father, it's time to move," Jacob pleaded. "We're losing animals for the first time. You've got to talk to Esau."

"I can't do that," Isaac said in his tired, gravelly voice. His voice had once been clear and strong, but those days were gone now. He was sitting on a mat in his tent while Rebekah did her work, listening. She motioned for Jacob to continue. It had been her idea for Jacob to talk with Isaac, but her son was convinced it was a waste of time.

"Father, you've got to listen to me. For some reason God has blessed us here. We've never had such harvests, and we've never had such increase in our herds. But we've got to use good judgment. Esau doesn't know much about the animals. He's too interested in hunting."

"You've always complained about your brother, Jacob. I don't want to hear it."

Jacob threw up his hands and would have left, but Rebekah intervened. "You've got to listen to him, Isaac. Jacob is right."

"And you always stick up for him, Rebekah. You've spoiled him."

"You've been listening to Esau," Jacob said bitterly.

"Everyone knows that you're your mother's favorite."

"And everyone knows Esau is *your* favorite!" Jacob spat out before he could think. He saw that the words hurt Isaac, and he immediately apologized. "I'm sorry, Father, but there's some truth to it."

"Well, he's the firstborn."

Jacob bit his lip, and Rebekah spoke up. "You've got to do something for Jacob, Isaac. He needs a portion. He's worked hard all of his life, and he deserves a reward."

"The firstborn must be the head of the clan," Isaac insisted. "I'll talk to Esau. He's a good man. Just a little rough."

Jacob knew it was useless to say any more. "Father, I've been thinking of going away and starting over. Perhaps you could give me just some of the flock."

Isaac shook his head. "Your brother will take care of you," he said.

Jacob stared at his father, then turned to his mother. But he saw only the helplessness in her expression. "I wish Grandfather were alive," he muttered quietly, then rose to his feet and left the tent.

"That boy is wrong," Isaac said. "Isn't he, Rebekah?"

Rebekah loved Isaac, but she loved Jacob fully as much. "No, he's not wrong. You've got to show more concern for him."

"Esau is the firstborn. Now, let's have no more talk about it!"

CHAPTER
5

Standing outside the tent, Rebekah felt a calm possess her as the night passed away and the new day was born. She sighed deeply, for the last month had been hard. Jacob had been restless, and it had taken all her persuasive powers to keep him from leaving home. Esau had been hard on his younger brother—arrogant and constantly harping on Jacob's shortcomings. As for Isaac, there was nothing to be said. His appetite was good, but he usually kept to his bed and rarely ventured more than a few yards outside his tent. His blindness had dimmed his appetite for the outdoors he had always loved, and it was all Rebekah could do to persuade him to get a little exercise.

The camp was beginning to wake up with the usual morning vigor. The sky was still dark and Rebekah stared up at the stars, which looked like sequins on black velvet. As she turned to face the east, she saw the horizon crack apart as if a fissure had divided earth from sky.

Pleasure came to her as the light of morning broke, and for a long time she stood there, simply drinking in the birth of a new day.

The noises of the camp gradually became more pronounced, the voices of children with their treble cries, men from the outskirts shouting at the cattle, and the singing and chattering of the women as they began the morning meal. The air was soon filled with the smell of woodsmoke, and the heat of the sun began to warm the camp. With a sigh Rebekah turned and began her day. She entered the smaller tent, which adjoined the large one where she and Isaac slept and spent most of their waking hours. The smaller tent held the cooking supplies, and she began, after a moment's thought, to select ingredients for the morning meal.

As she worked, her mind went back to the problem with Jacob. She ground corn into fine flour to make the mush that Isaac liked so much without thinking about her labor. She was good at blocking out everything except what was in the center of her thoughts, and now this was Jacob and his brother, Esau.

She had always striven to be fair to Esau, but he had been a hard child to love. Whereas Jacob was affectionate, often showing his love with caresses and pats, Esau was never demonstrative toward her. At first Rebekah had tried to share her caresses equally between the two boys, but Esau had early drawn away or laughed at her. As her sons had reached manhood, the differences between the two had become more pronounced. Rebekah sighed and shook her head at the thought.

Maoni, the sixteen-year-old servant girl, came in yawning and rubbing her eyes.

"Start preparing that fruit, Maoni," Rebekah commanded.

The girl was attractive and was already drawing the attention of young men. Rebekah was making plans for the girl, selecting which of the suitors would be best. Even as she thought of this, she was suddenly disgusted with herself. *Why do I think I have to manage everyone? Maoni's old enough to know which man she likes the best. As long as he's suitable, I'll have nothing to say about it.* Satisfied with her decision, she said, "You go get some water from the spring, Maoni. I'll finish this."

"Yes, mistress."

By the time Maoni had returned with a jug of fresh water, Rebekah had milked a goat and filled a cup with the frothy liquid. She arranged the mush and the veal she had pounded into small bits on a platter, preparing to take the breakfast to Isaac. She had left the small tent and started to enter the larger one when she halted abruptly. She could hear Esau's voice inside, which was a surprise. He was rarely seen about the camp in the early morning because he was either out hunting or sleeping late. She started in, but then stopped and stood listening instead, deciding to come back later. She had developed a suspicion, and what she heard confirmed what she had feared for some time.

"What can I bring you, Father?" Esau's voice was clear, strong, and throbbing with life. "Anything you would like in particular?"

Isaac's voice by contrast was weak and feeble. "My son, is it you, my son Esau?"

"Yes, Father. Shall I get you something to eat?"

Rebekah listened intently during the long pause that followed, and then she heard Isaac say, "Son, I am old, and I know not the hour of my death."

"Why, you'll be here for many years yet, Father. Never fear."

"No. My death is coming." The voice was pleading and frail—almost as if he were afraid, Rebekah thought. "Take your weapons, your quiver and your bow, son. Go out to the fields and bring me some venison."

"Why, of course. I was going hunting anyway."

"Good, son! Make me some savory meat such as I love and bring it to me so that I may eat."

"I will be back by nightfall. Game has been a little scarce lately, Father, but I promise you will have your venison."

"Yes. The savory meat that I love. Fix it for me." And then Isaac's voice became clearer. "And when you bring me the meat, my son Esau, I will bless you with the blessing of the firstborn."

Rebekah's heart grew cold. This was the final step. For once the father's blessing was given, it was irrevocable. She heard Esau's voice quivering with excitement, saying, "Yes, my father, I will go at once."

Immediately Rebekah whirled and dodged into the smaller tent. She heard Esau's footsteps as he left; then she took a deep breath. There was a struggle within her for a moment as she stood holding the breakfast she had made. But her mind was on her son Jacob.

"Esau must not have everything!" she whispered into the silence. "Jacob must not be left out. Oh, Lord God, you spoke to me and said that the elder would serve the younger. And now, Lord, help that I might bring this to pass."

Quickly she went into the tent and found Isaac almost asleep again. "Here, husband, you must eat."

She fed Isaac his breakfast, but her mind was elsewhere. As soon as he finished his breakfast, she said, "You get dressed now, and you can sit out in the sun this morning. It's a fine day."

"I think I'll sleep a little more, wife."

"Very well, then."

Leaving the tent, Rebekah went at once to Jacob's tent. She spoke as she approached the flap. "My son, are you awake?"

"Yes, Mother." Jacob stepped out fully dressed. "I was just coming to have breakfast with you."

"There's no time for that."

"Is something wrong, Mother? Is Father ill?"

"No, he's not ill, but something has happened that I've feared for a long time."

Jacob stepped closer and looked into his mother's face. "What is it?"

"It's your father. I heard him speaking to Esau. He told him to go hunting and bring him some venison. You know how he loves savory meat." She hesitated as if reluctant to bring out the news, but she knew it was necessary. She put out her hand and grasped Jacob by the arm. "Son, he's going to give your brother the blessing of the firstborn." She saw Jacob's face fall and said, "But I have a plan."

"A plan? But there's nothing to be done, Mother. Father has the final say."

"Yes. Listen to me now and do everything that I command you. Will you do it, Jacob, no matter what I say?"

"Why, Mother, I've always been obedient to you. You wouldn't tell me to do anything that wasn't for my own good."

Relief washed through Rebekah, and her voice grew stronger. "Listen to me. Go now to the flock and bring me two good kids, the best you can find. I'm going to make savory meat for your father such as he loves, and when I have prepared it, I want you to take it in to him."

"But Esau is going to bring him savory meat."

"He won't be back until late in the afternoon. By the time he finds the game, kills it, dresses it, and cooks it, it may even be tomorrow."

Jacob shrugged his shoulders. "Of course I'll do as you say, Mother, but what purpose will this serve?"

Rebekah felt for one moment as if her entire existence hung in the balance. She had prayed for years for the prophecy God had given her to come true, and now she felt a rush of exultation. Everything was falling into place! She kept her grip on Jacob's arm, squeezing it even harder. "Listen, my son. When you go to your father, he must think that you are Esau, for then he will bless you with the blessing of the firstborn."

"Why, Mother, he would never mistake me for Esau!"

"Yes, he will. He is confused in his mind now and is expecting Esau to come back. When you take the food in, simply put it before him and say as little as possible."

Jacob ran his hand through his hair, confusion sweeping across his face. "But Esau is such a hairy man, and my skin is smooth. You know how father sometimes likes to touch. If he puts his hand on my arm, he'll know that I'm not Esau." His voice sounded alarmed. "If he finds me out, he will put a curse on me and not a blessing."

Rebekah reached up and locked her hands behind Jacob's neck, compelling him to look straight into her eyes. She had always had the most beautiful, expressive eyes Jacob had ever seen, and now they were glowing with life and excitement. Her voice had a slight tremor in it, but it was strong and clear. "The curse be on me, my son, if there be one! I have waited for this moment for years. The strong God has chosen you to be His own special being. Esau is a man of the earth. He is my son, and I love him, but *you* are the one God has chosen. God himself told me that."

"But, Mother, are you sure? After all, Esau is the firstborn."

"God can do anything He chooses, Jacob. He's chosen you, and He will put you over your brother. Only do as I say, and you will see that I speak the truth."

For a moment Rebekah thought Jacob was going to refuse. He had grown up, like other Hebrews, with strong feelings about the firstborn. Rarely was the oldest son's position ever challenged. Rebekah knew she was asking Jacob to go against the teachings and traditions of the tribe, but she was absolutely certain that God had spoken to her. She could see no way other than this to bring about what God had said would come to pass. "Go now, my son. Quickly. We must hurry."

Jacob straightened up, and a determined look changed the set of his features. His eyes narrowed, his lips grew tight, and his very body seemed to grow taller. "Yes, Mother. If this is what God has said, then we must take whatever steps are necessary." He turned at once and left.

Rebekah stood watching him go, and for one moment doubt assailed her. She, too, was strongly taught in the ways of the Hebrews, and the tradition of the oldest son as the leader was very strong in her. But stronger than this was the memory of God's message to her, which over the years had not grown fainter but had only increased. Even now she could recall every detail of that moment when God had spoken to her. She lifted her hands and said, "Oh, God, Jacob and I will do your will, and it will come to pass as you have said—that the older shall serve the younger." She turned quickly then and left the tent.

———————

The sun was high in the sky, beaming down its warmth and life-giving qualities. Jacob had paced throughout the camp all morning after he had delivered the dressed kids to his mother. He knew she had started cooking the meat, and she had warned him not to get too far away.

Now he started toward the cook tent, and when he stepped inside, his mother turned to face him. She was pale, he saw, but her back was straight and her eyes glowed with an intensity he had never before seen.

"All things are ready, my son. Come, let me prepare you."

Jacob stepped forward and saw that she held something in her hand.

"What's that, Mother?"

"Let me tie these on your forearms."

Jacob obediently put out his right arm and leaned forward as she quickly put something over him. "What is this?" he said. "It looks like a skin of the kid."

"It is. Your father, as you say, loves to touch. He will put his hands on you, and your smoothness will tell him at once that you are Jacob." As she spoke, Rebekah fastened the woolly skin over his forearm. It fit exactly, and she tied it on with leather thongs through holes she had pierced. Jacob ran his left hand over it. "It does feel like hairy skin," he murmured.

"Here. Let me put on the other one."

Jacob watched as she finished the work and held his arms up. "How did you ever think of this?"

Rebekah did not answer. She turned and said, "I've prepared the meat. Your father won't be able to tell it from venison. I've seasoned it the way he likes." She went outside and Jacob followed her. Bending over, she picked up a bowl and then a wooden ladle. Dipping it into the black pot that was sitting over the fire, she filled the bowl and put a smaller spoon in it. She turned and held it out to Jacob. As he took it, she stared at him intently. "Speak as little as possible. Your brother's voice is stronger. So speak loudly."

Jacob swallowed hard, a touch of fear gripping his stomach. "If he finds me out, I'll be ruined, Mother. I will have to leave forever."

"You will not be found out. He's expecting Esau, and his mind isn't clear. Go now. This is our time, Jacob, yours and mine. God has told us to do it."

Jacob had always envied those who heard the voice of God, especially Abraham, his grandfather. Isaac had also been in the presence of the all-powerful God who ruled the world, the Eternal One who made all things. Jacob believed implicitly his mother's words that God had spoken to her, and now he steeled himself and said, "I'm trusting in the word that you got from the Eternal One, Mother."

"That is good, my son—now, go!"

Jacob walked quickly to the door of the tent, pushing back the front flap. A burning oil lamp threw its yellow corona of light over his father, who lay as if asleep. For one moment Jacob hesitated. His father's face looked so wan and tired that he thought, *I can't take advantage of a poor old man.* But his mother's words overcame his objections. Besides, as he had wandered the camp that morning, he had reasoned for the acceptability of their plan from the behavior of both his father and his grandfather. Both of them did a wrong thing in order for a good thing to come. *If I do this one thing that is wrong, I will be able to do many great things. Esau has much cruelty in him. He would not be kind to our people, but I will be.*

Grasping the medallion through his tunic with his free hand, he firmly imitated Esau's voice as well as he could. "My father, I am here. Are you awake?"

Isaac opened his eyes at once and said, "Yes, I am. Is it my son Esau?"

"Yes, Father, I am Esau, your firstborn. I have done what you have asked. Sit up now and eat of the venison; then give me your blessing."

Isaac struggled to a sitting position, then took the bowl. He fumbled eagerly for the spoon, but the meat was hot. He blew on it, and as he waited for it to cool, he said, "How is it you have found the game so quickly? It's not past noon, is it?"

"Because the Lord your God brought it to me," Jacob said quickly.

Isaac turned his head to one side slightly. He blew on the meat again, took a bite of it, and sighed. "That is very good." Reaching out his free hand, he said, "Come here, Esau, that I may feel whether you are indeed my son Esau."

Jacob's heart sank, and fear pierced him like a sword. *He knows I'm not Esau.* But there was nothing else to do. He came forward and said, "Yes, I am your son Esau." He put out his hand and touched the old man's shoulder. Isaac ran his hand over Jacob's forearm. Jacob was petrified. Any man of discernment would know the difference between a man's skin and a kid skin! He was fully prepared for his father to cry out "You're an impostor!" and his mouth was as dry as dust.

Isaac sighed then and removed his hand. "You are indeed my son Esau, and you have brought me such good venison."

The panic that had been rising in Jacob subsided, and he sat beside Isaac as the old man ate.

"Give me some wine, my son."

"Yes, Father." Jacob rose and took the bottle of wine that hung from a peg, poured it into a wooden cup, and handed it to Isaac, who drank gratefully.

Isaac handed back the cup, and when Jacob had set it down, the old man said, "Come here now and kiss me, my son."

Again Jacob became fearful. *Esau is a big, burly man, and I am not. He will know by the feel of me that I am not Esau.* But he need not have feared, for Isaac merely placed his hands on his shoulders. Jacob felt them lightly at first, like the touch of a bird; then Isaac drew him closer and kissed him.

Isaac's grasp grew firmer, and he put his arms around Jacob's neck and drew him close. "The smell of my son is like the smell of a field that the Lord has blessed." His voice then fell into a rhythm and became much stronger—so strong, in fact, that Jacob was shocked. He had not heard his father speak with such power and authority in many years, and he knew that this was the patriarch passing his mantle and staff along to the one who should succeed him.

"May God give you of heaven's dew and of earth's richness—an abundance of grain and new wine. May nations serve you and peoples bow down to you. Be lord over your brothers, and may the sons of your mother bow down to you. May those who curse you be cursed and those who bless you be blessed."

The blessing went on for some time, and the voice remained strong. But then Isaac began to weep. "My son, I shall soon pass from this earth, and I pray that you will be a man of strength and honor. A man like your grandfather Abraham, who was the friend of God. Always be the friend of God, my son, always!" Jacob felt Isaac's hands loosen, and then he saw that the old man had exhausted himself. He laid him down gently, and when he stared at the worn, tired features of his father, tears filled his eyes. He could not bear to look upon him, and he turned and left the tent.

"I heard him give you the blessing." Rebekah was standing there waiting. She threw her arms around Jacob's neck and drew him close. "Oh, my son, you have received the blessing of the firstborn! You will be the great man of our people!"

Jacob stood holding his mother, and there was a war inside his breast. He felt the triumph of all that she had said, and yet he knew that for a long time he would see the face of his father—pale, worn, and tired—the man whom he had deceived.

———

Late in the day, Esau returned from hunting and entered his father's tent with a bowlful of venison stew. The hunt had been difficult. His wives had made the stew under his direction, and now it was dark outside. As he entered the tent, he saw that his mother was not there, which surprised him. Nonetheless he went directly to Isaac and said, "Father, arise and eat. I have brought you the venison. Let your soul bless me."

Isaac sat up straight and looked around wildly. "Who is this? Who is speaking?"

"Why, I am your son. Your firstborn, Esau."

Esau was shocked at his father's expression. His face seemed to fall apart. His mouth opened, and he tried to speak but could not. He began to tremble, and Esau leaned forward. "What is it, Father? Are you ill?"

Isaac could not speak. He put out his hand and touched Esau's face and then let his hand run down his side and over his forearm. His voice rose, and panic threaded his tone. "Who is this? Who comes to me?"

Esau stared at his father. "It is me, Esau. Your firstborn, Father. Don't you know me?"

Isaac fell back and put his hands over his face. "I do not know you. Who brought me the venison earlier? I have already eaten of it and have blessed the one who brought it. And he shall be blessed."

Esau's mind went blank. He could not understand his father's words. "What do you mean, Father?"

Isaac did not remove his hand, and his voice was muffled. "One has come before you, my son Esau. I thought it was you. He said his name was Esau, and he brought the savory venison such as I love."

"But you did not bless him, my father."

"Yes. I blessed him. He received the blessing of the firstborn."

Esau angrily flung the stew from him. It splattered on the floor, and he fell forward on his knees and grabbed Isaac's arms. He put them on his own head and cried out, "Who was it?"

"It was your brother, Jacob! It must have been. He came and took away your blessing."

Esau began to shake with a white rage. "Is he not rightly named Jacob? He has usurped me twice. First he tricked me into renouncing my birthright, and now he's taken away my blessing." His shoulders shook, and he held his father so tightly that the old man winced. "Give me a blessing also, my father!"

But Isaac shook his head. "I have made him your master, and all his brothers have I given to him for servants. I have given him new grain and wine. I have nothing left to give you, my son."

Esau was not a crying man, but he began to weep, tearing at his robe and loudly lamenting, "Bless me. Even me also, oh, my father!"

And then Isaac reached out his hands, groping for his son, and they fell on Esau's head. The big man had bowed over him and put his head down on Isaac's chest, and Isaac began to speak. "Your dwelling will be away from the earth's richness, away from the dew of heaven above. You will live by the sword and you will serve your brother. But when you grow restless, you will throw his yoke from off your neck." He then embraced his son, clinging to him tightly. "Your brother has the blessing of the first-born, my son Esau. You must accept it."

Esau rose. Tears ran down his face, and he turned and stumbled blindly out of the tent. Rage began to fill his entire being, and he stopped and stared at the tent where Jacob lived. His mind was crazed with murderous thoughts, yet for once he restrained himself. Staring at his brother's tent, he whispered, "I will not touch him while my father lives—but as soon as he dies, I will kill my brother for stealing my place!"

CHAPTER
6

Everyone in the tribe walked widely around Esau in the days that followed Isaac's granting of the blessing to Jacob. Always a violent man, Esau did not hesitate to state his intent that he would have his revenge on his younger brother after his father's death. His threats were joined by a rash act, which was typical of Esau. His wrath against his brother so flowed through him that he was not reasoning well. He was never a man to think things through, so knowing that his parents despised his Canaanite wives and hoping to gain their favor, he went to Ishmael and took his daughter Mahalath as a wife. When questioned about why he added a third wife to his already conflict-filled household, he said, "My parents do not like the Canaanite women, so I will win their favor by marrying one of our own people."

But Rebekah was not deceived. She knew Esau was capable of murder, and she did not miss the looks of hatred he always gave his brother, Jacob. Finally she devised a scheme and went directly to Jacob with it.

She found him out in the fields with the flock, for he often stayed away from the camp now. She knew he was troubled over having deceived his father and was fearful of his brother's revenge. When he turned to her, she said, "Jacob, your brother will kill you as soon as he has a chance."

"I know it," Jacob said bitterly. He stared at his mother and shook his head almost violently. "I wish I'd never done it, Mother."

"It was necessary," Rebekah said. She put her hand on his chest and felt his heart beating. "It will be all right. In time he will forget it."

"Not Esau. He *never* forgets a wrong."

"Listen to me, Jacob. I want you to go to Haran."

"To Haran? What for?"

"I want you to go stay with my brother Laban."

"Stay with him? For how long?"

"A few days ... or weeks, perhaps. Even a few months would not be too much. You must stay away long enough for Esau to lose this hatred for you." She spoke quickly and persuasively. "Esau is an impulsive man. He will forget what you've done to him, and when he does I will send word for you to come home again."

Jacob felt a weight lift at her words. "I will go, Mother, but what will we tell Father?"

"Let me talk to him. We've already talked about your finding a wife. You must not marry one of these Canaanite women. You must find a wife among our own people."

Jacob shrugged. "I'm not worried about finding a wife. All I want to do is stay alive."

Rebekah leaned forward and pulled Jacob's head down and kissed him. "All will be well," she said. "You will not be gone long, and you may find a woman there to love. A woman of our own people. Get ready. I will go tell your father."

———

Isaac never spoke of the blessing Jacob had tricked him into making. Rebekah had prepared Isaac to meet with Jacob by saying, "You must be kind. What's done is done, and Jacob must not marry a Canaanite woman. He must go to my brother Laban. There will be young women there, and my brother will help him choose."

Isaac reached out toward his son, and when Jacob took his hand, he said, "My son, you must not take a wife from among the daughters of Canaan. Your mother and I want you to go to Paddan Aram, to the house of Bethuel, your mother's father. Take a wife from one of the daughters of Laban, your mother's brother." He hesitated, then seemed to grow freer. He lifted his head and strained to see his son's face. "May God Almighty bless you and make you fruitful and increase your numbers until you become a community of peoples. May he give you and your descendants the blessing of Abraham, so that you may take possession of the land where you now live as an alien, the land God gave to Abraham."

Relieved that Isaac had not mentioned his deceit concerning the blessing, Jacob kissed his father and left the tent. His mother had gathered his things together, and now she embraced him. "Go quickly, my son."

"I will miss you, Mother!"

"It will not be long," Rebekah promised. "You will be back in a short time. Now, God be with you."

Jacob shouldered his belongings and, taking his staff, left the camp. As he did, a sinking feeling came to him. He turned back to see Rebekah standing in front of her tent. Something about her posture disturbed him. He waved and smiled and called, "Good-bye, Mother," but she did not move for a long time. Finally she lifted her hand in a gesture of farewell, but he saw she was weeping.

Why is she weeping? I'll soon be back—maybe with a fine wife. With this thought he comforted himself and hurried out of the camp.

———————

The night was coming on, and Jacob sought a place to rest. He had been on his journey four days now, and his provisions were almost gone. He had brought a bow and arrows but had been unable to take down any game. The game was plentiful, but Jacob had never honed his skill with bow and arrow. Bitterly he thought, *If Esau were here, he'd be feasting by now.*

When he stopped for the night, the place was filled with rocks. He had to search to find some softer ground in between them.

Opening his bag, he ate the portion of mutton that was left and saw that he was practically out of food. He drank the last of the wine in the goatskin and then sat back and watched the sun set.

All day he had walked under a bright, full sun, and now the crimson disk was settling into the west, far away behind the mountains. The air was becoming chilled, and he shivered. Drawing out his blanket, he wrapped it around himself, lay back, and tried to sleep. All around him, as the sun disappeared, pearl-colored shadows covered the rocks, and the rough terrain with its scrub bushes took on soft, silver shadings. The peace of evening magnified distant sounds, and a sense of loneliness came over him as he heard the far-off cries of a wild dog. He watched as dust whirled in the small wind gusts, skimming along the surface of the world. Then night settled almost at once.

Jacob lay awake for a while, his mind full of his life history. He had the gift of almost total recall, and time and again he relived the scene when his father had put his hand on him and given him the blessing of the firstborn. He tried desperately to believe that his real motive had been to fulfill the prophecy his mother had been given. He tried to convince himself that what he and Rebekah had done had been a good thing. It had been necessary for God to achieve His purpose. But when Jacob tried to pray, the scene came before him, and he could sense God's displeasure. The thought chilled him.

Finally he built up a fire and sat for a long time watching it. From time to time he would light a twig and watch the yellow flame as it glowed briefly in the darkness. Overhead, stars spangled the ebony skies. There were no clouds, and when he looked up and saw the stars, he remembered his grandfather repeating the promise God had made him—that he would have descendants as many as the stars in the sky.

Jacob tried to count them, then shook his head, feeling foolish. "No man could count them," he said aloud. The sound of his own voice startled him, and he picked up a stick and poked the fire. The action sent hundreds of tiny sparks flowing upward, twisting and turning in the breeze. They rose high in the air and seemed to mingle with the distant dots of fire in the sky.

Finally weariness overtook Jacob, and he wrapped himself as warmly as he could. But for a long time he lay thinking of his past, wishing he could undo some of the things he had done.

A light came so abruptly and sharply that Jacob could not bear it. He was confused and put his hands over his eyes to blot out the intense brightness. He was frightened also, for such brilliance out of such darkness was not natural.

And then he knew he was dreaming. This had happened to him before when in a dream he knew he was dreaming. It always gave him an eerie feeling, and the thought troubled him now as he lay shielding his eyes. *What if I never wake up? What if this is the Strong One coming to kill me?*

A sound came to him then that he had never heard before, and in his dream he sat up and removed his hand from his eyes. What he saw that moment he would never forget. A stairway glowing with light appeared before him. The bottom of it was planted on the desert, but it went up and up and up, higher than any mountain Jacob had ever seen or could even conceive of. It rose high into the air, and the size and magnificence of the stairway, which glowed like pale gold and glittered like diamonds, would have been enough to frighten him.

But even more frightening was the fact that the stairway was occupied! The beings were glorious beyond anything he had ever seen. Their faces— what faces they had! Jacob realized they were angels, some going up the ladder, ascending out of sight, and others coming down. They were older than the hills yet younger than the morning dew, and they were innocent. He knew he had never seen such innocent faces in all his life! Every face he had seen on earth was a mirror reflecting guilt and wrongdoing and sin.

But these beings had no sin, and they exuded joy. And as they sang, the melodies they lifted were songs of praise such as Jacob could not have imagined. There were as many of them, it seemed, as stars in the sky, and they sang together—some in basso profundo tones, others with climbing, soaring soprano voices reaching the heavens. He could not understand the words, but he knew they all united to praise the glory of the everlasting God.

Jacob watched and listened, and the glory of the angelic beings and the stairway that reached far beyond the stars filled his soul. He was wishing he could stay there forever when he heard a voice he knew he would never forget.

It was as deep as the sea, as powerful as a storm with the strength to rip the earth asunder . . . yet as gentle as a breeze that might barely stir the tiny feathers of a small bird. There was comfort in that voice—and love and joy and strength—and it seemed to soak into Jacob like water to a man dying of thirst. He looked up and saw a mighty light above the stairway, majestic in its power and radiance. Yet the voice was close—in his ear . . . and in his heart.

"I am the Lord, the God of your father Abraham and the God of Isaac. I will give you and your descendants the land on which you are lying. Your descendants will be like the dust of the earth, and you will spread out to the west and to the east, to the north and to the south. All peoples on earth will be blessed through you and your offspring. I am with you and will watch over you wherever you go, and I will bring you back to this land. I will not leave you until I have done what I have promised you."

And then the angelic hosts lifted their voices in a triumphant song that seemed to move heaven and earth. It rose above heaven and went down to the deepest parts of the earth, but most of all it sank into Jacob's soul. He never forgot that melody, and he mourned the rest of his life because he knew he would never hear it again on this earth.

———

Jacob sat straight up, frightened, and looked around wildly. He saw that it was morning, and he knew that the dream had taken all night. He would never forget the stairway, nor the voice, nor the words. He felt a great surge of joy, and he jumped to his feet, lifting his arms and crying, "Oh, Lord God, you are real! You have spoken to me as you spoke to my grandfather Abraham and to my father, Isaac, and to my mother. I praise and thank you, my God, for stooping down to speak to a sinner such as I!"

Jacob walked around praising God, tears flowing down his face. He took the stone he had used for a pillow and heaved it on top of an upthrust rock, forming a pillar. Then going to his pack, he pulled out a small jar of oil. He returned to the stone and poured the oil over it, tears filling his eyes. He stepped back and fell on his knees and lifted his voice toward heaven. "I call the name of this place Bethel—'house of God.' If God will be with me and will watch over me on this journey I am taking and will give me food to eat and clothes to wear so that I return safely to my father's house, then the Lord will be my God. This stone that I have set up as a pillar will be God's house, and of all that you give me I will give you a tenth."

Then Jacob fell on his face sobbing, and he felt again in his heart a trace of the glory he had seen. He lay facedown, simply giving thanks to God, knowing that one day he would come back to this place. Finally he got to his feet, gathered his pack, and took one last look around. "This place is none other than the house of God, and this is the very gate of heaven!"

PART TWO

THE SISTERS

CHAPTER
7

Jacob had begun to think that Paddan didn't exist! Ever since he had seen the vision of the great stairway reaching up into heaven, he had marched hard across the arid lands. Water holes had been scarce, and at times his tongue had grown as dry as the sand and stones under his feet. His sandals had worn out, and he had cut pieces of leather off his pack in order to fashion new ones. Walking barefoot across the burning sand and rocks was intolerable.

As he approached the crest of the rise before him, he had little hope of seeing anything other than more desert. He had come over many such rises, and every time he had been greeted not with the sight of human habitation but only with more low, barren hills stretching endlessly over the horizon. With tongue swollen, feet torn and bleeding, and stomach shrunken from lack of food, his thoughts went back to Bethel, where he had met God face-to-face. Despite the discomforts his body suffered now, the memories he had of his past life were even harsher. Even with the glory of the vision still fresh in his mind, he could not help thinking what a wreck he had made of his life. *If I'd set out to ruin myself, I couldn't have done it better!* He shut his eyes as if to blot out the bitter thoughts. He caught his toe on a rock, and pain shot up his leg. Hopping on one foot, he held his toe, wanting to fling his staff far from him in a rage. But that would not do, for he needed something to lean on.

Stumbling on, he berated himself for his stupidity. *What did that vision mean? How can God use such a sorry fellow as I am? He knows everything I've done. You can't hide from God.* He remembered his mother's words: *"Soon you will come home again."*

"Fat chance of that," Jacob groaned. "Esau will never forget what I did to him. Never! I might as well get used to never seeing home again."

The sun rose higher in the sky as the lone figure stumbled along. A wild dog emerged from behind a rock, and the two stared at each other. For a moment Jacob thought the dog meant to attack him, but when he shouted and waved his staff, the animal ducked away and disappeared into the low-growing shrubs—the only vegetation the desert offered. Looking up, Jacob spotted three buzzards circling over to his right, and a shiver went through him. "They're just waiting to get me, but they won't," he muttered grimly.

Less than half an hour after seeing the dog and the buzzards, Jacob reached the top of yet another crest. His legs were trembling with weariness, and he had never been so dirty in all of his life. When he topped the crest, he stopped dead still. There lying before him was a large valley with lush green grass that bespoke of springs and human beings.

He stumbled forward anxiously, nearly falling, and saw spots of white that he realized were sheep. He moved as fast as he could, but he was using his last reserves of strength. Then he remembered the promise God had given to protect him. Gratefully he uttered, "Thank you, God, for bringing me safely here!"

The valley opened up beneath his feet, and soon he was walking on a thin crust of dirt, dotted with tendrils of grass. But Jacob was looking for water, not grass.

Soon he heard the bleating of the sheep, and the grass became thicker. A sigh of relief washed through him as he saw two men leaning on their staffs watching him stumble forward. Jacob lifted his hand and croaked, "Greetings."

The two men nodded but did not speak, and Jacob realized with chagrin that he was not much to look at. He was filthy from head to foot; his hair was clogged with the dirt of the desert and hung lankly around his shoulders. His knees were bleeding from the numerous falls he had taken, crusted with brown blood, and his clothes were ripped by the many thorns he had encountered along the way.

"Water!" Jacob gasped. "Please give me a drink!"

One of the two men looked at the other, and an unspoken message passed between them. He shrugged and said, "There's your water. Help yourself."

Jacob turned and saw a rock and beside it clear water bubbling forth. It fed a small stream that wound its way in a serpentine fashion, outlined now by the sheep that gathered around both sides of it, making a white line across the valley floor.

Dropping his staff and his pack, Jacob fell on his face and stuck his mouth under the water. It was cold and the best drink he had ever had in his life! He drank until he could hold no more and could almost feel the fluid seeping into his dry tissues. He stuck his whole head under the stream, letting it mat his hair, then rolled over and came to his feet. Wiping the water from his face and pressing it from his hair, he said, "Thank you, sirs."

"You look like you've had a hard trip."

"Yes. All the way from Beersheba."

Both shepherds shook their heads, and the taller of the two said, "That's not a good trip for a man to make alone. There are bandits and bears between here and there."

Jacob smiled wryly. "I know. But it was a journey I had to make."

"Where are you going?"

"Do you know of Laban?"

The shorter of the two grimaced. "Laban?"

"He's a relative of mine," Jacob said.

"My name is Doni and this is Razo," the taller man said. "We live over in that direction."

"But you know Laban?" Jacob asked again.

Doni laughed. "Yes, we know him, but we don't know much good about him, even if he is your relative."

Jacob's heart sank, and he saw the two watching him closely. "What evil do you know of him?"

"Oh, he's not a criminal or anything like that." Razo shrugged his scrawny shoulders.

"He would be if he had the chance, though." Doni grinned. "But I guess the worst thing I can say about him is that he spends most of his time in the village drinking when he ought to be tending to his business." He peered closely at Jacob. "You haven't let him borrow any money, have you?"

"No, certainly not!"

"Well, I wouldn't if I were you." He laughed, saying, "He's got two sons, Lomach and Benzar, dark-skinned fellows."

"That's right. They were born to a black concubine when Laban was a young man. He's too cheap to hire good help, so those two take care of what work is done—which isn't much."

"Is that all the family he has?"

"Oh, he's got a wife—who scares me somehow. She's some kind of a witch, I think."

"Yes, and he's got those two girls."

"Two girls? How old are they?" Jacob asked quickly.

Razo winked at his companion. "This fellow's already checking out the women, and he hasn't yet washed all the dust off of himself! One of them is too young to interest you now, but she'll be a beauty someday. Her name is Rachel. The other is Leah."

"She won't do you any good either," Razo said. "She's the brains of the family. If it weren't for her, they would have gone down a long time ago. But talk is she's going to marry."

"I don't know about that," Doni said. He scratched himself vigorously and then shook his head. "That Mehor, he's a rough one. He's already killed one man over a woman."

"Mehor?" Jacob asked. "Who's he?"

"He's from another tribe. Lives over those hills to the west. He's a big, bruising man. Swears he's going to marry Leah no matter what she says."

"It sounds like she doesn't care much for him," Jacob murmured. He turned as he saw a small flock of sheep approaching, being led by a young woman. "Who's this?" he asked.

"Why, that's Rachel. Your kinswoman, if what you tell us is true."

Jacob stood absolutely still, watching the girl with curious interest. He recalled having heard his mother speak of her. Rebekah had never seen Rachel, but she'd heard reports from a traveler.

The two shepherds grinned and ambled away, warning, "Watch out for that Leah. Don't fall for her, stranger, or Mehor will get you."

Jacob paid them no heed. His eyes were on the young woman. She was barely more than a girl but clearly on the verge of womanhood. Her hair was tied back, and she wore a simple light-blue robe that came down only to her knees. Had she been older, she would have worn a robe to her feet, as was the custom. As she came closer, Jacob studied her face. Her eyebrows were thin and arched, and her face was round with smooth, delicate skin. She pursed her lips, her lower lip more pronounced, as if she were pouting. She smiled at one of the sheep, and a dimple appeared on her right cheek. She was a slender girl but of pleasing proportions.

Jacob moved forward to greet her. The loneliness of the desert made his heart swell at the sight of one who was of his own blood. The girl turned to meet him too, her eyes wide with anticipation. He saw then that they were of the darkest possible blue, and her complexion was impossibly smooth. "Greetings, my kinswoman."

Rachel blinked with surprise. "You are a kinsman?" she asked breathlessly. Her voice was almost childlike, as was her attitude. Jacob suddenly remembered how the shepherds had spoken of her youth and how they expected she would blossom into a beautiful woman before long. He came forward and stood before her. "Yes, we are kin," he said. He leaned over and kissed her on the cheek as one would kiss a small child. He smelled a faint scent like a wild flower, and the weariness of his trip swept over him. "I am Rebekah's son," he said. "My name is Jacob."

Rachel broke into a bright smile, and her eyes danced. The dimple reappeared in her cheek, and she said, "Why, I've heard you spoken of, sir, many times. If you'll tend my sheep, I will go fetch my father."

"Yes, I will. Is it far?"

"No. Not far at all. You look tired and weary. Rest and I will run as fast as I can."

Jacob nodded, and as the girl whirled and ran away, he sat down, overcome with fatigue. "At least I found the place I was looking for," he muttered.

"Father, there's a man who says he's Rebekah's son. He's down at the spring."

Laban looked up, his eyes growing suspicious. "What do you say, girl? Rebekah's son?"

"His name, he says, is Jacob. He's all worn out and tired, and he's dirty, but he says he's a kinsman."

"He could be anybody," Laban muttered. He was sitting back leaning against a tent pole with a wineskin in his hand. He lifted it, squirted a stream into his mouth, and swallowed. He was a scrawny man, and his robe was filthy. He got to his feet. "I'll go see this fellow," he grumbled.

"Be sure he's who he says."

Laban turned to look at the woman who had spoken. She was tall with strange light-colored eyes and reddish brown hair. He had taken her from a desert tribe as a wife. "I guess I'll know my own kinsman, Ziva."

"You're so drunk you wouldn't know a horse if you saw one," Ziva snorted. "I'd better go with you."

"No, you stay here. I can handle this."

Laban staggered out of the tent with Rachel by his side. She skipped along, running ahead and coming back to the old man, who clumped along with his eyes to the ground. He had a seamed, sour-looking face with eyes too close together that squinted constantly with suspicion.

When they reached the spring, Laban watched cautiously as the young man, who was sitting down, stood to his feet. *Not much to look at,* he thought. *Looks like a wastrel. Well, he needn't think I'll feed him!* He kept these thoughts to himself, for he still had some idea in the back of his mind that Rebekah, or her family, might somehow be of use to him. He had heard reports for years about Isaac's wealth, and more than once he had been tempted to go on a journey to make some profit out of them. "Greetings, sir. You've come far, I see."

"My name is Jacob. You are my uncle Laban, I think."

"If your mother is named Rebekah, then she is indeed my sister. I'm surprised to see you in such condition."

"It was a harder trip than I imagined." Jacob's knees were shaking.

"Father, take him home. He's bound to be starved."

"Well . . . I suppose we must. Welcome, nephew."

The greeting was given grudgingly, Jacob noticed, but he was too weary to argue. The three made their journey back to the camp, and by the time they arrived, Jacob was trembling all over. He was aware that two tall women had come out. One was old and the other young, but they were obviously related. They both had strange hazel-colored eyes, oddly shaped, and the younger woman had a direct stare about her that discomfited him.

"This is my wife, Ziva, and this is her daughter, Leah."

Jacob bowed low. "I am sorry to have come in such poor shape. The trip was much harder than I thought it would be."

Leah came forward at once. She was as tall as Jacob, and her unusual eyes were round and staring, with such pale eyelashes they appeared almost snakelike. But there was a sensuous beauty to her form, and Jacob, even as tired as he was, found himself interested in her.

"Come, sir, I will provide you water so that you may wash while we prepare the evening meal."

Jacob smiled. "Thank you, Leah. You're very kind."

Laban suddenly laughed. "That's the first time you've ever been called kind, isn't it, daughter?"

Leah shot a venomous glance at her father, and he immediately shut his mouth and dropped his head, unable to meet her fierce glance. "Come along," Leah said. She led Jacob away to one of the tents, provided a bronze basin, and then brought a vase full of water. She poured it into the basin, and when he thanked her, she smiled.

Even though Jacob had found her eyes extraordinary, her lips now caught his attention. They were as full and sensuous as any lips he had ever seen on a woman.

"And you are very welcome," she said with a gleam in her eye that acknowledged his attraction to her. "Wash now and rest yourself. I will come when the food is ready." She reached out and touched his cheek in a familiar gesture. "You are tired and weary now, but after you rest, we will want to hear about your journey." She smiled then and left the room.

Jacob's cheek felt as if it were burning where she had touched him. He stared after her and then shook his head. "Never saw anyone like her!" he muttered as he began to wash. He had kept one clean robe in his pack, and after washing as well as he could, he put on the robe and gave in to his weariness. He lay down on the mat and was asleep at once.

———

He came out of his sleep with a start, for he found Leah kneeling over him touching his chest. In confusion he put his hand out as if to push her away and found himself shoving against the fullness of her figure. She did not protest but laughed. "Now, sir, you mustn't take liberties even with a kinswoman."

"I'm sorry," Jacob muttered, embarrassed. He got to his feet and saw that she had put on another dress of some rather sheer material that outlined her figure plainly.

She was watching him, and Jacob knew she was aware of his feelings. It clearly did not displease her, however, and she said with an inviting smile, "Come. The meal is ready."

Leah led him from the tent across a wide open space, around which were circled several tents. The children stopped their play long enough to stare at the stranger. Leah said, "This way," and led him inside the largest of the tents.

Laban and his wife were already seated, and Rachel was bringing food in and putting it down. "Hello," she said. "You look much better."

"I feel better, Rachel. I hope I look a little better. Thank you."

"Sit down," Laban said, motioning to a place.

Two women began serving the food. They were introduced briefly with a grunt as Bilhah and Zilpah. Bilhah was younger than Rachel and plump and short. She was a mere child, shy and backward. Zilpah, the older of the two, was tall and lean and in her midtwenties. She gave Jacob a careful look as she set a large platter of food down by him.

Jacob was ravenous, and the food, though plain, tasted as wonderful as any he had ever eaten. There was freshly baked bread, olives, and bowls of thick porridge prepared with sesame oil. There was also plenty of goat's milk and red wine to satisfy his thirst. As Jacob ate and drank, he noticed that his uncle Laban seemed cowed by his wife. Ziva was indeed an imposing woman. It was almost impossible to guess her age, but as the shepherds had told him, she had come from a desert tribe, and even in her older years, some of that wildness still clung to her.

Of the two daughters, Rachel spoke the most. She babbled on almost constantly, firing questions at Jacob until finally Leah said, "Rachel, hush, let the man eat. Can't you see he's starved?"

"Oh, I'm sorry! I do talk too much."

"No, you don't, Rachel," Jacob assured her. "But this food is so good! Just let me have my fill, and I'll answer any question you'd like."

The mealtime was pleasant and polite, but it was obvious that Laban was suspicious of him. *He's afraid I've come to live off of him. I suppose I don't look like much of a prize,* Jacob thought.

When the meal was over, Leah said, "Why don't you rest, Jacob, while Rachel and I clean up."

"Thank you. I'm afraid I still feel pretty tired, even after the sleep I had earlier," Jacob admitted. "Rachel," he said, looking at the girl, "perhaps we can talk again later and you can ask me any question you want to."

"Oh, that will be fine, Jacob," Rachel said. "I'll think up some more while I'm helping my sister."

Jacob laughed, got up, and bowed to his hosts. "Thank you, sir, and to you, Ziva, for your hospitality."

He returned to his own tent and lay down again. With a stomach full of warm food and wine, he went to sleep instantly.

"I think he's handsome, don't you, Leah?"

Leah was cleaning the dishes and turned to give her younger sister a smile. "Yes, I think so."

The two girls were very different, but they had different mothers. Ziva had imparted to her daughter her own height and sensuous qualities, as well as the strange-colored eyes and reddish hair. Rachel was barely out of childhood, and had an air of innocence about her.

Rachel's mother had been named Lewanna—which meant "the moon." She had been a beautiful woman. Laban had paid a great price for her, and if he loved anyone, it had been this wife. She had died giving birth to

Rachel, and the child had grown up with only whatever affection she could get from Ziva and from her sister, Leah. Actually they were rather fond of the girl, but she still led a lonely life.

"I don't think he's married," Rachel said. "He didn't say anything about a wife."

Leah turned her hazel eyes on the girl and laughed. "You're starting to think about a husband already? And here you've only been a woman for less than three months."

Rachel's fair skin reddened with a blush. "I have a right to think about a husband now, even if I am young! What about you? He'd be a good husband for you . . . if it weren't for Mehor."

"Well, I don't know about this man either. I don't know if he could satisfy a woman."

Rachel stared at her, not able to grasp her meaning, and then she saw the glint in Leah's eyes. "Oh," she said, "I hadn't thought of that."

"Well, you'd better start thinking of it. You'll be sleeping with some man for the rest of your life. Better make sure that he will be a good lover."

"What do you mean? I don't understand."

Leah laughed and put her arm around the girl, looking down at her. "You're young yet. You've got plenty of time to think of such things."

Rachel looked up into her sister's face. Rachel was intensely curious about the details of marriage. Having grown up around animals, she knew only the fundamentals of such things, and now she said, "Tell me how you can know if a man would be a good lover."

Leah sat down and pulled the girl beside her. "All right. First of all you have to be sure that he looks at you with something in his eyes."

"With what, Leah?"

"He has to want you like a thirsty man longs for water. You have to see it in his eyes." Leah continued to speak, and soon they were giggling. They were close friends despite the difference in their ages—more like mother and daughter, really—and Leah had a genuine affection for Rachel. As she spoke, she knew someone had to enlighten the girl, and her mother, Ziva, was not likely to.

Rachel listened avidly as Leah spoke on. She was in that time of youth when thoughts of love and marriage both drew her and frightened her. A woman was born to be with a man—she knew that much—but which man? And what would happen after the marriage ceremony? Would she be able to please her husband? And how does a girl know about such things? As she pondered her sister's instruction, she began to think of Jacob in ways she had never before thought of a man.

Even as the two young women were giggling and talking, Laban was speaking to his two sons, Lomach and Benzar, who had come in late from the fields. They were both dark complected and short and stocky as their mother had been. Laban had been barely out of his teens when he had bargained for the woman, and she in turn had given birth to the boys within two years.

Now Laban was telling them of Jacob's arrival, and like their father, they were suspicious of strangers—even family.

Lomach, the more talkative of the two, shook his head. "I don't like it," he said. "We don't need him here."

Benzar opened his mouth to agree, but Ziva suddenly appeared. The three lived in fear of her and did not know why. There was something in her strange eyes that repelled them, and each of them were sure that if they crossed her, their throats would be cut.

Ziva stood looking down at the three, her lips curling with disdain. "The man's got sense."

"How do you know that? He just got here," Laban barked.

Ziva did not deign to argue. "Mind what I tell you. He's got sense, and we need some of that around here." She looked at her husband, for whom she had lost respect years ago, and at the two dark men, who were lazy drunkards like their father. "He's got more sense than the three of you put together, and if somebody doesn't take hold here, we're going to lose everything! He's got sense," she repeated. "He stays!"

CHAPTER

8

As Jacob awoke one morning after a month in Laban's camp, he found himself longing for his home back in Beersheba. The intensity of his desire was not unlike that of a starving man craving food. *Maybe I can go home if I return the birthright to Esau....* The thought lingered, but then bitterness gripped him as he realized that the word of his father was binding, and Esau would never accept such a simple solution anyway. Jacob knew his brother well, and as the sunlight entered through a fissure in the tent, throwing down a pale beam that struck his face, the reality of his situation overwhelmed him with grief. In his time with Laban, the old man had proved to be stingy beyond belief. True enough Jacob had not starved, but Laban's hints that it was time for Jacob to earn his keep were getting plainer each day.

At a swishing sound by the tent flap, Jacob turned to see Leah enter.

"Are you awake?" she asked, and leaning down, she touched his cheek—half playfully and half seriously.

"Yes, I'm awake." Jacob arose and shoved his feet into his sandals. "I didn't mean to sleep so late."

"I like to sleep late myself," Leah said, smiling. She had a way of holding him with her gaze that affected him deeply. It was as if her eyes had some sort of magical power! He knew that predatory animals had this ability to fix their prey with such a stare that they could not move. He did not know if this was what Leah was doing—he only knew that her presence was both subtle and powerful. It was not so much what she said as the inflections of her voice. She had a way of moving her shoulders and torso that struck him as being an invitation—but to what, he could not be sure.

"Will you tell me something?" Leah said slyly.

"Why, of course."

The corners of her broad mouth were turning upward into a smile, and her wide eyes seemed to envelop him. "Rachel tells me that when you first met her, you gave her a kiss. Is that true?"

"Why . . . I suppose it is. Just greeting a kinswoman, you know."

"Well, am I not your kinswoman too, Jacob?" The voice was low-pitched, even lower than Leah's normal voice, her tone intentionally beguiling. "Don't I deserve a greeting from my cousin?"

Jacob felt uncomfortably stirred by her voice and by the way she held herself before him. He had never before known a woman who could issue an invitation in such a manner. He took her by the shoulders and started to kiss her on the cheek, but she turned her head so that her lips were waiting instead. He put his arms around her and felt her lips on his. It was like nothing he had ever experienced! It was like falling into a softness he had never known, closing about him and shutting out all reason. He felt her hands behind his neck pulling him closer, her soft body pressing against him, and he gave in to the ravishing sweetness without so much as a thought as to what Laban might think about the situation.

A fine sweat broke out all over his body, and he realized he was holding her too tightly—yet her own arms were tight about him. Finally Jacob lifted his head, his breathing shallow. Leah did not move back but still leaned against him. She put her hand on his cheek and whispered, "My! There must be many women saddened because you left your home."

"Why, not at all!" he said, surprised at her suggestion.

"Oh yes. You can't lie about that, Jacob. You're a strong man. You're able to stir a woman."

Jacob said nothing, but his throat tightened as she smiled and ran her hand down his cheek.

"I'll have to be more careful with you, Jacob. A woman has no protection against a man with your power."

Jacob was not greatly experienced with women. He felt a surge of pride at her assessment of him and at the desire in her eyes that assured him that she was—for herself, at least—speaking the truth. He had never before had a woman say things like this to him, let alone had a woman kiss him like this.

It was only when they heard someone calling Leah's name that she stepped back. "I'll see you later," she whispered with a promise in her voice that stirred him again.

"Get out of that bed before I drag you out!"

Ziva reached down and grabbed Laban by the hair. He cried out with pain as she shook him, but she was relentless. "Get out, I say!"

Laban had been in the village until late last night and had come home blind drunk. He had a splitting headache and now protested, "Turn loose of my hair! You're killing me!"

"You need killing! What do you mean staying out carousing—no doubt with a woman."

"No. That's not so."

"You were gone for three days with those drunken friends of yours. What do you think is happening to the stock?"

"Lomach and Benzar are taking care of them."

"Those loafers! They went off as soon as you left."

Ziva's words awakened Laban at once. In a panic he said, "What about the stock?"

"Jacob's been taking care of them. He hired two men."

"Who's going to pay for them?"

"You are, you old fool! They're your cattle, aren't they? Now, get out of bed!"

"I need something to eat."

"Then fix it yourself!"

Ziva argued more out of habit than for any other reason. She had long ago lost any illusions she might have had about Laban. He was a shiftless, drunken man—selfish, lecherous, and greedy to the bone. She knew he was afraid of her and well he might be. He had beat her once shortly after their marriage. Determined never to be humiliated by him again, she waited for him to go to sleep that night, then poured boiling water over his bare chest. It had left huge blisters that had taken weeks to heal. Since that day she had dared him to touch her, but he never had.

Now Laban stumbled around getting his clothes on, and when she put a bowl of porridge before him, he ate it with trembling hands. His head felt as if someone were driving huge thorns through it, and he endured her nagging until he finally said, "What's my nephew doing now?"

"Why, he's enjoying your gracious hospitality," Ziva said sarcastically. "He's been doing the work *you* should have been doing."

"Well, he needs to work. I can't just feed that fellow forever."

"He'd better stay, then. He knows more about animals than you and your worthless sons or anybody else I know." Seeing his bowl was empty, she dipped out another huge spoonful of the porridge and slapped it into his bowl, then reached down and pulled his head up by the chin. "You'd better wake up, Laban. If you don't do something soon, we're going to lose everything."

Laban could not answer but sat there intimidated. When she removed her hand and turned back to her work, he drew a shaky breath. *She's right,* he thought bitterly. *Somebody's got to take hold around here. Those two sons of mine are worthless.* He might have added that he himself was worthless, but he would never admit that.

Suddenly Ziva turned and said, "I think he ought to marry Leah."

"Marry Leah! Why, Mehor would kill him! You know that."

"He doesn't own her, you know. Besides, if Mehor marries our daughter, he'll take everything you have."

Laban argued faintly, but he knew that Ziva was right. She was always right about things like this, and finally he heard her say, "Leah despises Mehor. You ought to tell that beast to leave her alone."

"Are you crazy!" Laban shouted. "He'd kill me! You know how he is when anybody crosses him. He goes into a blind rage."

"Well, you've got to do something or we'll be beggars."

The cool breeze was delightful after the heat of the day. Overhead the clouds were rolling along lazily like huge, fluffy sheep. Jacob watched them for a time, then continued on his way toward the camp. He had been out treating some sick animals and wondered why in the world Laban had let the herds get into such a terrible state. There was so much to be done, and neither Laban nor his sons seemed to care anything about it.

He heard a cheerful voice behind him and turned to see Rachel skipping toward him. She had a delightful way of running in a childlike fashion. He almost never saw her walk. She either ran or skipped or danced—always in motion. Now the sun highlighted her black hair in a way that pleased him. She came up to him and said, "Are you going home?"

"Yes, I am, Rachel."

"Come on. I want to show you my special place first." She took his hand and chattered constantly as she half pulled him along. Jacob smiled down at her, for she was, indeed, the most cheerful element in Laban's camp. He could not understand how she kept such a happy spirit and decided she must have inherited it from her mother. She got nothing at all, it seemed, from Laban, and at times Jacob even wondered if Laban were truly her father.

Finally Rachel stopped beside a small stream that made a crook like an elbow around some small trees. Their shade sheltered the two from the sun, and she pulled him down to sit beside her.

"This is my special place," she said.

"It's very nice. It's cool here. Do you come a lot?"

"Oh yes. Every chance I get. Nobody else knows about it but you."

"I feel very honored that you'd share it with me, Rachel."

Rachel turned to face him. Her teeth were white as milk, which was unusual for anyone in this country. Her eyes were clear, and the blue was prominent today, he saw. They seemed to change color from time to time, and he was fascinated by them.

"What do you do when you come here all alone?"

"Oh, I sing and make up stories."

"Why don't you tell me one."

"Really? Nobody else wants to hear them."

"Well, I do."

Rachel had a vivid imagination and told a story about a huge bear that was about to devour a beautiful young woman. But he was killed by a strong warrior who drove a spear all the way through his heart.

"And did the warrior marry the young woman?"

"Oh yes! My stories always end happily."

Jacob laughed softly. "That's a good story. I like it."

"Oh, I know lots more."

Jacob sat there, letting the fatigue from the day's hot work drain out of him. It was the quietest and most peaceful moment he'd had since coming to Laban's camp. Finally Rachel turned to him and said, "Are you going to marry Leah?"

"Would you like it if I did?"

"No, because you'd be dead."

"Dead! What do you mean by that?"

Rachel's eyes were large, and she put her finger on her lips. "Mehor would kill you. Don't even talk about him. He's awful!"

"But he's going to marry Leah, or so I hear."

"You'd better stay away from Leah when he's around. The last time he was here one of the young men flirted with Leah, and Mehor just grabbed him and beat him half to death."

"Well," Jacob said, a bit ill at ease, "I'd better leave her alone, I suppose."

"It would be best."

"I'll tell you what. I'll wait until you grow up, Rachel, and then I'll marry you."

Rachel gave him an insulted look. "I *am* grown up! I became a woman four months ago." She stood to her feet, and he scrambled to stand beside her.

"I'm sorry," Jacob said quickly. "I didn't mean to insult you."

Her moods changed quickly, and she smiled and shook her head. "Come on. Let's go back home. I've picked some fresh figs, and you can have them dipped in honey."

"That sounds good to me."

————

Four days after Rachel's warning about Mehor, Jacob came back from the herds to find the man had arrived in camp. He had no doubt who he was, since the burly man towered over Leah. "He's big as an ox!" Jacob muttered. He would have left, but the man turned and demanded, "Who is this?"

Leah said, "This is my cousin Jacob. His mother is my father's sister. He's from Beersheba."

Mehor released Leah's arm and came over to confront Jacob. "You come for a visit?" His voice was rough, but no rougher than his appearance. He towered over Jacob too, and Jacob thought he was the largest man he'd ever seen. His eyes were a murky brown, his hair unkempt. But the most spectacular thing about him was the pads of muscle that covered his body. His hands were large, and now they were clenched as he placed them on his hips.

"Yes," Jacob answered, trying to keep his voice steady. "As Leah says, Laban is my uncle."

"Are you staying long?" The question propelled out of the burly man's lips.

Jacob cleared his throat. "I haven't decided yet."

Mehor stared at him, then looked suspiciously at Leah. "You know I'm going to marry Leah."

"So I've heard," Jacob said.

Mehor stared at him. "Who told you that?"

Leah came forward and said, "Leave him alone, Mehor. He's tired."

Jacob was relieved to see the man turn away and follow Leah.

Rachel had been watching, and she came to whisper, "Don't have anything to do with him."

Mehor was walking away, but he kept casting glances back at Jacob. "See that you don't have anything to do with that fellow."

"I'll do as I please, Mehor. You know that," Leah said boldly.

"If you do—"

Leah laughed at his threat. She was fearless. She looked up at him and said, "You think I'm afraid of you, Mehor?"

He grinned at her. "No. You're not. You're the only one who isn't. I guess that's the reason why I'm going to marry you."

"That'll be a long day coming."

"It will come, though. You might as well get ready for it!"

———————

Mehor stayed for two days, and during that time Jacob carefully avoided him. He took Rachel's warning seriously, and not only hers—Laban himself had muttered, "Stay away from that man. He could kill you with one blow."

"There's no reason for that," Jacob had insisted.

"He doesn't *need* a reason," Laban said grimly. "He's like a mad bull when he loses his temper."

Late on the afternoon of the second day of Mehor's visit, Jacob had gone down to water the cattle. It was the quiet time of evening, the time he liked best. He was sitting there thinking about his mother and wishing he could see her and his father too, for he found that he missed both his parents. He blocked Esau out of his mind, except for those times when they were children before the enmity had come between them.

"Are you daydreaming, Jacob?"

Jacob turned quickly to see that Leah had come silently down the path.

"I guess I was," he said. "What are you doing here?"

"What a rude thing to say! I came to see you, of course."

Jacob stared at her and could not help remembering the kiss they had shared in his tent. "Where's Mehor?"

"Oh, he's on his way home. I'm glad of it."

"You don't care for him, I take it."

"Of course not. Who could love a beast like that?"

"Everyone says he's going to marry you. That's what he himself says."

"I'll never marry him!"

"I'm glad to hear it, but making *him* believe that might be difficult."

The two stood talking of other things, and Leah questioned him about his home and family.

For some reason he didn't understand, Jacob began to tell this woman things he had kept bottled up. He even told her about his robbing his brother of his birthright and finally of the blessing of his father. When he had finished, he said, "I wish I'd never done that. It was wrong."

"Don't be sad, Jacob." Leah put her hand on his arm, and he turned quickly to face her. "All of us do things that are wrong, but we can't change what we've done."

"I wish I could."

"But you can't." She stepped closer, and he smelled the fragrance of the musky perfume she sometimes wore. "We can't change what we are."

"Oh, but that's not true."

"Of course it is! I am what I am—you are what you are." She stopped and searched his eyes. "Don't you like me as I am, Jacob?"

Jacob felt the pull of this woman, and he was powerless to resist her. He put his arms around her and kissed her, and she clung to him. The kiss lingered but ended suddenly when Jacob heard a savage cry.

He wrenched himself backward and saw Mehor running toward him. The big man's face was red and contorted with rage. Jacob started to protest. "Now, look—I didn't mean anything by this!" He heard Leah crying out, "Mehor, leave him alone!" But then the man was on him. He saw a huge fist coming at him, and then a wrenching pain followed. He felt blood running down his face and his body falling backward. Then everything went black.

Leah threw herself on Mehor, who was kicking the unconscious Jacob in the side and head. She put her hands across his face and clawed him with her nails. When he cried out and threw her from him, she scrambled to her feet. "Leave him alone!"

"I'll leave him alone when he's dead!" He turned and kicked him again. "I'll kill him if he's here the next time I come! You tell him that!"

"Get away from here, and don't ever come back!"

"I'll come back, and when I do, he'd better not be here."

Mehor whirled and lumbered away, and Leah went down on her knees. Jacob was totally still, frighteningly so. His face was battered, and blood flowed over his eye and out of one ear. Leah thought for one sickening moment that he was dead, but then she saw his chest moving. She pulled him up and held his head against her breast and began crying, "Jacob— Jacob!" And as she held him there, she knew only one thing. She had to have this man. She had to!

CHAPTER

9

Everything was cloudy, obscure, the objects before him hidden behind a fog. Then a faint glow caught his attention, like a cat's eye gleaming in the dark. He struggled to see through the haze—then everything seemed to clear. It was like the wind blowing a fog away, and the light proved to be a candle with the flame flickering wildly, then standing straight up in a sharp tear shape.

He tried to breathe, but the pain in his chest felt like a sword piercing him clean through. He tried to speak, but his dry, cracked lips and swollen tongue stopped the words he attempted to form, and he closed his eyes in frustration.

"Jacob . . . can you hear me?"

The voice came from somewhere over his head. He opened his eyes to see a woman's face. She stood between him and the candle, and the tiny light created a corona of brightness around her hair. He felt a hand resting on his face, and he tried again to speak. "Rachel . . . is it you?" he managed to whisper.

"Yes. How do you feel?"

Licking his lips, Jacob moved his shoulders cautiously. Slivers of pain sliced through his chest, and he stammered, "I . . . I . . . feel terrible!"

"You've been very badly hurt."

He carefully raised his hand and found a roughness over his eyebrow. Someone had sewed him up, he understood, and then opening his eyes wide, he said, "How long . . . have I been here?"

"You were hurt yesterday. It's night now."

Jacob tried to move, but again the pain smashed against him. "What's wrong with my chest?"

"I think some of your ribs are broken."

"Could I have a drink?"

"Yes. I've got it right here."

Jacob lay flat on his back and heard the delightful sound of water tinkling from a large vessel into a smaller one, and then her hand was behind his head.

"Try not to move," she said. "Just lift your head."

Obeying her, Jacob felt the cup against his lips. He guzzled at the water, spilling some of it so that it ran down the sides of his lips and onto his chest. He enjoyed the wonderful coolness along his tongue and in his throat. "That's good!" he said.

Rachel moved to fill the glass again, and as she did, Jacob's memory returned. "I . . . I thought he was going to kill me."

"I think he would have if Leah hadn't stopped him. You're going to be all right, though. You won't feel as much pain after a while."

Jacob tried unsuccessfully to smile. "Good. I'd hate to feel this bad for the rest of my life." She had moved to one side now, and he could see her face more clearly. Her features were outlined by the yellow halo of light from the candle, and she reached out and touched the side of his wounded head. "You were unconscious all the time Ziva was sewing you up. She's very good at such things. You're going to have a scar, though."

Jacob sighed deeply. "I've made a fine mess of things, haven't I?"

"It wasn't your fault," Rachel insisted. "It's that Mehor! I wish somebody would kill him!"

Surprised at the vehemence of her tone, Jacob stared at her face. She had a little girl's eagerness about her, though her feelings were constantly changing, coloring every expression her face revealed. She leaned over then, and he felt the warmth of her eyes and managed a smile. "Have you been taking care of me all this time?"

"Leah and I have. She's sleeping now."

Jacob lay still for a moment; then his lips twisted with a sour expression. "I think she's going to get me killed."

"Mehor once killed a man who took a woman he wanted."

A silence fell between them, and finally Rachel said, "You'll have to stay away from her, Jacob."

"I will," Jacob said fervently. "I'm no hero, Rachel."

"But you love her, don't you?"

Jacob stared at the girl's face. She seemed very young, but at the same time there was the promise of maturity in her expression and features. A few years would bring her to full womanhood, and he could easily imagine the beauty that would emerge. "I don't think so," he said.

"I saw the way you looked at her," Rachel said. "You looked at her like a man who wants a woman."

"I suppose many men have looked at her like that. But I can't risk getting killed over her." He saw that the remark pleased Rachel for some reason. "What's the matter? You don't want me for a brother-in-law?"

"I think whoever marries Leah will have to kill Mehor, and even then I think there would be trouble."

"Trouble? What sort of trouble?"

"Leah draws men to her. Have you ever noticed how moths are drawn to a candle flame? They burn themselves up in it, but they can't seem to help it. Some women are like that, and I think Leah is one of them."

Jacob was amazed at the girl's wisdom. He had thought the same thing about Leah but had not formulated it as Rachel had. He studied her. His mother had a bracelet made of lapis lazuli, a valuable stone used by the Egyptians, and Rachel's eyes, at the moment, seemed that same shade of lovely blue. Her hair, however, was as black as the obsidian arrowheads he had seen his brother Esau use. Black as a raven's wings that reflected a blue-black sheen when the sun struck it.

"I'm glad you came, Jacob," Rachel said shyly.

"I don't know why. I've been nothing but trouble to you."

"You could never be that," she whispered.

Jacob felt a sudden rush of affection for the young woman, but he was depressed. "I know where I've been, but I don't know where I'm going, Rachel." He sighed, and the sigh hurt his chest. "I guess I'm like a man in the middle of a bridge. I know where the ends are, but I can't go back, and I don't know what's ahead of me. So I'm just standing there leaning over and looking out over the waters flowing under my feet."

Rachel put her hand on Jacob's head. It was as gentle as a touch could be, and it comforted him. "You'll find your way," she said. "I know you will."

As the two sat there, Rachel began to speak of everyday things. Finally she saw that the pain was getting worse. "Ziva has made up some medicine for you. It's from a desert flower. She crushes it and puts it into water. It'll help the pain."

Jacob was indeed struggling with the waves of pain that rose and rushed through his body. She lifted his head, and he drank the mixture and shuddered. "It tastes terrible."

"But it'll make you sleep." She carefully placed his head down and then stood over him. "You're not going to be able to do much for a while, but I'll come sing to you and tell you stories."

"Will you, Rachel?"

"Yes." She reached out and touched the end of his nose with one forefinger, and her eyes danced. "I've got you in my power."

Jacob smiled. "What are you going to do with me, then?"

"I haven't decided yet. As soon as you get well enough, we'll go to my secret place, and then I can sing some more and tell you some more stories."

Jacob quickly felt the effects of the drug. It was like a tide starting at his feet and rising up. When it reached his eyes, he closed them and knew no more.

———————

When Jacob woke again, someone was washing his face with a cool, damp cloth. His eyes flew open, and he asked, "Is it you, Leah?"

"Yes. I need to clean you up."

Jacob was aware that his robe was gone and that he was naked from the waist up. He looked down, and the sunlight revealed the terrible bruises on his body. "He nearly killed me, didn't he, Leah?"

"Yes."

"He would have if you hadn't stopped him." He reached out and took her hand. "I guess I owe you my life."

"I never had anyone owe me their life."

Leah continued washing him with the damp cloth, and finally she stepped back and put the cloth away. "You're going to be fine."

"Rachel tells me Mehor will kill any man who gets close to you."

Leah's face changed instantly. She ceased to smile, and unhappiness came into her eyes as if he had stirred some old memory. He saw her lips flatten into a straight line, and she stared down at him in silence. "I will never marry him. I hate him."

Jacob did not know what to say.

Her voice rustled like rubbed paper as she said, "I wish he were dead."

Jacob was shocked at the words, even though he felt much the same way. The pain in his body reminded him of the man's cruelty, yet he saw that Leah's hatred exceeded his own. She had a rocky, drawn expression that made the feminine contours of her face appear almost masculine.

Jacob did not know what to say, but finally he managed, "I'll have to stay far away from you, Leah. You understand that. He'll kill me the next time."

"You feel something for me, Jacob," Leah said, and her breathing grew more rapid. She leaned forward and put her hand on his bare chest.

He felt the heat of the woman and saw the intensity of her eyes. "Maybe so, Leah, but a dead man can't feel anything."

Leah did not remove her hand. She leaned forward and said in a whisper so faint he was not sure he heard it at first, "Mehor will have to be . . ." She did not finish the sentence, but she may as well have, for Jacob knew what she was intimating. He saw something in her eyes he had never seen before in a woman, and even in the heat of the tent, a cold wave passed over him. He knew he had to end this at once.

"I don't want to hear about murder," he said hurriedly. "I may not even stay here, Leah, but if I do, I'll have to stay away from you."

Leah then leaned forward and kissed Jacob on the lips. "Yes, you will stay," she said. "And I will have you, Jacob. You know it and I know it." She rose at once, turned, and left the tent. Jacob lay there wondering what sort of woman this was, but a resolve rose in him, and he declared aloud, "I can't have anything to do with her. She'll have to understand that."

Jacob took a deep breath rather cautiously and then expelled the air. He twisted his torso to the right and to the left and was relieved to find that the pain was minimal. Six weeks had passed since he had been beaten by Mehor, and the healing had been slow. Ziva had told him that only time would heal his ribs.

"You're better, aren't you, Jacob?"

Jacob turned and looked at Rachel, who was seated beside him underneath the shade of the trees. She was smiling, and the sun had left its bloom on her fair skin. "Yes, I am," he said. "It took a long time. I don't know what I would have done without you."

"I didn't do much."

"Yes you did. You cooked for me, and you even gave me a bath when I couldn't move. And you talked to me. That helped more than you'll ever know."

Indeed, it had been Rachel who had made Jacob's inactivity bearable. Leah was there a great deal of the time, but Jacob never responded to her overtures. He saw the resentment in her eyes but knew that whatever he had felt for her—and whatever he still might feel—had to be put away.

Mehor was a killer. Since the attack, Jacob had heard more stories about the man's brutality, and there was no question in his mind that Mehor would kill any man who reached out for Leah.

But Rachel had filled in the gaps. She had brought cheer into his tent and fixed him special delicacies, and delighted him with her special stories. As he had healed, it had been Rachel who had encouraged him to exercise and had taken short walks with him at first, and longer ones as he got stronger.

Now as he sat beside the young woman, he felt a warm gratitude. Turning to her, he said, "You know, Rachel, I think you saved my life."

"That was Leah, not me."

"Yes. She saved me from Mehor all right, but I've never had to lie still for six weeks and do nothing. I think I would have lost my mind, gone stark, staring crazy if you hadn't come to me and brightened those hours."

"I didn't mind." Rachel smiled at him shyly. "I never had anyone to listen to me before."

Jacob reflected that this was true. The girl's mother had died years ago, and Leah was so strange that the two had little in common. Leah was very practical, and it was due to her that much of the work was organized and done. She knew about the household affairs as much as her own mother, but was not of an imaginative turn of mind.

Rachel, on the other hand, was full of the love of life, always singing, with a keen sense of humor and playful imagination—sometimes almost wild. She had so amused Jacob at times during the early part of his in-firmed condition that he had laughed until his ribs hurt him greatly. He had to plead, "Stop it, Rachel! Don't make me laugh anymore!"

Now as he sat beside Rachel, feelings that had been growing in him for a long time seemed to suddenly blossom. He could not explain it to himself, but he knew it had to do with the loveliness of this young woman and her kindness and her spirit, which was unlike that of any woman he had ever seen. She was childlike, and yet she was blossoming into a woman before his eyes. The thought had been in the back of his mind, and now, sitting in the shade watching the light filter through the trees and brighten her features and her dark eyes, he knew that this was what he wanted.

She was in the middle of telling a story, and a small dimple came and went winking at him, so it seemed, and he realized that there was a hint of will and pride in the corners of her lips and her eyes. The light was kind to her, showing the full, soft lines of her body, the womanliness beginning to develop, and the fragrance of her clothes came powerfully to him as he seemed to inhale the warm tone of her personality. She had a way of laughing that was very attractive, her chin tilting up and her lips curving in pretty lines. At that moment he knew she was not a child anymore but a woman with a mystery and feminine softness.

"Rachel?"

"Yes, Jacob?" She turned to him trustingly, and when he reached out and took her hand, her eyes opened wide. "What is it?" she whispered.

"You are the loveliest woman I have ever seen, Rachel."

The compliment caused Rachel's lips to part, and she flushed. She could not speak but waited for him to say more.

"I've come to care for you," Jacob said. And even as he spoke, a certainty was growing in him. He had been uncertain about so many things and had made so many mistakes, but now it all seemed to come together in a way that brought great joy to him. "I want you for my wife, Rachel," he said. "Could you ever come to love me?"

Rachel dropped her eyes for a moment, and when she lifted them, he saw the warmth he had longed for. "I've loved you since the first day you came, Jacob," she said simply.

"Then shall I speak to your father?"

"Yes!"

Jacob reached out, lifted her hand to his lips, and kissed it. She leaned forward and lifted her face. He kissed her on the lips and felt the fullness of them. When he lifted his head, he smiled. "I kissed you the first time I saw you."

"Yes, but you thought I was a little girl then."

"Well, I know better now. Come. I must speak to your father."

Laban glared at Jacob. "You want my daughter Rachel? Is that what you're saying?"

Jacob had braced himself for the old man's greed. He knew it well. "She loves me, and I love her. I want to marry her, Uncle."

Laban argued for a time, but finally he said, "Very well. You serve me for seven years, and you may have her."

Jacob shook his head. "Seven years! That's far too long. She might be dead in seven years—or I might be. I'll tell you what. I'll give you two years."

The argument went on for some time, as Jacob had known it would.

Finally Laban began to plead. "I have so little. I'm a poor man," he said, "and she's such a treasure."

Jacob shook his head. "I will accept seven years, but you must give me a dowry. I will not accept her without it."

Laban had been prompted by Ziva, who had said, "Don't be a fool. You know how smart the man is. He'll make us rich, but you must tie him to us for a long time. Make him agree to work seven years."

Finally Laban threw Bilhah in almost as an afterthought. "It'll be like having a concubine," he said.

"I'm not interested in that, but she'll be a help to Rachel. I agree to the terms."

And so the bargain was made. Rachel was ecstatic, but Leah threw a magnificent fit of rage. She screamed and spat and would have used her fingernails on Rachel for stealing her husband, as she put it. Jacob had to step in between the two, and it ended most unhappily. Leah glared at Jacob and said, "You'll be sorry for this, Jacob! You don't care for Rachel. You crave me, don't you? You can't deny it!"

With Rachel standing there Jacob *had* to deny it, but he knew he was not speaking the exact truth. "I don't care anything about you in that way, Leah. I love Rachel."

After the scene was over, Jacob and Rachel went to what had become their secret place, in the shade of the trees by the bend in the river. They sat there holding each other, and Rachel said, "It'll be such a long time before we can be married."

"But it'll be a good time. I'll court you. I'll sing songs to you, make up love songs for you, and I'll steal a kiss every chance I get."

Rachel laughed. "I'll be hard to get," she said. Then she asked quietly, "Do you really love me, Jacob?"

"You know I do."

"What about Leah?"

"No. It's you I love." Jacob put his arms around her and held her and thought of the seven long years that lay ahead. But he was still glad.

CHAPTER
10

"Just think, mistress, in another week you will be a married woman!"

Bilhah drew the brush over Rachel's gleaming black hair and caressed it lovingly. The hair now came down below Rachel's waist and was, in Bilhah's opinion, the most beautiful hair any woman had ever worn. "Aren't you a little bit afraid?"

"Afraid? Of course not." Rachel was sitting up straight, staring out of the opening of the tent while Bilhah brushed her hair. The camp was especially busy, for the celebration of Rachel and Jacob's wedding had brought many visitors. She had been surprised that her father had been willing to spend so lavishly, but she suspected that Ziva had been behind that.

"It's been a long time, hasn't it, mistress? I never knew a man to wait so long for his bride. Seven years!"

"It has been a long time," Rachel whispered. She was turning a ring around and around her finger, conscious of how Jacob had given it to her only recently. During their long courtship he had given her other gifts, none of them particularly valuable, but this one had been brought by a traveling trader all the way from Beersheba. The ring had belonged to Jacob's mother, Rebekah, and to his grandmother Sarah before that. With it had come a message from Jacob's parents, delivered aloud by the trader. Jacob had later repeated the words to Rachel as he gave her the ring. *"May your bride be as beautiful as the moon,"* the message had gone, *"and may she bear you many sons."* The entire message had been quite long, but Esau was never mentioned, which did not surprise Jacob in the least.

Twisting the ring on her finger, Rachel suppressed a sigh. It had indeed been a long seven years. There had been times when Jacob was so consumed with passion for her she did not think he could restrain himself for that long. But the seven years had proven Jacob's love for her. He had never wavered in his devotion, and now, at last, she was about to be his.

Leah had made life difficult for Rachel. She had never given up on trying to win Jacob's love for herself, and Rachel, at times, was consumed with jealousy whenever she saw Leah anywhere near Jacob. Once she had exploded with anger, accusing Jacob of dallying with her sister, but he had convinced her there was nothing between the two of them.

Jacob had survived Leah's attempted seductions, for he was more in love with Rachel than he could possibly express. Rachel thought about the tenderness he had shown her, the poems and songs he had made up celebrating their love, and she grew warm at the thought of the wedding to come—and what was to follow.

"This time next year you may have a baby," Bilhah said. She was a mature woman now but was still shy with everyone except Rachel. She adored Jacob, however, and thought that he was the only man fit to be the husband of her mistress. She spoke of him now as she continued brushing Rachel's lustrous black hair. "He's been able to make the herds so large over these years," she said. "Your father's a rich man now."

"Yes, and he doesn't give Jacob anything." Rachel's tone was bitter, for her father continued to display his customary stinginess despite Jacob's success in managing the flocks. Laban had refused to raise Jacob's wages, giving him only what pitiful few coins he deigned to spare. "I'm going to have Ziva speak to him," Rachel went on. "Jacob deserves more honor. He's worked like a slave these seven years! Those two brothers of mine are nothing but drunken louts, and my father's no better. They all stay drunk in the village while Jacob works night and day. It's not fair!"

"No, it's not. Has he ever thought about leaving here?"

"He would if it weren't for me, I know." Rachel softened then. "He's told me so."

"Maybe when you're married you can take some of the herd and we can go away and begin all over again. Jacob's so good with animals. He would be a success anywhere."

Rachel nodded. "Maybe so. We've talked about it."

Bilhah stopped brushing the hair and moved around to where she could look into Rachel's face. There was no one more beautiful than her mistress! She ran her hand over the smooth cheek. "You're so pretty," she whispered. "Jacob is a lucky man!"

———————

The wedding feast had begun, and the camp was filled with visitors. Ziva and Leah worked steadily along with the servants to keep the food cooked. The wedding ceremony was the next day, and Leah's face was stony. More than once she had thought about leaving, for she could not bear to see her sister's happiness, and especially not Jacob's.

Now she turned the spit that held the roasting lamb and, from time to time, sprinkled some spices on it. She remained there, ignoring the shouts and laughter and music that were going on all about her. She knew she was the only miserable person in the place and resisted an impulse to kick the lamb into the fire.

"Leah . . ."

Leah turned to see her mother approaching. "What is it?" she said.

"Leave that thing to the slave girl. I've got to talk to you."

Leah shrugged, then reached over and pulled the hair of the slave girl who had been hired. "Watch this lamb. Don't let it burn!" she snapped. Getting up, she moved away to follow her mother. She had no idea what Ziva wanted, thinking she probably had more work for her to do.

Ziva, however, went toward the tent where she lived with Laban. Glancing about as she followed her mother, Leah spotted her father groping after a plump young woman who was laughing at him. "The old goat!" she muttered. "Look at him, Mother."

"I know. I gave up on him a long time ago. The man is worthless!" Ziva ducked into the tent, and as soon as Leah stepped inside, she turned to face her daughter.

Leah was shocked at the intensity of her mother's expression. She knew her mother was totally immersed in the worship of her idols, and now when she saw the statuettes displayed in the tent, covered with flower petals and surrounded by burning lamps, she surmised that Ziva had been fasting and praying to them. Her mother normally kept her gods well hidden. "What is it, Mother?" she asked curiously.

"My gods have given me a word." Ziva's face was stark, and her eyes glowed fiercely in the lamplight. Her lips were drawn into a tight line, and when she spoke they barely moved—as if another being was speaking for her. This had happened several times in Leah's memory, and she grew very still.

"What is it, Mother?"

"You must have Jacob. There's no other man for you."

"Do you think I don't know that! I've tried every trick to get him to love me," she said bitterly.

"There is a way. My gods have told me."

Leah blinked with surprise. "There is no way!" she snapped. "What are you talking about, Mother? Have you lost your mind?"

"No. My gods have told me," she repeated in a rhythmic manner. "You must take Rachel's place."

"Take Rachel's place? What are you talking about? How can I do that?"

"Listen, daughter. Just before the wedding ceremony, you and I will be with Rachel. We will be dressing her. She will be wearing her bridal dress and a veil—but she will not wear it for the ceremony. *You* will wear it."

Leah's eyes narrowed. There was something different about her mother. Leah really believed in her mother's gods, although not to the extent that Ziva did. "What are you talking about? How can I do that?"

"I will give her a drugged drink. She will go to sleep almost at once. You will put on the bridal outfit, and it will be you whom I lead out to meet Jacob to become his wife."

"Jacob's not a fool. I'm taller than she is. Jacob would know instantly I'm not Rachel."

"Not if we make him drunk enough, and I'll see to that. And you can stoop down a little bit. Everybody will be so drunk by that time, nobody will notice."

Leah listened as her mother spoke rapidly, and slowly she began to see that the plan was possible. "What will Jacob do when he finds out?"

"He won't know until it's too late. He'll take you to his tent, believing you're Rachel. It'll be dark. You'll love him there. He had feelings for you once before, and you can win him back." Ziva's eyes glowed. "I know you can please a man."

Leah stood as still as a statue. "Yes," she whispered, "I can certainly please him."

"We will do it, then. Afterward, no matter what Jacob says, you will be his wife. He can't change that."

"What about Rachel?"

"She could have had a dozen men in the past seven years. You know how they've come swarming around her."

"Yes," Leah said bitterly, a glitter in her eyes. "I know exactly how that is."

"Come. We will do it together, daughter. You will have your man."

Suddenly Leah laughed. The sound was hard and metallic. "Yes, I will have a husband, and I will make him love me!"

————————

Jacob found Rachel outside her tent, and he pulled her around to the back, out of sight of the celebrating wedding crowd. "This is the last time I'll see you before we're married," he said, embracing her. "I wanted to tell you one more time how I adore you, Rachel."

"Do you, Jacob?" She put her arms around Jacob's neck and kissed him. She was delighted when he held her so tightly she could hardly breathe.

Jacob said hoarsely, "You're the only woman for me, Rachel. I could never love another."

"Go now before they see us. In a few hours you can have all of me that you want." Rachel suddenly giggled. "Does that please you, Jacob?"

"Yes, but I doubt if I could ever have all of you that I want."

Rachel kissed him again, shoved him away, and then ducked into her tent. She was pleased he had found this opportunity to tell her one more time of his love before they were married.

————————

The sound of singing and music filled the air as the wedding celebration reached a climax. Everyone gathered around Jacob, waiting for the coming of the bride. Jacob's eyes were slightly unfocused, for he had accepted all the flagons of wine that had been offered him, including several from Ziva. He had been surprised at this, for the old woman had been bitter toward him for years. She had wanted him to marry Leah and had never been pleasant. But on this day she had smiled at him while handing him a large cup of wine, saying, "May the gods bless you and your bride!"

He had drunk it down, then when she poured him another, had asked, "You're not angry with me, Ziva?"

She had merely laughed, but there had been a strange and troubling glow in her hazel eyes.

Now the wine was catching up to Jacob, and he knew he was on his way to being totally drunk. *No way for a bridegroom to act*, he thought, but then he heard shouting and looked up to see that the bride had come from her tent. Hands grasped him and pulled him toward the center of the crowd, and voices were whispering suggestions into his ear for the wedding night.

He stood across from his bride, who was clad in a colorful gown with a heavily embroidered veil completely covering her face. His head was spinning now, and he had to make an effort to remain upright.

The ceremony was brief, and it included the bride circling the groom three times in one direction and then three times in the opposite direction. Jacob tried to watch her but became dizzy as he swiveled his head. He fell backward but was caught by the men behind him. He laughed foolishly and tried to concentrate on the rest of the ceremony.

Finally all was over, and he found himself beside his bride. He grasped her arms, and while a song went up, he staggered toward the tent. He managed to make it inside, but when he turned to his wife, he found his lips were numb—so numb he could barely speak.

"Rachel ... my ..." He began to sway, and then he felt hands guiding him. The tent was dark except for one oil lamp, and he said, "Lemme see ... your face!" But she simply turned and blew out the lamp. She didn't speak but began to remove his clothes. He fell back onto the bed, crying out hoarsely, "My bride ... my Rachel!"

CHAPTER

11

Jacob stirred from a sound sleep as the pale morning light slipped through the small opening of his tent and touched his face. As consciousness returned, his senses took over, and he heard the distant barking of a dog and the faint babble of voices in the camp. The aroma of roasting meat piqued his hunger, but an overriding aroma puzzled him as he lay in that twilight state between sleep and wakefulness. At the same time he threw his arm out and encountered something soft and yielding. Awareness came with a rush, and he drew himself up on his elbow and opened his eyes as he twisted around. By the pale light he saw a woman's back—smooth, strong, and unmistakably feminine.

Joy flooded Jacob as he thought of his wedding night. He could barely remember the wedding and berated himself for drinking too much. He remembered how Ziva had forced several cups of wine on him, which had strongly affected him and clouded his mind. Despite his hazy memories of the ceremony, he did remember very well reaching out for his bride. And as the thought of their lovemaking came to him, his face flushed. His hand lovingly ran down the silken flesh beside him, and leaning forward, he whispered, "Rachel. . . ?"

The woman turned over, and Jacob stared—unable to believe his eyes. He drew back his hand as if he'd been burned and gasped, "Leah!"

Leah smiled slowly and lazily, her eyes half lidded. She leaned against him and put her arms around his neck. "Yes, it's me, husband. It's your bride." She kissed him fully on the lips, and despite the confusion that held Jacob, he was still aroused by her touch.

Pulling back and pushing Leah away, Jacob gasped, "What are you doing here? Where's Rachel?"

Leah did not lose her smile. She was satiated with love, and her voice was uncharacteristically soft and silky. "I am your bride, Jacob. I love you."

Jacob shook his head and sat straight up, trying to think. He looked around the tent hoping to find Rachel there, and then Leah sat up too and put her arms around him. When he turned to face her, still unable to speak, she said, "I've always loved you, Jacob. You're the only man I ever loved. I know you loved me once and you still do deep down."

Jacob said, "What have you done, Leah?" Jacob's voice was angry, and his eyes glinted. He ripped her arms from around him as they clung to him and then understanding dawned. "You've done something with Rachel. You took her place in the wedding, didn't you?"

"Yes, I did, and I'm not ashamed! I'm the oldest daughter, and older daughters marry before younger ones. Besides, she can't stir you like I can."

Jacob's world had suddenly turned upside down. He stared at her and said, "You know that I love Rachel."

"You're a man," she said. "You can love the woman who satisfies you, and she would never be able to."

"That's a lie!" Jacob shouted. He started to get up, but Leah caught him and clung to him. He struggled with her, but she was a strong woman. "Let me go," he said.

"No. I'll never let you go."

"I won't be your husband!"

"You *are* my husband," Leah whispered. "Don't you remember last night?"

Despite himself, Jacob remembered very well—as clearly as he had ever remembered anything—the night he had spent with this woman. True, he had been half drunk, but she had pleased him in ways he had never dreamed of.

"You are my husband, Jacob." Leah's voice was insistent, and her strange hazel eyes seemed to swallow him. She pulled at him, saying, "You are my husband. I made you happy last night. You know I can make you happy for a lifetime."

Jacob tried to resist, but she pressed against him and whispered, "Come, husband. Love me. I'm your wife."

And then Jacob felt himself unable to resist. He hated himself for being so weak, but in response to her pleas he found himself reaching for her. He thought of Rachel, but only for a moment, for Leah was whispering his name, and he came to her as she fell back.

———————

Ziva saw that Rachel was waking up. She had stayed in the tent with her all night and now during the morning, and as soon as Rachel's eyes opened, she saw her confusion. "Are you awake, Rachel?" she asked.

Rachel was wearing a simple undergarment, what she'd had on under her wedding gown. Now she looked down and cried out, "What? What. . . ?" She could not finish, and she looked at her stepmother. "Where's my wedding dress? Where am I, Ziva?"

"I must talk to you, Rachel. Here, put your clothes on."

Rachel slipped into her robe, trembling. "Where's Jacob?" she cried.

"Listen to me, Rachel," Ziva said. "Something has happened, and you're going to have to learn to accept it. . . ."

Rachel listened, stunned, not able to take it in. Her stepmother ended by saying, "So Leah is Jacob's wife."

White-hot anger surged through Rachel. "You drugged me, didn't you? You and Leah did it!"

Ziva did not deny it. "Yes, we did."

"You've robbed me of my husband!"

Rachel flew at her stepmother, striking out at her, but the old woman was strong and quick. She grabbed Rachel's wrist, and her voice crackled with energy. Her strange eyes, so much like her daughter's, seemed to hold Rachel. "Now, you listen to me, Rachel. It was not something I wanted to do."

"Why did you do it, then?" Rachel cried.

"I did it for my daughter's sake. You are a lovely woman, the most beautiful woman I've ever seen. Men have been coming for you ever since you were fifteen years old wanting to marry you, but they haven't wanted Leah as a wife. No suitable men have sought her."

"But Jacob loved me."

Ziva ignored this. "You can find another husband. One richer than Jacob. But my Leah can't."

As Ziva spoke, her eyes bright with passion, Rachel felt herself giving in. She had never been able to stand against this strong old woman, and she knew that what she was saying was true. No matter how evil the deed had been, it was done. Leah was Jacob's wife, and nothing could change that.

She collapsed on the bed and began to sob. Ziva stood over her, and the fierce intensity of her eyes softened. Her shoulders sagged, for she loved this girl in her own way. She had practically raised her after Rachel's mother had died, but Leah needed her and Rachel did not. She leaned forward to touch the girl with a show of compassion but then stopped short. She drew her hand back and said in a practical voice, "It's done, Rachel. The best thing you can do is to accept it and move on with your life." She watched the weeping girl and shook her head slightly. Her mouth compressed as she thought, *She's a good girl, but good people get hurt in this world.* She turned and walked away, wondering if Rachel would be able to survive this blow.

———————

"What . . . ? Stop that!" Laban came out of his drunken slumber with his head splitting, gasping and clawing at his face. "What have you done?" He looked up to see Ziva standing over him. She had a wide-mouthed jar in her hand and had thrown the water in his face. "I'll kill you!" he shouted.

"Shut your mouth, old man," Ziva spat back. When he reached out for her, she lifted the jar in both hands and cried, "I'll break this over your head if you come any closer!"

"No! What are you doing? What's wrong with you?"

"Listen to me, Laban. . . ."

Laban pulled himself together and listened—not comprehending at first—and then when the truth of what Ziva had said broke in on him, he stared at her. "Leah is married to Jacob?"

"Yes. It's done, and there's nothing to do about it."

"Why did you do this, you foolish old woman?"

"Leah needs a husband, and she loves Jacob. You know she's never loved anybody else."

Laban stared at his wife. "You know what you've done? Mehor will kill us all!"

"No he won't," Ziva replied grimly. She cackled suddenly, a harsh laughter coming from her thin lips. "I've taken care of that."

Laban struggled to his feet, still wiping his face. He was dripping with the water she had thrown over him, and he stared at her in disbelief. "What are you talking about?"

"There's one man meaner and tougher than Mehor, and that's his father. I went to him and bribed him. He's been paid, and Mehor will do whatever he says."

"What did he say?"

"He said if his son bothered any of our family, he would break his head. He'll do it too—and maybe worse. You know what a vicious old goat he is. Like a bear."

Laban took that in slowly and then nodded as he stroked his scraggly beard. "Well, that's good. I'm glad he's out of our way. The man always frightened me."

"Listen to me now—you're going to have to talk to Jacob. He's going to come to you, and you need to get ready for him."

"You mean he's going to kill me?"

"Don't be foolish—any more than you can help. He's not going to kill anybody, but he's going to be very angry."

"Well, you talk to him."

"I would, but the world is run by men," Ziva said bitterly. "Now, listen. This is what we'll do, and this is what you must tell him. . . ."

Laban was well prepared for Jacob's visit, but if he had not been, he might have collapsed immediately, for Jacob rushed into his tent with his eyes burning. Laban said nothing at all as Jacob shouted and ranted and raved. Once he even started for Laban as if to choke the life out of him, but Ziva had taught her husband well, and he simply sat there saying nothing until Jacob's fury began to subside. "You crazy old man! You're all crazy! Your wife is worse than you are."

Laban tried to put a word in. "Listen, Jacob. This isn't all that bad—"

"I've worked for a woman's hand for seven years, and now you give me different one! You think that's not bad? I worked like a slave for you, Laban, and you've given me nothing! I ought to wring your scrawny neck!"

Laban raised his hand in a frightened gesture, for he had never seen such fiery passion, and he actually feared for his neck. "Listen to me, Jacob, just for one minute."

"What do you have to say, old man?"

Laban hesitated, then said, "I had nothing to do with this. You've got to believe me. It was Ziva's idea. She and Leah cooked this up between them. I didn't know a thing about it until this morning."

Jacob knew that his new father-in-law was capable of lies and deceit and of almost anything else, but somehow he believed the old man. He stared at him bitterly and finally nodded. "All right. It's done, but I'll have satisfaction."

"Look, son," Laban said and tried to smile, "it's a custom in our country that the elder daughter marry before the younger ones."

"But I love Rachel, and everyone knows it. Don't you feel any sorrow or grief for her? She's been robbed too!"

"It doesn't have to be that way."

"What are you talking about? We can't undo a marriage."

"No, but you can take Rachel as your wife as well."

Jacob stood stock-still. He had been so befuddled with passion for Leah, and then afterward had become so angry with Laban, he had not thought straight. Suddenly he lifted his head. "Yes," he said firmly, "I must have Rachel for my wife."

"That's easy enough. We'll make the same arrangement we made with Leah."

Instantly Jacob's rage rose again. "You crazy old man! You think I'm going to wait seven more years for her?"

"No, no! You can marry her right away. We'll have another wedding— yours and Rachel's. In a week you'll have her for your wife, and I'll give you Bilhah, her handmaiden." He smiled shiftily and added, "But you must work for me another seven years."

Jacob stood before the twisted old man and thought rapidly. He knew he could not go home. He had no other place, and he also knew he must have Rachel. He made an instant decision. "All right. I will work for you seven more years for Rachel, but I claim her as my bride within a week."

Laban sighed with relief. "It shall be done. Now perhaps you'd better go talk to her. She's probably in poor shape."

———

Jacob entered the tent and found Rachel stretched out facedown on her bed. He knelt down beside her and touched her shoulder. "Rachel," he said softly, "come up."

Rachel did not move at first, and then when she turned over, he saw that her face was red with weeping and her eyes were swollen. The sight of her touched his heart, and he said, "Come. Let me hold you."

"I can't. You are a married man."

"Listen to me, Rachel. I knew nothing about this. Do you believe me?"

"Yes, I know," Rachel sobbed. "It was Ziva and Leah! Oh, Jacob . . . what are we going to do?"

"It's going to be all right, Rachel."

"No, no, no! It's *never* going to be all right!"

Jacob saw that reasoning with her was impossible. He pulled her across his lap and held her. With his left hand he supported her and with his right hand he pushed back her silky black hair, then wiped the tears from her face. "Don't cry, my little moon!"

"How can I help it? My life is ruined."

"No, it's not ruined."

"I hate Leah and that mother of hers!"

"I can understand that."

"You mustn't be doing this." Rachel pushed at him, and her eyes were filled with tragedy.

"Rachel, I've loved you ever since I first saw you," Jacob said quietly. He felt her trembling, and he smoothed her hair with his free hand. "In my sight you're the most beautiful creature the Lord ever made, and in one week you and I will be married. You and I will be husband and wife."

Rachel grew absolutely still. Her eyes flew open, and her lips parted. "You . . . you mean it, Jacob?"

"Of course. I've just been talking to your father. It's all settled. I'll work for seven more years, but we'll be married. We'll have another wedding in a week, and you and I will be one."

"But what about Leah?"

"She will be my wife too." Jacob then kissed Rachel and felt a great wave of tenderness. "She will be my wife . . . but you, Rachel, will always be the Beloved Wife. It's the title I give you, and you will always be the one closest to my heart."

With a short, passionate cry, Rachel threw her arms around Jacob's neck and put her face down on his chest. He held her as he would a child and stroked her back. "Don't cry. We're going to be happy, and you will always be the Beloved Wife."

CHAPTER

12

A flight of dark birds divided the air over Jacob's head, forming evanescent shapes in a beautiful pattern. He paused, fascinated, and stared up into the sky as it turned crimson over in the west. When the birds disappeared over the horizon, he continued to walk rapidly toward the flock of sheep that fed at the base of a low hill ahead of him. When he was close, he called out, "Hello, Nomar."

"Hello, master." A young man approached and stood before Jacob. He was no more than sixteen, but bright-eyed and lean as a skinned rabbit. "Are you a father yet, master?"

Jacob smiled briefly. There was no privacy among the people, and everyone he had met had asked him the same question. "I wasn't when I left home this morning, but any day now."

"May you have a beautiful boy and many of them." Nomar smiled.

"Thank you, Nomar." Jacob put his hand on the young man's shoulder. He was the best of his hired herdsmen. The young man had come into the camp one day starved, dirty, ragged, and half dead. Laban had ordered him out, but Jacob had overridden that order and fed the boy. He had made a herdsman out of him and now could see in him the promise of a fine man to come. "How are the sheep?" he asked.

"Four ewes gave birth last night," Nomar said proudly. "I had to help with one of them, but the lamb is fine. You are richer now, master."

Not me. Laban is richer. Laban never gave him anything. Still, he did not need to say this to the boy. "When you come in tonight, I'll have Rachel fix you some special cakes as a reward for helping that new lamb into the world."

Nomar's eyes lit up. "Thank you, master. I look forward to eating them."

"Come in as soon as you are relieved."

Jacob turned and began jogging toward the hill that lay before him. He wanted to hurry home to Rachel, as he did every day. Life had been hard trying to keep his two wives happy. He loved Rachel more than he could have ever imagined loving a woman. She satisfied the deepest needs of his heart, filling his eyes with her beauty and his ears with her stories and songs. Rarely was she far from his thoughts.

Leah, however, was another story. She still had the power to draw him into bed with her wiles, but since she had become pregnant, she had become difficult to live with. It was impossible for Jacob to conceal his preference for Rachel, and Leah had begun taunting her younger sister with her lack of a child. She did this openly and with scorn, and Rachel had no answer for it. Jacob had taken Leah aside twice already and threatened her sternly that she must never do such a thing again, and Leah had behaved— but only for a time.

These thoughts troubled Jacob as he increased his speed. He was pleased that he had grown tougher and more physically able over the past years at Paddan Aram. He gloried in his strength. As the camp came into view, he saw Rachel's tent. She had dyed the hides a light sky blue, and anyone coming into the camp saw it instantly. It stood out among the tents for its beauty, exactly as Rachel stood out among women for her beauty. Men's eyes could not miss the tent, nor did they ever miss seeing the beauty of Rachel.

As he came into the camp, he saw that Rachel was waiting for him. She came running quickly, and when she stood before him, breathless, her eyes were wide. "Leah is with the midwife. Her time has come."

Jacob forgot everything else and broke into a dead run toward Leah's tent. He halted by the tent flap, where an old woman was stepping out. "Lamah, how is she?" Jacob said anxiously. "Is the baby here?"

The old midwife glared at him. "Where have you been?" she squeaked. "No time for a husband to be running off!"

"Is the baby here?" Jacob demanded.

"Not yet but soon." The old woman turned without another word and disappeared into the tent. Jacob fidgeted, unable to stand still. He began to pace, and soon Laban came by and said, "A son, you think, boy?"

"I hope so," Jacob said shortly. He had little use for Laban, for the old man cheated him constantly. Jacob continued to pace, saying no more, and Laban shuffled away.

The wait was agonizingly long. Four hours after Jacob had arrived,

Rachel brought him some food. While he ate she said, "It will soon be over, and you will be a father."

"I hope so." He lifted his head and heard another muted cry from Leah. She had not cried out much, but every time he heard her moans, Jacob had wiped the sweat from his brow. He hated to see anyone suffer. Now he handed the tray back to Rachel, and as he did, he heard his name called. He turned to see Lamah coming out of the tent, beckoning him. "Come in, Jacob."

Jacob instantly turned and went inside, leaving Rachel to stand there staring after him. She felt a keen pang of loneliness at being left outside at such a time and knew this was something she had no part of.

As Jacob entered the tent, he saw Leah lying on the bed with the baby within the crook of her arm. He walked over and looked down at the tiny red face, the little eyes pulled together, and then the child broke into a loud, squalling cry.

Leah said, "I have borne you a fine boy, husband. Hold your son."

Jacob reached down and picked up the baby. Holding the morsel of life in his arms, he felt his heart swell with pride.

"His name is Reuben," Leah said. "That means 'behold a son.'"

Leah reached up and took Jacob's hand, and he squeezed it and knelt down beside her. "He's a fine son, wife." He leaned over and kissed her.

At the invitation of the midwife, Rachel came into the tent at that moment. Jacob and Leah did not even look up as their attention was solely on their new son and each other. Rachel stood watching the tableau before her, and it went straight to her heart. Tears came to her eyes, and she choked back sobs. Whirling, she left the tent without congratulating the new parents. She went to her own bed and fell on it, deep sobs racking her body. She pushed her face into the pillow, muttering, "He will love Leah more now that she has given him a son." Grief overwhelmed her, and she wept long. Finally she rolled over on her back and looked up toward the roof of the tent, as if she could see heaven above. "Oh, God," she wept, "what have I done to displease you that you have given me no child?"

PART THREE

THE FAMILY

CHAPTER

13

As Rachel slapped a waterlogged garment on a flat rock and pounded it with a smaller stone, she heard a sound and lifted her head. A fish had broken the surface of the small stream, making a widening ripple. The sunlight sparkled along the water lapping at the rocky banks, and in the distance a long line of mountains cast a sharp, jagged shadow against the flat land. The breeze stirred the scrub bushes along the bank, and the plants at the water's edge gave off a musty, pungent odor.

Rachel turned quickly at the noises the boys were making as they played a game nearby on a flat piece of ground. She smiled as she watched them, thinking how different each of Leah's four sons were. Not one of them resembled the other. They had been born one after the other, and Rachel had learned to love them—but not as if they were her own, for Leah would not allow her to get that close to her sons.

Arching her back to relieve the strain, she slipped her feet into the water, enjoying the coolness of it, and continued to watch the boys. She had made them a ball out of soft leather, stuffed with dried straw and sewn together with sheep-gut twine. She had taught them several games with it, and now they were playing one that they called Keep the Ball, which consisted of one of the boys grabbing the ball and trying to keep the others from taking it away from him.

As she watched, Reuben, the largest and the oldest of the brothers, made a wild grab for the ball. He was a rather clumsy boy and not swift in thought, but he was good-hearted and gentle nonetheless.

Simeon, the second-born, was as lean and quick as Reuben was large and clumsy. He had snatched the ball and laughed as Reuben made an ineffectual grab at it. He shoved Reuben backward so that the larger boy stretched headlong on his back, and then Simeon laughed and shouted. There was a cruelty in this boy that Rachel hated to see.

The third member of the quartet, Levi, was short and stocky with black hair and dark eyes. She expected him to lose his temper, for he often did. In this he was like Simeon and also in the fact that he could be cruel at times.

A shout went up, and Judah grabbed for the ball. Rachel smiled, for Judah was a miniature edition of Jacob—the same chestnut hair and warm brown eyes, not overly large but quick and strong. He was the best of the boys in Rachel's opinion, and she watched fondly as he snatched the ball away from Simeon and tore out as fast as his little legs would take him, pursued by the other three.

As the boys ran off and their voices grew fainter, a mixture of regret and grief filled Rachel. These were not *her* boys, and as she watched and listened to their play, a sharp sadness touched her, a pang that hurt deeply.

"You cheated!" Simeon shouted and shoved Judah backward. The smallest of the four went sprawling in the dirt, but he jumped right up, screaming, "I didn't either cheat!"

"You did too!" Simeon retorted. His small, close-set eyes flared with anger. "You grabbed the ball when I wasn't looking!"

"That's fair!" Judah said. He was an even-tempered boy, even sweet most of the time, but Simeon was a bully, and Judah felt he had to stick up for himself. The two boys began to argue, and finally Simeon snatched the ball and struck Judah in the face. Judah cried out, "I'll tell Rachel on you!"

"Go on and tell her! She's nothing anyway!"

Judah was on his feet, his eyes flashing. "Don't you say anything bad about Rachel!"

Simeon laughed. "She doesn't have any sons! She's no good for anything."

Judah could not bear to hear anyone verbally abuse Rachel, which Simeon often did and even Levi did on occasions. With an angry cry, Judah threw himself at his brother, and the two rolled in the dirt. Judah was getting much the worse of it. The other two simply watched, although Reuben had concern in his eyes.

Suddenly Rachel was there pulling the two boys apart. They were covered with dirt and Judah's lips were swelling.

"Shame on you!" Rachel cried. "Brothers shouldn't fight like this. You ought to love each other." She glared at them, and Simeon avoided her eyes. She had a fair idea that the fight was his doing, but she asked, "What's this all about? What are you fighting about?"

"Simeon said something bad about you."

"You shut your mouth, Judah!" Simeon cried furiously. "You're nothing but a talebearer!"

Judah started to answer angrily, but Rachel put her hand on his shoulder. "That's enough, Judah."

Judah blurted out, "He says you're not good because you don't have any children!" He looked up, his eyes filled with pain. "Why don't you have any little boys, Rachel?"

The question went right to Rachel's heart. She had heard this kind of talk often enough from Leah and knew that Simeon had been absorbing it, as had his brother Levi. "God hasn't given me any little boys, Judah," she whispered.

Simeon was still furious. "God blesses those He loves with children!" he said, then turned around and ran away. Levi followed him, but Reuben came closer and put his arm around Rachel. "Don't you pay any attention to them, Aunt Rachel. They're just soreheads."

"That's right. God does love you, and I do too," Judah said. He threw his arms around her, and Rachel held him tightly, her eyes blinded with tears. She could not speak, her throat was so tight, and the two boys held on to her as she fought back the tears.

———

Jacob stumbled into camp, his strength drained. He had been off caring for the sheep for two days. He had slept little and had only a few pieces of cold meat to eat, bringing his temper near the snapping point. He stopped long enough to take a drink of water and wash the grit from his face. When he stopped he saw Laban lying in the shade, asleep. A nearly flattened wineskin was beside him, and Jacob knew the old man had been doing nothing but sleeping and stupefying himself with wine. Anger washed through Jacob at the sight. He set his teeth, then stalked over to Laban and leaned down, shouting, "Get up!"

Laban startled awake and sat up at once, confusion in his eyes. He rubbed his face and tried to speak, but his tongue was furry. "What ... what is it? What's wrong?"

"I'll tell you what's wrong," Jacob said with scarcely concealed fury. He bit off the words, and they struck against Laban with all the force of arrows. "I've been out for two days working to keep your flocks and your herds. I haven't had anything to eat, and I haven't slept."

Laban quailed beneath Jacob's glare and rubbed his hand across his face. He cleared his throat and said, "Well, you should have gotten some help."

"Help? What do you know about help? All you do is sit here and stay drunk all day long."

"Well, Lomach and Benzar, they—"

"Those no-good, worthless sons of yours! I'll tell you where they've been. They've been in the village, drunk and consorting with harlots—like always!"

Jacob's raised voice was drawing the attention of the camp. He became aware that Leah and Rachel and everyone else within hearing distance had stopped their work and were staring at him. He did not often lose his temper, but now it was gone, and he grabbed Laban's thin arms and pulled the old man to his feet. "You listen to me! You're going to lose everything if you don't make those worthless sons of yours work!"

Laban was shocked. Jacob hardly ever spoke back to him, and now he had jerked him up as if he were a child. The old man sputtered, "You turn me loose! Who do you think you are?" He jerked himself backward and shook his fist in Jacob's face. "You're nothing but a poor relative. You don't own anything! You be careful how you talk or you'll be sorry!"

Jacob laughed harshly. "All right, old man. *You* take care of the flocks, then—you and those worthless sons of yours. I'm through! We'll see how long it takes you to lose everything you've got!" He turned on his heels and stalked away, anger in every line of his body.

Leah, who was watching the scene, waited until Jacob disappeared into his tent, and then she hurried over to her father. She was taller than he was, for age had stooped him. She was also stronger in every way, physically and emotionally. "You old fool!" she hissed. "You're losing your mind!"

Laban ducked his head and whimpered, "Don't you talk to your father that way! It's not respectful."

"Why should I respect you? Jacob's right. All you do is drink and sleep all day. You never give Jacob any help, and you never say a word to Lomach and Benzar. Those pitiful sons of yours! You should have taken a stick to them years ago. The three of you are absolutely worthless!"

Laban began to whine in self-pity. "I can't help it. I'm an old man. I can't work—"

"Be quiet! Are you so drunk you don't know that if it weren't for Jacob, we'd be beggars? He's the one who, for years, has stayed out and done the work while you and your sons have loafed and consorted with harlots."

As her tongue lashed at him, Laban glanced around, noting that everyone was listening. The worst of it was that he knew Leah was right. In his more lucid moments, he recognized that Jacob was the one who had brought prosperity to his family. He hated to admit this, but now he knew he was going to have to pacify Jacob. "You don't think he'll really refuse to work, do you?"

"Yes, I do, and I don't blame him! You might as well get ready to go take care of the flocks yourself—you and your boys."

"But I'm too old for that!"

"You're not too old to make a fool out of yourself!"

Alarmed, Laban said, "Now, Leah, listen. I know I was harsh, but I didn't mean it."

"You think that's going to mean anything to Jacob? It wouldn't surprise me if he took Rachel and me and the children away. *Then* see how long you'd last! You'd have nothing."

Laban's face broke then, and he clawed his beard anxiously. "Wait a minute now, Leah. I was too harsh. Be nice to him."

"I always am. You're the one who mistreats him. I've begged him to leave you, and I hope he does. We have to do all the work."

Laban realized he had gone too far. He cleared his throat and took his daughter by the arm. He had to look up into her face, and he pleaded, "Leah, don't be so cruel to your old father." He smirked then and said, "Be nice to Jacob. Fix him some good food and get him into bed. You seem to be good at that."

Leah stared at her father. "You are a pitiful old man!"

"You can do it, Leah. You get him in a good mood, and tomorrow I'll do something nice for him."

———

Jacob was sitting in his tent seething over the harsh scene with Laban. He looked up when Leah came in.

"Your father is an idiot," he spat.

"I know it, Jacob. He's old and doesn't know what he's doing half the time." She came over and ran her hand through his hair. "You're absolutely filthy. I've cooked a lamb just the way you like it, with all the fixings. Would you like to clean up first or eat first?"

"Let's eat. I'm starved."

"You stay right here, and I'll bring your food. We'll have a good meal together."

Jacob nodded, and soon Leah was back. He began to eat the olives and kemach bread, and afterward the lamb that had been boiled in sour milk; then he washed it all down with a fruity wine Leah had saved for him. He ate until he could eat no more.

Then Leah said, "You're so dirty."

"Who wouldn't be after two days out in the desert with those filthy sheep?"

Leah began to remove his clothing, then brought a deep basin of water and began to wash him. Her hands were strong, and Jacob started to relax. She washed his body, then his hair, afterward anointing it with sweet oil.

She even washed his feet, and Jacob grew sleepy.

"Now, do you feel better?"

"Yes, I do. But your father . . . I don't know what to do with him."

"We'll think of something. Come to bed now."

Jacob lay down, and Leah settled down beside him. The warm food and the washing had relaxed him, and now she began to rub her hands over his face. She whispered, "You're my sweet husband, and I'm your obedient wife." She moved against him, and he could not see her smiling in the darkness. She knew she always had power over him at times like this, and even though Rachel might be the Beloved Wife, she was the one who had given him sons. Besides, she knew how to comfort him in ways that no other woman could.

———

Rachel had watched the scene between her father and Jacob. She had started for him too, but Leah had reached him first. Then Rachel had seen Leah follow Jacob into his tent and knew she could not interfere. She watched as Leah brought food and fresh water and then she stood there as the lamp in the tent went out. Turning, she went to her own tent and found Bilhah there, making a shirt for Judah. When Bilhah looked up and saw the expression on Rachel's face, she put the sewing down at once. "What's wrong, mistress?"

"Nothing."

"Yes, there is. I can tell. Are you troubled because Jacob had a fight with your father?"

"No."

Bilhah was puzzled. She was a simple girl, not particularly attractive, but warmhearted. She had large, warm brown eyes—her best feature—and was totally devoted to Rachel. "It's Leah, then, isn't it?"

Rachel shot a quick glance at Bilhah and then bitterness tinged her speech. "She gives him sons, and I give him nothing!"

"No. That's not so." Bilhah came and put her arms around Rachel. "He loves you the best. He calls you the Beloved Wife. You know he loves you best."

But Rachel would not be comforted. She went to bed that night and could not keep back the tears as she thought of Leah with Jacob.

"Where's Rachel?" Jacob asked Bilhah as she passed by. He had not gone to the fields the next day but had rested in the camp, and now the late afternoon sun was going down. "I haven't seen her all day," Jacob said.

Bilhah said with some surprise, "Well, I haven't either. I thought maybe she was with you."

"No. I don't know where she is." Jacob got up immediately and began to search the camp. No one had seen her, it seemed, and he began to worry. Suddenly a thought occurred to him, so he left the camp and made his way through the scrub brush over the sands until he came to the small familiar stream. He followed its winding curves until he came to the clump of trees that overshadowed it. As he approached, he caught a glimpse of bright color inside the thicket of trees and felt a gush of relief. Making his way through the bushes, he came upon Rachel, sitting with her feet tucked under her, staring out over the stream.

"Rachel, here you are!" He went over and sat down beside her. "I was worried."

Jacob waited for her to speak, but she turned her face away. He heard her give a little sob, and he reached around and put his hand on her cheek. When he turned her face to his, he saw that her cheeks were tearstained. "Why, Rachel, what's wrong?"

"Oh, Jacob, everything is wrong!" She fell against him and began to weep great sobs, and he held her, making comforting noises and stroking her hair.

When her sobs abated, he said, "Now, tell me what's wrong."

"Jacob, do you ever pray for me to have a child?"

Jacob had suspected this is what had brought grief to Rachel. "Yes, I do, all the time," he said. His brow furrowed, and he shook his head sadly.

"But you know God hasn't spoken to me, not since I left home. It was such a wonderful thing, Rachel, when I saw the angels on that stairway, and God made such amazing promises." His voice grew sadder, and he bit his lower lip. "He promised me wonderful things, but they don't seem to be happening."

Rachel looked up at him. "Do you doubt the Lord?"

"No," Jacob said firmly. "But I know His time is not like ours. I don't think time concerns Him at all."

"How can that be?"

"I don't know." Jacob shrugged. "I don't think there ever was any begin-ning, and there never will be any end. But you and I and all humans, we're caught in time—like someone caught in a river. Yesterday is gone. We're sitting in the middle of today. Tomorrow may come if we live. We can't think any other way, but I don't believe that the Almighty is like that. He just always *is*."

Rachel lay quietly in his half embrace. She loved it when he talked to her like this. Finally she said, "It's hard to believe, isn't it?"

"It is when you can't really see anything happening." But he shook his head and shoulders and said, "But God will be faithful."

"I don't know why God is silent. Why doesn't He talk to us all the time?" Rachel whispered. "I've prayed to Him until I can't stand to hear my own prayers."

"I know what you mean, but we must not give up."

"Jacob?"

"What?"

"I've been thinking about something."

"What is it?"

"I'm not sure that I should say."

"Rachel," Jacob said tenderly, "a husband and wife should not have any secrets. I want to tell you all that's on my heart, and I want you to do the same for me."

"All right," Rachel said slowly. "I've been thinking . . . that you should take Bilhah as your concubine."

Jacob had expected anything but this. "Why would I do that?"

"You know the custom, Jacob. If a woman's bondservant has a child, it belongs to the mistress. The child would be mine in all but blood. It's the only way I can give you a son, Jacob."

Jacob was stunned. He had never thought of such a thing. He didn't like the idea in the least, but she was insistent, and finally he said, "I'll think about it."

"Please. I would have a baby to hold and to raise. It would be *our* son."

"What about Bilhah?"

"She would do it for me. I know she would."

"She'd have to, I suppose. But I wouldn't want to force her. She would have to agree."

"Then you will think about it?"

"Yes, I will. But no matter what happens, you're still the Beloved Wife."

"Oh, Jacob, I love you so much!"

Later that night Rachel went to her father's tent. He had gone to the village, and Ziva was out helping to deliver a child. Rachel knew where her father kept his household gods, for he had always put great stress on his idols. She unfolded them out of the soft leather he kept them in and stood them upright on the shelf. She stared at them for a long time, and her thoughts were thick within her. *Jacob's God hasn't heard my prayer, but maybe my father's gods will. I know Jacob thinks there's only one God. Everyone else I know thinks there are many.*

For a long time she stood there, but she could not bring herself to pray to the idols. Jacob's stories about his father and about his grandfather had sunk deep into her spirit. She had learned to have faith and confidence in the God that had spoken to Jacob.

Finally she wrapped the gods back up, replaced them, and left Laban's tent, determined to trust only the Almighty One.

Days passed, and Jacob said nothing about Bilhah, but Leah seemed to grow more cruel. She made her remarks openly now in front of the family and the servants, continually insulting Rachel for having no children.

Finally the day came when Rachel said to Jacob, "I must have a child."

"You still want me to take Bilhah and have a child by her?"

"Yes. It will be our son."

"All right," Jacob said. "I will do it, but I'm not sure it's wise."

"It will be wonderful!" Rachel threw her arms around his neck, kissed him, and then ran away to her tent. She found Bilhah churning milk, and when her maidservant looked up, Rachel said, "Bilhah, I have something to tell you."

"Yes, mistress?"

"I want you to have a child by Jacob."

"Yes, mistress, if that's what you wish."

Rachel was shocked at the ease with which Bilhah agreed. "Are you sure? You understand what I'm asking you to do?"

"It's a common custom." Bilhah shrugged. "I never had any plans to marry, and this will be your child."

"You understand that clearly, Bilhah?" Rachel sat down and put her arm around the young woman. "You will have the child and nurse him, but he will be *my* son."

Bilhah was a meek little thing, and she smiled winsomely. "I'm so glad I can do something for you. You've been so kind to me, mistress."

"Oh, thank you, Bilhah!" Rachel said, hugging her maidservant. "I hope you will bear me many fine sons!"

CHAPTER
14

"Don't get up, Bilhah. I'll get the jug."

Bilhah, who was heavy with child, smiled gratefully. "You spoil me, Rachel," she said. "I can do my work."

"No. You sit still." Rachel got up to fetch one of the heavy jugs of water that one of the servant girls had brought. She poured the water into a shallow clay dish and began breaking some bread into it.

"It's not fitting for you to do that, mistress," Bilhah said. "Let me do it."

"We'll do it together."

Rachel moved the dish over to where the two of them could mix the lightly baked bread with the water. After it was thoroughly mixed, they would pass it through pottery sieves and set it aside to ferment into a beer.

Bilhah smiled with gratitude, for surely no bondwoman had ever been so carefully treated! Throughout Bilhah's pregnancy, she and Rachel shared Rachel's tent, and as the months passed, Rachel coddled Bilhah and demanded to know every physical sensation the surrogate mother was feeling. Rachel was very pointed with her questions, demanding to know if Bilhah had known when life had first begun in her. Did she feel pain in her back? Was there a craving for anything special she could get for her?

As the child in Bilhah had grown, draining her, Rachel had been happy. She had laughed and played with Leah's boys. She had done Bilhah's work as well as her own. Even such tasks as making cheese and grinding grain, which she had never liked before, had become a joy.

When the bread and water mixture was ready, she stood up and began to strain it, thinking of how close she had gotten to the woman during her pregnancy. There was no jealousy, for Bilhah repeatedly insisted that the child was Rachel's, and the two women had grown closer than Rachel had ever been to her sister, Leah.

"I wonder if your child will be a girl or a boy," Bilhah remarked. She put her hand on her stomach and said, "Lamah thinks it will be a boy, but Ziva thinks a girl."

Rachel moved over and put her hand on Bilhah's swollen abdomen. Her eyes widened as they always did when she felt movement beneath her hand. "I hope it will be a boy." She leaned over and kissed Bilhah, saying, "We will raise him to be a fine man, won't we?"

"Yes. Your child will be the best of all Jacob's children."

Jacob had walked out to the river with Rachel, and they sat as the afternoon sun went down. The water ran by, making a sibilant whispering along the banks. The sky was a strange turquoise color, and Jacob, always sensitive to such things, mentioned it. "I wish you had a gown of that color, Rachel," he said. "It would look beautiful on you."

"I have never seen a dye exactly that color. Maybe we could mix up blue and green pigment and get something like it." She took Jacob's hand, lifted it and kissed it, and then laughed aloud. "I'm so happy, Jacob. I can't wait until our baby comes."

Jacob squeezed Rachel's hand. "I like to see you happy."

"You always did." The two sat there quietly, not speaking. It was a time of peaceful contentment. Jacob loved to come to this place, for the strain of working with the large herd he had developed drained him of strength. He had made a peace of sorts with Laban, and in return the old man had forced his sons to do more of their work. They were still lazy louts, but at least Jacob received some help.

"Jacob, will you love me better after I give you a son?" Rachel asked.

"No."

Rachel turned toward him, her lips open and a hurt look in her eyes. "You won't? But I thought—"

"Love isn't like that, Rachel."

"But I don't understand."

Jacob was a thoughtful man. He sometimes got an idea and would meditate on it for days. It so happened that this particular subject he had given long thought to. He stroked Rachel's hand for a time as he considered what to say. "I don't think we love people for what they do for us. We love them for who they *are*."

Rachel loved it when Jacob spoke of what was in his heart. "Tell me some more about love. You're an expert," she teased.

"I *am* an expert! And I have a likely subject to experiment with." He put his arm around her and drew her close. "I don't think we can make love conditional, Rachel. It's like this. If someone says I will love you only if you will do these things for me, then that's not true love. That's an *if* kind of love. Conditional, as I said. I think true love is when we love someone without any *if*s. No matter what they do or how they disappoint us, we love them anyway."

"That's so sweet," Rachel said. "But those we love do disappoint us."

"I didn't say they wouldn't, but we love them anyway. Not for their faults but in spite of them." He laughed and hugged her closer. "I'm sure you love me in spite of the fact that I snore at night."

"You sound like a bear!"

"And how many bears have you heard?"

"Well, you sound like what I *think* a bear would sound like. But I see what you mean, and it's a lovely thought."

"I've considered it carefully."

"You're the only man I know that thinks about things like that."

"I believe my grandfather did. I wish you could have known Abraham. There was nobody like him, Rachel."

"I think you must be like him."

"Oh no, he was a big, tall, fine man. Strong as an ox."

"I don't mean that. I mean, I think he must have been kind and loving as you are."

"I hope I am like him. My father's a loving man too. Much quieter than my grandfather. He's a thinker."

"Like you," Rachel said. "And your son will be the same way."

"Well, I hope he'll be larger than I am."

"I don't care about that as long he's good and loving."

The two sat again quietly, and after a while, Jacob said, "Sing me one of your songs, Rachel."

Rachel seldom had to be begged. She loved to sing, and most of the time she made up her own songs. But this time she sang an old song she had heard from someone else. It was about a woman longing for her lover to come to her. She lifted her voice and sang softly but with a clear, sweet tone. When she was finished, she reached over and kissed Jacob on the cheek. "There," she said. "Now you sing one for me."

———————

The birth was as simple as a first birth can possibly be. Bilhah felt the pains coming on, and at once Lamah, the old midwife, and Ziva had taken her to a special tent used for birthing. The maidservant groaned as she squatted on the birthing bricks, with Rachel standing right behind her. It was as if the two women were sharing the pains. Rachel fancied she could feel each contraction, and her face grew tense, and she cried out even as Bilhah did.

The baby came so quickly that all four women were astonished. The boy was delivered and the cord severed; then Lamah gave the baby to Rachel. Joyfully she held the squirming bit of humanity in her arms. Rachel helped wash the blood from the baby's body and checked to see that he was unblemished, then quickly put the child into Bilhah's arms.

Bilhah kissed the baby's head, and almost at once he began to nurse. "Your son is beautiful. What will you name him?" Bilhah whispered.

Rachel's voice was triumphant as she cried out, "God has vindicated me; he has listened to my plea and given me a son. I will call his name Dan."

Jacob had been waiting outside, and Ziva went to get him. When he came in, his eyes went not to the child but to Rachel. He smiled at her and saw her eyes filled with tears. "Your son is named Dan," she said, picking up the baby and handing him to his father.

Jacob, who loved all babies, passed his hand over the infant's head. "A fine boy," he said. Then he looked at Rachel and said, "Now you will have a baby of your own to care for." He bent down and passed his hand over Bilhah's head. "You have done a fine job," he said quietly. He had learned to have an affection for Bilhah and always showed kindness to her. He saw tears fill her eyes, and she took his hand and kissed it.

Jacob straightened up, and Rachel came over to him. They stood looking down into the face of the infant, and Jacob said, "I always wonder about the future of babies. Will he be strong? Will he be a warrior? Will he be a good man?"

"He will be a good man," Rachel whispered. She ran her hand over the baby's head and smiled. "We will see that he is."

———————

After the birth of Dan, Rachel's life assumed an even tenor. She had always loved caring for babies, but this one was very special. She could not nurse him, of course, but she could do everything else for him. She and Bilhah loved the child equally, it seemed, and they spent hours caring for the baby as he went through the problems of infancy.

The months sped by and quickly Bilhah became pregnant again. Again the two women looked forward to the birth of this child. As Bilhah grew heavier, more and more of little Dan's care fell to Rachel.

Finally Dan's brother was birthed as easily as Dan had been. For reasons she could not explain, Rachel was not as filled with joy this time. After the first excitement had passed away, she loved the new baby too, but something was still missing from her life. Rachel called his name Naphtali. Jacob was proud of this son as well, and Rachel gave him tender love and care. Yet an unsettledness lingered in her heart, a feeling she could not identify. The days passed slowly, and the feeling within her grew. It was like a memory she could not quite call up. As the days passed, she gradually acknowledged to herself that she still longed for a child born of her own flesh.

It was during this period of longing that Ziva grew ill. She had been sickly for a long time, passing blood and losing strength, and one day Bilhah mentioned, "I don't think Ziva will live much longer."

"I believe you're right," Rachel said. "I wish I could help her."

"When the time comes to die, no one can help except the gods," Bilhah said. She had never accepted Jacob's God. Indeed, he had not gone to many pains to help her understand. She cleaved to the gods of Laban, for she had grown up all of her life being told they were powerful.

The two women spoke of Ziva's possible death even as the old woman lay dying.

———————

"Come closer, daughter."

Leah had been sitting beside her dying mother for long hours. More than once she had thought that the woman had slipped away, but each time she had come back. Now Leah leaned forward and placed her hand on her mother's forehead. She had never been an affectionate daughter, nor had Ziva been an affectionate mother, but still it was blood answering to blood. "What is it, Mother?" she whispered.

"I am leaving this earth." The voice was thin and cracked, and Leah had to lean closer to hear it. "I want you . . . to do something."

"What is it, Mother? I will do whatever you say."

"You must . . . tie Jacob to you in a stronger way."

"How can I do that?"

"You have ceased childbearing. Give . . . give your maid Zilpah to Jacob as . . . Rachel has done with her maid."

Leah blinked with surprise. She had never thought of this; she had always considered her own children enough for Jacob. But she knew Ziva had a mysterious sense of discernment, and she could well be right about this. "I will do it, Mother," she promised.

"Every son you have ties him closer to you," Ziva whispered. She did not speak again, and a few moments later she passed from life to death. Leah stood beside her, thinking of the old woman's last request, and knew that she would do exactly as Ziva had said.

———————

After Ziva's funeral, Rachel was making a coat for Dan. She looked up when Jacob came in and held it up. "Do you like it?"

"Yes. It's very nice."

Rachel chatted for a moment as Jacob sat beside her, but then she saw that Jacob's face was troubled. "What is it, husband?"

"Leah wants me to have children with her maid Zilpah, as I have with Bilhah."

When Rachel did not speak, he said quickly, "The more sons a man has, the richer he is. Isn't that so?"

Rachel nodded, for she could not argue with this. She looked at him and made herself smile. "If that is what you want to do, I will not complain."

Jacob shook his head. He was troubled, yet he had spoken the truth. A man's sons were his protection. If Laban had had ten or twelve strong sons, he would not have needed Jacob.

"I don't love Zilpah or Bilhah in the way that I love you, Rachel. You know that. You're the Beloved Wife."

Rachel took his hand and waited for him to say that he didn't love Leah as he loved her, but she saw that he was preoccupied and troubled. She felt suddenly that if she asked him not to lie with Zilpah, he would honor her wishes. But she had taken the first step by offering him her own handmaiden, and now she gave up her will and said, "If it's a way for you to have more sons, then you must do it, husband."

CHAPTER

15

Rachel felt old beyond her years as she moved around serving at the harvest feast. The whole family was together now, and she filled her father's cup for what seemed like the hundredth time. Wine ran down his beard, and he was singing an obscene song in which her two brothers, Lomach and Benzar, joined in. *Were there ever three more vulgar men in all the world?* The thought had come to her many times before, and now she shook her head in despair. She moved back, and her eyes went around the family circle. Jacob now had ten sons ranging all the way from Reuben down to the youngest, Zebulun.

Somehow the passing years had left Rachel behind. Zilpah had done as Leah had asked of her and had become Jacob's concubine. She had produced two sons—Gad and Asher.

Strangely, during this time, Leah had a burst of productivity. In rapid succession, she produced both Issachar and Zebulun.

So here we are. Four wives and ten sons—and none of the sons are mine! Rachel thought bitterly.

Her eyes went to Jacob, and a warm pride came over her. He was a good man, loving to everyone, and a better father she had never seen. He took pride in all of his sons, carrying them with him as soon as they were able to walk out to the hills. He taught them the ways of managing the herds and spent long hours teaching them the skills of sling and spear.

Jacob had also attempted to impress upon his family his concept of one God. This was difficult to do, for no one in this part of the world believed in such a thing. Laban continued to put his utmost confidence in his idols. But Jacob never gave up, and he spent long hours, usually at night, telling the stories of his forefathers, of Noah and Abraham and his own father, Isaac. His eyes often glowed as he talked of how God had appeared to him on his way to Paddan Aram, at the place he called Bethel, and he had told the story of the stairway reaching up into heaven so often that everyone in the family could repeat it word for word. As for the boys, they loved their father and were always in competition for his favor. They cared less for their mothers, it seemed, perhaps except for Judah and Reuben. They were the most affectionate of the boys, giving equal loyalty to Rachel and Leah. This infuriated Leah, but nothing she could say would change it.

Now as Rachel kept her eye on Jacob's face, she saw that he was troubled. After their years together, she had learned to know him well. She had given up on the thought of having a child, but Rachel loved Jacob more than ever. She knew he was worried because he actually owned nothing. The flocks, the herds, the cattle, all belonged to Laban. After all these years of arduous labor, the only things he could call his own were the clothes on his back, his wives, and his children. He told Rachel often that this was riches enough for him, but she knew his heart—how he longed for his own possessions, his own herds. Laban's wealth had increased since Jacob had come years ago, but Laban had no spark of gratitude for his son-in-law, and his sons were always envious.

"Are you going to bring me something to drink or not, Rachel?"

Leah's voice rose. She was pregnant now with another child and had become shrill and irritable over anything. She seemed to look upon Rachel as a servant. She often said, "Bilhah and Zilpah and I have children. You don't have anything else to do. It looks like you could show me *some* consideration!"

Jacob's eyes went at once to Leah. He got up quickly and filled her glass and said, "There you are, Leah."

"Rachel could have done that. You didn't have to disturb yourself."

"I don't mind. Now quiet yourself. All is well."

Leah reached out and grabbed Jacob's robe and glared at Rachel. She had become more jealous over the years, for although Rachel had no children of her own, she was still the Beloved Wife. Jacob did not even try to hide this from people. Zilpah and Bilhah did not mind in the least, but Leah was jealous to the bone.

"You treat that woman like a queen!" Leah said. She flew into a fit, and when Rachel tried to quiet her, she took a cup of wine and dashed it into Rachel's face, cursing and raving.

Rachel wiped her eyes and left. Jacob looked down and put his hand on the back of Leah's neck. "Be quiet!" he said fiercely. "I won't permit you to behave like this. You have disgraced yourself."

Leah opened her mouth to scream again, but Jacob's hand tightened on her neck, and she began to whimper. "Be quiet and go to your tent. I'm ashamed of you!"

Leah got to her feet and lumbered off, heavy with child and weeping.

Jacob turned and looked straight at Laban. "That's some more of your raising," he said.

Laban started to speak, but Jacob said, "Close your mouth!"

Laban was an arrogant old man, but he had seen something in Jacob once before that frightened him. Now as he stood looking at his son-in-law, he knew this was not the time to assert his authority. He turned to Zilpah instead and ordered, "Give me some more wine." She rose at once and began to wait on him.

Jacob turned and left the tent. He sought Rachel and found her sitting inside her tent. She had not even cleaned her face, and he found a cloth and dipped it into a pot of water and began to clean off her face. "Don't let it anger you," he said. "She's not herself." As he stroked Rachel's face with the cloth she did not speak.

"Rachel, are you all right?" He put himself before her and saw that her eyes were looking right through him. Alarmed, he asked, "Are you all right, my dear?" Still no answer. Jacob had never seen Rachel like this. She had always been the most stable woman he had ever known, but now she seemed to have gone somewhere deep inside herself. Those lovely eyes he had always adored were staring at him blankly. Fear came over Jacob, and he sat beside her, his arm around her. The minutes went by, and from time to time he would speak to her, but she still would not respond.

Finally after an hour he got up and said, "Lie down, my dear, and sleep." She paid no heed, so he put her on the bed like a child, and she lay down obediently, her eyes staring straight up. "I'll stay right here beside you," he whispered as a fear grew within him.

What if something happens to her? he thought. *How could I live without her?* He took her hand and held it and kissed it, then he bowed over it and was shocked to feel tears forming in his eyes and running down his cheeks. He began to pray, "God, don't let her be destroyed. Bring her back from whatever place she's in."

But the heavens were silent, as they had been for so many years. The Almighty did not speak, and Jacob's shoulders shook as he wept for his beloved Rachel.

CHAPTER

16

As Jacob walked into the camp one evening, he saw Laban's two sons sitting with their backs against a tree in a drunken stupor. He stopped and stood stock-still. He had been gone since early morning doing the work these two should have done. All day he had been preoccupied with troubled thoughts about Rachel's strange behavior. She had been such a lively, outgoing woman, always cheerful and rarely complaining. But for over a week now she had been silent, speaking only when forced to. Her smile was gone, and she moved like an old woman. Leah had scolded her, telling her to snap out of it, but no amount of scolding would help. Jacob had been gentle as always, but whatever was wrong could not be fixed with kind words and caresses. With a cold dread, he thought she might be losing her mind, and now as he saw the two sots under the tree laughing, something snapped within him. His jaw tightened, and he swiftly crossed to where the two sat and stood over them. "Get up, you louts!"

Lomach looked up, too drunk to move. His words slurred together. "I don' hafta pay no 'tention to you. You're no relative. You're just a hired hand."

Jacob reached down and grabbed Lomach by the hair. The man let out a scream of pain, but Jacob paid no heed. Pulling him to his feet, he held on firmly and slapped his face back and forth three times.

Startled, Benzar scrambled to his feet and yelled, "You can't do that—"

But Jacob stopped his outburst, grabbing him by the hair and banging the heads of the two men together. He shoved them down, and when Benzar tried to struggle back to his feet, Jacob kicked him on the backside. Then he did the same to Lomach, shouting, "You get to work or I'll kill you!"

Laban had come out of his tent at the commotion, and he stood staring at the fracas, petrified. He had never seen Jacob in such a rage. He started to leave, but Jacob whirled and said, "And you, old man, you're not too old to work." He ran toward Laban, grabbing him by the robe and holding his arm. The old man struggled helplessly against the younger man's strength. Jacob's eyes were filled with rage, and he hollered, "You and your drunken sons can do your share of the work or I'm done with all of it!"

Jacob released him, and Laban staggered backward, staring after his son-in-law in a daze. Lomach and Benzar got to their feet, holding their heads. They staggered over to Laban, saying, "You won't let him do that, will you, Father?"

Leah had come out of her tent during the last part of the scuffle. She was close to giving birth and could not move quickly. Her eyes were cold at the sight before her as she laughed in scorn. "Aren't you three pretty ones! Are you going to let him do that to you?"

Laban shrank from her taunt and muttered, "That fellow is dangerous. He could kill somebody with that rage."

"The three of you are pretty babies indeed!" Leah spat. She was disgusted with her father and his sons. They were half brothers to her, but she never acknowledged any relationship to them. She was also furious that Jacob had been spending so much of his time with Rachel. She put her hand on her stomach and shook her head. "I don't need another son, and I pray he won't be like my father or those two worthless sons of his."

———————

Jacob stalked out of the camp and let his rage dissipate. His head swarmed with angry thoughts, mostly at Laban for the way he had cheated him out of his wages for years. The impulse came simply to leave, but as he walked off his anger, he realized he could not do that with Rachel in such poor shape.

Finally he turned and walked heavily back to Rachel's tent. He stepped inside and found her seated on a mat on the floor, just staring into space. Jacob hesitated, then went over and sat down beside her. Putting his arm around her, he held her close and said, "Did you hear that fight I had with your father?" He waited for an answer, but Rachel did not speak, did not even indicate she had heard him. Leaning closer, he saw in the faint light of the tent that she had been weeping. Her eyes were swollen, and he whispered, "Rachel . . . my beloved Rachel! What's wrong with you?"

Still there was no answer, and Jacob sat there for a long time. Fear gripped his heart as he thought about losing this woman. He knew he loved her more than he had ever loved anyone on earth, and he began to pray to the Almighty, asking His favor.

———————

To Laban's great relief, Jacob went to work the next day. Benzar and Lomach avoided him, keeping their eyes on him from a distance, but Jacob's rage appeared to be gone.

Jacob was ashamed of himself for having lost his temper, but at least it had accomplished one thing: his two worthless brothers-in-law had been frightened into working, at least some of the time.

When Jacob began work at the end of that week, he was met by Laban, whose face had a peculiar expression.

"What is it?" Jacob asked at once.

"It's Leah."

"Has the baby come?" Jacob was ashamed of his treatment of Leah. He knew he had neglected her lately, but he had been so troubled about Rachel, he could not think properly. Leah was a hard woman to love anyway. Her appeal for him had always been physical, but now even that had passed away. He was actually surprised when she had gotten pregnant again.

"Yes," Laban said, "and it's a girl this time."

"A girl?" Jacob said, astonished. After ten sons, the arrival of a girl was indeed a surprise. He shoved past Laban and went into the tent, where he found the old midwife Lamah cleaning up from the birth.

Moving over to Leah, Jacob bent down and put his hand on her head. "Was it a hard time?" he asked gently.

"No, not this time. We have a daughter."

"Yes. Let me see." Jacob picked up the baby and saw that her hair was the same chestnut color as his own. "A fine girl," he said.

"You always wanted sons."

"We have plenty of sons," Jacob said, smiling. "This one will be special." He kissed the baby's forehead and said, "What will we call her?"

"Her name is Dinah."

"Dinah. A fine name," Jacob said with approval. He held her up, bracing her back with one hand, and felt a gush of affection. A girl would be better. Someone he could pour his affection on openly. He could not do that with boys, especially as they grew. He laughed and said again, "This one will be very special indeed."

Leah was surprised at Jacob's pleasure; she had expected him to be disappointed. Wearily she closed her eyes and said, "I expect you will spoil her terribly."

"You're right about that. What is an only daughter for if not to spoil?" Jacob was surprised at the warmth he felt toward his little girl. He had not known he wanted a daughter, but now he was pleased and excited. "You and I will be great friends," he whispered. "You will grow up and please your father in everything you do."

"No woman could ever do that," Leah said jadedly, closing her eyes.

Jacob shook his head. "This one will," he said. "She'll be everything a woman ought to be!"

CHAPTER
17

A distant muffled voice spoke to Rachel. She struggled to understand, concentrating on who might be speaking to her. The voice spoke again—this time more clearly, right in her ear.

"Mistress, please let me help you."

The mist in Rachel's mind cleared away, as if she were coming out of deep sleep. The features of the woman next to her swam in disarray, then pulled themselves together, and she saw the face of Bilhah.

"What did you say, Bilhah?"

Rachel could see that Bilhah was relieved. Her wrinkled brow relaxed, and she reached out and touched Rachel's hair.

"Your hair is so dirty, mistress, and you need a bath. And look at your robe. You spilled food all over it."

Looking down, Rachel saw that her robe was indeed spotted with dried food. She tried to remember when it had happened but could not. She could not even remember the last time she ate. She touched the food smudges and looked up. "I'm sorry," she said.

"Oh, it doesn't matter. I can wash the robe—and let me clean your face and wash your hair."

Rachel touched her hair and found it stiff with dirt, and she pulled at it, not remembering when it was last washed. Events came and went in her mind, and she could not piece them together in a logical time sequence.

"All right, Bilhah."

The maidservant began to clean Rachel up. She removed her robe and washed her thoroughly with tepid water, then put a clean robe on her and had her lie back while she washed her hair. For Rachel it seemed to take a long time, and she listened to the sounds of children laughing outside the tent.

"Where are the boys?" she asked finally.

"Dan and Naphtali? That's who you hear outside. Would you like to see them?"

Rachel tried to concentrate on the question but could not. In terror, she felt herself slipping away, and she knew that something was dreadfully wrong with her. Random thoughts ran through her mind and memories of faces, especially Jacob's face. She cried out, "Jacob . . . husband!" But even as she cried, she felt herself going away again to that murky place she hated. She tried to stop herself, but it was as if she had fallen off of some high mountain cliff and was now plunging down. The voice calling her grew more distant as the depths below darkened and she could no longer hear the woman. She had forgotten her name in any case.

". . . and she came to herself, and I asked if I could clean her up, and I did, master. But while I was washing her hair, she slipped away again." Bilhah's face twisted with emotion as she looked down at Rachel. She had such a great love for her mistress, and now she picked at her robe and tears filled her eyes. "What's wrong with her, Jacob?"

"I don't know, Bilhah. Something dreadful."

Jacob had come quickly at Bilhah's urgent summons and had entered the tent to find Bilhah weeping and Rachel lying down, clean now but with her eyes closed. She did not awaken when he called to her.

"Sometimes she seems to know everything," Bilhah whimpered, "but at other times it's like she just goes away somewhere. I'm frightened for her."

Jacob bit his lower lip. "So am I, Bilhah. So am I."

"She's always been so careful to take care of herself. She loves to take baths and have me wash her hair, and now she doesn't care."

Jacob did not respond. Everyone could see that Rachel had been growing worse. Some said she was touched with evil spirits, and they refused to even get close to her. If it had not been for Bilhah, who had devoted almost all of her waking hours to taking care of her, Jacob did not know what he would have done. Now sitting beside his favorite wife—the Beloved Wife—he stroked her hair and tried to pray. But the words would not come. He had prayed and prayed until there was nothing left to say. He had fasted, and sleep had left him, but still Rachel had gone away from him.

Finally he arose and said, "I'm going out someplace where I can be alone."

"Keep praying for her, master," Bilhah said. "I'm afraid she's going to die."

———————

"She's not any better, daughter," Laban said heavily. He looked across at Leah, who was nursing Dinah and shook his head sadly. "Why has this come upon us?"

Leah stroked the infant's head but had no answer.

"I don't think she can live long if she doesn't get well," Laban said.

"There's nothing wrong with her physically, Father."

"Yes there is. She won't eat unless someone makes her. Haven't you seen how she's lost weight?"

Leah had indeed noticed how thin Rachel had become. Bilhah and Jacob had to almost force her to eat when she was at her worst.

"I thought it would help that she was praying to our gods," Laban remarked.

Leah looked up, her eyes narrow. "What are you talking about? She prays to the God of Jacob."

"No. She prays to my gods," Laban said, nodding his head firmly. "I've come into my tent several times when she's had my gods out praying to them."

"How do you know she was praying? Did she say anything out loud?"

"No, but her lips were moving. Why else would she get them out and her lips be moving if she weren't praying?"

Leah shook her head. "I don't think that's possible. She hasn't had any confidence in your gods for a long time."

"Well, she should have! I think maybe she must have displeased one of them or maybe more. That's the only reason I can think of why she's lost her mind."

Leah did not answer, but for a long time after Laban left, she pondered what her father had said. "Praying to those gods? That doesn't sound like Rachel," she muttered. Even though she herself was inclined to pray to the idols, she knew Rachel was not that way. Finally, she shook her head. "He must have been wrong about it."

———————

The stone was cool under Rachel's hands at first, but then it seemed to burn as if she had picked up a hot coal. Pain surged through her palm, and she dropped the stone and stepped backward as confusion swept through her.

What am I doing here?

She looked around wildly, recognizing that she was in her father's tent but having no memory of how she got there. And then suddenly she saw the idols her father so feared and that she had feared also until ... until what? Until when? She had learned to trust the God of Jacob. She stared at the idols as they were ranked on a shelf where her father customarily put them up from time to time so that he could kneel before them. They were of all shapes. One of them was a woman with a head like a bull. Another was a snakelike form with a woman's upper body and a snake's dotted eyes and fangs. Still another was an image of a fat man with puffed-out cheeks and eyes squeezed together.

Rachel stared at them and faint memories trickled down. She vaguely remembered having come to her father's tent to pray to these idols to give her a child. The memories became clearer, and she covered her eyes and fell down on the rug, sobbing. The sides of the tent seemed to close in upon her. She had grown from faith in the idols to doubt, and now she knew that whatever power they might have, there was also a dark power within her. She sobbed and cried out, "Oh, God, I didn't mean it!"

She hid her face and felt as if hands were picking at her, trying to get inside her. She was too weak to move at first, but finally, when she felt herself being invaded, she jumped to her feet and rushed out into the night. The stars were faint overhead, and the moon was hidden behind a filmy cloud. Rachel stumbled over a tent peg and fell headlong, then picked herself up and rushed out of the camp, fear driving her far from the idols.

She ran until she was gasping for breath. She fell to her knees and rested her hands on the earth. The sand was still warm, but the fear of what had taken place did not leave. She began to sob great choking sobs and curled up into a fetal position.

The fear that swept over her was like a great hand squeezing her, but inside her head or her heart was a tiny bit of resistance. Yet the eyes of the idols seemed to bore into her even though her own eyes were closed and her hands covered them.

"Please, God, help me!" she cried. And then again, "I'm sorry, great Lord! I didn't know what I was doing. Help me! Don't let me fall!"

She felt as if she were hanging on to a cliff and now her grasp was loosening. She dreaded falling into the darkness, for she knew that in that darkness were terrible, fearful things. She remembered how in the darkest hour of the wanderings of her mind she had felt them clawing at her, crying out with wild voices, pulling her down so that she would become one with them.

She lay sobbing, all light shut out as she pressed her hands against her face. Fear pierced her like a sword, and she shook from head to foot.

Finally, she somehow knew that her mind was being touched in a calming way. The weird cries of the idols as they pulled at her began to fade away ... farther and farther ... until her trembling ceased. She was still afraid to move her hands from her eyes, but then out of the silence arose what sounded like a wind far off in distant trees, a mere whispering. But it began to grow and gather force, and then Rachel heard a voice—a soft voice yet so strong! Stronger than any voice she had ever heard! She understood that this was the God of Abraham and of Isaac and of Jacob. She pulled herself up to a kneeling position and put her forehead on the earth, whispering, "Oh, Lord, God of Abraham, have mercy on me."

The voice seemed to come through her ears as a faint whisper, but down inside her mind and in her heart it grew stronger. She was almost afraid to breathe as the words became clearer.

"You have behaved foolishly, my child. You have turned from the one who is all-powerful to gods who have eyes but see not and have ears but hear not. Because you have turned from me, you have been troubled."

The voice went on, the very quality of it somehow calming Rachel. She knew that the one who spoke to her was the one who had created all the heavens and the earth. A part of her trembled at the power and strength in that voice, yet another part of her surrendered to the love in it—a love Rachel could not comprehend. It caused her to cry out, "Oh, God, forgive me!"

"You have doubted your God, but you must have faith. There is nothing too difficult for me, and you will bear a son if you will only believe my voice."

And then, as she knelt before God in the darkness under the stars, she cried out with a voice of praise, "Blessed be the God of Abraham, Isaac, and Jacob! I believe, O God. It shall be even as you say."

Rachel knelt for a long time after the voice had stopped speaking to her. A continuous river of love flowed into her and around her, and she knew that what had been promised would come to pass. She got to her feet, her strength almost gone. Not only was she half starved, but being in the presence of the Creator of all things had drained her. She stumbled back toward the tent with one thing in her mind. *I must tell Jacob what I have done and what I have heard!*

As she returned, bursting with the news, inexplicably Rachel felt the Lord telling her to keep silent about the promise she had been given. She could not understand this at all; nevertheless, the next day when Jacob arose, she was there, standing over him.

He sat up at once. "Rachel, are you all right?"

"Yes, husband. I am all right. I am fine."

Jacob got up and took her in his arms. She was thin and her face drawn, but he exclaimed, "Your eyes—they're clear!"

"Yes, and I must tell you what I have done and ask your forgiveness."

"What do you mean, Rachel? You've been very ill."

"I was ill," she said, "because I committed a sin against the Eternal God. The God of all the earth."

"Sin? What sin?"

"I was so anxious for a child that I forsook the God of your fathers, husband, and I prayed to my father's idols." Her trembling hand touched his chest. He covered it with his own hands, and she whispered, "I was so weak. I have watched my people pray to these gods all my life, but you have taught me of the true God, and I should have known better. I do know better now."

"What has happened?"

"I think God allowed my soul to be troubled when I chose to go away from Him, but last night I found your God, Jacob, and now He is my God too."

Jacob insisted on knowing everything, and she told of her experience in a voice filled with excitement. He held her tightly and kissed her, saying, "I'm so glad for you, Rachel. I was so afraid."

"I've been a trial to you, husband, but now it's over."

"Thank God," Jacob whispered. He held her tightly and felt the lightness of her body. "You're back again, Rachel, and now I feel that life is worth living."

Everyone was shocked at Rachel's return. It was as if she had come back from the dead. She began eating and gained weight rapidly. Her cheeks filled out, as did her body, so that as the weeks passed she became more beautiful than ever. Her hair, which had grown lank and dull, was lustrous again, and her eyes were wide with excitement.

Jacob, of course, was more ecstatic than anyone over Rachel's recovery. For a time he could not convince himself it was real, and he stayed with her constantly. He would reach out and touch her, anxiously asking, "Are you all right, Rachel?"

And she would laugh and say, "Yes. I'm all right."

Once, soon after Rachel had regained her full strength, the two of them were sitting before the fire late at night. She was singing to him and telling him stories, and Jacob was fully content. But finally he frowned and said, "You know, I'm so happy, but there's one problem."

"What is it, Jacob?"

"I feel like a slave here, Rachel," Jacob said quietly. "Your father is a hard master. He changes my wages so that I can never own anything. I want to leave here, and I want us to have a family where we can be our own masters and not be servants to anyone."

"If that's what you want, husband, then that's what you must do."

"Do you think I can?"

"Yes. You can do anything you want, Jacob. You remember the promise God made to you back when you saw the stairway reaching up to heaven?"

"I've thought of it every day since then."

"The God who spoke to you is real."

"But why hasn't He spoken to me again?"

"I don't know. He didn't speak to me until I was almost gone. But He loves you, Jacob. That's what I found out. He's the God of love as well as the God of power."

The two sat there, and Jacob drew her close. "I have you and that's enough."

"I have a gift for you, my Jacob."

"A gift? What is it?"

"Can't you guess?"

"No. I never did like guessing games." He smiled and then laughed. "What is it?"

Rachel reached over and took his right hand and placed it against her stomach. She held it there and whispered, "God has sent us a great gift."

Jacob remained absolutely still, then looked into her eyes and saw the truth there. Joy surged through him, and Jacob, the son of Isaac, knew complete happiness. He held her and the two of them rejoiced together. Rachel told him how the great and almighty God had promised her that they would have a son.

Jacob wanted to laugh and shout and cry out, but instead he held her gently, and after a long time he said, "This son. He's going to be a very special child."

"Yes," Rachel whispered. "I think he will be very special indeed!"

CHAPTER

18

Rachel's pregnancy was difficult. As she grew larger, she developed a fierce pain in her back, causing her to grow swaybacked. Her breasts swelled and grew extremely painful to the touch. She was sick every day—almost continuously—but she never complained, not once.

As the months went on, Jacob stayed with her almost constantly, whenever he wasn't working. Leah resented this, and she told Jacob's concubines, "Once this child is born, our sons will be as *nothing!*"

Bilhah answered sharply, "No, he will love them all!"

"You are a fool, Bilhah!" Leah said. "Rachel's always been the favorite wife—and this son will be the favorite son. Mind what I say, for it will come to be."

Finally the hour arrived for Rachel to deliver, and Jacob was beside himself. The labor pains seemed to go on forever, and Rachel cried out so pitifully that Jacob covered his ears as he sat outside the tent. No one could be of any comfort to him.

Finally he felt a touch on his shoulder and looked up to see Lamah, the ancient midwife, along with Bilhah, whose face was beaming.

"You have a son!" Bilhah cried out. "Come and see."

Jacob stepped into the tent and stopped, for Rachel looked almost dead. His heart nearly ceased beating, but then she opened her eyes and managed a smile. He ran forward, fell on his knees beside her, and held her.

"Your son," Rachel whispered. "Is he not perfect?"

Jacob turned and took the baby from Bilhah. He examined him carefully. It was as if he had never had a son before. Somehow this one was . . . *different*. He knew with one part of himself that it was so because this was the child of Rachel, whom he truly loved, whom he had always loved more than anything in life. Now as he held the baby, he wanted to crush it to his breast, but he held it tenderly instead. He put the boy down beside Rachel and said, "I've never seen such a beautiful boy."

"He's going to be a very special child, isn't he, husband?"

"Yes, he is."

Leah had by now entered the tent and heard the conversation. Displeased, she said sharply, "He needs to rest now." When Jacob rose, she went on, "I suppose you'll forget all your other sons now."

Jacob looked at her with irritation. "Don't be foolish, Leah! Of course I won't. I love all my sons and always will."

Leah stared at him and whispered something he did not catch. She walked out of the tent, and Jacob followed her. "What did you say?"

"I said this one will take all of your love."

"You're a foolish woman, Leah," Jacob said. She had spoiled his happiness momentarily, but as soon as she left, he began walking around, too excited to do anything else. Many friends came to him and congratulated him, and the warmth over the birth of this baby grew in him. He stayed up all night by Rachel's side simply watching her sleep, and many times he would reach out and touch the child. He would often pick him up and hold him, walking around the tent, quietly looking down into the infant's peaceful face.

Finally he sat down beside Rachel and began speaking to God. "Oh, God," he said, "I thank you for this child. I thank you for this wife. For all that you have given me. Lord, now I must leave Laban's house, and I ask that you will make the way."

Soon after this he saw that Rachel had awakened. "Did I wake you with my praying?" he asked.

"Yes, but it was good to hear."

"We'll have to leave this place sooner or later. I want this son to be free from all of this."

Rachel stretched out her hand, and when he took it and kissed it, she smiled. "Anywhere with you. That's where I want to be."

Jacob leaned down and kissed her gently. "Then we will ask God to deliver us from the bondage your father holds us in!"

PART FOUR

THE STRANGER

CHAPTER

19

Rachel looked up from her task and watched the two children playing a game with Jacob. "Joseph is growing quickly," she said to Leah. "He's caught up with Dinah and passed her." As the trio's screams of pleasure rose above the babble of voices in the camp, Rachel shook her head. "Jacob's like another child when he's with them, isn't he?"

"He makes a fool of himself over them," Leah said sharply. She was shoving a bone awl through a piece of leather, and looking up, she accidentally pierced her finger. "Ow!" She sucked at her finger and said sourly, "He's spoiling those two, just as I knew he would."

"I think it's good for all three of them."

Rachel was making a bowl on a simple potter's wheel. It consisted of a flat stone set in the ground with a hole in the top. Another stone carved with a protrusion on it was fitted into the hole of the stone below so that it could be rotated. Rachel had placed a lump of clay on the top and, while sitting on a low bench, began pushing the top stone with her big toe. It began to revolve, and with both hands she carefully shaped the clay. It was a slow method, but Rachel enjoyed it. Sometimes she used different colors of clay to make intricate designs.

As the top stone rotated, her fingers dug into the clay, and from time to time, she would reach down and dip her hand into a basin of water, sprinkling it on the work. Everyone in the tribe treasured Rachel's creations, and she found pleasure in the simple task. Finally Jacob walked over to where the two women worked. Sweat was running down his face. The afternoon sun was warm, but all of the summer scorch had gone out of it. Now the deep haze of summer had lightened, and the tawny land stretched into the distance. Far away the land smoldered with the tan and ash colors of fresh sunlight.

Jacob threw himself down, panting, then glanced back to where Joseph and Dinah were still running and throwing the ball. "They never get tired, those two." He laughed, and his eyes crinkled at the sides. "Makes me feel like an old man."

"You *are* an old man!" Leah grunted. "You're going to kill yourself wrestling with those two."

"No, I won't do that," Jacob said, smiling at her. "I didn't know a daughter could be so much fun. All I ever had was boys." He looked back and saw Dinah snatch the ball from Joseph and dash madly away. He laughed when Joseph caught her, and the two wrestled, shouting at the top of their lungs. Sighing deeply, he shook his head. "I wish I had their energy."

"They're a handful," Rachel said. She took her eyes off of the vessel that was taking shape and smiled at Jacob. "I was just telling Leah that it's like three children were out there playing. I never saw a man play with children like you do."

"I hate to see children grow up. I can remember when I played with Reuben like that. You remember that, Leah?"

"Yes, I do. You were always good with small children," Leah said. She smiled and shook her head. "Women have all the trouble of bringing babies into the world and then men have all the fun of playing with them. If it were the other way around, the race would die out, I suppose."

"You're probably right," Jacob agreed. He leaned back against a tree and studied the vessel Rachel was molding. "That's going to be a pretty piece," he said.

"If I had a better kiln, my pots would be stronger. But as soon as we get one built, we have to move away and leave it." This was indeed true. Jacob and some of the menservants had made her several kilns out of clay so that a fire could heat the interior. But they were too fragile to move, and Rachel always grieved when they had to be left behind.

Jacob shrugged. "We live by the animals and must move to find water and grass."

"I know it. I'm not complaining," Rachel said quickly. She touched her finger on the inside of the dish and took pleasure in seeing the clay form at her touch. She had developed a callous on her right toe as she turned the potter's wheel. She had become so adept at it that the rock turned smoothly.

Jacob studied her for a time, pausing once to get a drink of water out of the water bag that hung on a low limb. As she finished the job, smoothing it, he observed, "You do that so easily."

"It's not hard."

"It would be for me. I tried it once and just made a mess." He turned his head to one side and studied the deep dish. "It would be nice if it were as easy to mold people as it is for you to mold that clay."

Leah stared at him. He often made statements that irritated her. "That's a foolish thing to say. People are people and pottery is pottery."

"Well, I think in a way they're alike. They both have makers. Rachel made that dish and God made her." He winked over at Rachel and said, "I'm talking foolishly, aren't I?"

"Why, no, I don't think so. It's true enough."

"It *is* foolishness!" Leah snapped. She got to her feet and stalked off. She began calling out to Dinah, ordering her to leave her game. "Come with me!" she said sharply.

Dinah protested, and Jacob and Rachel watched as Leah dragged her away.

"I can never please her," Jacob said, shrugging, "no matter how hard I try."

Joseph came running over and said, "Come on, Father, play with me."

"I'm worn out, son."

"No you're not. You're more fun to play with than anyone."

Joseph was a sturdy boy and tall for his age. He had begun to talk at a younger age than any child Rachel or Jacob had ever seen. He had an abundance of chestnut hair exactly like Jacob's, and there was a faint resemblance in his features, but it was obvious that he would be a larger man than his father. He pulled at Jacob, saying, "Come on! Just a little bit."

Jacob groaned but got to his feet. "You're going to kill your old father." Rachel laughed. "Go on and play with him. It's what you want to do anyway."

Jacob reached down and tousled Joseph's hair. "All right, son. You'll have your own way as you always do."

Joseph looked up and laughed. His warm brown almond-shaped eyes revealed his cheerful, even pixyish, spirit. "Let me ride on your back," he said.

Jacob laughed. "All right. Get on." He bent over, and Joseph leaped up and settled himself. He leaned forward and said, "Father, when I get big you can ride on my back."

"What a thing to say!" Jacob laughed. "Wouldn't that be a sight." He trotted off, shaking Joseph while the lad yelled with enjoyment. Rachel watched them go, and she remembered then what Jacob had said the night she told him she was with child. *"He's going to be a very special child."*

She thought of Jacob's words about molding people, and she knew that the thought was deep. Leah had completely missed it, but Rachel had not. "It's true. We're molded by something," she said, "and it has to be God. The trouble is we won't let ourselves be molded. Now, you take this clay—" She gave the pot another spin and then paused the wheel to admire her work. "It doesn't argue back. It never disobeys my hands."

She looked over again to where Joseph and Jacob were careening around wildly, raising a cloud of dust. *The problem is that people aren't like clay. They refuse to let God mold them.* The thought troubled her, and she sat for a long time watching her husband and her son enjoying themselves. *It would be nice,* she thought, *if Joseph could always be small like this. It's when children grow up that they begin to cause trouble.*

———

Laban had drunk enough wine that the hard, sharp edges of his world had softened. He sat slumped with his elbows on the rough wooden table, listening as Lomach and Benzar argued over something. The three of them had come into the village and made straight for the house of an innkeeper named Rohazi. She was a fat woman with a round face and sharp eyes and had lost whatever beauty she had once had. She drew her trade from the dregs of the village and from visitors that came through from time to time. She kept two younger women—ostensibly to serve in the inn, but one look at them revealed their true profession.

Taking another long drink of the sour wine, Laban passed his hand over his face and began to listen to what his sons were arguing about. He studied them as through a fog and thought, *They're not much, but they're all I've got.* A feeling of self-pity washed through him, and when he heard Benzar say something about Jacob, he shook his head to clear it and listened more carefully.

"... and he's going to demand everything we've got one of these days. You see if it's not true! Rohazi, more wine over here." Benzar was younger than his brother and somewhat sharper. He held out his cup, and the woman poured it full. He reached out and pinched her, and she slapped at his hand. "None of that, now," she said.

Benzar laughed and drank deeply, then put down the cup and shook his head. "I've said he's a crook all along. There's nothing he won't do."

There was little basis for this accusation, but both men nodded as if Benzar had made some profound remark.

"Well, at least he does his work," Laban mumbled. His two sons stared at him, and he found that his lips were so numb he had to pronounce his words carefully to keep them from being slurred. "He knows a lot about animals. More than any man I ever saw. You have to admit the herds have grown."

"Yes, they've grown, but what good is that going to do us?" Lomach said bitterly. "For all we know he's selling off the best of them to other people."

"There's no way he could do that," Laban protested.

"Why not? He's out there by himself most of the time. A herd comes through. He sells them twenty goats. How would we know the difference?"

"You're right, brother. We've got to start keeping a closer count." He turned to his father and leaned forward, his small eyes shining with the wine he had consumed. "Have you heard talk about his leaving?"

Laban was startled. "What are you talking about? He's not leaving!"

"Yes, he is." Lomach nodded stubbornly. "And he'll take the best of the animals with him."

"We'd stop him," Benzar said indignantly. "They're ours—all of them."

"Look here," Laban said. "Jacob's not going to leave."

"That's what you think," Benzar spat out. "And when he does he'll take the best of all we have unless we do something."

The three men talked on, their voices growing louder. The other customers were accustomed to the three arguing. Their visits usually ended up in a fight between the two younger men.

Finally Laban said, "Something will have to be done. We can't let him leave here with our cattle." He got up and said, "I'll talk to him about it."

"You can't bargain with him. He's a deceiver—tricky as a fox!"

"I'm a little bit tricky myself." Laban grinned crookedly. "Don't worry, sons. I'll see to this business myself!"

———————

Jacob called a family council, consisting of his wives, Leah and Rachel, and his two concubines, Zilpah and Bilhah, and his older sons—they were still young but he thought it time they started learning about family affairs. He wanted to explain his plans about leaving. "I've talked about this for some time, but if we go now, we'll have to leave with only the clothes on our backs."

"You've worked so many years," Leah said. "Some of the herds are rightfully yours."

"You know how your father is, Leah." Jacob shrugged. "He's not giving anything away."

"Then you'll have to make some sort of deal with him."

"That's why I called you all together. Your father has talked to me about the future."

"That's the first time he's ever done that, isn't it?" Rachel asked, her eyes fixed on Jacob. "What did he say?"

"I think he's afraid I'm going to cheat him." Jacob grinned sourly. "He's the one who's been cheating me all these years. But it's what I've been waiting for."

"What are you going to do?" Zilpah demanded.

"I've been thinking about a plan, and I'm going to see to it that in a couple of years, we'll have enough livestock of our own to leave here."

"What sort of plan?" Leah, the practical one, asked.

"I've got to make it sound like Laban's getting the best of the deal. I've given this a lot of thought, and here's what I'm going to propose to him. . . ."

―――――――

"I don't *owe* you anything, Jacob," Laban argued. "I gave you your two wives and their two handmaids and dowries."

Jacob had expected this reaction from Laban. He knew the old man would give nothing away, but he had planned carefully. "You know I deserve more than that. I've worked for you for years, Laban."

After a heated argument, Laban finally said, "All right. I'll give you twenty head of sheep and twenty goats and twenty cattle."

"Any overseer would get more than that," Jacob said firmly. "You would have had to give any man that's done what I've done at least a tenth of the herd and the pick of them too. And I have to remind you, Laban, that most of your wealth has come because I've brought it to you. So make up your mind to it. You're going to have to give more than a few head of cattle."

This was actually the second meeting the two had had. The first one had ended in a shouting match, but both men knew that some agreement had to be made. Laban was terrified that his son-in-law might cheat him, and Jacob played on this fear by threatening more than once to simply walk out without due warning.

Finally Jacob said, "Laban, my God wants me to leave here eventually, and He will be hard on anyone who doesn't treat me fairly."

This troubled Laban greatly, for he was terrified of gods—those that he prayed to himself, but perhaps even more the great God of Jacob. He knew the history of Abraham and Isaac well and was convinced that their God was strong. "Now, wait a minute," he said. "I'm not trying to cheat you. I just don't want you to take more than what is right."

"All right. I'm going to make you an offer, and it will be my final one. If you don't take it, I am leaving."

"You're going to cheat me!" Laban protested.

"Listen to me, old man. I want to take only the animals that are streaked and spotted. Those are the least valuable ones, as you well know. Their wool and hides bring practically nothing at the market."

"You want all of those?"

"Yes, and I'll leave you all of the pure animals."

Laban's eyes narrowed. It seemed too good to be true, and he thought hard, trying to find some flaw with Jacob's proposal. It was true enough that the darker animals did not produce the best wool and there were fewer of them. He took a deep breath and, seeing the determination on Jacob's face, said, "All right. That will be our agreement. All the pure animals are mine, and all those that are marked or streaked or speckled will be yours."

"Agreed," Jacob said at once. The two did not shake hands, but Jacob was insistent on making the agreement known to everyone. He took the old man into town before the elders, and a scribe wrote it all down and made copies on pieces of sheepskin.

Laban held on to his copy, but his eyes were on his son-in-law. "Remember, the pure animals are all mine."

"Exactly right, and those that are marked with spots or streaks are mine."

————

"It sounds like such an awful deal, Jacob," Rachel said. She had gathered with Leah, Bilhah, and Zilpah again as Jacob had explained what he had done.

"It is a bad deal. You gave away the best of the livestock," Leah groaned.

"That's what Laban thinks." Jacob was smiling. He began to laugh and walked back and forth.

"Have you lost your mind?" Leah demanded. "You agree to work for the worst of the beasts and you're laughing?"

"Listen. What Laban doesn't know—and what *you* don't know—is that these streaked beasts, the brown ones and spotted ones, are far heartier than those that are pure white. I don't know why it is, but the white animals are much quicker to fall prey to disease. And I'll tell you something else," he said. "The brindled animals drop twins more often than not, and almost all of their offspring are female. That means more animals, more wool, more cheese. And the hair of all these mottled goats, why, it's different. It makes a much stronger weave than pure white."

The four women listened as Jacob went on about the future. Finally he said, "It's going to take a little while. I want to leave here with all of the animals I can. But in a year, or perhaps two, we'll have a herd as large as we can handle. In the meantime, start collecting things. When we leave here we're going to take the best we can with us. All of the oil, the grain, the wine, the tools. I'll keep my eyes open for herdsmen who'll leave this place with us."

"Well, I'm ready," Leah said, shaking her head. "We'll never get ahead the way we've been going."

"It will be very good, husband," Rachel said. "I'm proud of you."

"It's going to take a few miracles, but in a couple of years we'll be back in Canaan with my parents." He did not mention Esau, pushing away any thought of his brother. "I'll be home again after all these years!"

C H A P T E R

20

The world of Dinah and Joseph was unbounded by time, or so it seemed to them. Day followed day, and week followed week, and as the weeks turned into months, they were only vaguely aware of the stirrings within the family. They had both picked up, as children will, on the "secret" that one day they would depart from this place. But time meant little to them, and when they were told it would not be for many months, they threw themselves into the activities around them.

The family of Jacob had divided itself into two separate groups. Reuben, Simeon, Levi, and Judah were older and did the things that older boys enjoyed. They worked, they hunted, they went on expeditions—usually keeping to themselves and having little to do with the rest of Jacob's sons.

It was the younger children that mostly made up the world for Joseph and Dinah. Dan was the leader and Naphtali his lieutenant. Gad and Asher were headstrong and made difficult playmates, so Joseph, Dinah, Issachar, and Zebulun spent much of their time together. Being the only girl, Dinah was the one who instigated most of the games that the group occupied themselves with.

Dinah was a marvel to everyone, making up games and stories and songs without effort. It was Dinah who would make up some fabulous story and people it with her brothers. Sometimes one of them would be a monster, another would be a bird. Whatever came out of her head she wanted to act out, and her brothers usually went along with her ideas.

Joseph, although the youngest of all, was almost as imaginative as his sister. He threw himself into the games with all of his energy and added his own refinements to the dramas the children enacted.

Being the youngest, Dinah and Joseph were spoiled—no great secret to either the family or the servants. Quite often Dinah would forget or rebel against the tasks that Leah set for her. One of her jobs was to feed the goat they were keeping in a pen for a feast. She got so involved once in her games that the poor animal suffered with no food or water. Leah had discovered this and had come out to where Joseph and Dinah were playing with Zebulun and Issachar. Leah grabbed Dinah by the arm and screamed at her, "You didn't feed the goat!"

Dinah tried to pull away, but Leah was too strong. The girl was dragged screaming until Leah pulled the branch off of a tree and thrashed her, leaving stripes on her legs.

Finally Leah laid one last hard blow on the girl and said, "Now, you forget again and see what punishment you'll get next time!"

The three boys had watched in awe as Dinah had screamed and fought with her mother. There was no passivity in this girl! Any one of the three boys would have submitted—indeed, they had received thrashings by the elders without resistance—but not Dinah. They watched as she ran off, and Joseph turned and said, "She's going to tell Father."

"She always does." Issachar grinned. "What he needs to do is thrash her himself."

"He'll never do that," Zebulun said, shaking his head. "Come on. Let's go see if we can trap some hares."

———

Jacob was startled when Dinah burst upon him. He had been half asleep when his daughter came squalling and threw herself at him. He caught her and saw that she was in a temper—which was not unusual.

"What's the matter, daughter? Did you fall down?"

"No. Mother whipped me."

"Whipped you? What for?"

"For *nothing!*"

"Come, now. I don't think your mother would do that." Jacob put the girl down and was shown the stripes on the backs of her legs. He saw that she was not crying, however, for she was not a crying child. She would cry over a sad story or a sad song, but punishment simply hardened her. She would set her mouth, grit her teeth, and glare at anyone who was doing the paddling—even Jacob himself.

Jacob finally got the truth out of the girl and shook his head. "You should have fed the animal, Dinah. Your mother was right to punish you."

As young as she was, Dinah had become an expert in manipulating her father. She was an accomplished actress and could project any mood she chose. The role she chose now was to be the repentant sinner. She turned her face up to him and pulled her mouth down and opened her eyes wide and then said in a plaintive voice, "I know. I'm an *awful* girl."

Jacob was helpless before this young girl. He could handle men, or even his wives and concubines, but Dinah had a power over him he couldn't resist. He saw tears forming in her eyes and, not knowing that she had the ability to cry at will, his heart smote him. "Now, now, it's not that bad," he said.

For a time Dinah played her father as a man will play a fish before landing it, and finally Jacob found himself talking not about Dinah's disobedience but about something far different. He had even been aware of the transition to the subject of a red dress.

"Menna has a red dress, and I want one like it."

"You're too young for that kind of dress. Menna's a grown woman."

Dinah never directly disagreed with her father—not vocally, that is. He was sitting down, and she crawled up into his lap. She twirled his beard and stroked his hair and then turned a sad face to him. "I suppose you're right," she said. "I don't really deserve a red dress. I've been such a bad girl."

"Well, now, you haven't been all *that* bad. But the dress is a little old for you."

"You're probably right, but I want it so bad, Father. You can't imagine. I sometimes wake up at night thinking about it."

Jacob sat there holding his daughter and finally frowned. "Well, I'll have to think about it."

"All right. You're so sweet," she said, pulling his head down and kissing him. She knew she had won, and she ran off laughing on the inside at how easily her father was to manage. Her head was full of the red dress, and she wanted someone to share the triumph with.

When Dinah reached the boys, she found they had been joined by an older boy named Aaron. She did not like Aaron because he refused to play her games. Her brothers, however, looked up to him, for he was older and knew about things they didn't—things like hunting and fishing.

"What are you doing here?" Aaron said.

"I can come here if I want to," Dinah retorted angrily. "You don't own this place."

"You go on home. We're going out on a hunting trip and no girls are allowed."

A stubborn expression settled itself on Dinah's face. She had a well-shaped mouth. Her lower lip was more prominent, and when she wanted her own way she had a habit of sticking the lip out and staring at her opponent. "I can go if I want to."

"No you can't. You fellows tell her she can't go."

Joseph said nothing, but Zebulun said, "You'd better stay behind this time, Dinah. You can't keep up."

"I can too!"

Issachar glanced at Aaron and saw the anger gathering on his face. He said quickly, "Aaron's the leader, and he said you'd better not go."

"I will too go!"

Aaron scowled at her. "You're not going."

"I'll follow you!"

"Come on," Aaron said. He laughed roughly and came to stand over Dinah. "You'd better stay here and play with the rest of the girls. This is men's business. Come on, fellows, let's go."

Dinah did not hesitate. The boys took off, and when they saw she was following them, Aaron called, "Come on. Run as fast as you can. She can't keep up with us."

Dinah was a stubborn girl, to say the least. She did not stop to think about what her mother would say, nor her father. She only knew she had been challenged, and that was all it took. As the boys took off running, she ran as fast as she could. All of them barely flew over the ground, but age and strength began to tell. Joseph looked back once as she was being left behind, stopped, and called out, "Go on home, Dinah. When I come back, you and I will go on a hunting trip."

"I'm going with you, Joseph!"

But Joseph shook his head. "You can't keep up. Now, go home or you'll get lost."

Dinah shook her head and increased her efforts.

They aren't going to leave me behind, she thought grimly. *I can keep up with them.*

The boys were tired and hungry as they gathered around the fire where they were cooking two hares they had caught in a snare. Actually Joseph, Issachar, and Zebulun were too young to really know what they were doing, but Aaron was clever in finding game and at making snares. It was growing late now, but the scorched meat they held over the fire on sticks smelled delicious.

When the two hares were done, Aaron took the meat off the sticks and began cutting it with a bronze knife he was very proud of. The boys helped themselves to the pieces of rabbit and began blowing on them and gulping them down. They had built the fire by a small spring and satiated their thirst too while they ate.

Suddenly Issachar lifted his head. "What was that?"

The others boys looked around. "I don't hear anything," Aaron said. But they all knew that Issachar had the best hearing of any of them.

"Somebody's coming," Issachar said nervously.

The boys got up at once. They were out of sight of the camp, and they could encounter such things as bears or even a lion. Aaron took the knife out of his belt, but apprehension was in his eyes.

"Maybe we'd better get out of here," Zebulun whispered.

But then a figure appeared from out of the scrub bushes.

"It's Dinah!" Joseph cried, and he went forward at once.

Dinah stopped and felt relief wash through her. She had been lost, and the thought of being alone in the wilderness with wild animals had intimidated her. But now she covered that up and came forward to meet Joseph. "I told you I'd follow you, didn't I?" she cried triumphantly.

"Come on," Joseph grinned. "You can have some of the rabbit, and I'll bet you're thirsty."

"She's not getting any of this meat," Aaron said, scowling. He was furious that Dinah had been able to follow them, and he came to block her way. "You can't have any of our food. Now, go back home."

"I won't!"

Aaron turned her around and gave her a push. She fell down on her hands and knees, and Joseph, without warning, threw himself at Aaron. The sudden attack threw the larger boy back, and he tripped. He fell to the ground, but as Joseph fell on him, he easily rolled him over and straddled him. He punched Joseph in the face and was raising his fist to strike again when he suddenly yelled out in pain. He rolled off and grabbed Dinah, who had leaped on his back and was screaming with the full force of her lungs, clawing at his face, kicking, and spitting. Joseph got up and returned to the fray. Though he was much larger and stronger than either of them, Aaron was taken aback by the savagery of their attack.

Issachar and Zebulun dove forward. Issachar grabbed Dinah and pulled her back, and Zebulun did the same of Joseph. "You shouldn't fight," Issa-char said nervously.

Dinah shook loose from her brother and said, "Come on, Joseph. We don't need them."

The two walked off, and Aaron touched his bleeding face where Dinah's fingernails had clawed him. "I hope you get lost and a bear eats you!" he shouted.

Joseph took Dinah's hand. "Come on. I wasn't having any fun with them anyway."

"We would have whipped him if Issachar and Zeb hadn't got in the way," Dinah said.

Joseph laughed. "I believe we could have. Well, come on down to the river. We've still got time to play there. Maybe we can catch a turtle."

"All right, Joseph."

The creek was no more than six feet across, but it was easy enough to pretend that it was a mighty river like the Nile, which they had heard about in stories. Joseph and Dinah splashed and chased small fish and pretended bandits were attacking them. Soon they were submerged in a deeper pond. Their hair was soaked and night was coming on, but Dinah said, "Let's not go home yet."

"We'd better. It's going to get dark pretty soon, and you know how your mother is when you stay out too late. Mine too, for that matter."

"I'm going to get a red dress."

"What for?"

"Mother whipped me this afternoon."

"Yeah. I saw that."

"I went to Father, and he fussed a little. But he's so easy to manage."

Joseph suddenly laughed. "He is for you, but nobody else can do it. How did you get the promise of a red dress out of him?"

"Oh, I just patted his cheek and played with his whiskers and made my face look real sad—like this."

Joseph turned to look at Dinah's sad face. He grinned and said, "You're spoiled is what you are."

"Well, so are you. Father likes you best of any of the boys."

"I guess that's true, but it doesn't seem right."

"I don't mind it. I like being spoiled." She threw water at Joseph and caught him full in the face. He began throwing water at her, and finally he grabbed her. They wrestled, sometimes going under but then coming up and exploding with laughter.

After a bit Joseph said, "Come on. That's enough. We've got to start home."

"You know what, Joseph? We'll always have each other," Dinah said. "You and me. We're different from our brothers."

"That's right. It'll be you and me. We'll always be close, Dinah."

Dinah suddenly slapped at Joseph's chest and said, "Come on. I'll race you home."

Joseph let her get ahead and, of course, let her win as he always did. *I'm no better than Father,* he thought. *I let her do anything she wants to, but so does everybody else. I don't think that's always good, but who can help it with a girl like that?*

CHAPTER
21

After making the agreement with Laban concerning the flocks and the herds, Jacob worked harder than he ever had in his life. He wore himself thin training the other shepherds and moving the individual animals into herds where the breeding would favor his own. It was during this period of time that word came from traders passing through that Esau had become a prosperous herdsman and that he had changed from what he had been as a young man. This encouraged Jacob, for always at the back of his mind was the guilt over how he had treated his brother. As for his wives, both of them were anxious to leave.

The spotted and streaked animals that Jacob separated from the pure white ones prospered beyond belief. As Jacob had told his family, they were a far heartier breed, and the females often produced twins. Jacob tried to be secretive about his intentions, but he had to hire extra herdsmen as the flocks and herds grew. It was inevitable that some of these would pick up on the imminent departure and that Laban and his sons would hear of it.

The result of this was that Laban became more and more belligerent. He made frequent visits, along with his sons, to the flocks, and was stunned to see Jacob's herds proliferating far more than his own. He tried every way he could think of to go back on his word, but the agreement was recorded, and all he could do was shout, "You're cheating me!"

Jacob bore all this well, for the plan unfolded in his mind daily. Over a year had gone by when Jacob was suddenly stopped in the midst of his work by the appearance of the Lord God.

He had been breaking in the new shepherds, and now as he made his way wearily home, he stumbled from fatigue. He had missed two full nights' sleep and had eaten little. He paused by the spring, lay on his stomach, and lowered his head to drink. Rolling over onto his back, he tried to summon the strength to get up. The stars overhead were beginning to glow faintly, and he thought it would be so wonderful simply to lie there, but he knew that Rachel would be waiting up for him.

His eyes were almost closed when suddenly a brightness caused him to open them wider. He looked overhead and saw one star that glowed more than the others. He had a fair knowledge of stars, and for a moment he tried to recognize this one. It did not fit in with any constellation he had memorized, and as he watched, it seemed to grow infinitely bright, sparkling and flashing against the blackness of the sky.

And then the voice came to him audibly:

"Go back to the land of your fathers and to your relatives, and I will be with you. I am the God of Bethel, where you anointed a pillar and where you made a vow to me. Now leave this land at once and go back to your native land."

Jacob stiffened, afraid to move. He waited, but there was no further word, so he shook his head and closed his eyes. When he opened them again, he saw no star glimmering more than the others, but he knew he had been in the presence of the great and mighty God!

Getting to his feet, Jacob felt strength flowing through him. Gone was the fatigue, and he felt that he could run and leap like a young man. Indeed, he did run until he got back to the camp, where he burst into the tent and found Rachel not yet asleep. She sat up and, after one look at his face, asked, "What is it, Jacob? What has happened?"

"The Lord has appeared to me," Jacob whispered. His throat was tight as the memory of the visitation filled his heart. "He has not spoken to me for so long, but He is the same."

"What did He say?"

"He said that it was time for us to leave this place and go to my home."

Rachel made Jacob repeat everything he had heard, and when he had finished, she asked, "When will we go?"

"At once."

"My father and his sons have gone to look at some cattle over to the west. They'll be gone for at least a week."

"Then we will leave tomorrow."

Rachel came forward and put her arms around Jacob. "I'll be glad to leave this place," she whispered.

"So will we all. Come. We will begin to prepare tonight and leave as quickly as we can tomorrow."

———————

"Hurry, Mother. Everybody's ready!"

"I'll be right there, Joseph. You go on."

As soon as Joseph whirled and left, Rachel took one last look around the camp. Her own tent was packed, as well as all the possessions she could possibly take. Jacob had gathered camels for the heavy burdens, and they were all standing in the morning light.

Rachel stood irresolutely, for she had slept poorly. One thing had come to her over and over all night: she was troubled about her father's idols. *They are evil things. They nearly destroyed me, and they're destroying him.* By daybreak, the thought had grown stronger, and she shook her head and said aloud, "He hasn't been a good father, but he might be better if those terrible gods of his didn't control him."

Rachel devised a bold plan. Without hesitation she went into her father's tent, opened the chest where he kept his idols, pulled them out, and crammed them into a bag. She did not even look at them, for she still remembered the horror of her own experience with them. She now knew that they were nothing but pieces of wood and clay, but her father believed in them, and they were destroying his mind. Quickly she tied the bag shut and ran out of the tent. She found Jacob looking for her.

"Where have you been?" he said. "We must go."

"I'm ready."

"What's that?" he asked but then shook his head. "Never mind. Here, we'll pack it in with the other things on this last camel."

Thankful that she did not have to reveal what she'd brought, Rachel surrendered the bag. Jacob took it, stuffed it in with the other possessions, and moved quickly to the head of the caravan. "All right. We must leave now."

———————

The morning march was slow. The animals were not well trained, and it took all the men and dogs to keep them going in the right direction. The sun rose higher, and as Jacob trudged ahead, he paused often to look back at the ragged line of animals. Behind them the huge flocks and herds were scattered over a great distance. He could hear the barking of the dogs and was grateful that he had trained them to help with the herding; otherwise, moving such a large number of animals would have been impossible.

After a brief noon meal, they traveled until late afternoon. Everyone was tired, and the animals had been harder to drive than ever.

"We will camp here," Jacob announced, and everyone sighed with relief.

By the time dark had fallen, a hasty meal had been prepared and a tent had been put up where the women and the children slept. The men dropped on the ground, where they wrapped themselves up in their robes and blankets and slept like logs.

Jacob came by the tent and looked inside. "Is everyone all right?"

"Yes, we're fine," Rachel said.

Joseph was by her side, and he piped up, "Let me come sleep with you, Father."

"No, you stay with your mother, son. Maybe in a day or two you can come with us, but not tonight."

Joseph did not argue, but Dinah did. She ran to Jacob, begging, "Let me walk with you tomorrow at the head of everyone, Father."

Jacob shook his head, but she pulled at his hand and begged, "Please. I won't be any trouble."

"All right," Jacob relented.

Triumph glowed in Dinah's eyes, and she pulled him down and kissed him. "You and I will go together, won't we?"

"Yes, we will, Dinah. All the way to the land of Canaan."

———

Each day the herds moved forward like clouds across the desert floor, and the great beasts carrying the household effects moved on without ceasing. The journey did not get any easier. Six more days went by, and it seemed to Jacob that they had traveled forever. Every day Jacob was up well before dawn, urging the women to cook the morning meal. The women and children would gather what wood could be found, and by dawn he was so anxious to go, he was berating everyone to hurry and get moving. He was anxious to get far away, for he did not want a confrontation with Laban. He was to be disappointed, however, for on the eighth day of their journey, when the women's tent had just been erected and the animals were being watered at a small creek, Reuben came running to Jacob.

"Father," he shouted, "it's Grandfather—and he has a group of men with him!"

Simeon had come in with his older brother. "Everyone get your weapons," he said. "They may cause trouble."

Jacob protested, but by the time Laban rode in, all of the male servants, along with Reuben and Simeon, were behind him.

Laban pulled up his donkey and slid off of it. His eyes were flashing, and he was followed by Lomach and Benzar and a group of other men—some gathered, Jacob could see, from the nearby inns. Drunkards, most of them, but dangerous all the same. As they approached, Jacob stepped forward and lifted his staff. "Stop where you are, Laban."

But Laban advanced until he was only a few yards away, and his men came with him. The two groups lined up, and Jacob saw that his servants were all picking out the man they intended to take down if necessary. "What do you want, Laban?"

"I want what's mine! You're a thief, Jacob!"

Jacob's face flushed. "You call me a thief! You've stolen from me since the day I arrived in your camp! I worked without pay. I've not stolen anything from you."

"You have stolen away my daughters! Why would you steal away my children? You have not honored me." He hesitated and then lowered his tone. Clearing his throat, he said, "It's in my power to overcome you even now, but last night——" Laban swallowed hard, and his words were muted. "Last night the God of your fathers spoke to me, telling me not to harm you."

"I'm glad you're finally listening to the true God." Jacob smiled. He saw that there would be no trouble and was greatly relieved.

"But where are my gods?"

Jacob stared at the old man. "Your gods? What are you talking about?"

"Someone has stolen my gods—and it had to be you!"

Jacob grew angry. "Who do you think wants your gods? No one here has stolen them."

The two men began a shouting match, and finally Jacob lifted his staff and said, "Whoever has stolen your gods, let him not live! Look all you please, old man. You won't find any gods here."

Laban stared at his son-in-law, but then he nodded. He turned to speak to his sons. "Find my gods. Search everything."

The search began at once. More than once there was a scuffle as one of Laban's men got too rough.

When everything had been searched except for the women's tent, Laban himself went inside. He threw bedding and dishes aside, frantically searching for the gods. He came to his daughter Rachel, who was sitting on her camel saddle on the ground, with the idols hidden under the saddle. "Rachel, where are my gods?"

Rachel lowered her head. "Let it not displease you, Father, but I cannot rise. The custom of women is on me."

Laban stared at her but finally cursed and continued his search.

Rachel gave a deep sigh of relief. She had feared that if her father had found the idols, there would have been bloodshed, for she knew how her father treasured them. *Now,* she thought, *he will be rid of those dreadful things! Maybe he will be a better man.*

When the search was over, Jacob came to stand before his father-in-law. "Now, old man, you know we are not thieves here. You have behaved as usual, pursuing me and calling me a thief. For years I have worked like a slave for you, and you've changed my wages time after time. If the God of my father, the God of Abraham, and the fear of Isaac had not been with me, you would surely have sent me away empty-handed. But God has seen my hardship and the toil of my hands and has rebuked you."

Laban stared at Jacob and knew that he was beaten. "Let us make a covenant that will be a witness between you and me."

Jacob was familiar with the custom. He began to search for a stone and commanded his sons to bring stones until they finally made a heap.

When the stone pillar was done, Laban said, "May the Lord keep watch between you and me when we are away from each other. If you mistreat my daughters or if you take any wives besides my daughters, even though no one is with us, remember that God is a witness between you and me."

Jacob nodded. "So be it." He hesitated, then said, "Let us not part enemies. We will feed you tonight. You will sleep, and you can get a fresh start in the morning."

Among the men gathered, the tension flowed out of them at hearing this agreement, for most of them had been expecting trouble.

Jacob went to Rachel as her father and his men were being fed. He put his arm around her and said, "All will be well now." He shook his head. "That crazy old man accused us of stealing his gods."

Rachel wanted to weep. She hated to hide anything from Jacob, but it was too early to tell him yet. What frightened her were Jacob's words earlier: *"Whoever has stolen your gods, let him not live."* She believed that curses were terrible things, and the fear that was planted with those words of Jacob went with her from that day forward.

———————

The next morning Laban rose early. He came and kissed his daughters and his grandsons, and with one last despairing look, he mounted his beast and rode away, his men trailing after him.

Jacob waited until they had become small in the distance, and then he put up his hands and gave a cry. "At last we're free! Come, we will go to the land of my fathers!"

CHAPTER

22

The worst part of the journey, the barren desert, was behind Jacob. Still he could not shake off the sense of disaster that seemed to hover over him. The long line of cattle and sheep and goats and pack animals and ox carts seemed to crawl along like a worm in the dust, and he expected each moment to hear that Esau was approaching. If it had not been for this, he would have been excited, for he was approaching the land that he had loved in his youth. The bluish heights in the east, Moab and Ammon, were the lands of the children of Lot. Far off to the south glimmered Edom and Seir; ahead of him, the land of Gilead brought back memories of the day so long ago that he had fled his brother, Esau.

Jacob was so preoccupied with his dark thoughts that he did not hear Reuben, who approached and spoke to him.

"Father, did you hear me?"

Jacob started, turned, and saw Reuben standing to his right.

"Don't you think we should stop for the night?" Reuben asked.

Jacob had to collect his thoughts. "Yes, I think so."

"Is something wrong, Father?"

Jacob felt the need to talk to his firstborn. He loved Reuben, who was good-hearted and the largest and strongest of his sons, but somehow the two had never really been as close as Jacob had hoped. Still, Reuben was the firstborn, and gnawing on his lower lip for a moment, Jacob finally blurted out, "I'm worried about my brother, Esau."

"But he's your brother," Reuben said. "Brothers shouldn't have fears of each other."

The guilt that Jacob had felt for years had been rising like a flood within him ever since he had left Paddan Aram. "You are a good-hearted man, my son, and like to see the best in everyone. You don't realize what a bad young man I was when I was your age."

"I can't believe that!"

"I wish I were as good as you think I am, but in all truth, I was not." The words boiled out of Jacob's mouth, and he began telling the whole story, as if by confessing it to another the guilt would leave. Finally he shook his head. "I robbed my brother, thinking only of myself."

Reuben stood silently. This side of his father he would never understand. He had always revered Jacob, held him high in love and esteem, but as Jacob told his story, it was as if he were speaking of someone else. Finally Reuben suggested, "Maybe we could go someplace else."

"No, we've got to go back to my home. That's what the Lord has told me to do."

"Well," Reuben said slowly, "if God has told you to do it, then it must be that no harm will come to us."

Jacob's eyes lit up for a moment. "Why, perhaps that's the way it will be," he said hopefully.

"God wouldn't deliberately hurt you, Father."

Jacob patted Reuben on the shoulder. "You're a good man, my son. Let's pause here for the night."

"All right. I'll put up the tent for the women."

Reuben turned and left his father. The conversation troubled him, and as he went about the business of getting everyone settled in for the night, he mulled over his father's words. He had great difficulty believing that his father had cheated his own brother. It went against everything he knew of Jacob.

Dan and Simeon helped him set up the women's tent, and when the tent was up, those two left.

"Thank you, Reuben."

Reuben turned to Bilhah, who had come to smile at him.

"Why, you're welcome."

"You always look out after us."

Reuben had always felt close to Bilhah. She was as simple as he himself was. Neither of them were deep thinkers, and many times they had talked together about the simpler things of life, the things that they knew—the herds, the flocks, the equipment. He had always felt comfortable with her.

Looking across to Leah, who was unpacking the vessels for cooking the evening meal, Rachel asked, "What sort of a life do you think we will lead when we get into Canaan, Leah?"

Leah was in a bad humor. "We may all be dead," she said sharply. She threw a pot out on the ground and began to search for the flour she had brought. "I'm going to bake some bread tonight somehow."

"What do you mean we might all be dead?"

"I mean from what I hear about Esau, he's not a man to forget an injury. He might kill Jacob right off. Then what will happen to us?"

"Don't talk that way!" Rachel said sharply.

"Talk is that Esau's not a forgiving man."

"Maybe his parents will be able to reason with him—it's been such a long time."

The two women were arguing when Jacob came. Rachel took one look at him and saw the trouble in his face. "Sit down, Jacob, and rest. You're not sleeping enough."

Jacob slumped to the ground, and both women could tell from his face that he was preoccupied.

"Don't worry about Esau," Rachel said. "I'm sure he's forgiven you for what you did to him."

"I'm not sure at all about that," Leah said sharply. "A man never gets away from what he does—nor a woman, for that matter."

"That's right," Jacob said heavily. "A man's sins have a way of catching up with him."

Leah and Rachel exchanged glances. They had never seen Jacob so depressed, and Leah finally said, "Lots of people do bad things and never get punished. You know that. You've seen it."

"I think maybe they do," Jacob said. He lifted his eyes, which were full of misery, and said, "Maybe we don't see it, but somehow people have to pay. Maybe after they're dead."

Leah shifted uncomfortably. She did not like such talk. "It was a long time ago, Jacob."

"God has a long memory, I think," Jacob said. He sat there, a forlorn and dejected figure, and the two women were completely unable to cheer him up.

———

A simple evening meal was quickly prepared with the olives and raisins they had brought. Two of the sheep were killed, so there was plenty of good meat. When the meal was over, a tall man—one of Jacob's most trusted servants—came stumbling into camp.

"Where has Abez been?" Rachel asked.

Jacob hesitated. "I sent him ahead to try to find Esau and see how he feels."

Abez came in covered with dust and exhausted. One look at his face and Jacob knew that the news was not good. He had sent Abez with a message to Esau that he had hoped would soften the heart of the man. "Did you find my brother, Esau?"

"Yes, master, I found him," Abez said. He shifted his feet for a moment and could not meet Jacob's eyes. "He's coming to meet you."

"You mean alone?"

Abez shook his head, and there was fear in his eyes. "No, he's bringing a band of armed men with him."

A murmur of voices arose, and Jacob felt the cold clutch of fear in his heart. He shook himself, and his voice was tense with strain as he said, "Don't be afraid. God will be with us." But as soon as he had said it, he turned and walked away.

Rachel stared at Judah, who had come to stand beside her.

"It doesn't sound good," Judah said. "Maybe we should leave."

"It's too late for that." Rachel sighed heavily. "We can't go back."

Jacob stood under the skies and saw that night was coming on. The words of Abez had shaken him—the news that Esau was coming with an armed band. He fell down on his knees and said, "O God of my father Abraham, God of my father Isaac, O Lord, who said to me, 'Go back to your country and your relatives, and I will make you prosper,' I am unworthy of all the kindness and faithfulness you have shown your servant. I had only my staff when I crossed this Jordan, but now I have become two groups."

He began to weep and pray earnestly, and finally he said, "Save me, I pray, from the hand of my brother, Esau, for I am afraid he will come and attack me, and also the mothers with their children. But you have said, 'I will surely make you prosper and will make your descendants like the sand of the sea, which cannot be counted.'"

For a long time Jacob prayed, but the fear was still with him. "I've got to do something," he groaned, and getting to his feet, he went back to the camp. He found everyone in a state of confusion, and his eyes fell on Reuben. "Reuben," he called.

Reuben came at once, his face twisted with troubling thoughts. "Yes, Father?"

"I want you to select some of the finest of the cattle—the goats, the ewes, the camels, everything—and I want you to send them by faithful servants."

"Send them where, Father?"

"Send them to meet my brother, Esau. And when they meet him and he asks, 'To whom do you belong, and where are you going, and who owns all these animals in front of you?' then they are to say, 'They belong to your servant Jacob. They are a gift sent to my lord Esau, and he is coming behind us.'"

"Yes, of course."

Reuben left at once, and Jacob lifted his voice. "We will pass over the brook tonight and camp on the other side."

Confusion followed, but Jacob was adamant. When all of the servants had gathered up that which they had packed and were ready to go, the moon was already high in the sky.

Reuben came and said, "The servants have taken the gifts and gone to meet your brother."

"Reuben, I want you to take everyone across the brook and camp on the other side tonight."

It never occurred to Reuben to question his father's orders. "Yes, sir," he said and turned at once. He lifted his voice, and Jacob watched as the caravan pulled itself into order. He stood beside the brook and watched them as Reuben led them forward.

Rachel came to Jacob and asked, "Aren't you coming with us?"

"No. I will stay on this side tonight."

Rachel felt a sudden fear. "What are you going to do?"

"I don't know, but I must be alone tonight. Now go."

The caravan lumbered forward slowly, and Jacob watched as they splashed across the brook Jabbok. He heard the voices of the drivers as they herded the cattle under the moonlight, and he did not move until the last one was across. Even then he stood there until the sounds of their passage faded completely from his ear.

And then Jacob, the son of Isaac, the grandson of Abraham, looked around. He was completely alone now, and the silence bore down upon him. He did not know why he had done this, but as he walked slowly away from the brook Jabbok, he felt that his heart would break. The memory of his past treatment of his brother had been with him, pressing against him for a long time, and now it was as if it had happened only yesterday. Guilt sliced through him like a razor, and alone under the stars, he began to weep.

CHAPTER
23

From somewhere far off came the plaintive howl of a wild desert dog. Jacob had been sitting with his knees drawn up under him, his face pressed against them, listening to the sound that struck him as sad and plaintive and savage. He looked out but could see nothing.

"Oh, God, how can I get rid of this burden—this guilt that I've carried for so many years?" he cried aloud. He came to his feet painfully, looked up, and saw the stars twinkling and glittering high above. Many of the people he knew worshiped the stars, the sun, or the moon, but Jacob had gained a wisdom far beyond that. He knew that those worlds, strange and alien, had been created by *someone*, and it was that Someone he cried out to now.

He walked back and forth wringing his hands and, from time to time, falling on his face, beating his fists against the earth. More than once he had to restrain the desire to simply run blindly away, but he knew he could not do that. Finally he walked to the small stream and stared across it. The moonlight threw its silver beams on the water, which winked at him as it flowed over the stones. The water curled at his feet, whispering as if it had a voice of its own. Jacob turned from the stream, preoccupied and consumed with his thoughts, but then he halted abruptly, and his eyes opened wide.

Outlined by the silver moonlight, a man stood before him!

Fear ran through Jacob. *Who could be out at this time of night in this lonely desert place?*

The man stood not ten feet away, and his features were clear in the silvery light. He was neither old nor young. He wore a light-colored robe, and as well as Jacob could tell, his hair was a light brown. There was strength in his face, and Jacob's first thought was one of fear. *This might be a robber or someone who could kill me!*

But the eyes of the stranger held no threat, and he had the countenance of one whom Jacob could trust. He could not make out the man's nationality or much else about him, and finally Jacob said, "You're alone in this place."

"Yes, except for you."

Jacob waited for the stranger to speak again, but he made no further comment. "And might I know your name?" Jacob asked.

The man answered, "I have been called by many names."

Jacob hardly knew what to say to that. He was troubled by the appearance of the man in this place and said so. "I'm surprised to see anyone in such a lonely place as this. Might I ask what you are doing out here this time of night?"

"You are troubled, Jacob, son of Isaac."

Jacob gasped. "How did you know my name—and my father's name?"

The man approached, and Jacob resisted the impulse to flee. There was nothing threatening in the man. Jacob sensed an immense wisdom lying behind those eyes that were fixed upon him. He was not a large, bulky being, such as his son Reuben, but still Jacob sensed immense power and knew that it was not the power of pure muscle.

"Why are you here by yourself? Why have you left your family and your goods?"

Jacob was so stunned he could not answer. He opened his mouth but nothing came out, and he could not meet the eyes that seemed to bore into him. He had the feeling that nothing went on inside his own heart that this man did not know. "Sometimes it is good to share troubles."

Jacob swallowed hard. There was no reason why he should trust this man, but somehow he knew he had to break the silence.

"I am indeed in trouble, sir."

"Perhaps if you'd tell me about it, it might help."

And then Jacob began to speak. His legs were unsteady, and he had to hold his hands, they were trembling so hard. He tried to confess what he had done to Esau, but somehow he could not get the words out. There was such decency, and even nobility, in the being standing before him, he could not bring himself to confess the sort of man he himself was.

The stranger began to speak. "You are troubled, but all men are troubled. All men have their secrets that they will not speak to another. All women also. You know the story of Cain, who slew his own brother and became a vagabond and a fugitive?"

"Yes," Jacob whispered. "My father and my grandfather Abraham told me of him. I wondered if God abandoned him. I've often wondered that."

"No, God does not abandon men or women. They abandon God."

Jacob clenched his hands together and whispered, "Always?"

"Yes, all men and women abandon God and go their own way. They try to run from Him and hide their thoughts from Him, but there's no hiding from the one who sees all things. Sometimes they wander over the earth desperately trying to flee from the one who made them and the one who loves them."

"Why would a great God be concerned about a worm such as . . . well, such as I am?"

"Do you not know, Jacob? It is because He loves them."

A bitter taste came to Jacob's lips. "I can't see how God can love men and women who sin." Jacob bowed his head, and tears filled his eyes. "I don't see how God could forgive a man like me."

"Jacob, you have eleven sons."

Jacob knew with a certainty now that this was no ordinary visitor, and he felt more fear than ever. "You are a messenger from God," he cried.

"You have eleven sons," the man spoke, and the words came quickly. "Suppose one of them sinned against you. What would you do?"

"Why, I would perhaps chastise him."

"But would you continue to love him?"

"Yes," Jacob said fervently. "Yes, I am not such a bad man as that! I would love my sons even if they sinned against me."

The words that came next were summer soft. "And do you think you're more compassionate than the great God himself?"

Jacob could not speak, but he listened intently as the stranger went on to speak about men of God who had failed their God, and He spoke of Noah, who after being the greatest man of faith on earth, still fell into sin. "But God loved Noah. He was one of your ancestors. And there was a man named Lot."

"Yes, my grandfather's nephew."

"He failed God, but God did not fail him. He saved him from a terrible fate." The man went on speaking, and as Jacob listened to the voice, he felt a sudden compulsion to speak of his own crime—but somehow he could not do it. How long that conversation went on, Jacob could never afterward remember. It was like a wrestling match, in which the strange man who stood before him tried to penetrate to the center of Jacob's heart. And Jacob did everything he could to avoid speaking out his crime and his guilt and his shame. The two engaged in a tremendous struggle in the desert under the open sky, and Jacob knew that his life and his very being were on the brink of some terrible decision.

When Jacob was almost hoarse, the man said sadly, it seemed to Jacob, "I must go. Morning is beginning to break."

Jacob never knew what possessed him, but he ran forward. He somehow had to have freedom from the terrible guilt that was in him, and he knew that this man was the only one who could give it to him.

"Do not go!" he begged. "Please don't leave me." He grabbed the man by the arm, abashed at his own impertinence, but he held on tightly. The man tried to pull away, but Jacob would not let him go. He felt the strength flowing out of the man and knew that if he had so chosen, the stranger might have broken free easily. He began to cry and to plead, but the stranger would not be reasoned with.

"Bless me!" Jacob cried out. "Please, master, bless me!"

Afterward, as Jacob remembered this, it seemed as though the struggle that he then entered into took place on two planes. Physically he was scuffling with and clinging to the man who had come to him from God, but the real struggle was in his own heart, for he knew that this man had been sent by the Almighty One to give him one last chance.

Jacob felt a sharp pain in his hip, and he cried out but continued to hold on. "I will not let you go except you bless me!" he gasped.

He had fallen at the feet of the strange visitor, and he clung to him. But he twisted around until he could look up at the face.

"What is your name?" the stranger asked.

Jacob blinked. "You already know my name."

The man did not speak, but Jacob knew there was more in the question than it seemed. "My name is Jacob," he said.

"And what does that name mean?"

And then, hanging on to the feet of this strange man who had come to him out of the night and who was more than a man, Jacob suddenly understood. Bitterness rose in his throat like bile, and he knew he had reached the end of his rope. He knew there was no other place that he might turn, that his only hope lay in confessing what he was.

"Jacob is my name. It means *usurper*. Some have called me thief and deceiver. That was the name that was given to me," he said with his throat tightening up, "and I have been that kind of a man." He began to tell the story of how he had cheated his own brother, and as he did, he was aware of a lightening in the east. But it was the light in his own spirit that he felt the most. All of his life, since he had sinned against his brother, he had been carrying a heavy burden of guilt. Now as he spoke his confession, he felt as if he had stepped out of darkness into light. And he knew that it was not the light of the sun beginning to break in the east, but it was the guilt being lifted from his breast.

Jacob began to weep, and he felt strong hands on his arms lifting him up. Through tear-dimmed eyes, he looked into the eyes of the one who held him. He saw compassion and love and joy, and he felt these qualities seeping into his own spirit.

And then the man spoke, his voice low but powerful. "Your name will no longer be Jacob, for you will not be that sort of man anymore. Your name will be *Israel*, for as a prince you have struggled with God and with men and have overcome."

As these words were spoken, Jacob felt a sense—he could not describe it—of purity, of cleanliness, of goodness pouring into his heart. Joyfully he whispered, "Tell me your name."

"My name? I think when you have thought about it, you will know my name. And now, Israel, prince of God, I will leave you."

Jacob tried to speak, but the stranger turned and moved away. Jacob started to follow him, but suddenly there was no one there! He stood staring into the moonlit desert. He was trembling violently, but that was physical. Inside there was a newness and a freshness, and he lifted his hands and cried out, "Oh, thou great and mighty God, I thank you for finding me and making me new!"

And Israel looked up to the stars—and gave praise to Him who made them . . . and to Him who pursues men.

CHAPTER
24

"What's wrong with Jacob?" Rachel asked with alarm. She had risen at the sight of the figure that had come from the direction of the brook, and Reuben, who was standing close, shaded his eyes with his hand. "Something's wrong with him—he's been hurt," he said, a worried expression crossing his face. He hurried forward, and Rachel followed him. When they reached Jacob, they saw that he was leaning heavily on his staff and limping badly.

"What happened, Jacob?" Rachel cried out. Others were coming now, having seen their leader, and Jacob waited until they had all crowded around him.

"I'm all right," he said.

"But why are you limping, Father?" Reuben asked. "Did you fall?"

Jacob started to answer and then said, "I will tell you about it later."

Rachel was staring at Jacob's face. Something was different about it. When he had left he had been burdened down with care, his forehead lined. He had looked old and defeated, but now, although his age still showed, there was a brightness and clearness in his eyes she had never seen before. Suddenly she thought she knew. She came closer and put her lips to Jacob's ear. "Has the Lord appeared to you?"

"Yes," he whispered back. "I will tell you all about it later." Aloud he said, "Has Esau arrived yet?"

"No," Reuben said. "But according to Abez, he should be here any moment. I've had the men arm themselves."

"There will be no need for that," Jacob said, and confidence rang in his voice. He stood straighter, holding himself on his staff, and there was a new authority in his voice as he said, "All will be well. Let no one fear."

Leah stared at him. "Not fear! You were the one who was most afraid."

"We will put our trust in the Most High God. He will not fail us," Jacob said. "Now everyone go and begin a meal for my brother, Esau, and his companions."

————

"Everyone is wondering what you will do to your brother."

Esau was riding a camel beside his steward. "Are they, Moriel? What do you think?"

Moriel was a tall, well-built man, younger than Esau but a man well tried. He had sharp, dark eyes and wore a sword at his side. "I think you will kill him as the rascal deserves!"

Esau laughed. "You're a bloodthirsty fellow indeed."

"Well, everyone knows what a rascal Jacob is."

"How do they know that? It all happened a long time ago. You were just a boy."

"I'm not deaf, though. It is no secret how your brother cheated you out of everything."

Esau turned to smile at his steward. His red hair had dulled somewhat with age, but he still had a strong, athletic figure. The rich robes he wore proclaimed his wealth, as did the body of men that rode behind him.

There were twenty of them, all well armed and well dressed and riding fine animals. Esau did not speak for a moment, and then he said, "So you think I will kill my brother?"

"Yes, and I think you *should*. Just give me the word, and I'll take care of that chore. I'll cut the head off of that deceiver!"

For a moment Esau's smile disappeared, and a look of sadness came over him. "That's exactly what I would have done a few years ago. I was fully as bloodthirsty as you are, my son."

Moriel knew his master well. He knew him to be a fair man and a just man, capable of anger, but he could not understand this softness in him now. "Well, it's been a while since he cheated you, but the offense is still there."

"But I will not kill him."

"You should!"

"I'm glad I didn't catch up to my brother when I was a younger man," Esau said quietly. "I have a little more wisdom now."

"The men are betting that you'll kill him. I've got a bet on you myself."

"Then you'll lose your money—for I will not."

Moriel struggled with this concept. "But he wronged you! He deserves death."

"You do not know everything, Moriel. Jacob did a wrong thing—but so did I."

"He was the one who stole your blessing."

"But I was the one, Moriel, who sold my birthright simply for a pot of stew." Bitterness twisted Esau's lips as the memory came back. "I can't believe I was so stupid as to do a thing like that! But I was a heedless young fellow. I cared only for hunting and for having a good time. I despised my birthright, and though Jacob was wrong, I think now that I was more wrong than he."

Moriel was quiet for a time, but he was a talkative man and one who had to understand things. "The way I heard it, your own mother conspired with Jacob to steal what was rightly yours."

"Yes, she did, but it wasn't altogether her fault."

"I don't see why not! And your own mother!"

"My mother had received a word from God before the two of us were born, Jacob and I. God told her that the elder would serve the younger. When she saw that I was about to receive the blessing, she took matters into her own hands so that the prophecy would come true."

"Do you believe all that, sire?"

"Yes, I do. My mother's a good woman. She was wrong, perhaps, in her methods, but she was concerned that the word of the Lord would not be done. And if I had received the birthright, Jacob would have served me."

"Well, I don't understand it. Your mother and your brother cheat you, and you don't do a thing about it. I don't see how you could forgive that scoundrel!"

"Jacob did wrong, and that's his sin. Perhaps God will punish him—but I will not. Moriel," Esau turned and shook his head, "God has blessed me so greatly. How can I kill my own brother?"

"Well, he deserves it," Moriel said, shrugging.

"But what about all the gifts he has sent to us?" Esau asked. "Surely his heart has changed."

Moriel thought of the sheep and the cattle and the goats that Jacob's servant had brought. "He must be a rich man himself. At least," he grumbled, "you'll make a profit out of all this." He suddenly straightened up and said, "Look, there's the camp ahead. That must be your brother's family and his herdsmen."

"Yes, it is."

"I hope you give him a good thrashing. If you're determined not to kill him, he deserves at least that."

Esau did not answer. He had been speaking the truth when he had told Moriel that he would have killed Jacob years ago if he could have gotten his hands on him. But the years had mellowed him, and he had gained a respect for God, whom he had not known as a young man. His mother had been mostly responsible for this. For years she had told him of how God had spoken to her and begged him to forgive his brother. The change had been slow, but he had finally come to believe his mother's words. "You be respectful to my brother, Moriel."

"I'd like to chop his head right off."

"Mind what I say!" Esau said sharply.

"Very well. I will obey, but I think it's a shame that that rascal gets by with what he did."

"We all get by with wrongdoing for a time. But I suspect that we all reap a harvest in the end. Show some respect."

"As you say," Moriel grumbled.

———————

Jacob watched as the men drew up and dismounted. He picked Esau out at once, and for just one brief moment his heart failed him. But then he remembered the meeting with the Lord, as he had come to think of it, and he went forward and fell down. He bowed down seven times as his brother approached, and every member of Jacob's family and every servant practically held their breath as Esau came forward. He was a tall, strong, broad-shouldered man, and the weapons of his followers glittered in the sun.

Rachel whispered, "He could kill him right where he kneels."

But then everyone saw Esau reach down and take Jacob by the arms. He pulled him to his feet and was shaking his head. They were too far away to hear what was said, but suddenly Esau embraced Jacob and kissed him. He held on to the smaller man, and relief manifested itself by a great sigh and murmur that went up from Jacob's family and his servants. The two men then came forward, Jacob leaning heavily on his staff and limping.

Rachel could not believe her eyes. Was this the bloodthirsty man Jacob had so feared? How could this possibly be, for Esau's face was wet with tears? Rachel whispered to Joseph, "You need not be afraid, son. Your uncle is a good man."

As for Jacob, he could hardly speak. He believed that God had spoken to him. Still, old times die hard, and it was only when he saw the tears running down Esau's cheeks that he dared hope his brother had changed.

Jacob led Esau to where his family stood and introduced them. "This is Reuben, my firstborn, the son of Leah, and these are Leah's children. This is Simeon, Levi, Judah, Issachar, and Zebulun." He introduced the other boys, and then said, "This is Joseph, the son of my Rachel."

Esau smiled and said, "He is a fine boy indeed." He came over and put his hand on Joseph's head. "You look very much like your father—only better looking."

Joseph flushed. "No, I couldn't be better looking than my father!"

Esau laughed. "You're a polite young man." Then to Jacob he said, "You have a fine family."

Jacob said, "Come. We must sit down and eat. Leah, is the food ready?"

"There is plenty," Leah said, bowing before Esau.

"Come, then. We will eat."

Jacob and Esau stayed close together, and the meal was set out. Jacob asked eagerly about his parents and listened as Esau told him that they were well. He asked many more questions, and finally Esau laughed and said, "You will see for yourself, my brother."

Jacob finally said what was on his heart. He reached out and laid his hand on Esau's forearm. "You have changed, my brother."

"I hope I have."

"I have changed also." Jacob then spoke the words easily but with great feeling. "I wronged you greatly, and I ask your forgiveness."

Esau's eyes warmed. "Of course I forgive you! We are brothers, are we not?"

Jacob knew then that God had done a work, and his heart was lightened. He could not take his eyes off Esau and knew that God had done a series of miracles, not only in his own life but in the life of Esau. This was not the impulsive, violent young man he remembered, and he breathed a silent prayer of thanksgiving to God.

Esau and his retainers had left, and Jacob sent for his wives, maidservants, and children. As they gathered around him, a good feeling came to him. It was obvious in the warmth of his eyes and also in the excitement of his voice. "God has spared us all," he said, "and I must tell you that God has given me a second chance. Let us all honor the true God, the only God. The God of Noah and Seth. The God of Abraham and Isaac. Let us honor Him and serve Him." He hesitated, then said, "I have a new name." He saw the surprise on their faces and heard the questioning murmur of their voices. "God has taken away the name of Jacob and has named me Israel."

"A prince with God," Rachel whispered. She came to stand before him, and Joseph was with her.

Jacob put his arm around Rachel and his hand on Joseph's shoulder and looked out over his family. "It's been a long, hard journey since the time I left my home. I left there a deceiver and a wicked man, with only my staff, but now the good Lord has given me great possessions and more than that—he has given me a fine family. Let's thank Him for it." He bowed his head and began to praise the Lord. The sound of his voice filled the clearing, and as Rachel felt his arm around her, she too gave thanks, for she knew that this was in some way a new husband, a Jacob she had not known, and she was happy.

PART FIVE

THE DAUGHTER

CHAPTER

25

As Demetrius strolled along the paved courtyard, he lifted his eyes to the palace towering over him. The many-tiered stone-block structure seemed almost airy as it rose from the very rocks of the earth. Actually, the palace covered only five acres on the north central coast of Crete, and the colonnaded wings softened the outline of the block construction. Much of the palace was a delicate pink color, the color of some of the island's wild flowers, but the rounded and graceful colonnades, which held up the various tiered roofs, were a rose color that made the massive structure seem almost delicate. Trees added their green foliage—some sharp-pointed, some rounded, and all carefully tended—and flowers were everywhere, adding their yellows, blues, and brilliant oranges like paint splashed on a canvas.

Demetrius could not go more than a few steps without greeting those who spoke his name, for everyone knew him. He towered above most of those who were celebrating the festival, and his tall figure was draped with an intricately patterned kilt that hung low in the front. He was bare from the chest up, and the muscles of his fair skin made a pleasing symmetry that caught the attention of many. In fact, most of the Minoans (as the dwellers of Crete were called) had a horror of flabbiness. Men kept trim through gymnastics and other vigorous exercise, and most of them exaggerated their leanness with tight-fitting belts. Almost all of them were beardless and wore their hair long.

The women that crowded the courtyard were more elaborately dressed. They also worked hard to achieve their slim figures, and almost all wore narrow-waisted skirts flounced in gaily-colored tiers from hip to ankle. Above the waist they wore tight-fitting jackets that left their bosoms bare.

Most of them piled their dark hair high on top of their heads in coiffures that sometimes included delicate ringlets that curled over their foreheads and cheeks. The use of cosmetics was not spared either, for lips were redder than nature had intended. Their eyebrows were shaped, and eye powders enhanced their large dark eyes.

Music filled the air, and Demetrius stopped to watch a group of musicians. Their instruments included a string cithara, a rattle called a sistrum, and pipes that shrilled their music high in the air. A sacred dance was under way, and a circle of three women with arms outstretched were dancing around a fourth woman. The maidens wore long, light robes, and the men who joined them in the dance wore tunics of fine-spun cloth. All had anointed their skin with olive oil, and the sharp, acrid odor of incense hung on the air. The girls wore garlands on their heads, and the young men carried golden knives that hung from sword belts of silver.

More and more of the younger citizens joined the dancers and formed rows, which moved in a structured pattern for a time. Around the dancers stood a great multitude, pressed together, watching as acrobats joined in doing backflips and twisting and turning in the air.

"Come, Demetrius, we must join them."

Demetrius turned to face a young woman who was dressed in the height of fashion. Her tiered skirt was dyed all the colors of the rainbow, and a silver belt nipped her waist in, emphasizing the fullness of her upper figure. She wore a garland of fresh green leaves on her head, and her black hair hung down behind in carefully tended tresses. Her lips were full and rich with promise, as were her dark eyes that danced as she took Demetrius by the arm.

"I'm sorry, Adara. I'm on my way home."

Adara laughed. "Come now, you can't refuse to worship the Mother Goddess. That would bring bad luck indeed!"

Demetrius smiled. He had a strongly masculine face. His teeth were whiter than most, and his skin was fair—in contrast to most Minoans' naturally olive skin. His eyebrows were black as a crow's wing and so was his hair, which hung down his back in long locks. His jawline was firm, and his ears lay flat against his head. There was something intensely alert and masculine about his features, but when he smiled at the woman, there was an ease that was pleasing. "Ordinarily I would, but I've got to see my parents."

"Oh, you can see your parents anytime." Adara moved herself closer and pressed against him. He was aware of the delicate perfume she used and of the smoothness of her skin. Memories of his nights with her rushed through him, and he was tempted but shook his head. "I've got to leave before dawn."

"Where are you going this time?" Adara sighed, but she did not loosen her hold.

"Taking a ship full of olive oil and wine to Syria." He smiled and ran his hand down her smooth cheek. "I'll bring you back something very nice."

Adara was pleased but still clung to him. "You don't have to leave until dawn? Then we have plenty of time. Come with me."

"I can't do it, Adara, much as I'd like to. I've got to go to my parents' house, and after that I have to be at the ship to be sure everything is set. My men are a little careless sometimes."

"You're so restless, Demetrius," Adara said with asperity. She shook her head, her lips pressed together with displeasure. "Always sailing far away to strange places."

Demetrius laughed. "That's what sailors do, didn't you know?"

"I *know* what sailors do! I'll bet you have a woman in every port."

Demetrius laughed. "No, you're the only woman I care about."

"Oh? I've heard that before. Calandra told me you said the same thing to her."

"Oh, well, that was a long time ago."

"What about Ennea? You told her the same thing and that was just last month." Suddenly Adara laughed. "You're a faithless man like all the rest, but somehow I forgive you. I always do."

Demetrius put his arm around her and kissed her lightly. "I'll be back, and I'll bring you material that you've never seen before for a gown. I saw it the last time I was in Syria. I should have gotten it then. It's all the colors you can imagine and as delicate as this beautiful skin of yours."

Adara leaned against him. "Don't be long," she whispered. "I'll be waiting for you."

Demetrius kissed her again, then turned and walked swiftly away. He liked Adara, but then he liked other women as well. He filed away his promise in the back of his mind. *I'll have to bring that cloth back with me or she'll never forgive me.*

"He should have been here by this time." Metus was pacing the floor nervously. He was a handsome man with his dark hair just beginning to go gray at the temples, and he was still trim. There was authority in his features, and his dress and the ring and bracelets he wore proclaimed that he was not a poor man. Indeed, he was the king's counselor and one of the richest men in Minoa. He turned now and went over to the woman who was looking out the window. "Theodora, are you sure he said he'd come by?"

"Yes." The woman was small and dressed rather simply. There was a dignity about her, and her early beauty still revealed itself in her well-shaped eyes and lips. She put her hand out and said, "Husband, you know that Demetrius always does exactly what he says. He promised he'd be here to take dinner with us, and he will."

Metus stood there looking dissatisfied. He chewed on his lower lip briefly and then threw his hands out in an expression of helplessness. "I can command the whole kingdom, but I can't command one wayward son."

"Don't be foolish! Demetrius isn't wayward."

"How can you say that? He spends too much time with silly women!"

"You know that's not true. You're just upset."

"Well, he does!"

"So did you when you were his age."

Metus stared at his wife, his eyes wide. Then suddenly he laughed, came over, and put his arm around her. "You know me too well," he said fondly. He kissed her cheek, then released her. "I suppose he'll be here, but I can't see why he has to go on these voyages."

"He's restless, Metus. He's young, and he hasn't figured out his role in life yet."

"Well, it's high time he did. How old is he now? Twenty-five? Why, we were married and I was well on my way up into the king's council when I was his age."

Theodora was accustomed to her husband's impatience, especially with their son. She spoke soothingly. "He loves the sea, but he'll tire of it one day and settle down. And as for his antics, women chase after *him*."

"They certainly do," Metus growled. "Why can't he settle on one of them and marry and give us grandchildren?"

"He hasn't fallen in love yet."

"Love! I'd like to marry him off to the daughter of Haemon."

"That pitiful, plain thing! She's doesn't have the personality of a snail!"

"But she's the richest heiress in Minoa. She'll have all of Haemon's money when he has the good sense to die. He's old, you know."

"If you're so worried about riches, why didn't you marry Xenia, the daughter of Claus? She would have married you in a moment."

Knowing he was trapped, Metus kept his face straight. "I didn't like her voice—too shrill. Aside from that, I would have gladly taken her and all her money."

"You would not. You were so in love with me you would have married me even if I hadn't had any money at all."

The two argued amiably. The room they were in had a high ceiling and the walls were covered with colorful frescos. The Minoans were famous for this art, painting on wet plaster, and had spent much effort in developing the oils that gave them their colorful hues. Done in life-size patterns, some of them portrayed the Minoans at sport—such as that of two boys boxing, each wearing only one glove on his left hand. Others portrayed antelopes at a full run across the wall. There were landscapes with lilies and swallows, and one showed the Mother Goddess standing with her arms outstretched, holding a serpent in each hand.

At a voice, both turned to see Demetrius enter. He came at once, kissed his mother, and then clapped his father on the shoulder. "Well, I'm on time for a change."

"You're not on time. You are half an hour late," Metus snapped.

"Metus, be still." Theodora smiled. "Are you hungry?"

"Always."

"Come, then. Everything is ready."

The three of them went into the dining room and took their seats. The walls of this room were also covered with frescos, and as they sat down, Theodora glanced around at them. "I don't know why you painted that horrible picture there."

Demetrius turned to look at the fresco she indicated. It portrayed a monkey of a bluish color scrambling over orange rocks. Strange flowers of an unusual aqua color filled the background.

"I'd never seen a purple monkey, and I thought there ought to be at least one."

"You could have made a good career as a painter," Theodora said. "You have the talent for it."

"You could have made a fortune as a metal worker too, if you had set your mind to it," Metus put in.

"I'm just a simple sailor, dear beloved parents, nothing more."

This was hardly true, as all three of them knew. Demetrius had tried several careers, including painting and two years in a foundry learning the art of making bronze and other metals. He had a good ear for music and was an excellent dancer, as were most Minoans. Still, the many avenues he had tried had narrowed down his choices until finally, after his first long voyage, he had come back sparkling with excitement and announcing that the sailor's life was for him. Since then he had learned his seamanship well and was now captain of his own ship, the *Argus*.

"Why do you have to go just now? The festival has just started."

Demetrius had heard this protest often enough that he knew how to handle it. "This will be a profitable voyage, Father. I've got the ship loaded down with olive oil and the best wine, and I'm coming back with a cargo that'll make us a fortune."

"We *have* a fortune." Metus sighed. "You're still like a boy—always looking for some kind of adventure."

"Don't scold him—not on this night," Theodora pleaded, and Metus at once grew gentle.

"All right. I won't say any more."

They finished the meal without further talk of the voyage, but as soon as it was over, Demetrius said, "That was such a fine meal. I won't get one that good until I come back."

"I wish you would stay at home and marry and give us grandchildren," Metus said. Then he managed a smile. "But go on your way, son. Maybe you'll get enough traveling on this voyage."

Demetrius embraced both his parents and kissed his mother. "This is farewell, then, but it won't be a long journey. We'll unload our cargo at Syria, where we'll take on the return load, and we'll sail right back. Just a few weeks, depending on the winds."

Theodora clung to her son, and when he left she turned to Metus. "He's the only son we have left," she whispered. "May the gods give him safety."

Metus sensed that his wife was having difficulty. He himself hated these voyages of their only living son. They once had three sons, but two were now dead. Demetrius and his sister, Thea, were their treasures. Now they clung to each other, both of them silently yearning for the day when Demetrius of Minoa would have his fill of dangerous adventures at sea.

A gloom settled on Demetrius as he made his way through the city to the ship. Night was coming on now, and overhead the stars glittered. He looked up, recognizing his old friends, the stars, for he had learned much about them as he used them for navigation. As he pondered the starry expanse, a troubling thought occurred to him: *How easy my life has been! I've known no hardship at all.* He well knew that there was much misery in the world. He had seen the suffering of the slaves in Egypt, in Greece, and in other exotic places. He knew that the peasants on his island home had their share of trials. He himself had been born into a good family, rich enough to provide him whatever he needed, but he was aware of a world that was crueler than the one he inhabited.

He passed by a shrine of the Mother Goddess and hesitated. He was not particularly religious, but suddenly he felt the need to make at least a token sacrifice. He turned and went in and was greeted by the priestess, whom he did not know. He went at once to the glazed statue of the Mother Goddess, which stood with her large staring eyes, her hands holding up twin serpents. The enormous eyes of the goddess kept him transfixed for a moment.

Like most Minoans, Demetrius worshiped nature, and he had a reverence for almost everything in the natural world, including mountains, snakes, bulls, trees, and flowers. He considered these sacred. Most people kept private shrines in their homes but were just as likely to worship on the mountaintops or in one of the many caves formed in the limestone by dripping water. It was common to leave homemade offerings at the shrines and worship places in hopes of pleasing the spirits of the netherworld.

He stood before the Mother Goddess of the nation and noted the dove perched on her head and the writhing snakes in her grip that reminded the faithful of her close ties to the mysterious underworld. Quickly he breathed a prayer, left an offering, and exited from the temple. He made his way through the streets quickly until he got to the ship and drew a sigh of relief. *It won't be a long trip,* he told himself. *I need to stay home more and be with my parents. Maybe even give them grandchildren.* The thought pleased him, and he boarded the ship, greeting his first officer with a cheerful shout. "Hello. Everything loaded, Nestor?"

The ship keeled over so suddenly that Demetrius only had time to grab the mast. He screamed, "Take hold!" But it was too late. He saw four of the remaining hands go over the side into the crest of white water and then disappear. The storm had caught them unawares and blown them so far off course that he had no idea where he was. Demetrius had been in storms before, but now as he clung to the mast, he felt that the *Argus* was no more than a tiny woodchip, tossing in the churning water. It was a killer storm! The waves were twenty feet high, and he knew that most of the crew had already been swept overboard.

Struggling to his feet, he felt the *Argus* slowly right itself and turned to Nestor, who was clinging to the handle that controlled the rudder. "Forget that, Nestor!" he screamed to make himself heard. "Find something to hang on to. We're going into the breakers."

Nestor shouted something back, but the wind carried the sound of his voice away.

As Demetrius peered through the driving rain, his ears filled with the roaring wind and the fierce rushing of the surf, he thought briefly of how another storm had caught them almost a week earlier. They had been driven far off course, but there had been nothing to do except run before it. Now he figured they were somewhere off the coast of Syria, but he had no way of knowing.

He heard Nestor shout something and turned to look. His heart seemed to stop as he saw an enormous wave—a solid wall of green-gray water—taller than any he had ever seen in his life, moving toward them! It rushed forward, and Demetrius knew that all was over then. He had a sudden poignant wish that he had stayed at home with his parents. Now he would never marry. He would never give them a grandchild. They would go to their deaths without seeing their own blood in the faces of grandchildren.

He had no thought of praying, for the wall of water could not be prayed to. It was a monstrous thing that blotted out the sky, and Demetrius of Minoa felt despair as it struck the ship. He felt himself tossed high into the air, and then he was under the water upside down and whirling and being tossed. He tried to fight his way to the surface, but soon the breath he held was forcibly expelled, and as the cold water rushed up his nose and into his lungs, he thought, *This is death. . . !*

———

Demetrius coughed and at the same time felt something nudging at his ribs. Something gritty pressed against his cheek, and he moved slightly to get away from the nudging, but it only became more persuasive.

"Wake up! You're not dead!"

Demetrius felt a harder blow and in protest rolled over. His head was swimming, and he began coughing. His lungs felt raw, and the blazing sunlight blinded him for a moment. Finally he caught his breath and looked up, but the sun was brilliant overhead, and he quickly shut his eyes. The voice was rough, but he understood it, for his tormentor was speaking

Syrian, a language he had found it handy to master on his trips. He finally opened his eyes to slits and saw a man standing in front of him. He blinked his eyes, and then his vision cleared. The man was short and broad and held a whip in his hand. Demetrius started to speak, but he had no chance, for the man bellowed, "Masud, the fair one is awake!"

Another man came, a skinny man also bearing a whip. Demetrius's mind was spinning when suddenly the first speaker said, "Get up! You're all right."

The world seemed to whirl as Demetrius got to his feet. He swayed and looked around, noting that others were there. He saw that they were on a beach and that the figures he saw were all chained together. Startled, he looked down and saw that his own feet were shackled with chains.

"Well, he didn't die after all, eh?" The man called Masud laughed, stuck the butt of the whip under Demetrius's chin, and forced his head up. "He'll fetch a fancy price, Captain!"

Demetrius struck the whip away and stared at the two. "What am I doing in chains?"

The broader man who had spoken first said, "My name is Khalid. You are my property now and nothing else."

Instantly the truth came to Demetrius. Somehow he had escaped death and had been cast up on the shore. Looking down the line, he saw three of his sailors already chained in a line of captives. They cried out to him, but he had no chance to respond, for Khalid struck him a blow on the side of the head. "Keep your mouth shut and you'll be all right."

Demetrius had never been hit in his life, and without even thinking, his fist flew out and caught the short, bulky man and drove him backward. But Demetrius had no time to enjoy his triumph, for Masud struck him with the heavy end of his whip. It drove him to his knees, and as he struggled back up, the rawhide began to sing through the air. He felt the sharp pain as it cut across his shoulders, then again lashed across his face, narrowly missing his eye.

"That's enough. I think he knows who's the master now, Masud."

"Yes, Captain Khalid."

Demetrius struggled to his feet, the pain from the lashes stinging. "Look," he said, "you can get a large ransom by taking me home."

"Where is home, pale one?"

"Minoa."

Captain Khalid merely laughed. "I'll get my money out of you, and we won't have to cross the great sea to do it. You'll bring a good price. Put him in the line, Masud."

Masud flicked his whip at Demetrius, but he was ready. He caught the whip and gave it a jerk, and when Masud was dragged forward, he dealt him a hard blow right in the mouth. The slaver fell backward, but instantly Khalid shouted and Demetrius was swarmed by other guards.

"Hold him down!" Masud shouted, and he came forward and began lashing Demetrius furiously.

Khalid watched this and finally said, "That's enough. We want him in good shape for the sale."

Demetrius struggled, but there was no hope. His feet were now bound in the line of chains with the rest and his hands tied behind his back. A steel chain was forged around his neck, and the chain attached him in the line to the man in front and the man behind. Masud said, "All right, you scum, walk!" He moved up and down the line of slaves, slashing them with his whip and paying careful attention to Demetrius.

Demetrius stumbled forward. He was sick, and the beating had drained him. It was all he could do to keep up, and when he looked back, he saw the sea vanish as the long line of slaves headed off into the desert.

───────────

Demetrius could hardly move. For a week he had marched along the coast, and every day Masud had beaten him and starved him. He had developed a special hatred for Demetrius and missed no opportunity to mistreat him.

The break had come at high noon and the slaves sprawled out, panting under the sun. They had all swallowed their pitiful ration of water, but Demetrius's mouth was dry and his tongue swollen.

"Here, eat this."

Demetrius looked up to see the slave who was linked directly in front of him. He had something in his hand, and when Demetrius took it, he saw that it was a fragment of half-rotten meat. It was filled with maggots, and he doubted he'd be able to keep it down.

But it was a sign of kindness, not from the slavers but from one in as bad a condition as he himself. "You need it yourself," he said.

"No, eat it and listen. Don't fight them. Masud likes it. He'll kill you if you don't give in."

The slave had no chance to say more, for Masud suddenly appeared above him. He saw what had happened and struck Demetrius's hand.

"You'll get something to eat when you bow down and kiss my feet."

Demetrius looked up and cursed him, and immediately Masud began slashing at him with the whip. The beating continued until Khalid intervened. "Don't kill him, Masud. We'll get more for him if he's not all marked up."

Masud struck him twice more, cursed him, and then spat in his face. As he walked away, Demetrius wiped the spittle from his face and turned to the man who had given him the meat. "Thank you," he said. He picked up the offering, brushed the sand off, and began to eat.

CHAPTER
26

Joseph crept into Dinah's tent, tiptoeing and with his eyes alert. When he caught sight of her, he grinned broadly, and his dark eyes began to dance with merriment. She had her back turned to him and was looking into her bronze mirror. She was primping, as usual, and Joseph moved silently across the rugs that covered the floor of the tent. He made no sound, and then he leaped and grabbed her around the waist, lifting her high up and shouting in her ear, "I've got you!"

Dinah uttered a piercing scream, dropped the mirror, and began to flail with her arms and kick with her feet. Twisting around, she saw it was Joseph and grabbed a handful of his thick hair.

"You beast! You scared me! I'll kill you!"

"You can't. You're too little," Joseph said, laughing. He grabbed at her hand that was pulling at his hair, and the two wrestled around. He was a strong young fellow, and grabbing her, he pulled her down. He straddled her and grabbed her wrists and pinioned her. He leaned forward, ignoring her yells and whispered, "Happy birthday."

"Let me up, Joseph!"

"You promise to be nice?"

"No."

Joseph laughed and came to his feet. He helped her up and avoided her blows as she beat at him. "Happy birthday, Dinah. You're an old woman today."

"Seventeen isn't old."

Indeed, Dinah, the daughter of Jacob and Leah, did not look old. There was a freshness about her that reminded Joseph of one of the desert flowers early in the morning when the dew was still on it. Her hair was thick and glossy, brown but with a touch of auburn in it, much like Jacob's. Her gray-green eyes were a beautiful almond shape. They were her best feature, except, perhaps, for her complexion, which was smooth and very pale with only a touch of the olive coloring that her brothers had.

After Dinah stopped struggling, Joseph said, "I hope you're not expecting a present from me."

"Of course not. Father will give me everything I want."

Joseph glanced around the tent and laughed. "I guess he already has." The tent, indeed, was filled with Dinah's robes and sandals and headdresses. A small shelf contained several boxes filled with jewelry, and another set of boxes held ointments and cosmetics. Joseph shook his head. "I wish Father would give me things like he does you."

"You don't need as many things as I do," Dinah pronounced.

"What's Father going to give you for your birthday today?"

"A servant."

Joseph stared at her. "A what? A servant?"

"Yes. I'm going to have a maid of my very own."

"You can't own maids. A woman can't own servants unless she's married."

Dinah pouted. "She'll be mine, though. Father's already promised me."

"I'd hate to be her." Joseph shook his head and tried to look sorrowful. "She'll probably run away after about a week of your temper."

"No she won't. She's going to be very pretty, and she'll have to do everything I say—or I'll beat her." She went and picked up the mirror and studied her face and began arranging her hair again. "A slave trader has come to town, and the sale's today."

"I'll go with you. I'll pick out a pretty one."

"You're too young to think about girls."

"That's what you think. What time is the sale?"

"Late this afternoon, but you can't go. Father and I are going alone."

"You're not the only one that knows how to work him. I'll bet I could get him to let me go."

Dinah suddenly laughed. "You probably can. You're as spoiled as I am."

"Impossible!"

"Well, if you can get him to agree, then I suppose I'll have to put up with you."

Jacob looked down at the game board that lay between him and

Joseph. It was a very ornate game of Hounds and Jackals, much like he had played with his brother, Esau, when he was a boy. This one was made of ivory and had insets of gold and silver. The markers, which were carved sticks with either a jackal's head or a hound's head, had eyes of semi-precious stone. Jacob loved games of all kinds, and now he made a final move and said, "There, I win. You can't beat your father yet, young man."

"Let's play again," Joseph said, grinning impudently. "If you lose, you can buy me that bronze knife I've been wanting for so long."

"What if you lose?"

Joseph laughed. He had a good laugh, and it was often heard, for he was a cheerful young man. He was bright too, brighter than any of his brothers, even at his youthful age. Rachel had bequeathed him her imagination, her quickness, her sense of humor. Jacob knew he was wrong in making such a favorite of this boy, but he could not help it. "Well, what do I win if you lose?"

"If I lose, we'll play again until I do win. You've got to get me that knife, Father. I need it."

Dinah came in as Jacob was pondering his answer. She smiled, leaned over, and kissed him. "Time to go to the sale," she said.

"Oh, Dinah, I can't possibly go!"

"But you promised, Father."

"It's my hip," Jacob said. He tried to move, and pain etched its mark on his face. "It's very bad today. I just can't."

"Is it the hip you hurt when you wrestled with the angel of the Lord?" Dinah asked.

"Yes," Jacob said. "I can never forget that time. This hip of mine is a reminder."

"I wouldn't think an angel of the Lord would hurt you." Joseph's eyes conveyed puzzlement as he spoke. "God doesn't hurt people, does He?"

Jacob studied Joseph for a moment, then said, "Yes, He hurts people. Or He allows us to hurt ourselves. Most of the pain comes because we either make a bad choice or else God is trying to keep us from making a bad one."

Joseph leaned forward, his eyes clear and his features intent. He loved to hear Jacob speak of his encounters with the almighty God and would have asked for more, but he could not, for Dinah interrupted.

"Father, please! This will be the last chance. There may not be another trader along for a year, and you promised me."

Joseph leaned back and watched. A smile turned the corners of his lips upward, for he well knew what would be the outcome of this. Jacob would protest, and Dinah would hug him and play with his beard and stroke his hair. She would look up into his face and give him a mournful expression. Then in the end Jacob would give in. He always did!

Finally Dinah said, "You can just give me the money. Joseph and I can buy the servant."

It took a little more persuasion, but finally Jacob threw up his hands. "All right. You'll worry me to death if I don't. Joseph, you make sure she buys a suitable servant."

"You can count on me, Father," Joseph said. He winked at Dinah. Both of them knew he would have little say in the matter, but his words reassured Jacob.

Jacob got up and moved painfully to get the box that he kept the coins in. He counted out several of them and said, "This is all you get."

"Oh, just a little more! I want to get a nice servant."

Jacob tried to resist, but in the end gave in.

Dinah kissed him, and as the two left the tent, Joseph said, "I'll look after her, Father."

They went at once to Dinah's tent, and Joseph said fervently, "I wish I were a spoiled girl."

"You're spoiled enough as it is. Come on. We've got to hurry."

After Joseph and Dinah left Jacob's tent, Leah—who had sat quietly during the commotion—approached Jacob. "You spoil that girl, Jacob. She'll make life miserable for a husband. She'll expect him to give in to her like you do." Dinah was her only daughter, and she was proud of her, but she could not resist giving Jacob a hard time.

"No, I don't spoil her. I just like to give her nice things."

Leah sniffed. "You do that all right! She can twist you around her little finger, that girl! I wish I could handle you that well myself." Then a sour expression twisted her mouth. "Only she can manipulate you the way Rachel can."

Jacob said, "Well, Leah, I did promise her a servant. You had one when you were her age—Zilpah—and Rachel had Bilhah when she was no older. It's only fair."

"You should have insisted on my going with her."

Jacob knew he should have but said, "I didn't think of it. Don't worry. She's got a lot of sense. She'll make a good choice."

Dinah looked at the four female slaves, all of them older women, beaten down, and not at all pretty. "I can't buy one of those!" she cried, turning to Joseph. "I want a young, pretty girl."

Joseph shrugged his shoulders. "Men buy the young, pretty ones. They go fast."

Dinah was furious. She had her heart set on a servant girl, and she very rarely was disappointed. "Maybe they've got some hidden somewhere in those tents over there."

"You can ask," Joseph shrugged. "Maybe they have."

Dinah had been watching the master of the slaves. She approached him and said, "Pardon me, sir."

Khalid bowed low. He recognized the richness of Dinah's clothing and the jewelry sparkling in the afternoon sun. "What can I do for you, mistress? You need, perhaps, a good slave?"

"Yes, but I need a maid. A young, pretty woman."

"Ah, mistress, I regret that those are not available."

"You don't have any that you're holding back?"

"If I did," Khalid grinned, "I would certainly bring her out now. But I don't have any such thing. They go very fast, you know."

Dinah said, "Thank you," and turned and walked away. Joseph joined her, and they started down the line. They had not paid attention to the male slaves earlier, but suddenly Dinah stopped. "Look at that man."

Joseph turned and saw she was pointing to a tall man who was standing stiffly. His ankles were chained and his wrists also. "He doesn't look like the others, does he?"

"I've never seen anyone like him. His skin is so fair, almost as fair as mine." Dinah moved closer until she stood right in front of the man. "Look at his eyes. They're blue—almost like the sky."

Joseph was not impressed. "He's been whipped. Look at those marks on his chest and probably on his back too. And he's pretty stringy."

Dinah was walking around the man, studying him as she would an animal she intended to buy. He was dirty, and the whip marks were abundant and some of them had started to fester. "He stinks," she said, "but he looks like he'd be strong if he were fed well." She reached out and punched the man's chest and felt the firm muscles.

"Leave him alone, Dinah," Joseph said with alarm. "Don't be poking at him."

But Dinah was fascinated. His skin, if it had not been scarred, would have been smooth, and there was a strength in him that she saw, even though he was emaciated. She began to poke at his stomach, and suddenly the slave shoved her away. She staggered, taking small steps and flailing with her arms, then fell flat on her back.

Anger boiled over in Dinah. She screamed out and got to her feet as Khalid came forward. He had seen the whole thing. Another man carrying a heavy stick was with him. Both of them were furious.

"Do you let your slaves treat buyers like this?"

Masud lifted the stick and struck Demetrius on the shoulder. Demetrius exploded. He went for the man, wrapping his chain around the man's neck. He was strangling the man when Khalid raised his own stick and struck him on the head. It took several blows, but finally the slave went limp.

Masud freed himself and began to curse. He looked around for his stick and began pounding at the inert body of the slave.

"I'll kill him!" Masud screamed. "He's nothing but trouble."

Dinah took him seriously and was alarmed. "Wait," she said, "don't kill him!"

Instantly Khalid said, "Wait a minute, Masud." He turned to the young woman and remarked, "He's a troublesome fellow. I've made up my mind to do away with him. He'd be no good to anyone. Go ahead, Masud," he said. "Finish him off."

Masud raised his stick and struck the head of the slave. It made a thumping sound that sickened Dinah.

"Don't do that!" she said.

"He leaves me no choice," Khalid said smoothly. He had been watching the young woman as she had inspected the slave, and a sly thought had come to him. The rebellion of Demetrius had given him the idea. He had no idea of letting Masud kill him, but he shrugged now and said, "The fellow would be better off dead. He has a streak of violence, as you see."

Dinah swallowed hard. "You . . . you're really going to kill him?"

"Oh yes. We have to do that from time to time," Khalid said calmly. "I'll have him hauled off where you won't have to watch it. Take him and slip a knife into him, Masud, or beat him to death. Whichever you like."

"With pleasure!" Masud said.

Dinah watched as Masud motioned, and two of his men came to drag the limp body off.

"Wait a minute! You . . . you can't just kill him!"

"Oh yes. He's given Masud a lot of grief, and he's of no use. No one would buy him."

Dinah stared at the bleeding body of the pale slave and said, "How much do you want for him?"

"Oh, only twenty kalehiras."

"That's too much," Dinah said.

As she began to bargain, Joseph came along and argued. "Dinah . . . Dinah, you can't buy that fellow. He's a bad one."

"I can't let them kill him," Dinah whispered.

The bargaining ended with Khalid pocketing the coins Dinah had brought. "Take the chains off of him," he commanded Masud.

"I still say we should have killed him," Masud growled, but he removed the chain.

"Now what are you going to do? He can't even walk," Joseph said.

"I don't know." Dinah was furious with herself. She often did things like this, but she knew she had let herself in for a great deal of trouble. "You'll have to help me talk Father into this."

"Not me," Joseph said vehemently. "You made a fool out of yourself, but I had nothing to do with it."

The two stood helplessly until finally the slave began to roll over. His eyes were dazed, but he sat up and his hand went to his head, which was bleeding.

"What's your name?" Dinah demanded in Syrian—the language of the traders—hoping the slave would understand.

"Demetrius."

"What kind of a name is that?" she demanded, but he would not answer.

"Can you walk?" Joseph said. "Let me help you up." He leaned over and helped the tall, fair-skinned slave to his feet.

"Come along," Dinah said. "You belong to me now."

Demetrius gave her a look. He was in considerable pain, but he stared straight back at her. "I'm no slave," he said.

"Yes, you are. They would have killed you if I hadn't bought you."

"You should have let them," Demetrius said grimly.

Joseph noticed that a crowd was gathering. This would be all over the village and would, no doubt, drift back to Jacob. "Come on, Demetrius, we'll get you out of here." He pulled at Demetrius as Dinah walked away, her head held high.

"Who is she?"

"Her name is Dinah. We're the children of Jacob, the Hebrew. Come along. We'll get you cleaned up and give you something to eat. It looks like you could use it."

Dinah turned and demanded, "Will you come along?"

"We're coming," Joseph said quickly. He turned to Demetrius and whispered, "She's not as bad as she seems."

Demetrius stared after the young woman. "No, she couldn't be," he said grimly.

———————

Dinah wasn't quite sure how she was going to break this news to Jacob, or for that matter, how he would react. But she didn't think it would be good. As soon as they returned home, Jacob asked to see the maidservant she had bought. Dinah began to stammer, and Jacob eyed her with suspicion.

"What have you done?" he demanded, and finally the story came out. For once, Jacob was livid with Dinah.

Joseph tried to defend her, saying that the man would surely have killed the fellow, but Jacob simply shouted, "What business is that of yours? You mean you spent all your money on a half-dead male slave that you have no use for?"

Dinah tried all her wiles with Jacob, but for the first time in her life, nothing worked. Jacob's face remained grim.

Leah had entered while this conversation was taking place and learned what had happened. She was of no help to Dinah either. "I told you not to let her buy her own slave," she said to Jacob. "Now see what you've got."

Jacob ignored his wife and turned back to his daughter, saying sternly, "You're entirely responsible for that fellow. He'll try to run away. If he escapes, Dinah, I'll sell every ring and every robe and every garment you own to make it good. Now, get out of here! I didn't know you were so foolish!"

Dinah whirled, glad to get away, and Joseph quickly followed. "I've never seen him so mad," Joseph remarked in awe. "I thought he was going to take a stick to you!"

Dinah could not speak, she was so mortified. She was an astute young woman, spoiled but not at all stupid. She knew she had made a terrible mistake, but she couldn't bear being thought of as foolish by her own father. When she saw the slave standing nearby, being carefully examined by several curious onlookers, she walked right up to him. "I wish I'd never seen you!"

Demetrius said nothing, and this angered her as well. "All right. You belong to me, and you have to do what I say." She turned to Joseph and said, "See that he has a place to sleep. Chain him up. Make sure he doesn't get away."

"What are you going to do with him, sister?" Joseph asked. And when Dinah looked around, she saw that the curious onlookers were waiting for an answer.

"It's none of your business!" she shouted at them all with a dismissive wave of her hand. Then she whirled and stalked away.

Joseph turned to the slave. "Well, Demetrius, come along. At least we can wash you up. I imagine you'd like that."

"Yes," Demetrius said. He felt a sudden wave of gratitude for the young man, although the sister was unbearable. "I have never been this dirty in my life."

Joseph led Demetrius to his own tent, where he had servants bring water. It took several washings for Demetrius to get clean, after which Joseph said, "I've got some ointment here for cuts. My mother's good at things like that." He searched until he found it, and Demetrius began to apply it to his cuts and bruises.

"Here. Let me get your back," Joseph said.

Puzzled at this kind treatment, Demetrius asked, "Why are you helping me like this?"

"I don't know. Because you need it, I guess." Finally he said, "My sister's not as bad as she must seem to you."

"I doubt that. You, however, are kind, sir, and I thank you very much."

"Do you speak any Hebrew?"

"No. Just Syrian. But I pick up languages easily."

"I'll have to turn you over to Obed, Demetrius, but I'll have to warn you, you can't get away. He's a fine tracker and a dead shot with a bow. A rough fellow. I'm sorry, but I don't have any choice."

"It's all right. Did I hear correctly that your name is Joseph?"

"Yes."

"I'm too weak to run away now, Joseph, but I'll tell you one thing. I'm not a slave."

Joseph felt the truth of this statement—and the power of the man. He could not answer, for the blue eyes seemed to be boring into him.

"Someday," Demetrius said softly, "I'll leave here and go back to my home."

Joseph felt the impact of this, and he said, "I believe you will, but don't try it with Obed around. Come along. I'll get you something to eat."

C H A P T E R
27

"Look, Ada. Dinah and Demetrius—they're at it again!"

The speaker, a full-bodied young woman named Temira, put her hands over her mouth to cover her smile. "You'd think she'd give up trying to make Demetrius bow down and kiss her feet after all this time."

Ada, the older of the two, turned from where she was standing beside the vertical loom and studied the tall form of Demetrius as he stood facing Dinah. "She's not going to get anything out of him—that's for sure. Look at him! He doesn't look like a slave, does he?"

The two women were standing on opposite sides of a large loom, passing a shuttle back and forth between them as they wove a colorful rug.

Ada shoved the shuttle through, and as Temira pulled it her way, she laughed softly. "You'd think Dinah would know she's making a fool of herself. The whole camp has been laughing at her ever since she went to buy a maid and came back with Demetrius."

"Her father hasn't been laughing much."

"No, that's true. Probably the first time in Dinah's life she hasn't been able to make it right with the old man."

The two women continued to move the shuttle back and forth, from time to time pushing the horizontal strands of wool up to the top, where the pattern of the rug was beginning to take shape. They were both, however, more interested in the conversation that was going on, which they could hear plainly.

Dinah was irritated that she had to look up to Demetrius's face, but there was no help for it. He was such a tall man that most people had to look up to him. She stood facing him now, her hands on her hips and her voice strident as she said, "You didn't bring the cool water in from the well as I told you."

"Yes I did, mistress," Demetrius said. He was standing loosely, and his voice was lazy. He had picked up a little Hebrew during his month-long stay with Jacob's family, and most of the family knew enough Syrian so that Demetrius could communicate well enough. "It's right over there in that largest jar."

Dinah turned and saw the jar, which she had not noticed. She flushed, for she hated it when Demetrius was right.

"Don't be insolent to me!"

"Of course not, mistress. How could I be such a thing as that?"

Dinah's whole life had changed since Demetrius had come—and as far as she was concerned, it was not for the better. She had never seen a slave like him! Indeed, he claimed that he was not a slave, but she would fire back with the rebuttal, "You are now! I bought you and paid for you, and you're mine."

As she stood facing him, she could not help noticing that the welts he had borne on his body when he first came were very faint now. He had gained weight too and looked very fit. He had put on muscle and was attractive enough to catch the eyes of the maidservants, a matter which Dinah also abhorred.

"Did you grind that grain I want for my meal extra fine, the way I told you?"

"Yes, I did, mistress."

"I'll check it. It was too coarse the last time."

"I'm so sorry."

The words may have been humble, but there was nothing humble in the face of Demetrius. He looked directly into her eyes, and there was none of the servile bowing or nodding. He simply answered questions with as few words as possible—at least to Dinah. She had noticed that he spoke and often joked with Joseph and the other slaves, but he always seemed to be laughing at her. She longed to catch him at it, but he was clever!

"All right. I put a pile of clothes inside the tent. I want you to take them down to the stream and wash them, and I want them *clean*. Do you understand me?"

"Oh yes, I understand you very well."

Indeed, Demetrius did understand Dinah. She was the most spoiled young woman he had ever seen. He had noted almost at once that Jacob gave her everything she asked for, and that she had never learned humility of any sort.

"I'll be looking at them when you bring them back. Wash them and dry them and fold them. You think you can handle that?"

"I will do my very best, mistress. You may depend on it."

Demetrius nodded and headed for the tent. Dinah turned to watch him, and when he came out he said, "I will take great care with these clothes. You may be sure. As a good slave should."

Dinah did not miss the irony in his tone, but she could think of no retort. She whirled and walked away, saying sharply, "Be sure that you do!"

Temira and Ada had been watching the scene and both of them enjoyed it. Dinah was not the easiest person in the world to get along with and was not always careful to be gentle. Both had felt the weight of her anger, and now as Temira watched the tall form of Demetrius head for the stream, she said, "You know, Ada, I think I have a few things to wash myself. Get someone else to help with this."

Ada laughed as Temira winked at her. "Be careful. A good-looking man like that can get a woman in trouble."

"Or maybe the other way around." Temira winked again and turned to her tent.

———————

". . . and so we were blown off course, and we wound up in Greece."

"What's it like in Greece?" Temira said. The two had been washing clothes, but now they were finished. Temira had found herself sitting on a fallen tree beside the stream along with Demetrius. He had told her several fascinating stories of his travels, and she listened as he continued to speak.

As for Demetrius, he was amused at the young woman. It was obvious that she was one of the world's worst flirts, but he enjoyed being away from the sharp tongue of his mistress. He turned to Temira and saw that she was looking up at him with a rather enticing smile. *She's probably not listening to a word I say. She's a plum ripe for the taking.*

Demetrius was amused at how the other Hebrew women admired him too. Most of them tried to conceal it, but he was experienced in such things. Now as he saw Temira looking up at him, her lips parted and her eyes locked with his, he put his arm around her and kissed her thoroughly. She returned his kiss, and he felt her arms going about his neck, but at that moment Dinah's voice came loud and clear. "Demetrius! I didn't send you here to dally with slave girls!"

Temira jumped up, her eyes wide. She knew that Dinah was perfectly capable of beating her with a switch. She had done it before. "I was just washing clothes, mistress," she said with a voice that was not steady.

"Yes, I saw what you were doing. If you don't have enough work to do, I'll find some more. Now, get out of here!"

"Yes, mistress!"

Temira scurried off, and Dinah turned to glare at Demetrius. Most servants would have been quaking with fear, but he was smiling slightly. "I washed all the clothes," he said. "I was just telling Temira about some of my adventures."

"Yes, I could see how you were *telling* her."

Dinah picked up a lightweight white robe and flung it at him. "Look at that! It's still filthy! I'll just stand here and be sure that you do it correctly."

"I'm so sorry that I've displeased you," Demetrius said. He shook his head and tried to look sad, but he was amused.

Obviously the robe was perfectly clean, but he picked it up, stepped out into the stream, and began to rinse it in the water. "I'm afraid the creek is a little muddy. It's not clear enough for such dainty things as this. This must be one you wear right next to your skin."

Dinah flushed. It *was* an undergarment that she wore, but she knew he was just tormenting her. "Just wash the robe without comment."

Dinah stood watching as he leisurely washed the robe. She would never admit it, but she was fascinated by the tall, fair-skinned slave. She was somewhat mortified to find herself admiring him. He wore only the short kilt he had worn when she had first brought him home, and his upper body was lithe and muscular. He was humming slightly and paying her no attention whatsoever.

"Where do you come from?"

Demetrius looked up. "I come from a place called Minoa."

"I never heard of it." When he said nothing, she flung him another question. "Do all people there have blue eyes?"

"No. Most do not."

Dinah found the conversation was hard, for Demetrius would give only brief answers. Finally, she said, "How did you become a slave?"

"Bad luck."

And then Dinah said, "Are you married? Did you have children?"

"No," he said.

"Were you a criminal?"

"No, I was not."

Dinah was irritated with his short answers. She had heard him talking to others and knew that he was well able to carry on a conversation. "Bring those things. I have some more work for you to do."

"I'm sorry, mistress, but your father told me to help your brothers."

"You're my slave. You'll do what I say."

Demetrius came out of the stream with water dripping off of his lower body. He began to pick up the clothing, and when he had gathered every item, he said, "I'm sorry, but you'll have to take that up with the master. I can't disobey him."

Dinah glared at him but knew there was no answer for that, for Jacob did legally own him. Nonetheless, it made her furious to see the slight smile on his face. "We'll just see about that!" she cried and then turned and ran back toward the camp.

———————

Jacob was standing leaning on his staff talking with Judah and Zebulun when Demetrius came up. He had come out to look at the flocks and the three were in serious conversation. Jacob looked up and said, "Oh, here is Demetrius. You can use him to help build the fence if you want to."

Judah smiled. "I thought he was a ladies' maid, but I suppose he can do a man's work. Have you ever built a fence, Demetrius?"

Demetrius was by now accustomed to being teased about being a ladies' maid, and he merely smiled. "No, but I've built some big ships. A fence can't be more complicated than that."

"A ship!" Zebulun said, coming over to stand in front of him. "Have you ever sailed a ship?"

"Why, yes, as a matter of fact, I was the captain of my own ship. The name of it was the *Argus*."

Jacob threw up his hands. "Please, Demetrius, don't encourage him. He thinks of nothing but the sea and ships."

"Is that right? Well, there are worse things for a young man to think of."

"I don't want my sons to be sailors. Now, just build the fence." Jacob turned and limped off.

As soon as Jacob was out of sight, Zebulun began to fire more questions at Demetrius. "How big was your ship? Did it have one sail or more?"

Demetrius was amused at the young man's enthusiasm and had no compunction over talking to him about his experiences at shipbuilding and sailing. *Young Zebulun just might be a good friend*, Demetrius thought to himself.

―――――――

Jacob had come out several times to watch the work on the fence that was going to enclose the ewes that were bearing young. It had been Judah's idea to keep them fenced up. Usually they moved so often that building a permanent fence was not worthwhile, but the water and grass were good here, so Jacob had agreed to it.

He was pleased to see the progress being made. Demetrius was attaching a top rail to an upright, and Jacob said to him, "My, you certainly are skillful with tools."

"I learned a great deal of it by building ships."

Jacob was becoming very interested in the young man as he learned more about him. At first he had not been sure what to do with him. Obviously Demetrius could not be a ladies' maid for Dinah, although Jacob let her use him for whatever tasks she could think of.

"You come from Minoa?" Jacob asked him. "That's out in the great sea, I believe?"

"Yes."

"I've never been able to picture such a thing—sailing out of sight of land."

"Most people can't because they have never been out at sea. Would you like me to show you where my home is?"

"Yes, I would like that."

Taking a sharp tool in his hand, Demetrius sketched out a rude map in the dirt. "This is the great sea—and here we are. This is Canaan. Up north here is Syria. If you set sail from approximately here, you'll hit a large island named Cyprus. But if you bypass it and go straight across, you'll hit Minoa, named after Minos, one of the ancient rulers of our people. When you approach it, it has to be by sea. That's the reason we prospered, I think, master."

"What is your land like?"

"Well, it's an island, sir, and we've learned to build ships better than anyone else. That's why we can go all over the world. Even the Egyptians accept us, and you know how the Egyptians are."

"Yes, I do indeed!"

Jacob was fascinated to hear about Demetrius's homeland.

"What god do you worship in Minoa?" he asked finally.

Demetrius shrugged his shoulders. "Well, we worship many gods, master. Almost anything in nature, such as a tree or a mountain or a bull. The bull plays a large part in our worship."

"You would pray to a bull?"

Demetrius smiled. "Yes, sir, and of course, there's the Mother Goddess. There are many figures of her on our island, and most of us pray to her." Demetrius spoke about their beliefs for some time and finally said, "What gods do your people worship?"

"We have only one God," Jacob said.

Demetrius had suspected this. "I heard that, but I couldn't believe it. Only one God? What's His name?"

Jacob smiled. "He has many names. The Most High God is one of them, or Almighty God, but He is the only God. The rest are merely blocks of stone."

"What does He look like?"

"No one has ever seen Him." Jacob hesitated as he remembered his experience and then said, "He sometimes speaks to men, but He has no form."

Demetrius's eyes narrowed. "Has He ever spoken to you?"

"Yes, he has. But only on rare occasions. He also spoke to my grandfather Abraham and to my father, Isaac. He is a great and mighty God."

"Tell me about Him. What sort of a God is He?"

Jacob studied the young man and found honesty and openness in his clear blue eyes. He, therefore, felt free to speak frankly about the God he worshiped. His voice grew warm, and his eyes danced, and he began to saw the air with his hands, for every time he spoke of his God, he grew excited.

Demetrius listened and watched, and he thought, *This old man may be deluded, but he certainly does love his God! I've never seen anything like this before.*

Finally Jacob flushed and said, "Well, I didn't mean to say all that."

"I hope you're right. It would be much simpler if there were only one God."

"Perhaps we may talk of this more, Demetrius."

"Yes, master. I'll be glad to hear it."

———————

Judah was speaking enthusiastically about Demetrius at the evening meal. The bondwomen were serving the family, and Judah said excitedly, "Demetrius knows how to make bronze."

"What is bronze?" Rachel asked.

"It's a very fine metal. Nobody knows how to make it around here. If you have a sword made out of bronze, anyone with swords like ours will be lost. The bronze will cut right through them."

"How did he know how to do that?" Reuben asked.

"He learned it in his homeland in Minoa. The traders that come from there have a lot of things made out of bronze, but they're very expensive."

Judah turned to Jacob. "Father, I think we should use Demetrius to make tools and weapons."

"He belongs to me!" Dinah cried out. "You can't use him as though he were yours."

"He's too valuable to be a maidservant," Levi spoke up. "Judah is right. We need good tools and good weapons. If this man can do it, then I say use him."

Dinah put up an argument, then rose and looked at her father. "A fine thing! You give me a gift and then take it away." She whirled and ran out into the darkness.

There was silence for a moment, and then Issachar said, "My sister has a hot temper."

"You need to have a firm hand with her, Father," Judah said.

Simeon spoke up. "A woman can't own a slave, can she? I mean he's actually yours, Father."

Jacob held up his hand. "I will take care of it."

Everyone seated around that meal knew how Jacob "took care" of things with his daughter, but no one argued.

———

Dinah did not sleep well that night. She was furious with her father, for he had called her aside and told her that Demetrius needed to exercise his skills as a metal worker. She had argued, but even she had known it made sense.

She rose early, then went to look for Demetrius and found him playing a game with Joseph. They were tossing a ball around, and when Joseph saw her, he threw her the ball. "You can play too, sister," he said.

Dinah caught the ball and threw it to Demetrius. He caught it, threw it to Joseph, and soon the ball was being passed around. Shortly, however, Joseph's mother called him and he left.

Dinah hesitated, then walked over to Demetrius and said, "I need some more water from the spring."

"Yes, mistress, I will fetch it."

"I'll just go with you."

"Are you afraid I'll poison it?" Demetrius said slyly.

"Don't be foolish!"

Demetrius picked up the jar and headed for the spring. He walked slowly, and Dinah kept up with him. When they reached the spring and he was letting the jar fill, she said abruptly, "You're going to be doing some work for my brothers and my father."

"Yes, they want me to help them learn how to make tools. I think it would be good, mistress. They need it."

"Yes, it would be good." Dinah did not mention the argument she had put up. "Joseph told me a little of what you said about your homeland. Tell me about it too."

"Well, it's hard to explain to anyone who's never been to sea. When you approach the island I live on, you see three peaks sticking up in the air, so you can't miss them. All around, the sea is green or blue, depending on the color of the sky that day. Sometimes the water is gray. And if you've never smelled the sea, I can't describe to you what it smells like."

"Well, what about your home? Is it mostly farms?"

Dinah listened with awe as Demetrius spoke of the beauty of his homeland. When he paused, she asked, "Do you have a family there?"

"Yes, I have a father and mother and one sister. I had two brothers, but they died."

"I'm sorry."

"Are you really?" He raised an eyebrow at her.

Dinah stared at him. "Well, of course I am."

"Well, thank you, then."

"Tell me more about what it's like in Minoa. Are there deserts there?"

"No, just lots of rocks. We have to farm between them. We have many vineyards and olive trees and olive presses. We make some of the finest olive oil and wine you've ever tasted."

Their conversation was interrupted when Judah came up and called out, "Demetrius, come on! You need to show me how to make that furnace you were talking about."

Dinah was irritated. She got up and left without another word. Judah came over, but he had seen her face. "Don't mind Dinah. She's really nice. Just a little spoiled."

"Yes, she is a *little* spoiled," Demetrius said, smiling.

"Well, she's the only girl, so I guess it's natural. You've probably also noticed our father's favoritism for Joseph. Rachel is the Beloved Wife. Father loves her best."

"She's a beautiful woman, and a kind one."

"Yes, she is. You can see her beauty in her son. Well, come along. We want to know all about this furnace you keep talking about."

CHAPTER
28

Judah, Reuben, and Zebulun formed a semicircle around Demetrius. The smoke from the furnace that they had worked together to build stung their eyes, but they paid little heed to that. Zebulun edged closer as Demetrius carefully poured the molten contents of a thick, heavy pan into another container resting on a roughly made wooden table.

"How do you know how much tin to add, Demetrius?" Judah asked.

Demetrius did not take his eyes from the bubbling molten metal as it fell in a thin stream. "It's largely a matter of experience. You get it wrong a few times and that teaches you."

Demetrius tilted the vessel he was holding toward him and studied the metal that was bubbling over the fire. "That ought to be about right," he said with satisfaction.

"What do you do now?"

"We mix it up, and then we pour it into the mold we've made. Do you want to try it, Judah?"

"Yes!" Judah stepped forward at once and grasped the heavy tongs Demetrius had made. He gripped the jaws firmly over the vessel containing the mixture, lifted it, and turned to the table, where a mixture of heavy clay had been formed in the shape of a sword. Carefully he lifted and tilted the container, and the molten metal of a rich golden color poured out.

"That's good, Judah. Now each of you fellows try your hand at these other molds."

Demetrius supervised as the other two sons of Jacob tried their hand at the task. Reuben filled a form that made an axhead, and Zebulun created a series of daggers all in the same mold.

"How long do we have to wait before they're ready to use?" Judah wondered.

"They'll have to cool properly," Demetrius explained.

"Let me see that sword you made again, Demetrius," Judah said eagerly.

Demetrius nodded. "It's over there," he said, indicating a shelf to the right of the furnace. A crude shelter for the furnace had been built, consisting of only a roof held up by stakes, but there were several shelves to hold the tools and finished products.

Judah went and picked up the sword, which was perfectly formed but as yet had nothing to protect the hand from the raw metal handle. Nevertheless, Judah picked it up and began slashing it around in the air. "It's perfectly balanced!" he exclaimed. He ran his hand along the length of the blade, and his eyes sparkled with pleasure. "It's so much better than the old swords we had! We've got to make a lot of them."

"You'll have to buy more tin first," Demetrius said. He began to clean the vessels, adding, "The closest place I know of to get it is from the Hittites up in the north, but they don't like to sell to strangers."

"We can do it, though," Zebulun said, excitedly waiting his turn to hold the sword. "I'd like to make a trip up there and buy some. Maybe we could take a ship."

"You're always wanting to go on ships," Judah said, shaking his head. "I wouldn't want to get out of sight of land."

Zebulun argued, "Well, I would. I'd like to sail all the way across to where you came from, Demetrius."

"So would I." Demetrius grinned dryly.

His words made the three somewhat uncomfortable. Demetrius was a slave, but he had never had the attitude of one. During his stay with the Hebrews, he had proven himself to be an invaluable worker, especially in the matter of metal working. The three brothers who had gathered to help Demetrius were most interested in doing the metal work. The others had their eyes, as always, on the flocks and herds.

"Well, it's been a long day," Demetrius said. "Let's clean up here. We've got a little tin left. Maybe enough to make a couple more swords tomorrow."

"Yes. We need to make all we can," Zebulun said, "and I'll ask Father about buying some tin. Copper is easy to find, but tin isn't."

"What are you going to do the rest of the day, Demetrius?" Judah asked as they finished the cleanup.

"I'm going somewhere and hide so I won't have to do anything else."

"That's a good idea," Judah said, laughing. "You've put in a hard day. You do it, and we won't tell anyone."

———————

Demetrius sat with his back against a scraggly tree and closed his eyes. He held a wineskin in his lap and from time to time had taken a sip from it. The sun was lowering in the sky now, but there was still an hour or more of daylight left. The lowing of the cattle around him and the voice of the shepherd, who was softly singing a love song, lulled Demetrius into a light sleep. This was broken when he heard a voice calling his name.

"Demetrius, come here."

Opening his eyes, Demetrius saw Dinah approaching. She was wearing a light-blue colored robe and there was determination in her face—as there usually was! Getting to his feet, Demetrius waited under the sparse shade of the tree until she had come to stand before him. "What are you doing here?" she demanded.

"Nothing."

"Nothing!" Dinah's eyes opened wide, and her mouth grew firm. "Well, if you don't have anything to do, I've got some work for you."

"I put in a pretty hard day with your brothers working with our metals."

"That's none of my business!" Dinah snapped. She tilted her head back and, as always, resented having to look up at him. "I want you to go into the village."

Demetrius glanced at the direction from which she had come and did not seem to hear her question. "You shouldn't have come across that field," he remarked. "It's dangerous."

"What are you talking about? There are no bears or lions this close to the camp."

"No, but that bull over there can be more dangerous than either one of those."

Dinah turned and saw a large red bull mixed in with the cows. "I'm not afraid of an old bull," she snapped impatiently.

"You should be afraid of that one. He attacked Denzil just this morning. If the boy hadn't been so quick, that animal would have killed him."

Dinah did not like being told what to do by anyone, especially by Demetrius. "I'm not afraid of any bull," she said. "Now, I want you to go into the village and get me some kohl."

"Kohl? What's that?"

"It's something for my eyes."

"Are you having eye trouble? Is it a salve?"

"No. It's eye powder. You put it on your lids."

"What for?"

"To ... women use it to——" She broke off suddenly, embarrassed at his question.

"Use it for what?" Demetrius persisted. He actually knew what kohl was for, but he enjoyed embarrassing her.

"Women use it to make their eyes more noticeable."

"You don't need that." Demetrius almost smiled.

"*I'll* decide what I need and what I don't! You can find it at the house of Jamar. His wife knows how to make it just the way I like it. Here. Take this money and be sure you use it for what I'm telling you."

"I don't think it'd be enough to buy me passage back to Minoa," he said, looking at the coins in his palm.

"You're impudent, Demetrius. You need to learn some humility."

"I'll work on it. Maybe you could give me lessons, mistress."

Dinah could think of no reply. She was nearly always bested in a war of words with this man. She turned and walked away, her back straight.

"Don't go that way!"

"I'll go any way I please!" Dinah shouted without looking back. She made her way around the edge of the herd and found herself angry for losing at another encounter with the slave. "I wish I'd never *seen* him!" she muttered.

She had not gone more than fifty yards when suddenly she heard a shout. Startled, she glanced back at Demetrius, who was running toward her yelling something—calling her name. She twisted her head to see what he was gesturing at and saw that the red bull had left the herd and was coming straight for her. He looked much larger now, and she turned and started to run. She was a fleet girl, but she heard the sound of the hooves coming closer.

Suddenly she stepped in a hole that an animal had burrowed, and her ankle twisted. She fell headlong, scraping the palms of her hands, and when she rolled over, she saw that the bull had lowered his head and was charging right toward her. She cried out in fear, "Demetrius!"

What Dinah saw next she would never forget for the rest of her days. The bull was coming straight for her, but as she struggled to her feet, feeling the pain in her ankle, she saw Demetrius running at full speed. He had pulled a piece of cloth out of his belt, and his features were intent. Dinah knew she could not outrun the bull, but she did not see what good the slave could do.

The bull's eyes were small and were fixed directly on her, but suddenly Demetrius yelled and waved the cloth he was carrying toward the bull's head. It caught the red animal's attention, and he turned shortly, leaving his pursuit of Dinah. He was going so fast he skidded around with his hind feet and then headed straight for Demetrius.

Dinah held her breath as Demetrius simply stood there, holding the cloth in one hand, watching the animal closely. As the bull approached, he held the cloth out and flapped it. The bull turned his horns, and Dinah saw the tip of one of them pass through the cloth and rip it. The momentum of the bull carried him past Demetrius, and she cried out, "Demetrius, run!"

"Run from what?" he said. "We're not afraid of bulls, are we, mistress?" He turned to her, and she saw that he was laughing. Dinah saw the bull turn and charge again and she cried out. Demetrius turned, and once again, he held the cloth out and flapped it to catch the bull's attention.

Dinah stood there transfixed as time after time the bull charged. He was furious, she could see, but he was running out of energy.

Dinah's ankle was so painful she could not put any weight on it, so she stood with her weight on her left foot. "Run away, Demetrius!" she called out.

"From this baby? Not likely, mistress." He turned to her and said, "I'll show you a trick I learned when I was a boy."

She watched as Demetrius tossed the cloth to the ground. He stood facing the bull squarely. The bull was partly spent, but he came slowly forward, his head lowered. He got within twenty feet of Demetrius and then charged again.

Demetrius waited, his feet planted slightly apart. He had no cloth this time to distract the bull, and he held his arms directly out in front of him. The bull came straight as an arrow for him.

And then what happened next made Dinah doubt her eyesight!

As the bull ran into Demetrius, the man planted his hands right between the bull's horns. At the same time he threw his body upward. The bull tossed his head, and Demetrius flew high into the air. Dinah watched openmouthed as the man's trim body did a complete somersault over the bull! He landed facing away from the bull just behind where the animal stood.

And he was laughing! Dinah stood watching with amazement as he turned and ran back toward the bull. The bull turned as well and Demetrius struck him on the nose with a tremendous punch and yelled,

"Get out of here, you worthless animal!"

The bull was confused, but Demetrius continued striking him until the animal turned and loped away, uttering a hoarse braying noise.

After watching the bull run away, Demetrius turned and walked across to where Dinah was standing, still balanced on one foot, her mouth open. "Are you all right?" he said with a smirk.

"My ankle's hurt. I can't walk on it."

"I'll go get an animal for you to ride home—or do you want me to carry you?"

Still shocked at the scene, Dinah could only reply, "How did you do that?"

Instead of answering, Demetrius simply reached down and picked her up. He answered her question as he began to walk toward the camp. "It was a trick I learned when I was just a young fellow."

"But how did you do it?"

Dinah squirmed a bit as Demetrius looked into her face, which was only inches away from his own. She could see the clearness of his eyes and the firmness of his lips. He seemed to be unaware of her weight, but she was well aware of being pressed against him. She did not know what to do with her hands and her arms. His left arm was under her knees and his other around her back, exactly as she herself might have carried a child.

"It's something we do in our country," Demetrius explained. "Part of the way we live." He stepped sideways to avoid a pile of sharp rocks and then continued. "We have people in my land called bull leapers. They do what you've just seen me do. My brother was one, and my sister too."

"Your sister did it?"

"Yes. She was the best of all of us. Her name is Thea. She's married now and doesn't face the bulls anymore." He hesitated, was quiet for a while, then shook his head. "One of my brothers was killed by a bull. The three of us were performing. He missed his grip, and the bull killed him with one thrust of his horn."

Dinah whispered, "I'm so sorry!"

Her words caught at Demetrius. He was moving steadily along and did not break pace, but he shifted Dinah to better see her face. "You really are, aren't you?"

"Of course I am."

"Well, that's a good sign."

"What do you mean?"

"I mean I've never seen you sorry for anyone before."

"I'm sorry for lots of people," Dinah protested.

Demetrius did not answer. His face was only six inches away from hers, and he suddenly leaned forward and kissed her right on the lips.

Dinah had not even guessed he was going to do such a thing. No man had ever kissed her before. After a few seconds, she pulled away, trying to act shocked and offended.

"You . . . you shouldn't have done that!"

"No, I suppose not, but I did."

"I'm not one of those brazen young girls that you flirt with."

"I think they're very nice," he said. "A kiss isn't the end of the world."

"Put me down."

"Are you sure you want me to?"

"Yes."

Demetrius stopped and set her carefully on her feet. Dinah tried to walk, but she could not put her weight on the hurt foot.

"I'll go get you an animal."

"I think that might be best."

"Are you afraid of men?"

"No! I . . . I just won't be treated with impudence by a slave!"

Demetrius shook his head. "I didn't mean anything by it. We all kiss each other where I come from."

"That's not true!"

"No, I guess it isn't." He grinned playfully. "Well, I'll be back as soon as I can find an animal."

Dinah stood balanced on one foot, watching the tall slave as he jogged away. Slowly she reached up and touched her lips. "Impudence! A slave kissing me!" She tried to feel anger, but she was thinking more of how he had come to save her. *That bull might have killed me,* she thought. In her mind's eye she watched the scene play itself out as she waited, wondering at how graceful he was and how fearless.

It's too bad he's a slave. He . . . She did not finish her thought but sat down abruptly and waited for him to return.

CHAPTER
29

".... but tell me again, Dinah, exactly how it happened." Jacob had stopped Dinah as she was walking out of her tent, still limping on her injured ankle. Catching her by the arm, he had raised the subject of her rescue by Demetrius. He now stood expectantly, not noticing how Dinah's eyes flashed at his words.

"There was nothing to it really, Father," she said impatiently.

"But that's not what Belhu said."

Dinah had been embarrassed and humiliated by the encounter with the bull, and even by her rescue by Demetrius. Belhu, one of the shepherds, had seen the whole thing and had told the story back at camp, until everybody in the tribe knew it now. Dinah was sick to death of being asked to relate the incident, and now she shook her head angrily. "It was just that old red bull. He got after me, and Demetrius chased him off."

"But Belhu said that Demetrius did something wonderful with that bull. What was it?"

"If you're going to go around listening to servants, I'm not responsible," Dinah said petulantly.

Jacob stared at her. "You seem angry."

"I'm not angry."

"Yes, you are. Why is that?" Jacob asked, looking at Dinah more carefully. "From what Belhu said, Demetrius saved your life. You ought to give him a reward."

"He's a slave, Father!" Dinah said, wishing her father would release her arm. "It was his duty."

Jacob might be guilty of spoiling his only child, but he was not a stupid man. He knew well how to read the mood of both men and women, and he saw that his beloved daughter was behaving peculiarly. "Don't you like the man?" he finally asked.

"Like him! He's a slave."

"That doesn't mean you can't like him. I have affection for many of our bondservants and slaves."

Dinah succeeded in removing her arm. "I wish you'd stop pestering me," she said peevishly and, without another word, scurried away.

Jacob stared after her, a question growing in his mind. He turned and walked across the area where some women were working, churning milk and operating the loom.

He found Demetrius working at the metal works shed that had become so important to some of his sons. "Hello, Demetrius," he said. "What are you doing?"

"Good afternoon, master. Just experimenting a little bit." He held up an object, and Jacob took it in his hand.

"Why, this is silver!"

"Yes. I melted down one of Miss Rachel's bits of jewelry and recast it."

"Why, this is well done, Demetrius!" Jacob exclaimed, looking admiringly at the flat brooch, which was still warm to the touch. "It's beautifully done."

Jacob handed the brooch back, but Demetrius refused it. "You can give it to Rachel yourself, sir."

"I'm sure she'll love it." He admired the brooch for a time and then said, "Explain to me again how all of this works. It's just a great mystery to me how anybody can take dirt and make shields and knives and things like this out of it."

"Well, it's not exactly dirt," Demetrius said, laughing. "You have to have the right minerals."

Jacob listened as Demetrius spoke easily. He, like others, admired the tall, strong form of the slave, and after a time he said, "Demetrius, I haven't spoken to you about how you rescued my daughter. Don't think I'm ungrateful, however." He reached into his pocket and pulled out a bag full of coins. Removing several of them, he extended them to Demetrius. "I'd like for you to have these."

"Why, you don't have to do that, master."

"As a matter of fact, I do. Take them now. No argument." Jacob pressed the money into Demetrius's hand, then said, "Now, I've heard stories about how you leaped clear over the bull and pulled his tail and all sorts of wild things."

"It wasn't really difficult. You see my people practice what is called bull leaping. . . ."

Jacob listened intently as Demetrius described the ancient custom. He ended by saying, "I'm too old to be doing such things very often now and too heavy. It's a wonder that bull didn't get me, but he's smaller than the bulls we used at home in Minoa."

"That is an amazing thing," Jacob said, shaking his head.

Demetrius looked down at the ground. "My dear brother was killed by a bull. I've never forgotten it."

"Oh my, that's too bad!" Jacob exclaimed.

"Many were killed and injured. I never worried about myself, but I worried about my sister all the time. But she was the best of us, really."

"How did such a strange thing come about, Demetrius? I've never even heard of such a thing in Egypt or anywhere else."

"I don't think anyone really knows, sir. There is a story of the gods that's told. According to it, Zeus, the king of the gods, fell in love with a beautiful mortal named Europa, a princess from this very country. He appeared to her first in the shape of a bull, and later she bore him a son called Minos. This man established a kingdom on our island and became a great king indeed. Every year Athens was forced to send him a ship filled with young men and women. They were fed to a creature called the Minotaur. He was part bull and part man." Demetrius shrugged and shook his head, a smile on his face. "This monster, according to the myth, lurked in a labyrinth. It was a building full of passages so intricate that no one who entered would ever find the way out. In one famous story Theseus, a Greek, unwound a ball of thread as he stalked the Minotaur through the labyrinth. He killed the Minotaur with a magic sword given him by Minos's love-stricken daughter Ardine. And, of course, he could follow the trail of thread and escaped."

"Do people believe that story?"

"No, I don't think so really. It's just a pleasant story. We have movements of the earth often in my country. They are very frightening. The land shakes and wide cracks open up. Superstitious people say that's the Minotaur still alive and shaking the earth from somewhere deep down."

"And this bull. People worship it?"

"Well, it's very prominent in our religion. As you enter the palace, there's a giant painting of a charging bull on the east wall. And there are horns carved from magic blocks of stones in all the rooms and hallways. Sometimes the officials pour libations from the vessels fashioned in the shape of a bull's head."

"What about the afterlife?" Jacob asked. He was intensely interested in such things, and his eyes glowed as he added, "Do your people believe in that?"

The question seemed to make Demetrius uncomfortable. "Well, I suppose after a fashion, but you know how the Egyptians build huge structures to preserve the bodies of the pharaohs? We don't do anything like that. We build simple tombs, but it's almost as if our people have shut out of their minds such things as any life after death." Then he asked, "What do you believe about such things, sir?"

"I believe that we are made for more than this life."

"Has your God told you this?"

Jacob shook his head. "No, but the hope of such a thing seems to be in our people. I think one day God will tell us more about himself and about the life that is to come."

"I'm very interested in this God you call the Lord."

"Are you, now?" Jacob needed no other invitation. He drew Demetrius down to sit on a bench and began to tell him about his God. "God has always sought men," he said. He continued to speak of God's dealings with men according to the old tales passed down for generations. He spoke of the flood and of Noah and said, "Our family comes from Noah's son named Shem."

"I've heard," Demetrius said cautiously, "that you actually wrestled with your God and that's how you hurt your hip."

"I don't know if it was the Lord or merely one of His servants. I think He probably has many."

"But you've said that He is a God of love. He crippled you. Doesn't sound like a God of love to me."

Jacob's eyes burned, and at that moment Demetrius realized the depth of this old man who sat across from him. "Sometimes men are so stubborn that God has to get their attention any way He can. If He has to break me, that's a small price to pay for finding the God of all power."

Demetrius listened with interest. "I'd like to know this God, but I'm not a Hebrew."

Jacob thought for a moment and then said, "I don't think God is only interested in the Hebrews. As a matter of fact, the most godly man my father ever mentioned was a king called Melchizedek. He wasn't a Hebrew, but he knew God better than anyone my grandfather Abraham had ever met."

The two men sat there silently, and finally Jacob looked at the young man and said fervently, "I think the Strong God, the Almighty, will hear any man or any woman who calls on Him with a hungry heart." He rose up and said, "I didn't mean to keep you so long."

"It's very interesting. If there is such a God and you're right, a man would be a fool not to seek after Him," Demetrius said.

"Perhaps, then, we can talk more at another time," Jacob said, smiling.

"Indeed, I would like that, sir!"

Dinah sat impatiently as Leah brushed her hair. She was looking at herself in the highly polished bronze mirror that Demetrius had made for her. It was so much better than any of the other mirrors, that she had grudgingly admitted it, even to him. Lowering the mirror, she said, "I'd have a maid if I hadn't bought that Demetrius."

Leah stopped brushing and smoothed Dinah's hair down with her free hand. "Why don't you have Jacob sell him? Then you could buy a maid."

Dinah didn't answer for a moment and then she said, "Maybe I will the next time he's impudent."

"Aren't you the least bit grateful that he kept you from getting killed by that bull?"

"I wouldn't have been killed. I would have gotten away."

"That's not the way I heard it," Leah said dryly.

"Aren't you about through there, Mother?"

"Yes. And if that's all the thanks I get, you can brush your own hair next time. Or get Demetrius to do it." She laughed, saying, "That would be a sight to see."

"Don't be foolish! I don't want him touching me." She flushed as she said this, for she had not been able to forget the kiss that Demetrius had given her. It infuriated her that she could not laugh it off, and now she said, "When are we going to leave for the festival?"

"As soon as your father says so."

"Men!" Dinah exclaimed. "They get to decide everything."

"You should have been born a man."

"I wish I had," Dinah said. She got up and walked about impatiently, then looked out the door of the tent and said, "Have you ever seen King Hamor?"

"Of course not. None of us have. Not even your father." Leah tossed the brush down on Dinah's chair and said, "We don't exactly move in the same world as kings and princes."

"I've heard his son Shechem is the handsomest man in the country."

"If he's rich, then everybody would think he was handsome."

"I wouldn't. If he's ugly, he's ugly." She pouted for a moment and then said, "I wish we could hurry up and go. I get so bored of being stuck out here in the middle of nowhere. I don't know why we can't live in the village."

"Because we make our living with sheep. You can't keep thousands of sheep in the middle of a village. Now, don't be so foolish. We'll be staying three or four days during the festival," she added, "so be sure to take plenty of clothes."

"I will." Dinah suddenly smiled. "I'll pack it all and let Demetrius carry it." The thought pleased her, and she laughed aloud. "I'll wear him out by the time we get to the village." *I'll have the best time there,* she thought. *There'll be singing and dancing and lots of good food. I may not meet the prince, but there'll be lots of handsome young men there, I'll wager.*

———

The screams and laughter of the young girls who were trampling out the grapes in a large wooden vat caught King Hamor's eye. He turned around to stop and stare at them. "It's a wonder we don't taste their feet in the wine we drink. There must be a better way to get the juice out of grapes and make good wine."

Hamor was a man of no more than average height and was running toward being fat. His clothes were rich, and the turban on his head contained flashing jewels. He turned to the young man beside him. "Do you see any there worth your trouble, Shechem?"

The prince was as slender as a knife blade. He was somewhat taller than his father, and his clothes were even more ornate. Even his shoes were imbedded with red and green stones that glittered in the sun. From his turban he had exotic plumes, brought from some far country, that trembled in the breeze. He had a thin face and was dark complected, but his eyes were large and well shaped, and his mouth full, with a sensuous look about it.

"Who are these people? Are they farmers?"

"No. They're shepherds."

"I don't know anything about them. Do they have a king?"

"Oh no. They don't own any land. How could they have a king? Don't be foolish, my son."

"Well, who are they, then? Where do they come from?"

"I don't know, but I know one thing. They've got more cattle than anyone I've ever seen in my life. Their herds are huge. They call themselves Hebrews."

"Hebrews! I've never heard of them."

"They're just wandering shepherds. The leader is a man of some stature. His name is Israel, so I hear." His eyes went back to the young women who were laughing as they trampled out the grapes and then to the men, strangers to him but all bearing the earmarks of a shepherd. "I rode through their herds one day. They seemed to stretch out forever." A crafty look came to his face. He was no fool, this Hamor, and always kept his eyes out for opportunities to increase his fortunes. He glanced back toward the women and said, "Those are their women, I suppose. Do they please you?"

Shechem's back arched, and he looked and said, "That one there might be nice to taste. A real desert flower."

"Which one?"

"That one. The one with the reddish hair. See what pale skin she has and a body to drive a man crazy, at least I *think* so. It's hard to tell under those robes."

Hamor suddenly laughed. "How many wives do you have now in your House of Delight?"

"None prettier than that one."

Hamor ceased to smile. He studied the young woman carefully, then turned to face his son. "An alliance with these people wouldn't be all bad." He smiled. "We'd never run short of meat if we had herds like these people have."

Shechem stared at his father, and an understanding came to him. "There's always room for one more in the House of Delight, and that one would be a delight. She's probably never known a man. I'd like to teach her a few tricks."

"I wouldn't say no to an alliance with the House of Israel."

"You don't care about Israel," Shechem said, laughing scornfully. "You just want his flocks and herds."

"Don't be so cynical, my son!"

Shechem knew his father well. He nodded and moved over toward the young woman. "I'll see what can be done."

———————

Dinah had not been wrong about the festival. She had enjoyed every-thing tremendously. The music delighted her, for there were musicians from all over the land. They played timbrels and flutes and pipes and some stringed instruments she had never heard before.

The trip had not been hard, and she had delighted at forcing Deme-trius to carry more clothing and gear than she would ever use. He had complained about it, and she had enjoyed saying, "Be quiet, Demetrius. You belong to me, and that's all there is to it."

Now the young women of Jacob's retinue had joined together and were performing a dance. Dinah was especially pleased at this, for she loved to dance. Along with the other young women she moved in an intricate rou-tine they had practiced ever since she was a child. It was a rather sensuous dance, even though they were all clothed in modestly concealing robes. She took a special delight in the movements, lifting her hands and swaying from side to side, and when they broke out into song, her voice could be heard above all the rest.

After the dance, Dinah was laughing and speaking with her friend Shamar when suddenly she heard a voice right behind her.

"That was a beautiful dance indeed."

Dinah turned and saw a slender young man approximately her own height. He was dressed in such rich apparel that she knew he was of the royal house. She curtsied and said, "Thank you very much."

"And what is your name, if I may ask?"

"My name is Dinah. I am the daughter of Israel, the Hebrew."

The slender man bowed, his dark eyes smiling. "My name is Shechem."

Dinah instantly flushed and was almost tongue-tied. "Prince Shechem?"

"That is my title. You must be warm after your dance. Come over in the shade and let me have my servants bring you some refreshment."

The other young girls watched enviously as Shechem escorted Dinah to a tent that had been erected for the purpose of refreshment. He called for refreshments and the servants scurried around, quickly bringing two flagons of wine. Shechem took both of them and then handed one to Dinah. He bowed low, saying, "This will not be as good as the wine at the palace, but it will have to do."

"It's very good," Dinah said. She was well aware that everyone was staring at her and this pleased her.

Shechem spoke pleasantly of the dance, asked her how she had learned it, and commended her fulsomely. Finally he said, "It would please me for you to meet my father. Would you mind?"

"No, Prince Shechem, not at all."

Shechem led Dinah to the king, who greeted her with a smile and a slight bow. He listened as Shechem spoke enthusiastically of Dinah's dancing, and when he had finished, he said, "I believe I have heard of your father. His name is Israel?"

"Yes, Your Majesty."

"Is he here? I would like very much to meet him."

"Oh yes. He would be very honored."

Jacob was indeed there and had been watching the proceedings. When he saw Dinah looking for him, he stepped forward slightly. She called his name, and he came at once and bowed low before the king as Dinah made the introductions.

"It is an honor to meet you, sir," the king said. "I have seen your beautiful cattle. I'm very interested in such things. Perhaps you would tell me a little of your methods."

Shechem laughed at his father. "I don't think Israel's daughter and I want to hear about raising cattle."

"One day when you are king you will have to take care of such things, but run along, son."

Shechem skillfully guided Dinah out away from the king and her father. They walked through the activities for some time, and finally Dinah said, "I think I must go back to my father now."

"Of course. It has been a great pleasure." Shechem's eyes were warm and his smile even warmer. "It occurs to me that we're going to have a celebration at the palace in a week. My father's given me leave to invite any friends I choose. It would please me greatly if you would come."

Dinah whispered, "Oh, Prince Shechem, I would be delighted—but I could not come without my father's permission."

"Why, of course you couldn't! Naturally you must ask him. But I will assure you that I could send a group of our soldiers to escort you and also to bring you home again, and you will, of course, bring a chaperone with you."

"I will ask."

"I will look forward to it." He reached out and bowed low. When he smiled his teeth were white, making him look even more handsome. "The festival will be a failure for me if you do not come."

"I will try," Dinah whispered. And as she turned from the prince, she immediately began the campaign to wheedle permission out of her father. *He's got to let me go. He just has to!*

———————

Jacob proved to be hard to persuade. Dinah, however, had seventeen years' experience of getting her own way from him, and in the end he grudgingly granted permission.

Judah was not pleased. He came to Jacob after hearing of the trip to the palace by his sister and said bluntly, "Father, I don't think you should let Dinah go."

"Why not, my son? It's an honor for her."

"She's too young for such things. Visits like that to the palace could turn her head. She won't be satisfied with a plain tent anymore."

But Judah's words fell to the ground, and Dinah was ecstatic as she began to prepare.

Demetrius heard of the visit from Jacob himself. The patriarch had called him to one side and said, "I want to send a good guard with her, so you and Amasa will go." Amasa was one of the boldest of Jacob's servants, a proven warrior. "I'll also send Tersa with her as a maid."

Demetrius said merely that he would be very careful to guard Dinah, but he spoke more plainly to Dinah.

Dinah was shocked when Demetrius walked straight up to her and informed her of his father's command to accompany her to the palace.

"I don't need you to guard me."

"Your father insists on it, but I don't think you ought to go."

Dinah stared at him. "It's none of your business, Demetrius. You're always meddling with things that don't have anything to do with you."

Demetrius shook his head. His lips were set stubbornly. "Servants and slaves hear things."

"What sort of things?"

"Things about Prince Shechem. He uses women."

"You don't know that."

"Everybody talks about it," Demetrius said. "When he sees one he likes, he just takes her if she's a poor girl. With the richer ones like you, he has to use more strategy."

Dinah stared at Demetrius, her anger rising. "You shut your mouth right now, Demetrius! Get out of here! I don't want to listen to you!"

Demetrius knew he could say no more. He turned and walked away, anger in every line of his body.

"He doesn't know anything. I'll show him that I'm able to take care of myself!"

CHAPTER

30

Dinah was in a flurry of excitement planning for her trip. No robe was good enough, and she had almost driven Leah crazy with her demands for new jewelry and new robes. Leah had finally said, "I wish your father hadn't agreed to let you go. No good will come of it!"

Dinah had paid no attention to her. She ignored her mother's concern as she had Demetrius's warning. She was taken off guard, however, when she looked up one day to see a group of camels making their way toward the camp. At once she knew this was some sort of noble procession, and then she saw that Prince Shechem was on the camel in the lead. Her breath began to come quicker, and she flew to her tent and made herself ready. She did not have time to change clothes, but she gave her hair a few brushes and moistened her lips and cleaned her face.

When she stepped outside her tent, she saw the prince getting off his camel. She also saw that Demetrius was standing off to one side. None of her brothers were in evidence as she walked forward.

"Ah, it is the lovely daughter of Israel." The prince bowed low. "I've come to escort you to the palace."

Dinah stopped. "But, Prince Shechem, my father was going to send me tomorrow."

"I know, but the desert is dangerous. I thought it might be better if you would come with some of my own personal guard. You will be perfectly safe that way."

Dinah was confused. The arrangements had already been made, and she knew it would not please her father if they were not carried out. "I'm so sorry, my prince, but I could not disobey my father."

Shechem laughed. "Well, you are an obedient daughter. That is good to see."

"I trust that I am." Dinah hesitated, then said, "It was kind of you to think of such a thing."

"Perhaps you would like to go for a ride on one of our beasts, you and I."

Dinah actually had ridden on a few camels but not in years. The idea of going for a ride with the prince intrigued her.

"Yes, that would be wonderful."

"Good. Casmir, assist the lady on your beast. She and I are going for a ride."

"Mistress, I do not think that would be appropriate."

Both Dinah and Shechem turned to see Demetrius, who had approached.

"Who is this fellow?" Shechem asked, anger beginning to show itself in his features. "He's not one of your brothers, is he?"

"No. He's only a slave. Demetrius, mind your own business!"

But Demetrius well knew what Jacob would have done. "I don't want to be impertinent, mistress, but you yourself know that your father would not approve of such a thing. Nor would your brothers if any of them were here."

"I tell you go away, Demetrius, or I'll have you whipped!"

"You should," Shechem cried out. "We don't put up with this sort of insolence in the palace. Go away, fellow."

Demetrius bowed slightly. "I am the servant of Israel, and this is his daughter. As a good servant, I could not permit such a thing as you suggest, Your Highness."

Dinah was furious. "Demetrius, I told you to go away! Now, will you obey me or not?"

"I'm sorry, but in this case I cannot obey you."

"Such a fellow needs to be beaten!" Shechem exclaimed.

"Yes, he does!"

"Casmir, take care of this fellow!" Shechem ordered.

The burly servant of the prince laughed and motioned to the others. "Come along, fellows," he said. "This slave deserves a thrashing."

Dinah was suddenly confused. She saw the five servants of the prince advancing on Demetrius, who stood calmly awaiting his punishment. She called out, "Wait a minute—"

But it was too late. Casmir had thrown himself forward. He was a big muscular brute, and the blow he threw should have demolished Demetrius. But Demetrius simply ducked under it and drove his fist into the guard's face. Casmir stumbled backward and sat stupidly, with blood running from his nose and dripping onto his white tunic.

"Grab him!" Casmir shouted.

Dinah started forward, crying, "Oh no!"

But the prince took hold of her arm, saying, "That fellow needs discipline. My men will take care of it."

Dinah was appalled when she saw all five of the men throw themselves upon Demetrius. He fought hard, but there were too many for him and they were too strong. Finally three of them were holding him down, and the one called Casmir had run to his camel and come back with a cane. He began lashing Demetrius across his fair back.

Dinah cried out, "Don't do that!"

But Shechem said, "You must not allow servants that liberty, Dinah. It is dangerous."

"Let him go!" Dinah cried. She saw the red welts beginning to ooze blood as the huge man struck with all of his strength.

Dinah could not free herself from the prince's grasp, but at that moment three of her brothers came rushing in—Reuben, Judah, and Levi. Reuben took the situation in with one glance and ran forward. He was a huge, strong man, and his first blow knocked one man completely unconscious. His next blow hit another in the back of the head, and the man dropped as if struck by lightning. The three brothers made short work of the guards, and finally Reuben strode toward Dinah and the prince. His eyes for once were not mild but were blazing in anger. "What is going on here, Dinah?"

Shechem was taken aback. His men were chosen for their ferocity, but these sons of the desert had made short work of them. Quickly he saw that it was time for a strategic retreat.

"I am Shechem, son of King Hamor. I fear we've had a misunderstanding."

"I fear we have indeed! Why were your men thrashing another man's servant?"

Dinah spoke up. "It was a misunderstanding. These are my brothers."

"Prince, it is no misunderstanding when you put your men on another man's servant," Reuben said.

Reuben was the mildest of men, and Dinah had never seen him so incensed. She knew he had become a close friend of Demetrius, and now as he stood towering over the prince, she knew that in his present state he was entirely capable of attacking the prince himself.

Quickly she intervened. "It was all a mistake, and it was my fault."

"No indeed, the fault was mine," Shechem said quickly. "I will ask your pardon, sir, and I will take my men away at once." He turned and called, "Get that man on his camel. All of you prepare to leave." Then he said to Dinah, "I am terribly sorry for all of this. I thought I was doing the right thing. I hope it won't interfere with your decision to visit my father's kingdom."

"Of course not, Your Highness."

Reuben did not relent. "I will inform my father of what has happened. I'm not at all sure that he will allow his daughter to make her visit."

"I will send my apologies by an emissary," Prince Shechem said quickly. He turned and moved to his camel. He mounted, and his battered guards follows suit. One of them had to be tied on his camel, and they rode off as quickly as they could manage.

Judah had been standing beside Reuben. Now he turned and ran back to Demetrius. "Poor old fellow. This was bad."

"Yes, it was," Demetrius said grimly.

Reuben was still furious. "Dinah, I'm going to ask Father not to let you to go. Look at what they did to Demetrius!" He went to the injured man on the ground. "Let me see," he said.

"It's not so bad." Demetrius tried to make light of his wounds.

By this time Dinah was heartily sick with shame. She knew she had brought it on, and now she went at once to Demetrius and said, "Let me see." She saw his back bleeding from the cruel strikes of the cane and cried out, "Oh, that's terrible! Come to my tent. We must clean your back and put some ointment on it."

"It's not necessary, mistress."

"Of course it is. Come along."

Dinah insisted, and Judah and Reuben accompanied the two to her tent. They watched as Dinah sat him down and scurried around finding water and cloths to wash his bloody wounds. Then she found a healing salve and began to apply it gently with her fingertips. "This ought to cool it off. It's what I put on my own cuts."

"What in the world got into you?" Reuben demanded of his sister.

"Don't scold her," Demetrius said.

"She *needs* a scolding—or better still, a whipping! I'm going to tell Father. I hope he keeps you home."

As he left the tent, Rachel entered, and when she saw Demetrius's back, she shook her head, her lips grim. "What a terrible thing! I'm so sorry, Demetrius."

"So am I," Dinah said. Tears were in her eyes, and for once in her life she was ashamed of herself.

"You're the one who could use a caning," Rachel said bitterly to Dinah.

Demetrius rose and shook his head. "It's all right. I've been hurt worse." He gave Dinah one look and then turned and walked out of the tent.

"I hope your father will show a little reason and sense," Rachel said. "You don't need to be around such a man as that Shechem. He's vicious."

Dinah could not speak. She had been shocked by the scene that had exploded in her face, and now she knew her father was fully capable of forbidding her to go to the palace. "I didn't mean for it to happen," she whispered.

"You never *mean* anything, but you must learn that you are a woman now and not a child."

––––––––––

Jacob was furious when he heard of the incident. After Reuben explained what had happened, he went at once to Demetrius. He insisted on looking at his back and said, "You'll do no work for a while."

"I'm all right," Demetrius insisted. He was weary of the whole thing.

Jacob said, "You'll need to care for that back. I'll have Rachel see to it." He left and immediately went to Dinah, speaking more harshly to her than he ever had in his life. Finally he said, "I'm afraid for you to visit such a man as that."

"It really wasn't his fault," Dinah pleaded.

"He's used to having his own way. I'll have to think about it. I'm not at all sure you should go."

As Jacob left her tent, Dinah drew a deep breath. She was still trembling over the incident. The sight of Demetrius's back cut so badly had shocked her. She had seen slaves beaten before, but somehow this was different.

––––––––––

"Demetrius. . . ?"

Demetrius had been watching the sunset outside of camp where he could be alone to enjoy the evening quiet. He turned to find Dinah, who had come so silently he had not heard her approach.

"Good evening," he said quietly. "A beautiful sunset."

"Yes, it is." Dinah tried to find the words she had prepared and finally stammered, "Demetrius, do . . . do you hate me?"

Demetrius turned and saw the pain in her eyes. "Of course I don't hate you," he said. "One can't hate a child." He smiled and shook his head. "It's not as bad as all that."

"Yes, it is. I feel terrible about it. I would have never done such a thing myself."

"It's all right. Don't worry about it."

Dinah did not know what else to say. He was looking at her in a strange way, and she laughed tremulously. "I'm always doing the wrong thing."

"Not always. This isn't the wrong thing. I wager it's been a long time since you asked someone to pardon you."

"Yes, it has. I know I'm spoiled rotten. And so is Joseph. We're a pair, the two of us."

"I can understand that. He's the son of the Beloved Wife. Jacob loves Rachel very much. Anyone can see that. As for you, a man always loves his daughters—and as you are Jacob's only daughter, he must especially love you. My father was that way about my sister."

"Was he really?"

"Oh yes. It used to infuriate me. She could get anything she wanted out of him. It reminds me of someone I know."

Dinah suddenly felt better. She had seen glimpses of gentleness in this man, and now she knew it was his true nature. Any other man would have been furious with her and hated her forever after being so humiliated as the result of her foolishness.

"You saved my life from that bull and now I reward you by getting you badly beaten."

"It wasn't really your fault. It was Prince Shechem's doing."

"I know. He was wrong, and he's sorry."

"I'm not sure about that, and I'm not sure you should go visit him either."

"Oh, Demetrius, I get so *bored* out here! It can't hurt anything. I'll make a little visit. I'll see the people of the palace. You'll be there, and Amasa. Tersa is going with me too, so nothing can happen."

Demetrius saw no sense in arguing. Dinah might be sorry for what had happened, but she still had a stubborn will.

"Well, you'll have your own way, I suppose."

And then Dinah did something she would not have dreamed of doing before all this had happened. The sight of Demetrius being beaten had done something to her ideas about him. As she had watched the cane cut into his flesh, it almost felt as if she were the one being whipped. Now she put out her hand and laid it flat on his chest. She felt the muscles there and the warmth of his body. She looked up boldly, and her face was flushed. "I'm so sorry that I've caused you all this trouble. Can you ever forgive me for being such a spoiled girl?"

Demetrius was surprised at the sincerity he saw in her eyes. He covered her hand with his own and pressed it against his chest. "Of course I can. That's the good thing, I suppose, about being a beautiful woman. You can always get your own way."

"Do . . . do you really think I'm beautiful?"

Demetrius kept his hand over hers. He reached out and touched her cheek, feeling the smoothness of it. "You know you are," he whispered. "If you lived in my homeland, Minoa, and I saw you there at a festival singing and dancing, I would do exactly what Prince Shechem did. I would come to you at once—as would every other young man in Minoa, and I'd have to fight them off. Does that please you?"

Dinah was extremely conscious of his hand over hers and even more so of his hand on her cheek. His hands were rough but strong and gentle at the same time. She looked up into his eyes and felt the goodness and strength of Demetrius. "Yes, it does," she whispered. Suddenly she did not trust her own impulses. She found herself wishing he would kiss her again, but that would never do! She drew back, and he released her at once. "Good night, Demetrius. Thank you for your forgiveness."

"Good night, Dinah," he said. He used her first name without the title of "mistress"—and somehow this gave a warm intimacy to the moment. Dinah turned and walked away, leaving Demetrius standing there.

He watched her go and then laughed shortly to himself. "What am I doing? Falling in love with that spoiled child? I can't believe I'm behaving like a love-sick calf!" He tried to put his attention on the sunset, but he kept remembering the faint fragrance of her perfume and the smoothness of her cheek. "Here, stop this," he said, striking his forehead. "Don't be a fool. She would drive a man crazy inside of a month!"

CHAPTER
31

Much of Dinah's pleasure as she traveled toward the palace was diminished by Demetrius's attitude. She had bidden good-bye to her father and mother and taken her place in the wagon drawn by two donkeys, the back filled with clothing and other necessities. Tersa, a sturdy young woman whom Jacob and Leah trusted for her common sense, sat beside her.

At first Dinah had been excited, but all day long she kept glancing at Demetrius, who walked alongside the wagon. His face was set, and she knew he was displeased with her decision to proceed with the visit. He had brought with him not only Amasa, a rather fierce man who was an expert in all sorts of fighting, but also Tascar and Moack to strengthen the guard. These two followed along behind, and for most of the journey their voices had been raised in arguments. They were close friends and argued about everything under the sun.

Tersa was a good woman but no company at all for Dinah. She was in her midthirties, had buried two husbands, and was likely to take a third when the opportunity arose. She was completely without imagination but was a practical soul who could see to Dinah's comfort and serve as a chaperone inside the palace walls.

They had stopped at noon and had eaten a meal of cold meats and bread, washed down by sour wine. Demetrius had stayed with the men, but now he came to Dinah and asked, "Are you sure you want to go through with this?"

"You mustn't be angry with Shechem. He's really not what you think," she insisted.

Demetrius did not answer. He gave her an odd look, shook his head in disbelief, and then turned to go back and speak to the men.

Dinah was troubled by Demetrius's attitude, but she put it behind her as they approached the city, which was called Shechem in honor of the prince.

Shechem was not a large place, but it was very old. It was composed of a ring wall of unmortared blocks of stone, which enclosed two cities—one in the southwest and one in the northwest. The upper one in the northwest stood on an artificial mound and consisted almost entirely of the palace of King Hamor and a massive temple dedicated to Baal.

These two structures were the first things that met Dinah's eyes as they entered a valley and approached the gate. Dinah studied the inhabitants of the lower city and was disappointed to see it was hardly more than a village. The inhabitants seemed dull and slow-moving, but she hoped for better things inside the palace.

As they passed through a bazaar, the peddlers called out their wares, begging them to stop and bargain, but Dinah paid them no heed. She was looking at the gate, which was highly ornamented with carved wood and had heavy brass hinges and handles.

The gates opened, and they were met by no less than Prince Shechem himself, who had evidently been informed of their coming. As soon as the wagon stopped, he ran to hold up his hands. Smiling, he helped her to the ground and said, "Our palace is honored by your presence, mistress. Come, and I will show you to your quarters myself."

"Thank you, Your Highness."

"This is your companion?"

"Yes."

Shechem nodded toward Tersa, and then his eyes fell on Demetrius. He stood still for a moment, and since he was turned away, Dinah did not see the hatred that flashed in his eyes. His eyes locked with those of Demetrius, who also stood still, not bowing but resting his hand on the hilt of his sword. For a moment the two men glared at each other, but when Shechem turned back to Dinah, his expression became pleasant again. "Come. You must be tired after your long journey."

"Oh, not at all! I'm anxious to see the palace."

"Then you shall." He waved his hand to his servants and ordered, "See that the attendants of the princess are cared for."

"Princess? I'm not a princess," Dinah said, laughing. "I'm only the daughter of Israel."

Shechem turned toward Dinah, admiring her. "You're beautiful enough to be a princess, and who can say what time will bring us?"

Shechem escorted Dinah into the palace, and she was impressed with the furnishings. He showed her to her quarters and said, "When you have refreshed yourself, inform my servant, and I will show you the rest of the palace."

"Thank you, Prince."

Dinah went inside the quarters and found them to be far more ornate than she could have imagined. There was a bed that was so soft she could not imagine what it was made of—feathers of some sort, she suspected. The walls were covered with paintings, and some of the statues had precious stones for their eyes. The servants of Shechem provided her with enough water for a bath, so she washed away the grime of the travel, and then she put on fresh clothes. She had brought a new robe of a pale rose color, which had cost a great deal. Finally, when she was ready, she informed the servant, and ten minutes later Shechem arrived. "Come along. We will see the palace, and then you will have an audience with my father and his first wife. Then there will be a feast in your honor and much entertainment. I am sure you will find it pleasing."

"I know I will," Dinah said, smiling. She was tremendously excited, and for the next two hours she accompanied the prince as he showed her the magnificent features of the palace, which included many fountains. She did not know what powered them but somehow they bubbled up, some high into the air. There were artificial waterfalls too, so inside the palace one was never far from the sibilant sound of the rushing of water.

The audience with the king was flattering to Dinah. He introduced her to his first wife, Marza, a quiet but attractive woman with sharp black eyes. She was gracious to Dinah, asking her many questions about her life and her family.

The meal was overwhelming. It consisted of pots of thick porridge prepared with sesame oil, warm cakes of barley flour, radishes, cucumbers, sprouts of cabbage palm, and several cuts of roasted meat, including lamb, beef, and chicken. For drink there was goat's milk and wine.

The room itself was ornate and luxurious. Two large earthenware chests on the outer walls of the room held copper basins, milk vessels, and goblets. The family sat on a low leather-covered dais. Dinah sat with her legs curled under herself, while the king had a backless chair gaily painted with gorgeous colors and a footstool to match. There were cow's-horn spoons for the porridge and knives for cutting the meat.

The meal went on for a long time, it seemed, and Dinah, who was not accustomed to much wine, felt herself reeling. She finally laughed and said, "No more wine! I'm not used to it."

"Oh, this is very mild," Shechem insisted. "See how clear it is? Almost like water."

Indeed, the wine he insisted she take was almost like grape juice—or so it seemed.

After the meal, Shechem described the entertainment that was to come at the celebration the following day. "We have acrobats from the Far East and jugglers. There will be demonstrations of swordplay by our finest warriors. Dancers, singers, musicians of all kinds. I'm sure you will enjoy it."

By this time Dinah was finding it difficult to concentrate. She was relieved, finally, when the king said, "Shechem, you are not thoughtful. Can't you see our guest is tired from her long journey?"

"My most abject pardon, princess," Shechem said. "Come. I will show you to your quarters."

Dinah said her good-byes to the king and the queen, hoping she was following the rules of protocol, but as she walked back, she found her legs not quite steady.

Shechem said, "Pardon me. You're very weary. We kept you too long at the meal."

"Not at all. It was wonderful."

When they got to the door of the quarters, Shechem opened the door and led Dinah inside. As soon as they were inside, however, he put his arms around her and began telling her how lovely she was.

Dinah was confused. She tried to resist, but Shechem was kissing her lips and neck, and his hands were roving over her in a way that shocked her.

"Please, Prince Shechem, this is not proper!" She put her hands out and tried to get away. It proved to be quite a struggle, and she grew angry. "Your Highness, I must ask you to leave." Her tongue was thick, making it difficult to speak, and she realized that the wine had some sort of drug in it. She began to shake with fear as she saw the blazing passion in his eyes. Desperately, she cried out, "Tersa—Tersa!"

The maid appeared at once, as if she had been waiting nearby. The prince immediately dropped his arms.

"I am not well, Tersa, and must lie down," she said, trying to control her speech. "Please see the prince out. Good night, Your Highness."

Shechem's face was flushed and anger flashed from his eyes, but he recovered quickly. "Of course. Forgive me, Princess. I will see you in the morning. Sleep well."

"Are you ill, mistress?" Tersa said. She had heard some of what had gone on, and her face was set. "He didn't hurt you, did he?"

"No. I just had too much wine, I'm afraid. I must lie down."

Tersa helped her change into a sleeping robe, and Dinah fell into the bed. Her head was swimming, and for a time, it seemed the whole room was swirling around. She began to grow quite ill, and finally she rolled out of bed and threw up.

Tersa held her head, washed her face, and then put her back into bed. "You're not used to these rich wines, mistress," she whispered. "Sleep now."

Dinah felt better, but she was disappointed. *I didn't think he would be like that*, she thought wearily, *but I suppose princes are used to getting what they want.*

Sleep would not come, and Dinah realized she had made a mistake. *I shouldn't have come here without some of my family*, she thought. *I really shouldn't have come at all.* She had been warned of Shechem's ways with women, but she had not thought he would try to force himself on her. As she lay there, she felt a gush of relief. *If Tersa hadn't been here, he would have forced me. This is a bad place.* As she finally began to fall asleep from exhaustion and the effects of the drugged wine, she told herself, "Demetrius was right. We'll leave this place tomorrow."

———————

Tersa sat straight up. She had been sleeping on the floor beside her mistress, but she was a light sleeper. Coming to her feet, she glanced at Dinah, who was sound asleep. The sound came again, and she went to the door. "Who is it?" she whispered.

"A messenger from the king."

Tersa hesitated but suddenly the door opened—there was no lock on the inside—and she saw a burly man standing there. "What message is—?"

Tersa had no time to say more for the burly guard grabbed her, wrapping her up in his arms and clamping his hands over her mouth. She struggled, but she was like a child against his strength. She was picked up bodily and carried out, but as she went, she saw Prince Shechem waiting. He gave her not a glance, but she saw his eyes were burning. As Tersa was carried away, trying but unable to scream, she knew that Dinah was trapped and there was no hope for her!

———————

248 + GILBERT MORRIS

Dinah came out of her drugged sleep quickly. Someone was touching her, mauling her, and she awoke to find the prince in bed beside her. He was pulling at her, and when he saw her eyes open, he laughed. "Well, you play hard to get, Princess. But you're a woman and I'm a man, and we must have each other."

Dinah uttered a cry. "Tersa!"

"She won't be harmed, but we don't need her to interrupt again."

Dinah had led a sheltered life but not so completely that she didn't know exactly what Shechem had on his mind. Terror filled her, and she lunged away from him, rolling out on the other side of the bed, but he was after her in a moment. He grabbed her and began tearing at her clothes.

"Let me alone, you beast!" she screamed. "Tersa! Help me!"

"Come, now. You're a little bit shy, but I like fresh women. Have you ever known a man?"

Dinah made up her mind that he would not have her willingly. He was larger and stronger than she, but she would never give in. She reached out and ran her fingernails down one side of the prince's face. She saw the blood come and heard his wild curse, and then his fist began to rain on her face. She protected herself as well as she could, but there was only one end. She fought like a wild animal, but finally the blows had their effect, and blackness closed over her.

———————

Demetrius sat up at once. He was camped outside the palace grounds with the other guards. In the darkness he saw a form coming to the door, and he grasped his sword. "Who is it?" he demanded.

"It's me, Tersa."

"Tersa, what are you doing here?" Demetrius came to his feet, and the other guards began to stir.

"It's the mistress . . . she's been hurt!" Tersa cried, and Demetrius saw by the light of the single candle that tears were streaming down her face. "We've got to get away from here."

Demetrius demanded, "What's happened?"

"She's been raped and beaten! I couldn't help it, Demetrius! They came and took me away, and then I saw the prince going into her room. They just released me a few minutes ago at dawn. As soon as I saw her, I ran to get your help."

Shaking Amasa, Demetrius said, "Wake up!"

Amasa rolled over and came to his feet. He was a huge man, towering over Demetrius. "What's wrong?" he growled.

"It's Dinah. She's been attacked by the prince."

Amasa stiffened and began to curse. He glanced over at the others, who were still sleeping, and said, "Tascar, Moack, wake up!"

"Take me to where she is, Tersa," Demetrius demanded.

"We'll go with you," Amasa growled. "Maybe take a few heads off."

"No, you wait here and get the wagon ready. We'll be back very soon," Demetrius said.

Tersa turned and ran back toward the palace, with Demetrius right by her side. There were no guards along the passageway, and Tersa stepped back at the door to Dinah's room. "She's in there," she whispered.

Demetrius entered the room and stopped dead still. Dinah was lying on the bed facedown, absolutely still. Demetrius moved to her side and turned her over. Her face was bruised and swollen, her lips cut, and there were bruises all over her body.

Anger came in waves of white-hot rage, but Demetrius knew there was no time to give in to it. He had to keep his wits about him. "Tersa," he called. "Come. Let's get her dressed. We're leaving this place."

Ten minutes later Demetrius stepped outside the palace carrying Dinah and followed by Tersa. The wagon was drawn up with Amasa and the other two guards standing waiting.

Dinah was whimpering; one of her eyes was swollen shut and the other was a mere slit. Demetrius heard her whisper something and leaned forward but could not make it out. Gently, he said, "You're all right now. I've got you."

"Demetrius?"

"Yes?"

"Take . . . take me home, Demetrius!"

Demetrius lifted her up and set her gently in the back of the wagon. "Tersa, you ride with her. I'll drive."

Demetrius turned, but before he could get into the wagon, Amasa called out a warning. "Demetrius, they're coming!"

Demetrius whirled to see a group of white-clad guards boiling out of an entryway. At their head was Prince Shechem, who was screaming, "Cut them down! Cut them down!"

A grim and fierce pleasure came to Demetrius then. He called, "Amasa, are you ready?"

Amasa laughed. He had a huge sword in his hand, but it looked small against his bulk. "A little blood is what I need." He stepped forward, and when the first of the wave reached them, he sheared the man's head off with one blow.

Demetrius threw himself into the fray, and he and his three companions hewed and hacked. He tried to get to Shechem, but the prince remained back, shouting, "Kill them! Kill them all!"

The battle did not last long. After three more of the guards lay bleeding and writhing like cut worms, the rest retreated.

"Come, Prince Shechem, let's you and I have a bout!" Demetrius shouted, but the prince turned and disappeared inside the portal, followed by his guards.

"Come. Let's get out of this place," Demetrius growled. He leaped up into the seat of the wagon and grabbed the reins, and the animals moved forward at once.

Dinah awakened to pain such as she had never known. She seemed to hurt all over and could barely see. Reaching up to touch her face, she found her hair stiff with blood.

"Don't try to move, mistress."

"Tersa, is that you?"

"Yes." Dinah felt the soft touch on her head. She was being held almost like a child, and she clung to Tersa and began to weep.

"Don't cry. It's all right. It's all over."

Dinah clung to Tersa, her body shaking with sobs. "No, it won't ever be over. . . !"

————————

Levi and Simeon were beside themselves with fury when the entourage arrived back at camp, the guards limping behind it. Seeing the bloodied and swollen face of their sister as Demetrius lifted her out of the wagon and carried her toward the tent, both of them seemed to go insane. They were shaking, their faces pale with rage. Levi began screaming, "We'll kill him! We'll kill the king! We'll kill all their servants!"

Simeon was even worse. He and Levi had always been the most violent of Jacob's sons, and now they ran around trying to gather together a party of men to go attack the king.

Reuben, pale and shaken by what had happened, grabbed them by the arms. "It's no time for that. We've got to see that our sister is all right."

"All right? She'll never be all right! She's been ruined by that monster of a prince. I'll kill him! See if I don't!" Levi shouted.

Jacob heard his sons shouting, but he quickly pushed past them into the tent and fell on his knees beside Dinah. He was crushed at the sight of her and began to weep when she turned away from him, crying, "Don't touch me, Father. I'm unclean."

Jacob whispered, "Don't be foolish, child." He pulled her over and took her in his arms. She clung to him, and weeping came like a storm. He held her and looked up to see Demetrius still standing there. He saw the grim rage in the eyes of the tall young man and knew he would get the full story later. Now, however, all he could think of was his daughter. He held her as she wept, and he wept too, inwardly calling out, *O God, why did you allow this to happen?*

CHAPTER

32

King Hamor was furious with Shechem. As soon as he had discovered what had happened during the night, he stormed into Shechem's House of Delight and jerked his son out of bed by the hair. He ignored the women who scattered like frightened chickens. "You idiot! You crazy imbecile!" the king raged. "All you had to do was wait and we would eventually have had the girl and all of her father's possessions."

Shechem's face grew pale. He had never seen his father in such a rage. He tried to speak, but his father merely slapped his cheeks and cursed him. So he sat there and waited until his father seemed to get a grip on himself. Clearing his throat, the prince said, "I was wrong, but it's not too late."

"Not too late? That's what you think! Don't you know how violent these people are? They still tell the story about how this man's grandfather took a few hundred men and defeated a whole army, and this man Israel is of the same blood."

"But they'll listen if I ask her to marry me."

Hamor stared at his son. Bitterness marred his face and soured his expression. "You'd better hope so," he said, "or you'll wake up one night with your throat cut from ear to ear." He paced back and forth and said, "I'll have to talk with the father. I'll have to crawl on my hands and knees—figuratively speaking, of course."

"Yes, the girl really is a sweet little morsel—"

"Shut your foul mouth before I shut it for you!" Hamor shouted. "You've put me in a bad position. Now I've got to get us out of it!"

Jacob stared unblinkingly at the king. He had risen, and the king, who had come with only four men, had bowed before him, saying, "A terrible thing, my brother, but we must talk."

Jacob stood for a moment, but the rage that filled some of his sons suddenly boiled in his own veins. He wanted nothing more than to pull out his dagger and slice this man's throat, but he knew that this was an idle thought. He stood like a stone, facing Hamor, and dropped his eyes so that the king would not see his anger.

Hamor began to speak. He apologized most abjectly for what had happened. "My son is hot-blooded and not the wisest young man in the world. Nevertheless, he loves your daughter, and I have come to ask that you give her to him in marriage."

If Hamor had expected to see Jacob overwhelmed with joy at the offer, he was disappointed. When Jacob lifted his face, Hamor saw nothing but a mask. *This man would kill me if he could* was the thought that passed through his mind, and he began to panic. He was helpless here before this man with only a token of a guard. He began to apologize profusely and finally said, "You and I are older, my friend. We know that out of bad things sometimes good will come. So let it be with this. My son will treat your daughter as a princess. You have my word on that. If he does not, I will have him beaten as I would have the lowliest slave in my kingdom. My sacred word on it!"

Jacob said, "I will speak with my sons about your offer."

Relief then came to Hamor. "That is as it should be. Shall I wait for your answer?"

"Yes, you may wait here. I will have refreshments sent."

———

The sons of Jacob were stone-faced as they listened to their father. Jacob spoke of Hamor's offer and then said with a weariness in his eyes and a shrug of his shoulders, "We have no choice."

"Yes, we have a choice," Simeon hissed, his face contorted. "We can kill him right now! He only brought a few guards with him. Kill them all!"

"We cannot do that."

"But, Father, you can't give Dinah to this man—not after what he's done to her."

"The king has given me his word that he will personally see to it that Dinah is never abused again."

"His *word!*" Levi shouted. "What kind of word does he have? He just covets our flocks. That's all he wants."

A murmur of assent went around, and for a time a heated argument raged. But finally Jacob called for quiet.

"We have no choice," he said, looking more like a beaten man than his sons had ever seen him.

"Father's right," Judah said. "No other man would have my sister after she has been so disgraced. The whole countryside knows about it."

"That is right," Reuben spoke up at once. "The prince is a vile man, but I will have a word with him. If he mistreats Dinah again, I will kill him myself." From the meekest of the brothers this was, indeed, indicative of their feelings.

But Jacob knew they had no choice. "It must be," he said.

Levi had said nothing, but now he spoke up. "I ask only one thing."

"And what is that, my son?"

"That Shechem, his father, and the members of the royal family be circumcised."

Jacob blinked. His own sons were circumcised, as was he himself. It was a covenant for them with their God, the Supreme Lord of all. But he did not understand why Levi would want this of the king and his people. He stared at Levi. "Why should I ask that?"

"They deserve some physical pain for what they have done to our sister."

Instantly Simeon agreed, and the others were not opposed.

"Very well. I will make this offer."

"He will accept," Simeon said bitterly. "You won't believe me, Father, but all he wants are our herds."

"Enough of that," Jacob said wearily. "I will go talk with King Hamor."

———

"No, Father, you can't make me marry that man!" Dinah cried. "Please don't do it."

Jacob had broken the news to Dinah, and her reaction was exactly what he had expected. He had tried to prepare himself for her pleas, but he could see no other way out. "It has to be this way, Dinah. There is no alternative."

Dinah had kept to herself since she had been brought back to camp. She had seen no one, keeping to her tent. Now she stood looking at her father, her face still swollen, although not so badly now. The physical damage would soon repair itself, but Jacob knew Dinah's wounds were inward, and his heart cried out to her. But as head of his family, he had to make this hard decision. He did the best he could to get her to see there was no other way, but she turned away and threw herself facedown on the bed.

Jacob could say nothing more. He left the tent, bitterness welling up in him. He was walking almost blindly, preoccupied with his troubles and with his daughter's heartache, when Demetrius stepped beside him. "How is she, master?"

"She's torn apart on the inside." The two walked together, and Jacob said, "I don't know what the right thing to do is. She doesn't want to marry the prince."

"Can you blame her?"

"No, I can't. But I don't see any other way. No man would have a woman who is not a virgin."

"They do it all the time," Demetrius said sharply. "If a man loves a woman, he won't hold her past against her."

Jacob was surprised. This man was constantly surprising him. "Do you think there are men like that?"

"You're a man like that yourself, master. If such a thing had happened to your Beloved Wife, Rachel, would you have turned from her?"

"No, I would not have." Jacob suddenly felt ashamed at what he was doing, but he shook his head. "It has to be, Demetrius."

Demetrius did not answer, but one look at his face and Jacob knew that the tall young man violently disagreed. He bade him good-bye, saying, "Thank you again for what you did for my daughter."

———————

The bargain was made, along with agreements concerning dowry and mundane things that Jacob and his family were not really interested in. The king agreed to submit all of the men of his country to the rite of circumcision, and Simeon professed himself satisfied. He said little, and Jacob was surprised at this, for he and Levi had been the loudest in their cries for vengeance. Now they seemed satisfied with the agreement of Hamor and Shechem to be circumcised along with all of their house.

"I can't understand Simeon and Levi," Jacob said to Rachel. "They were all ready to form an army to go wipe out the king—or try to."

"I don't understand them either," Rachel said, shaking her head. "But I'm glad they've become more peaceful."

"They're not peaceful men," Jacob said. "That's why I don't understand it."

"It will be all right. Dinah, though, is the one who will never get over the shame of this. She can't bear to look anyone in the face. Have you noticed?"

"Yes. It tears me to pieces, Rachel." He reached over and took her hand. "You must stay very close to her. Leah's not enough. She needs a tender heart like yours."

"You know that I love her and will do all that I can, but I'm not sure it will be enough."

———————

As it happened, Jacob was with Dinah when the news came. He was sitting beside her, speaking of unimportant things. She was silent, answering only when asked a direct question. Jacob heard feet running and commented with surprise, "Somebody's in a hurry."

Reuben suddenly burst into the tent. His eyes were wide and his face twisted with shock.

"What is it? What's wrong, Reuben?" Jacob cried, coming to his feet.

"It's ... it's Simeon and Levi. They've murdered the king and the prince!"

For one instant Jacob could not take in what Reuben was saying. He stared at his tall, broad-shouldered son and could not even speak.

Reuben burst forth then—he who usually spoke so slowly. The words flowed from his lips. "They hired some of the hill people—killers—and this is the third day after the circumcision, and the king and his men were still recovering. Levi and Simeon invaded the palace and killed every man they could find. They were too sore to defend themselves. The king is dead and so is the prince."

"How do you know all this? It can't be true," Jacob cried. But somehow he knew in his heart that it was.

"They're on their way back. Simeon came ahead. He's outside now."

Jacob could not move, and when he looked at Dinah, she was staring at Reuben with an expression such as Jacob had never seen on her. He could not tell what it meant.

Then Simeon came in. He looked victorious, and he came at once to Dinah and stood before her. "Do not worry, my sister. Your shame is avenged."

Jacob found his voice. "What have you done?" he cried. "You have ruined me, you and Levi! We are so few among these people. We'll all be killed."

But Simeon merely stared at Jacob. His voice was harsh as he shouted, "Should he treat our sister like a harlot? I have taken much plunder. Our sister's shame is now avenged."

But Jacob turned to face Dinah, and he saw no joy there. The shame was still in her eyes, and she did not speak.

"Leave us," Jacob said, and as soon as Reuben and Simeon were outside, he went to Dinah and put his arms around her. He could not speak for a time. He did not know what she was thinking, and finally he said, "That was an evil thing your brothers did."

"Yes, it will not bring back my innocence."

"No man will blame you for it."

Dinah's voice, usually so light and lilting, was dead. "Yes, they will. No man will have me. I will never marry."

Jacob stared at her but knew that talk was useless.

"I will never marry," she said again, then turned from him.

Jacob stared at her helplessly. Without another word, he left the tent and saw Levi coming in to join Simeon. Fierce anger stirred within him, rising over his grief. "Levi and Simeon, you will never rule over my other sons! Reuben is the firstborn, but you two—never!" He stood helplessly, not knowing what to do next. His plans for an easy, peaceful old age seemed to be slipping away from him. He began to cry out in his spirit, *O Most High God, show me your tender mercies. Be with my daughter, who needs you so desperately. You have given me the name of Israel. Let me now be a prince indeed.*

His prayer seemed feeble and the future looked grim. Jacob, the son of Isaac, the grandson of Abraham, turned away, and tears coursed down his cheeks as futility washed over him.

PART SIX

THE LION

CHAPTER

33

The wind in the branches above Demetrius's head made a soft sound like the tearing of cloth. Lifting his eyes, Demetrius watched the colors of the land run and change along the horizon, touching the low-lying peaks to the east. As the sun dipped westward, it touched the ragged rim on the foothills, and the livid red ball seemed to break, spilling out against the humpback mountains. The light began to break up, creating a fan-shaped aurora against the blue, and then it began to fade. Soon the blueness of twilight trickled down from the heavens, and after that the heat of the earth would pass away and the stillness of nightfall would come.

Demetrius dropped his head and started to doze, his chin resting on his chest, but a sharp pull at the line tied around his index finger brought him back. He sat up straight, coming alive as he always did when he caught a fish. The line straightened out and then ran madly as the fish tried to escape. Demetrius hauled it in and, as he pulled it out, laughed softly. "You'll make a fine supper tonight." He carefully removed the fish from the bronze hook, pulled up a sack anchored at his feet, and dropped the fish in, then let the sack settle back in the water. He had discovered when just a boy that keeping fish in this manner kept them fresh much longer.

Glancing over, he smiled at Joseph, who was lying flat on his back in the shade of a tree. His mouth was open, and he snored slightly. "You're going to catch flies that way, but no fish," Demetrius murmured, then rebaited his hook and cast it out again.

Catching the fish had driven away his drowsiness, and as he waited for another fish, he thought of Joseph and how fond he had become of the young man. He'd had opportunity to study all eleven of the brothers and had reached the conclusion that Joseph was the best of them all——with the possible exception of Judah. These two were his favorites, and he was not surprised that Jacob seemed to have the same feelings.

He doubled up his legs, reached around and grasped them, then put his chin on his knees. The sun reached long fingers of light through the trees across the river and was now touching the earth with gentleness instead of a scorching power. The strong but pale light pooled between the trees, and he took pleasure in the sight. He had learned to love the desert—which he had never expected to do when he had first been forced into slavery. He knew that part of his love was the affection he had come to feel for Jacob. The old man had become very close to the heart of Demetrius. Jacob loved to talk about God, and Demetrius loved to listen. Now, for some time, he sat there amid the sounds of the late afternoon, thinking of all that his master had told him about his God.

Another thought brushed against his mind. He thought of the small hoard of money he had managed to save. It had come from different sources. He had managed to save bits of silver from some of the metal working he had done, which he had sold to passing traders. He had done extra work more than once, for which Jacob had rewarded him, and he had carefully kept the money. It was well hidden, buried in the tent he shared with some of the other men, underneath the pad he slept on.

I could have gotten away before this. What am I doing here? Why haven't I made a run for home?

For a time he struggled with this question. It was not that he did not love his home, for he had a poignant longing to see it and be among his own people again. But something had kept him here. One thing was clear. He was fascinated by the God of the Hebrews. He knew well that he could never go back to worshiping the gods of his ancestors. They seemed foolish to him now, and his will had become fixed on finding the God of the Hebrews for himself. Perhaps on even hearing Him speak to him personally, as Jacob and his ancestors had heard Him!

But as Demetrius sat there mulling over these things, another thought came that he kept trying to push away from his mind. But it would not leave. He knew that Dinah had something to do with his remaining in Canaan. She had never recovered from the attack of Shechem. The young woman he had known before was gone, replaced by a woman marred with sadness. She kept to her tent almost entirely now, and he missed her lively eyes, her songs, even the way she had of trying to boss him around.

I've come to care for her. . . . But I'd care for any woman who got hurt.

A tug on the line pulled his thoughts away, and he drew the line in quickly. It was a small fish, not worth keeping, and he unhooked it. He almost tossed it back, but then humor danced in his eyes. Getting up, he tiptoed to where Joseph lay with his arms flung out, his mouth open as he snored. Carefully Demetrius pulled the neckline of Joseph's robe open and tossed the fish in, then jumped back and watched as Joseph reacted.

A long muffled cry rent the air, and Joseph jumped up, beating at his chest. He danced around wildly, slapping at his clothes, and Demetrius laughed as the fish fell out.

Joseph stared at the fish that flopped along the ground, then whirled to glare at Demetrius. "That wasn't funny!"

Demetrius shook his head in mock amazement. "I didn't know you could move so fast, Joseph."

"I ought to shove this in your ear," Joseph said. But he picked up the fish and threw it back into the water instead. Then he began to laugh but warned Demetrius, "Wait until I catch *you* asleep! I'll drop a worm down your throat while you're snoring."

"Fair enough, but I expect we'd better get home. It's getting late."

Demetrius wound up his line, stored it in a pack, and threw the rest of the bait out as a reward for the fish he didn't catch. Pulling the sack of fish out of the water, he was pleased at the weight of it. He wrapped the end around his wrist, and the two started back for home.

Joseph was a talkative young man, given to telling tall tales. Finally, however, he mentioned his brothers. "They've been running off from their work, leaving the cattle with some of those sorry hired men. I'm going to tell Father about it."

Demetrius did not answer for a moment and then he shrugged. "It's best not to tell on your brothers—or anyone, for that matter."

Joseph twisted his head to look at Demetrius. "Maybe not, but they're doing the wrong thing."

"What would you think if I told your father about some of the things I know about you?"

Joseph was offended. "I'm not like they are! They're older. They ought to behave better." He was silent for a while and said, "Most of them don't like me very much."

"Well, that's right, and it's because you're the favorite. They resent you."

"I can't help that," Joseph said. Actually he loved his brothers and was troubled at the ways of some of them. He got along fairly well with the younger ones, but his older brothers, except for Reuben, caused him problems. He had gotten in the habit of carrying tales to his father, and naturally his brothers resented this.

Joseph blurted out, "Why haven't you tried to run away, Demetrius?"

Demetrius was surprised by the question but knew that this young man had a sharp mind. "I don't know," he said.

"I do," Joseph nodded with authority. "You're worried about Dinah."

"Well, of course I am. Aren't you?"

"Yes, but I'm not a slave. She's my sister. I've watched you around her, and I can tell when you're worried." He stopped then, and Demetrius turned to face him: "You like her, don't you, Demetrius?"

"Well, she hasn't always been the easiest slave owner, but I feel sorry for her."

Joseph did not answer. He examined the face of Demetrius, then said, "No, it's more than that. I think you have a feeling for her like a man feels for a woman."

"Well, that would be useless, wouldn't it? I'm a slave and she's the daughter of a wealthy man."

Joseph considered these words, then went on, "I think you do like her. You know, Demetrius, I miss what she was before she got hurt. I try to cheer her up all I can, but she cries a lot when she's alone."

"I know. Sometimes even when she's not alone." Demetrius hesitated, then said, "I hope we'll get the old Dinah back one day. I miss her like you do." He was afraid to carry this conversation on any further, for he had feelings he did not want Joseph to know about. "Come along," he said. "It's going to be late when we get home, and we've got to clean these fish."

When Demetrius broke into a run, it was all Joseph could do to keep up with the man.

———

Dinah sat in her tent, staring at the wall and trying to blank out her mind. She was aware that Leah was moving around and wished she would leave. Finally her mother came over and stood directly in front of her. "Why don't you go out and join the other young women, daughter? They're having a fine time working on a new dance."

"Not right now."

"Dinah, you can't hide in this tent all your life." Leah was worried about her daughter. She was not a woman given to affectionate gestures, but she put her hand now on Dinah's shoulder, and her voice was soft. "You can't stay in here forever. I know it's been hard, but other women have had to go through this. Just put it behind you. Forget it, and go out and have some fun."

"I think I'll just stay here."

Leah stared at Dinah, then snorted and left the tent. Her impatience was evident from the line of her back, and Dinah knew that she was trying everyone's patience, including her mother's.

The sounds of the young women singing came to her through the wall of the tent, but she had no inclination to go out and join them. At first, she had tried to make some effort to pick up her life, but everyone seemed to be looking at her, most with pity but some not so kindly. She had had to fight off the questions from the young women who had avid curiosity, who wanted to know all the details of the attack, while Dinah wanted nothing more than to blot it out of her mind. She had, indeed, spent much of her time trying to do exactly this, but she had learned by bitter experience that memories will not be confined. It was like putting something in a box and clamping the lid down, only to find out that it would come out again when least expected. At first, time had slipped along with a rapidity that amazed her, but now every day seemed to pass on leaden feet. And even when nightfall came and she could hide herself in the darkness, there was no escaping the sharp, bitter memories of the past.

Sometimes the whole terrible scene played out before her with a sharp clarity that brought pain, and which would not be denied. She had wept over how she had ignored the warnings of Demetrius and her father and had cried out—a thousand times, it seemed—"Oh, why did I have to go to that place?" As she sat there, the futility of wishing for the past to be changed, to be blotted out, seemed to drop over her, pressing down with an unbearable weight. "It can never be changed!" she whispered. And then she began to weep. She did not attempt to stem the tears but sobbed and let them run down her cheeks. Weeping had become a part of her as much as laughter had been before.

At the sound of someone approaching, she quickly made a grab for a cloth and wiped her face. She thought it was Leah coming back, but it was Demetrius's voice she heard. "Mistress, are you there?"

"Yes . . . just a minute." She did not want to see anyone, especially him, but she knew he could be persistent. He had come several times to try to cheer her up, but she could never face him. Quickly she grabbed a cloth, dipped it into the basin of water, and ran it across her face. Tossing the cloth down, she said, "Come in."

Demetrius stepped inside. It was not quite dark outside, and his form was outlined darkly against the twilight rosiness. "Joseph and I caught some fish. Some nice ones. How do you want yours cooked?"

"Just any way."

"Well, I don't suppose you'd like to eat them raw. I'll fry them for you in some fat. How does that sound?"

"It's all right, Demetrius."

The hopelessness in her voice and the sight of her shoulders brought Demetrius a feeling of great compassion and perhaps of something more. He had a passionate desire to bring back some of the liveliness he had always admired in her, even when she was at her worst. He knew that there was a depth to this girl that had never been drawn out, but this tragedy was accomplishing just the opposite. It was robbing her of her youth, her vivacity, all that made her lovely and attractive. Suddenly he made a decision. "I have a present for you."

The words caught Dinah by surprise. "A present? Why?"

"Oh, I just wanted to give you something."

"Not a fish, is it?"

"No," he smiled. "Not a fish. You stay right here, and I'll get it."

As Demetrius turned and dashed out of the tent, Dinah sat down. She wished he would go away, for the very sight of him reminded her of how right he had been about Shechem and how wrong she herself had been. He had shown not one bit of the avid curiosity about Shechem that others had shown, but then, he had been there. It disturbed her to think that he had found her bloody and bruised and beaten, and somehow she knew the memory could never be washed from his mind.

Soon Demetrius was back. He came in holding several flat objects in his hands.

Placing himself before her, he said, "Guess what your present is."

"I can't."

"Well, try."

"They look like flat pieces of wood. Are they trays of some kind?"

"No. Guess again."

"Oh, Demetrius, I can't."

"All right. Here's what it is." He held two of the pieces away from her in his left hand, and with his right he turned the other around.

"There's your present," he said.

Dinah gasped. The oil lamps burning in the tent threw off considerable light, and she stared down at a beautiful painting on a flat board. It contained brilliant colors, and she leaned closer to study it. It was so full of life! A bull was charging across an arena of some kind, and a young woman was somersaulting over the bull's head. Two more young people were there, one in front of the bull and one behind to catch the woman who was turning the flip.

"Why, it's so real! Is this what you were telling me about when the red bull almost got me?"

"Yes, this is bull leaping."

Dinah was mesmerized by the sight. "How did you learn to paint like this?"

Demetrius shrugged and smiled. "Well, at one time I was sure that painting was going to be what I did. I had good teachers."

"How do you get these colors?"

"Oh, I collect the materials from different places. You have to collect oils and minerals and mix them together."

"I'd love to see this thing that you've painted—this bull leaping."

"It's something to watch, but it's dangerous. I think I told you I had a brother that got killed doing it."

She looked up and remembered he had told her. "That must have made you grieve a great deal."

"We were very close. Here. Here's another one." She turned another one of the frames around, and Dinah stared at the picture of a couple— obviously mature people. "These are my parents," Demetrius said.

"They're fine looking, Demetrius."

"Yes. That's why I'm so handsome. I didn't have a chance to be ugly, not with parents like these."

Suddenly Dinah laughed, not realizing it was the first time she had laughed since the attack. Her eyes were bright, and at least for a moment she forgot her misery. "Are they as modest as you are?"

"About the same. The pity of it is we don't have anything much to be modest about."

He continued to speak of his parents, and Dinah stared at the painting. "I don't see how anybody does this. We don't have any painters among our people at all."

"All Minoans learn a little bit about painting. Some are better than others."

Dinah considered the picture carefully. "Your mother looks so lovely."

"Yes, she is. Almost the loveliest woman I've ever met."

Dinah looked up quickly and saw that he was smiling at her. "What's the other picture?" she asked.

"I can't tell you."

Dinah blinked with surprise. "What do you mean you can't tell me?"

"I don't think it would be good for you to see it, mistress."

Dinah could not help grinning. The dimple on her cheek leaped into prominence, as it always did when she smiled. "It must be a very naughty picture."

"I wish you could see it," Demetrius said. He looked at it and shook his head with admiration. "Too bad, but I'm afraid it's not for you."

Dinah reached out and snatched at the picture. She got her hand on one edge of the frame, but Demetrius suddenly held her wrist. She struggled harder, crying, "Let me see it!"

"Well," Demetrius finally said, "you're the mistress, so I suppose you'll have your own way. Here."

Dinah turned the picture around and held it in her hands. She studied it and said nothing for a long moment. "She should look familiar," Demetrius said. "It's you, Dinah."

Dinah was looking at the picture of the young woman that was painted on the surface. She did recognize herself. She was outside somewhere and half turned, with her profile showing. She was wearing her favorite robe, a light blue, and he had caught the hue exactly. "I never look this good," she protested.

"Yes. I've seen you many times with that look. I think it's the best painting I've ever done."

Dinah could not look up. She was staring at the girl and something changed in her face.

"Do you like it, Dinah?" he asked.

Dinah suddenly looked up, and her eyes were swimming with tears. "It's a beautiful painting. I . . . I wish I was still the girl that you painted here."

Demetrius felt the compassion that had been in him for some time come to the surface. He stepped closer to her and took the painting. He set them all down and then turned to her and took her hands. He saw surprise leap into her eyes, but she did not try to get away. "Dinah, if someone you loved had been attacked and harmed by a wild beast, a bear or a wild dog, would you think less of him?"

"Why . . . no, of course not!"

"Then why can't you understand that no one thinks less of you? For you were attacked by a beast worse than any bear or lion." His hands tightened, and she could not tear her eyes away from him. "You're still the same sweet, lovely girl you were before it all happened."

"No, I was never sweet!"

"Yes, you were. I saw it in you. Oh, you were layered over with a silly selfishness, but I watched you, Dinah. I've seen the kindness you show to everyone. You must never call yourself selfish. A selfish woman would never have paid all her money for a slave . . . as you did to save me."

"I wish I could believe that . . . but I can't."

Dinah was very much aware of the warm pressure of his hands. She was suddenly possessed with a longing such as she had never known before. It came so sharply that the poignancy of it almost took her breath. She wanted to simply fall into his arms and stay there so that the world could not hurt her anymore.

"Demetrius, I can never be the same again. My heart is broken."

Demetrius pulled her down to the bed and sat beside her with his arm around her. She was caught off guard by this, but it was exactly what she had been longing for. She turned to face him to see what was in his countenance and saw the deep compassion in his fine eyes. "You could never heal my heart."

"Well, you just don't know me, mistress! Why, I have a reputation in my country for healing broken hearts."

"Oh, don't be foolish!"

"It's true. I could have made a good living at it instead of being a sailor." Demetrius saw that she was watching him with a childlike expression. She was longing for someone to say these things to her, but nobody had been able to.

"Parents came to me from all over Minoa, begging me to help their children who had been hurt. Many of them"—he nodded firmly—"were young women who had been disappointed in love."

Despite her grief, Dinah could not help smiling. "And did you do it, Demetrius? Did you cure them?"

"Every single one!"

"And how did you do that, if I may ask?"

"Ah," Demetrius said, shaking his head with mock sobriety. "I'm not giving any secrets away. Why, you'd steal them. You'd become the famous healer of broken hearts. You'd become rich and have nothing to do with a poor sailor."

"No, I wouldn't do that, Demetrius." She took his hand then, the first time since he had brought her home that she had reached out to anyone. She clung to him and said, "I would never turn away from you."

"You wouldn't? Well, now I'll take you on as a special patient. Dinah, the daughter of Israel the Hebrew."

He got to his feet and lifted her up by the hand. "Come. It's time for the first treatment."

"What? It's almost dark!"

"It has to be that way. The first treatment always begins just at twilight."

The heat had gone out of the earth and the night breeze was cool. Out in the distance, under the full light of the moon, the full shadows of night had fallen, and the earth nearby had a gray, lucent shine to it as the two stood beside the same stream where Demetrius had been fishing earlier. The sun had dropped down in the west, and the clear light of the moon seemed to bring a fragrance to the land. The stillness was complete, except for the murmur of the stream at their feet. They had been there long enough for the full moon to clear the horizon and turn to a butter yellow haze in the air.

Overhead the stars were great crystal masses, almost bright enough to hurt the eye. And the coolness of the night air was a relief after the heat of the day. The wind softly roughed up the leaves that had fallen from the trees, and the smell of the land rising with the dissipated heat whirled in streaky currents in the moonlit air. The two figures beside the stream were facing each other. Demetrius sat in front of Dinah, his voice softly rising in excitement at times, and his hands waving in the air to outline his tales.

Dinah suddenly said, "You've been telling lies for two hours, Demetrius. When does your treatment for broken hearts begin?"

Demetrius smiled. His teeth looked very bright in the moonlight. "I *have* begun. Don't you feel it working?"

Dinah stared at him and realized that she *did* feel better. The tales of his homeland and of his adventures on the sea and in foreign places had taken her out of herself. She smiled and said, "Yes, I do feel better. Is this all your treatment, healer of broken hearts?"

"Of course not. It's just a beginning. Now the second part is very important."

"What is it?"

Demetrius rose to his feet. Dinah's eyes widened as he reached over and picked her up off the ground. "The second step is that you must be totally immersed in running water."

Demetrius stepped to the bank and swung her back as if he would fling her into the river.

"Demetrius, you can't!" Throwing her arms around his neck, she clung to him. "Don't you *dare* throw me in that water!"

"Well, that's part of the treatment. Of course, there is one alternative that will keep you dry."

"What's that?"

Demetrius turned then to face her. His arms felt strong and capable, and she suddenly loved the strong planes of his face as they were laid into chiseled planes by the moonlight. She had always thought him handsome, but never had he seemed stronger and more masculine and virile than at that instant.

"You must sing me a song."

"Oh, Demetrius, I can't sing!"

"Too bad. Good-bye, then."

He swung her back and actually started the forward movement, but she wildly grabbed at him, saying, "No, don't! I'll sing!"

"Good. Let's hear it."

He did not put her down but held her, and she saw that he was smiling.

Dinah began to sing. She had a beautiful voice and sang an old song she had learned as a child. It seemed to draw her back into the past. She was aware of his arms holding her close. The strength of his body seemed to give her strength. Her voice grew stronger, and when she finished the verse and he insisted on another, she sang another song she had learned while growing up.

When she ceased, Demetrius said, "That was lovely. You're just like my old mistress again." He suddenly put her down and said, "Come. It's late."

Dinah was filled with amazement at how the time had flown. She walked alongside Demetrius, and when they approached the camp, she said, "Thank you for coming to me . . . and for the paintings."

"Well, tomorrow the *real* work begins. Get a good night's sleep."

"The real work! What is it?"

"I never reveal my methods." Demetrius was smiling, and suddenly she found herself smiling back at him.

"You've got to tell me."

"No, it's so drastic, mistress! I used it once on a young woman from Greece. She was in poor shape, but I'm afraid it worked too well."

"What do you mean? What happened to her?"

"Oh, she fell madly in love with me." He laughed then and said, "Tomorrow we'll have another treatment, won't we?"

Dinah was filled with a sense of gratitude that seemed to fill her breast. She took his hand and whispered, "Thank you, Demetrius. I . . . I like your treatments."

Demetrius suddenly grew serious. He lifted her hand to his lips, kissed it, then said quietly, "The best of life lies ahead of you."

"I wish I could believe that."

Demetrius dropped her hand. He grabbed her shoulders and shook her slightly. "It's true. My methods never fail. I hope you can live through what you will face tomorrow. You'll have to be strong."

Dinah suddenly felt light and free. "I'll try to live through it no matter how bad it is. Good night, Demetrius."

She went into her tent, undressed, and got into bed. For a long time she lay there, and then she realized as sleep came to her that for the first time since the horror at the palace, she was excited about waking up the next day.

CHAPTER

34

"Well, it's time for another treatment from Master Demetrius—healer of broken hearts, magician, and expert in all matters known to human beings."

"I don't see how you could possibly be as wise as you pretend to be." Dinah turned to look up into the face of Demetrius. He was staring upward, and his profile was outlined against the sky, blocking out the stars.

Turning to her, Demetrius said, "You must have faith. All my patients are required to have faith, and I must say I'm rather pleased with myself. You laughed three times tonight. That's a good sign."

"Yes, it is. I do feel strangely content tonight."

The two of them were standing on a flat plain quite a ways from the closest tent in the camp. The stars were sharply glistening overhead, and the scented wind frayed at the odors of the wilderness about them. The mystery of the night had closed down, and loneliness had moved in with its questions and its majesty. The breeze coming in from the mountains over to the west flowed around Dinah, and she sensed the timeless swing and vast rhythm of all the starry bodies that glowed above her.

From somewhere far off, a wild dog broke into a half bark, adding an indescribable note of wildness to the night. "That's a lonesome sound," Dinah said.

"I kind of like it. We don't have wild dogs where I come from. I admire those fellows."

She stared at him, noting how the silver light brought out the boldness of his features. "Nobody likes wild dogs." She waited for him to answer, and when he did not, she asked, "Why do you like them?"

"Oh, they're free. They can go where they please."

Dinah opened her eyes with surprise. She had never heard him speak of his bondage before. "Are you really so miserable, Demetrius?"

He did not answer but suddenly said, "Look!"

Dinah turned to look and saw a star make a scratch on the heavens. "I've always liked that," she said. "What causes such a thing, do you suppose?"

"I'm sorry. That's a trade secret to us professional heart healers. But it's a good sign. It means you're going to get something very nice in the future."

"What will I get?"

"Ah, you'll have to wait. But for tonight the treatment includes learning something about those fellows up there."

"What fellows?"

"Those. The fire people up in the sky."

Dinah turned to look upward. "You think those are people?" she whispered in awe.

"Nobody knows what they are, but I know them pretty well. A sailor has to know them. They're the only way he can find out which way he's going or where he is."

Dinah was staring upward. "They all look alike to me."

"Well, they won't in a few minutes. I'm going to teach you how to recognize some of my good friends. Now, look up there." When she obeyed, he reached over and put both hands on her head. "No, right up there." He kept his hands on her head, and she was conscious of the strength that always seemed to flow out of him. "You should see a big cup with a long handle, a small cup with a crooked handle, a bear, and a strange-looking beast like a snake with a big head."

Dinah stared. "I don't see any of those."

"You don't! Well, you have eyes, don't you?"

"Yes, but it's just a bunch of stars. There must be hundreds of them."

"All right. Here, I'll show you. Wait a minute."

Dinah watched as he scrambled around. The silver moonlight flooded the plain, and she felt the peacefulness of the night. The past days had been good for her. Demetrius had not done a great deal of work but had instead spent as much time with her as possible. He had encouraged her to travel with him to see the flocks, to go to the river to fish. She knew her parents were glad that she was getting out. Now as she watched, she asked, "What are you doing?"

"Gathering stars," he said. He came back with his hands full of small stones and got down on his knees. "Now, sit over here right across from me."

Dinah obediently moved to where he indicated and knelt, leaving some space between them. She watched as he put stones out in a peculiar pattern. Once he stopped and said, "That won't do. Come over here by me." She got up, dusted off her knees, and knelt down beside him, so close he could feel the pressure on his side as she touched him. "Now," he said. "There's what you see overhead."

Dinah stared at the stones. They seemed to be scattered in a random pattern. "They just look like rocks on the ground to me."

"All right. Look up at the sky again. You don't see a cup with a handle?"

"No. I don't see anything at all but a bunch of rocks and up there just a lot of stars."

"All right. Look at this." He picked up a stick and began to draw lines between some of the stones. "Now," he said, "do you see the cup with the handle?"

"Well, of course I see it now."

"Of course," he mocked. "Okay. Look up. Right up there you should see it. The same thing in the sky."

Suddenly the pattern seemed to leap into her eyes. "Why, I *do* see a cup, and it's got a long handle that's bent."

"That's the Big Cup," he said. "That's your first lesson in learning the sailor's friends. All right. Do you see a little cup?"

She tried but could not see it. "No."

"Look at this then." He drew a dotted line from the end of the big cup across to a very bright star. "Now, this is the end of the handle. See? This is the Little Cup."

At once Dinah saw it. She exclaimed with delight, "Why, I do see it! It's right up over the other one."

"That's right. Now, this is very important. It's going to make you a wise woman and a happy one. Do you see the star right at the end of the handle of the little cup?"

"Yes, I see it! It's so bright!"

"That's the most important star in all of the sky."

"Why is it so important, Demetrius?"

"Because it never changes position. All these other stars move around, but this big cup goes around in a circle and the little cup also. And all the other stars are always moving, but that fellow up there"—he pointed up—

"never moves. Sailors call it the unchanging star. I guess some put a proper name on it, but I've never heard it."

"Why, I can see them as plainly as anything now!"

"Can you? Well, you should be able to see the bear."

"A bear?" Her tone was puzzled. "I don't see anything like that."

"Look down at the stones." He began to draw lines between some of the stones at the bottom of the pattern. "Now do you see it?"

Dinah looked down at the earth for a moment and then exclaimed, "Why, I do see it!"

"Then look up there. You'll see the bear. The Big Cup is the saddle right on his shoulders.

"There's his hind legs. One of them is crooked, you see, and he's holding his snout up in the air like he is sniffing something. And there are his front legs."

Dinah laughed with pure delight. "I can see them now!"

"Can you see the serpent?"

"Serpent?" She studied the stars again and shook her head. "No, not really."

"Well, look at this." He moved her back to the stones and began to draw lines. "There is his head, a big head, you see. And here's his two feet, and here's his slimy body twisting around and ending up right between the Big Cup and the Little Cup. Now, look up and see if you can find it."

Dinah looked up then and at once exclaimed, "I do see it! Why, this is wonderful, Demetrius. Do you know any others?"

"Oh, there are lots of others, but these are where you start."

"Teach me some more."

"Not for tonight." He laughed and got to his feet and then pulled her up. "It's hard work putting young women back together again."

"You know, Demetrius, you're like that star, the unchanging star, at least to me."

Demetrius grew serious. He reached out and put his hands on her shoulders. "Do you really feel that way about me?"

"I don't know what I would have done," she said simply, "if you hadn't helped me over these past few weeks."

"Well, my treatment is working, then."

"I don't think you knew," Dinah whispered, "how bad off I was. I'd even thought about killing myself."

Demetrius said quickly, "Don't even mention that. What would your family do without you?" He gazed at her, then asked quietly, "What would *I* do without you?"

Dinah was startled. She looked up, not knowing what he was thinking.

Suddenly he asked, "What were you like when you were a little girl?"

"Why, like all other girls, I suppose."

He grinned. "What are girls like?"

"What a question! You might as well ask what boys are like. Girls are what they are, Demetrius. Some are sweet and gentle, others are sharp and rough. Some are pretty and some are plain."

She fell silent for a moment, and then she said, "When I was a girl I did what all girls do. I played with the other children and by myself. I learned how to work, but, of course, there's a fine line between being a little girl and a woman. Women are different from children."

"Yes, they're bigger," Demetrius said with a straight face.

"Why, of course they're bigger, but that's not the only thing. They're different in other ways too."

"How are they different?"

"I thought you were the expert in women," she said, smiling. "Why, they think of different things. Men can do what they want to do, but women can't. They have to get married and they have to have children."

"Isn't that what you want?"

"Yes, of course." She laughed, and it made a tinkling sound on the air. "I had two men that I grew fond of. One of them was Ebor. He was the strongest man anywhere. He could pick up the hugest rock, bigger than anybody else could lift, and throw it."

"I suppose every woman wants a strong man."

"But a little later after Ebor, I fancied myself falling in love with Remelu. He was so *smart!*"

"Why, you could marry both of them," Demetrius said, "and the strong fellow could throw rocks for you, and the smart one could entertain you with his wit."

"Don't be a fool," she said. "I was just a growing girl. I didn't know what I wanted."

At that moment, as they were talking lightly and even foolishly, a thought came to Demetrius. He had known women before, but there was something in this young woman that touched him as no other woman ever had. He realized that he had been, for all of his acquaintances and through all of his activities, touched with a loneliness he had not recognized until now. He felt a longing he could not identify, but he knew it had something to do with Dinah, the daughter of Israel. He did not speak, and when she looked up at him, he knew he could no longer hide his feelings for her. His heart ached at the wonderful innocence he saw in her uplifted eyes. He stepped forward and put his hand on her shoulders, watching her lips and the expression in her glance. She said nothing, but there was a layered darkness in her eyes. He bent down and kissed her gently, holding the kiss for a time. The words almost formed in his mind, *Why, this is what I've been looking for!* He lifted his head and saw tears in her eyes. "What is there to cry about?" he asked gently.

"You're so . . . so *gentle.*" The whisper was almost inaudible as she leaned forward into his arms. She put her head down on his chest, and he held her. He understood her need for his strength and gentleness as she wept quietly.

Finally she looked up, and the tears that welled in her eyes caught the silver of the moon.

"Do you care for me, Dinah?" he said and waited for her to speak.

As for Dinah, there was a riot of emotions within her. She had thought never to let a man touch her again, so deeply had she been scarred, but there was such honesty in this man. He had been so patient, and she knew that what she felt for him was more than a casual thing. She also realized that she had touched him deeply and believed now that no matter what other men were like, this one was different and would always be different with her.

"What is it, Dinah?"

She looked into his eyes and saw that he was waiting for an answer. She didn't know what to say, for despite the progress she had made, at times the terrible memories of Shechem came back to her in a fearful way. She was afraid to trust herself to any man. It was not that she was afraid of Demetrius. Far from it! But she was afraid of the past and of what lay within her.

"I'd better go home, Demetrius."

He nodded and said, "All right."

The two of them walked back along the path, and from time to time he mentioned one of the stars overhead, pointing it out to her. She felt a rush of gratitude that he did not press her, and she wondered if he would ever ask her again if she cared for him. She hoped someday she would have an answer for him.

Dinah had gone to sleep with a smile on her lips, but some time during the night the bad dream came back again. It was always the same, with Prince Shechem tearing at her, violating everything she had always treasured. She woke up trembling. She got up off her bed and saw Tersa sleeping soundly over on her pad on the carpet. She tried to control her trembling, and looking out, she saw that it was almost daylight.

I've got to get away! I've got to think things through! The thought possessed her as she stepped over to her handmaid and bent over the sleeping woman. "Tersa, get up."

"What . . . what is it?"

"Help me get dressed. I'm going to make a trip."

"A trip? You never said anything to me about a trip." Tersa got to her feet, rubbing her eyes and staring at her mistress wildly. "Where are you going?"

"I'm going to see my cousin Deborah."

"The master didn't say anything about it, nor your mother."

"They don't know, and I don't want you to tell them."

Tersa stared at Dinah in consternation. "You're running away?"

"No, I'm just going on a visit for a day or two. Now help me get dressed and get some things together."

"But what will I tell your mother?"

"Don't tell her anything until at least noon. Give me time to get away. It's not far over to where my uncle lives. I've been there before."

"But you were always with your brothers or your parents. You'll get lost."

"I won't get lost. Now, promise me you won't tell them until noon."

Tersa struggled but finally gave in. "All right, but they won't like it, and they'll probably thrash me."

"They won't do that. Just tell them I've gone for a short visit and that I'll be back in a few days."

Dinah quickly made the preparations. She had traveled to her uncle's camp several times. It was a long day's journey, but there were water holes along the way, and she would take a water bag. As soon as she was dressed and had her things in a sack, she made Tersa promise again not to tell her parents right away and then left. She had a donkey that was very gentle and that she had often ridden. She offered him some bites of bread she had brought as bait, and the donkey came quickly. She slipped the bridle on, swung herself on, then kicked her heels against his side. "Come on," she commanded. "We've got a long way to go."

She left the camp just as dawn was beginning to show a faint light in the east. She was thinking of what Demetrius had asked her: *"Do you care for me, Dinah?"* She knew as she left the camp and started her journey that she did care for Demetrius. What she did not know was whether the ghost that rose in her in such a frightening manner would ever be still enough that she could give herself freely and completely to a man.

CHAPTER
35

Rachel lifted her eyes from the robe she was mending and gazed out over the camp. There was a stillness on the air, for at high noon most of the people tried to take shelter from the midday heat. She could see the mountains far off, a jagged line against the horizon, and wondered what lay beyond them.

A slight breeze lifted a whirlwind of dust and drove it through the camp. She felt its coolness on her cheeks. Not for the first time, she thought of how much better it was to live in a tent than in a regular house of stone or wood. Some people thought of tents as being a poor sort of home, but she had known nothing else since she had been married to Jacob. The tent could be sealed tightly, more tightly than most stone houses, but even more important, the sides of it could be lifted to catch every breath of breeze.

She watched a group of children playing some sort of a game, chasing each other and screaming, and a smile touched her lips. She tried to remember when she had been such a child, but it all seemed so long ago. For her, life had started when Jacob had come to Paddan Aram. She still remembered with startling clarity how she had met him for the first time. He had been dirty, bedraggled, and fatigued, but even at that moment she had somehow known that they were meant to be together. She had never regretted for one moment marrying him. She was the Beloved Wife, and she knew that Leah resented this, but there was nothing she could do about it.

She glanced across the room to Jacob, who was studying the accounts on clay tablets. It never ceased to amaze her how he was able to keep track of his animals. There were so many! But when someone would ask him how many sheep he had, he would say without hesitation, "Three thousand, four hundred, and twenty-three as of yesterday." This was a miracle to Rachel, but it appeared to come naturally to him. She took great pride in knowing that the name of Israel the Hebrew was known all over the region. He was known as a fair man, one who watched over his kingdom with a sharp eye, yet never abused anyone under his authority.

She looked at his face again as he pored over the accounts and saw the seams and marks that time had left on him. When he had first come to Paddan Aram, he had been almost as fresh cheeked as she herself. But time and sun and wind and rain had weathered him. Yes, he was older, she thought, but also wiser, with an inner strength that had not been there when he had first arrived at her home.

Jacob looked up and caught her watching him. "Why are you looking at me like that?" He smiled. "Am I so handsome you can't take your eyes off me?"

"Oh yes—you always were."

He put down the accounts and came over to sit down beside her. Putting his arm around her, he leaned over and kissed her on the cheek. "You're probably planning something for me to do—buttering me up for something that I don't want to do."

"Why, I never do that."

Jacob laughed. "Yes you do. You do it all the time. What is it now?"

Rachel hesitated, and Jacob picked up on it right away. "Is there something wrong?" he asked with surprise. "You can tell me anything, you know."

"Anything?"

"Why, of course."

"Suppose I were planning to run off with another man."

"Who would you run off with?"

"Oh, that handsome tentmaker that lives in the village."

"You'd be sick of him in a week," Jacob said, grinning. "Come, now. What is it?"

"I have some news for you." Rachel looked up, and he saw that there was joy in her eyes. "We're going to have another baby, Jacob."

For a moment Jacob could not move. He had assumed Rachel was past the age of bearing children. He gaped at her, and she laughed at his expression. "You look like a sheep," she said. Reaching up, she put her hand on his cheek. "I hope it'll be a son."

"Another son who'll be ours," Jacob said. He hugged her, and she saw that he was delighted. "How long have you known?"

"Not too long. I wanted to be sure."

"Well, this is good news," Jacob said, beaming. He got up and paced back and forth. "I'll have to start getting ready. Raising a boy is an important matter."

"Well, he won't be here this week."

"I know, but I like to prepare for things."

Rachel was happy because Jacob was happy. They talked for a long time; then he got up and said, "I must go tell people."

"Wait a minute. There's one more thing."

"What is it?"

Rachel hesitated. "I should have told you this a long time ago, but I didn't. You remember when we left my father's house and he came after us. He was looking for his idols."

"Yes." Jacob's face turned into a grimace. "The old fool said I'd stolen them. As if I would steal such a thing!"

Rachel licked her lips and said, "I took them, Jacob."

"What!"

"I was afraid for him to keep them. They were so horrible. They were what caused me to be so ill—to lose my mind for a time. I took them so he wouldn't have them."

Jacob stared at Rachel. He had a clear memory of the encounter he'd had with Laban, especially when he had shouted, *"What would I want with your idols? Let him that has taken them die!"*

The words echoed in Jacob's mind, and he tried to keep the fear he felt from showing on his face. He had heard about curses all of his life—in fact, he had seen them work. He would have given everything he owned to take those words back! He saw that Rachel was watching him strangely, and he quickly shrugged his shoulders. "Well, that was a long time ago, and you were thinking of your father."

"You're not angry?"

"How could I be angry with you?" He came over, bent down, and kissed her, then said, "Don't let this worry you. Don't let *anything* worry you. You just bring our child into the world. That's your job for now." He would have left the tent, but at that moment Tersa came in. Jacob turned and asked, "What is it, Tersa?" He saw that she was agitated and immediately asked, "What's wrong?"

"It's the mistress. She's gone."

"Gone? Gone where?" Jacob demanded.

"She said she was going for a visit to her uncle's camp."

Jacob turned. "Did you know anything about this, Rachel?"

"Why, no. Not a thing. Tersa, when did she leave?"

"Very early this morning."

Jacob shook his head. "Did she take anybody with her?"

"No. I don't think so."

An alarm went off in Jacob's mind. "That's a long day's journey through wild country. She shouldn't have done it. I'm going after her."

"No," Rachel cried. "Zebulun and Issachar are in the camp. Send them."

"We'll all three go. We'll spread out in different directions. Don't worry, Rachel. We'll find her."

"Come back and tell me as soon as you do. I'll be worried."

"Yes, I will." Jacob left the tent and immediately went to look for Issachar and Zebulun. He found them working at the furnace with Demetrius. "Issachar, I want you and Zebulun to go out after Dinah. She left early this morning to visit Deborah."

"By herself?" Issachar asked, surprise washing across his face.

"Yes!"

Zebulun shook his head. "That's bad country, Father. What possessed her to go off by herself?"

"I have no idea. She's been doing so much better lately."

Issachar said, "We'd better go mounted and take water."

"Yes, and we'd better start now," Jacob said.

Demetrius said nothing, but as soon as the three had left, his mind worked rapidly. He did not know that country himself, but the words of Jacob indicated it was no place for a young woman to be out alone. Determined to help Dinah too, he went looking for Tersa and found her scraping a hide.

"What's this about Dinah going out by herself, Tersa?" He listened as the woman explained it and questioned her closely. "Did she go on foot?"

"No, she rode that donkey she likes so much."

Demetrius asked a few more questions, then walked away. He was accustomed to making quick decisions at sea, but this was different. His first impulse was to rush out into the desert and start calling her name, but he knew that would be useless. He paced back and forth for a time and then a plan began to form in his mind. He made his way through the camp out to where a small herd of cattle were being watched over by a man called Olam.

"Hello, Demetrius. What are you doing out here?"

Olam was a big man with a cheerful expression, but when he saw the look on Demetrius's face, he demanded, "What's the matter?"

"It's Dinah. She's gone off by herself to visit her cousin Deborah."

Olam whistled a low note and shook his head. "By herself, you say?"

"Yes. She went off alone. Olam, they say you're the best tracker in this part of the world. She rode that little donkey she's so fond of. I want you to come with me and see if you can track that thing. We've got to find her."

Olam looked at the cattle and shook his head. "We'll have to get someone to watch these cows."

"Beoni will do it. Come on. I want to get started."

The two got some food and water bags together, and Demetrius asked, "Should we ride or walk?"

"You can't track on top of a camel. You have to stay on the ground. It's faster that way in the long run."

"All right. Go as fast as you can. I'll be right with you."

The two men left camp, and Olam picked up the tracks of the donkey almost immediately. "She's headed right into that wild country, all right."

"Come on. We've got to hurry," Demetrius said, and the two men hurried on.

———

Dinah slumped down in the shadows of a rock. She had tied up the donkey, which she called Noisy because of the startling noises the animal made, especially when he was hungry or thirsty. She was filled with fear, for she had become totally lost and would be forced to spend the night in this wild land. With trembling hands, she picked up her water bag and drained the last few drops out onto her parched tongue. There were water holes in the desert, and the men knew where they were, but she had not seen one.

The sun was low in the sky, and night was coming on. She had expected to be at the camp of her uncle late in the day, but somehow she had taken a wrong turn. Now the heat seemed to press down upon her, even though it was growing cooler as night came on. She sat there and wanted more than anything else to break out in tears, but that would be useless. She felt stupid and wondered how she could have even thought of trying to take such a trip by herself.

"They'll be looking for me," she muttered and licked her lips, which were as dry as the dust beneath her feet. "They'll find me. I know they will."

She was so weary that she leaned her head back against the rock and, without meaning to, dozed off. She woke up with a start and saw that night had gathered all around her. The blackness was oppressive, pushing down upon her, squeezing her, and the shadows seemed to move. She heard small stirrings and rustlings around her, and finally she got up to go to Noisy. She stopped dead still when she saw that the animal was gone. "Noisy!" she cried out. "Noisy, where are you?"

Fear rushed through her veins. "I should have tied him more tightly," she whispered. "Maybe he'll come back." She called again and again, but the animal did not return. The immense distances stretching out before her were frightening. Overhead, the stars were hidden by clouds and there was no moon. Groping her way back to the rock, she sat down and placed her back against it. Thoughts crossed her mind like the fluttering of wild birds. She doubled up her legs, placed her arms across them, and buried her eyes on her forearms. She trembled at the night sounds, which came more clearly now. The howls of a wild dog seemed very close. She knew they traveled in packs and could pull down a full-grown cow, and a shiver went through her. She tried to make herself appear small, but she knew the wild dogs had a keen scent. She had heard the shepherds talking about how dogs could track down lambs or ewes that had wandered off from the herd simply by their sense of smell.

She began to weep as terror filled her at the brooding menace surrounding her in the darkness. Finally she began to pray. She had prayed before, or tried to, but it had never meant much to her. Now she called out, "O God of my father, Jacob, hear your handmaid, I beg you! Preserve me and save me from the wild animals. Bring someone to find me!"

The prayer brought her a measure of peace, but she longed for morning light.

She was startled at a noise and jumped up to stare wide-eyed in that direction. She had no weapon and knew that it would be useless to run. The sound came closer, and she could not tell what it was. Finally she cried out, "Go away! Leave me alone!"

Total silence followed, and she pressed her hands against her breast, calling out wildly for God's protection.

She saw a bulky shadow approach, and she feared it was a bear. But then she heard a voice calling her name! It was Demetrius, and he was suddenly there in front of her! She fell against him. Her mouth was so dry, and she was trembling so violently she could not speak. His arms were around her, and she held him tightly as if he would run away. She pressed her face into his chest and knew that tears were running down her cheeks.

"It's all right," Demetrius said, gently stroking her hair. "We're here now. You'll be all right." He lifted his voice and said, "Olam, let's get a fire going here."

"All right."

"Do you have any water?" she whispered.

"Of course." Demetrius took the water bag from his shoulder and held it. She opened it wide and allowed the stream to run into her mouth and spill onto her face and down her neck. It was the most delicious thing she had ever tasted.

"Not too much, now. Just little sips. Come, sit over here. Everything's all right."

Dinah would not let him go. She pulled him down next to her and clung to him while Olam got a fire started. He went off muttering, "Got to find more wood."

The amber-orange cone of light from the small fire broke the velvet density of the night. The two of them sat close together, and Dinah could not help holding tight to Demetrius's robe. She knew he would not run away, but she still pressed ever closer to him.

The familiar smell of woodsmoke calmed her, and she gradually stopped trembling.

"Why did you go off by yourself, Dinah?"

Dinah had been thinking about this, and now she had no hesitation about what she knew she must say. She turned to him and said, "You've been so good to me, Demetrius, and the other night you asked me if ... if I cared for you." She reached up and put her hand on his cheek. "You must know I care for you, Demetrius! I think I have for a long time." She hesitated and then went on, "But I was afraid of what ... of what ..."

He saw she could not finish and said, "That's all over. We'll never mention it again. I forbid you to do so."

"Yes, Demetrius," she said and there was gladness in her voice. "I never will."

"You don't have to be afraid, Dinah, because you'll always have me. You'll marry me, and we'll go to my home. My parents will love you. We'll have children, and we'll bring them back for your parents to see. All of this will happen."

Dinah listened as he spoke on, and a great warmth began to grow within her. She knew what it was now to love a man without selfishness, and she reached up and pulled his face around. When he lowered his head and kissed her, she knew somehow that she had passed into womanhood. She would never again be the selfish, thoughtless girl she had been. "I love you, Demetrius. I want to be your wife more than anything."

Demetrius held her tightly and after a time said, "There is one detail that will keep us from marrying."

"No, don't say that!" She hesitated and then said, "What is it?"

"I'm a slave. I belong to you."

"No," Dinah cried out, "I belong to *you*, Demetrius. I always will."

Olam stepped into the light of the small fire and looked at the two, his arms loaded down with chunks of wood and sticks. He began to pile them on the fire and noticed that the girl and her slave were clinging to each other, paying him no heed whatsoever. He built up the fire until it flickered upward, reaching for the sky, then shook his head. *What's all this about? Her father will give her a good caning, and that'll cure her.* He looked over at the two and saw that they were lost to him and to the world. Despite the incongruity of the situation, it gave him a good feeling, and he laughed deep in his chest as he piled more wood on the fire.

CHAPTER

36

A shadow fell across Bilhah, and she looked up from the stone she was using to grind grain. She smiled at once, saying, "Hello, Reuben. I thought you had gone with the other men to the flocks."

"I did, but I came back." Reuben knelt down beside her and, reaching over, took the round rock Bilhah held in her hand. "Let me do this for you."

"You don't have to do that."

Reuben smiled and pulled the grinding stone before him. His hands were so large that the stone looked very small. "Pour some of that grain in here," he said.

Bilhah reached into the large pot, scooped out some grain, and poured it onto the hollowed out stone. "This is woman's work," she said.

"I don't see why it should be." Reuben took the round rock in his hand and began to crush the grains. With a few turns of his strong hand, the grain was mashed into smaller fragments. "Is that fine enough?"

"No, not quite."

Reuben continued to grind while Bilhah sat beside him, scooping out the crushed flour and adding more whole grain.

"There ought to be a better way to grind grain than this," Reuben observed. "Somebody ought to invent something."

"I wish they would. It seems like I've spent half my life doing this kind of work." She held out her hands and looked at them ruefully. "It makes the hands so rough."

"Let me see." Reuben pulled Bilhah's hand toward himself. He rubbed the surface with his thumb and observed, "Not rough like mine. As a matter of fact, I've always thought you have pretty hands."

Bilhah grew flustered. She was aware of the strength of Reuben, who was by far the biggest and most powerful of Jacob's sons. She glanced around to see if anyone was watching, then whispered, "You shouldn't be holding my hand, Reuben."

Reuben gave her a startled look and then flushed. "I suppose I shouldn't." He released her hand and continued to grind the grain silently.

Bilhah attempted to make conversation. She had always known that Reuben was attracted to her, but she now saw something disturbing in his eyes. A faint flush came to her face, and she rebuked herself inwardly.

When the day's grinding was finished, Bilhah's eyes swept the camp and she said, "Oh my. Look at that."

Reuben's eyes followed to where she indicated across the camp, and he saw Dinah and Demetrius laughing together. He was holding her arm, and she was gazing up at him.

"They're having a good time, aren't they?"

"Yes. Dinah's so different."

"I wonder what happened? She hasn't been the same since Demetrius brought her back from that crazy trip she tried to make. She's like her old self again."

"She's in love," Bilhah said simply.

Reuben gave her an incredulous look. "In love with Demetrius?"

"Why, of course. Can't you see it? All you have to do is look at her."

"But he's a slave!"

Bilhah smiled and shook her head. "Do you think that matters when a woman loves a man?"

"Why, of course it does!"

Bilhah had already reached her own conclusions about Dinah and Demetrius. She felt a sudden pang for Reuben, for he was such a simple man. He had never married, although he was the oldest of the boys and had had many chances. She studied his blunt face as he sat watching Demetrius and Dinah. Finally she said, "When a woman loves a man, it doesn't matter what he is."

Reuben turned to face her. "I never thought of that," he said. An odd expression flickered in his eyes, and suddenly he seemed embarrassed. Getting to his feet, he said, "I'll carry that grain for you."

"Thank you for helping me. You're always so thoughtful, Reuben."

THE GATE OF HEAVEN ❦ 291

"Why, of course my parents will love you. Why wouldn't they?" Demetrius had been telling Dinah more about his home and family. Dinah had grown uncomfortable hearing about his parents and had said, "They might not like me."

The two had been standing on the outside edge of the camp when Demetrius had noticed Reuben helping Bilhah grind grain, and now he said, "That looks odd."

Dinah looked over and saw the big man kneeling awkwardly grinding grain. "He's always been partial to Bilhah."

"She's a sweet woman."

"Yes, she is." Dinah felt uncomfortable, however, with Reuben's obvious attraction to Bilhah. She was much too old for him, and she was their father's concubine. "I wish Reuben would marry. I'm surprised he hasn't already."

"I've wondered about that myself."

Dinah ran her hand over her hair and said, "If we marry and I go back with you to Minoa, will we live with your parents?"

"No. I want to build a house right on the seashore. Every morning we'll get up and there'll be the sea, all fresh and beautiful, and at night we can sit out and watch it. Sometimes the moon rises and forms a silver track in the ocean, very broad close to you, but it narrows down as it reaches toward the horizon. It looks like a silver road leading right to the moon."

"It sounds so wonderful," Dinah said wistfully. "But I'm not sure it will happen."

"Of course it will happen," Demetrius said. He wanted take her in his arms, but he dared not do that here. He was aware that they had an audience wherever they went. "I'm going to talk to your father today."

"Oh, Demetrius, I don't know what he will say! He's very partial to me."

"And you think he might not want you to marry a foreigner?"

"I don't know what he'll think." She looked up at him anxiously. "Maybe . . . maybe we should wait awhile."

"No, we won't," he said firmly. "I'm going to marry you, and we'll go to Minoa. We'll have children. I'll teach the boys to sail, and you can teach the girls to be as beautiful as you are."

Dinah laughed then and the fear left. Whatever this man set out to do, she knew he would do it. He wanted her and that was all that mattered.

Jacob looked up to see Demetrius walking purposefully toward him. He had come out, as he often did, in the late afternoon to look over the flocks. Sometimes he grew tired of the hubbub and the talk about the camp, and it was out here in the open spaces that he felt comfortable. The sun was already dropping behind the low-lying hills in the west.

"Master, could I speak with you?" Demetrius had come up and stood before Jacob. "I have something to say."

Jacob knew what was coming, but he let nothing show in his face. He had been so filled with joy and thanksgiving that Dinah had been rescued, and he had always felt that this young man had something in him most men of his age lacked. He had humor and could make people laugh, and he was an expert in working metals, which had been handy—but it was Demetrius's hunger for God that drew Jacob.

"Come. Let's go sit down. My legs are tired."

"As you say, master."

The two men sat down on an outcropping of rock, and for a while neither man spoke. Jacob surveyed the sky and studied the thin moon that already lay askew in the south. He lifted his head and savored the dry, sweet odor of the country. A highly perceptive man, he could feel the life in the earth, could hear small animal feet scampering through the dry grass, could see a vulture several miles away making beautiful circles in the sky. He said, "You know, Demetrius, vultures are ugly creatures when you're close to them, but when they're up there like that, there's nothing more beautiful."

Aware of Jacob's love of wild things, Demetrius said, "You're right. There's only one thing more beautiful I've seen, and that's the porpoises when they come up out of the water and make an arch."

"What's a porpoise?"

"A very large fishlike creature. They're not actually fish because they don't have gills. They breathe air. Sometimes they'll follow a ship, a dozen of them. They'll all come out of the water and arch over. They're very friendly. Once I was swimming and one came right up and got in front of me, his head out of the water. I could have sworn he wanted to speak to me."

Jacob listened, questioning Demetrius more about the creatures of the sea. Finally Demetrius took a deep breath, and Jacob knew that he would now speak of the real matter he had come about.

"I don't know how you'll take this, sir, but I must tell you that I love your daughter."

Jacob smiled. "I would be a blind man not to see what's been going on. She has blossomed. It was you who saved her from Shechem, and then you found her in the desert." He shook his head and said, "You know, I think she would have lost her mind after that terrible experience with that awful man if it hadn't been for you."

"I care for her a great deal."

"And she cares for you."

Demetrius blinked with surprise. "Yes, she does. We love each other." He hesitated and let the silence run on. Then he said firmly, "You probably will be shocked at this . . . and perhaps angry. But I want to marry Dinah."

Jacob remained totally still, and thoughts scampered through his head. He had prepared himself for this, however, and now he said, "You are not of our race, son."

"No, I'm a foreigner. I'm a slave here," he said. "But back in my own home, I'm not without honor." He went on to explain how his father was a counselor to the king and how he himself would inherit his father's possessions and even some of his prestige.

"It was a great tragedy when you were shipwrecked and sold into slavery, but I think the great God above brought you to us to save my daughter."

"I know I'm a slave—"

"No, you are not a slave. I grant you your freedom from this day onward."

Demetrius could not have been more relieved! He had already been making plans to run away, to steal Dinah if necessary, but this wonderful old man had seen into the heart of each of them. He felt tears gather in his eyes, and he whispered, "You are good, sir. Very good indeed."

"I am but a servant of the Most High, but I have a little more wisdom now than I had when I was a young man, as you are. God had to run me down and break me before I would really listen to Him."

"One thing I must tell you," Demetrius said. "I must know the God that you worship. I could never go back to worshiping an idol."

"That is good, my son," Jacob said eagerly. "He is the only God, and there is happiness only in serving Him."

"I must go back to my parents. They think I am dead. I've been gone so long, and sailors lead a perilous life. Do you think, sir, that the great God will hear me even if I'm not in this land?"

"He is the God of all lands. He is everywhere. You cannot find a place where He cannot come. If you were put into the deepest dungeon under the earth, God would be there."

Demetrius listened, as he always did when Jacob spoke of his God, and a resolution formed within him.

"When I get back to my home, I will tell others of the true God. They will be very shocked, I'm afraid."

"You must grow accustomed to that. The worshipers of the true God are few. The worshipers of idols are many. But when those stone and clay idols have gone back to dust, the Strong One, the Eternal One, will still be God."

The two men spoke for hours, and finally Jacob said, "I will bless you, my son, and I will pray for you."

"You will give me your daughter, then?"

"I can do nothing else, for I see the hand of God in all of this."

Dinah saw Jacob and Demetrius coming into the camp. They were moving straight toward her, and her heart was in her throat. She could not speak, but then she saw the expression on Demetrius's smiling face, and she flew to her father. He took her in his arms and said, "Well, as always, you will have your own way."

"Oh, Father, I love him so!"

"Then always do so. I have told him that he will have you with my good will."

Dinah lifted her head and saw that Demetrius was as happy as she was herself.

Jacob stepped back and said, "Tomorrow I will announce to everyone that you are a free man, Demetrius. I will also announce your betrothal, but first, daughter, I must tell your mother." He kissed Dinah and said, "A man has a daughter and learns to love her, but one day he must step aside, for she must find her own love. And I think you have found the one that God intended for you."

Jacob turned and moved quickly toward Leah's tent while Demetrius stepped forward and put his arms around Dinah. "Your father is a great man. Not many would do what he has just done."

"I know," Dinah whispered. She leaned back and said, "Now I will be your wife, and you will be my husband."

"Yes. And we will go to Minoa."

"When will we go?"

"Not until after the wedding. Then we will go."

———————

Rachel was not asleep when Jacob came to her tent. She was lying on her bed and said, "You're late tonight."

"Something has happened." Jacob came over and sat down beside her. He took her hand and studied her face. "You're not well."

"I'll be fine."

Jacob knew that this was her way of saying that she was having considerable pain. He hesitated, but finally said, "I have just agreed to give Dinah to Demetrius as his wife." He waited for her to speak but saw that her face, tired and pale as it was, broke into a smile. "You're not surprised!" he exclaimed.

"No—nor will anyone else be too surprised."

"But it's never happened before, that one of our people will give a daughter to a foreigner."

"Demetrius is different. He will be one of us. You've always told me how hungry he is for God."

"Yes, he is, and he's agreed to be circumcised. And I've freed him this night. He's no longer a slave. You know, back in his own country, he's quite an important person."

Rachel lay there listening. She had had a hard pregnancy and knew that she was really too old to be having this child. She listened as Jacob told her more of the details about Demetrius and Dinah, and then finally he began to speak of the child that was to come.

"He will be a fine boy just like his brother."

"Yes. I pray God that he will be." Rachel suddenly shuddered with pain. She closed her eyes and whispered, "I'm very tired, Jacob."

Jacob sat there holding her hand. Ever since she had told him about her father's gods, he could not stop thinking about the curse he had put on the one who had stolen them. He had begged God to take those words away and remove the curse, but he was not sure God would do such a thing. Now as he held Rachel's hand, he felt a dark heaviness in his spirit. Up till now, he had been only happy about the child to come, for the child would be Rachel's, but there was a fear growing in him that he could not ignore.

———————

Jacob's face looked drawn, and Rachel, who had risen late, saw that he was troubled. "What is it, husband?" she asked. "Are you troubled about Dinah and Demetrius?"

"No. I'm happy about that." Turning to her, Jacob said quietly, "The Lord came to me last night while you were asleep."

Rachel grew very still. "What did He say?" She could tell that Jacob was troubled, and as always, she knew he would obey whatever God commanded.

"He said we must leave this place and go up to Bethel. He told me I must make an altar to God in that place."

"Does He mean for you to go alone?" Rachel was disturbed because she was far along in her pregnancy and hated for him to leave her.

"No. He told me that we must move there and make that our home."

Rachel's heart sank. She was sickly and weak, and traveling would be an agony for her. She let none of this show in her face, however, saying only, "Then we must go."

"It will be hard on you. Perhaps we'd better wait."

Rachel shook her head. "No. When the Lord speaks, we must obey. You must tell the people this morning."

———————

Except for the few who were left to watch over the flocks, all of Jacob's people had been gathered together. He waited until they grew quiet, noting the curiosity on their faces. His sons were ranked before him, but he had already told them of his decision. There had been little argument, except from Simeon, who thought it best to stay in this place. Other than that, the other sons agreed.

"We will be leaving this place," Jacob announced. His voice at first was weak, but it grew stronger as he went on. "The Lord God has appeared to me and told me that we must move back close to my old homeland in Bethel." He waited until the mutterings and whisperings had ceased. He saw surprise in faces, but no one seemed utterly disturbed. His next words, however, did bring a stronger reaction.

"Some of you are harboring strange gods. I command you this day to bring all of those to me. Anyone who will not do so will be put out of the family, out of the camp. The bondservants will be sold." He saw fear, surprise, and resentment among different faces, but he was firm.

"We have a hard journey, and the true God must be obeyed. I will wait right here. Make your decision now. Either bring your idols and your false gods to me, or take the consequences."

Judah, who was standing next to Joseph, leaned over and whispered, "I've never seen him so immovable."

Joseph said, "He is doing the right thing, Judah."

"I believe he is, but some resent it."

———————

Jacob put the last bit of dirt over the cavity he had dug. He stood looking down and said aloud with grim satisfaction, "There. That should have been done a long time ago."

The sun was falling in the west, and dark would be coming soon, but Jacob had felt an urgency to gather up all the false gods. When he had done so, Reuben loaded them onto a donkey. Jacob mounted the donkey and made his way out of the camp. Everyone stood silently watching him, but he said nothing.

He traveled a long distance from the camp and finally stopped beside an oak. He labored hard to dig a hole with the implements he had brought, dumped in all the idols, then covered them up.

He looked skyward and said, "O God, I have obeyed your voice. And now, Lord, we must leave this place as you have said. I pray you will go with us and before us and protect us." He prayed for a long time and waited for the voice of God, but it did not come. Quickly he mounted the donkey and rode back. *Now we will obey the voice of the Lord*, he thought, *and all will be well.*

C H A P T E R
37

Of all the preparations Jacob made for going to Bethel, he spent the most time working on the wagon that would carry Rachel. He and Demetrius tried to make it as comfortable for her as possible. On the floor of the back was the softest bed they could possibly contrive. It consisted of a pad of straw covered by a softer pad of feathers that had been saved over the past years. Demetrius had even designed a set of steps which Rachel could mount easily from the back.

The day had come to leave, and Jacob was leading Rachel to the steps. He walked up them with her and helped her to lie down. "We will go very slowly," he said. "The best driver will be driving this cart. He will avoid the bumps as much as possible."

"This is beautiful, Jacob. It's like you to be so thoughtful."

Jacob leaned over and kissed her. "All will be well," he said. "We will stop early, and when we get to the place where God is sending us, you will have this child."

Rachel, he saw, was deathly ill and in pain, but she tried to smile. He kissed her again and said, "Shall I ride beside you for a time?"

"No. You need to be at the head of the people. They need to see you, husband. I will be all right."

Jacob kissed her yet again and said, "We will be joyous with this child, my beloved."

"Yes," Rachel whispered, and it took all of her strength. "He will be the child we have dreamed of along with Joseph."

———————

Dinah chewed on her lower lip, a sure sign that she was nervous. Turning to Demetrius, who was sitting beside the fire, she said, "I'm worried about Rachel."

"So am I." Demetrius picked up a stick, held it in the flame until it caught, and then held it up before his eyes. He watched it burn for a time and then tossed it onto the fire. "I wish we could have waited until she had the child."

"That's what Father wanted to do, but she insisted."

"It's been a hard trip on everybody, but most of all on Rachel."

Indeed, the trip had been hard. They had passed through some dry, arid land, and water had been hard to find. The heat had been terrible, and the herders had been hard put to find enough water to keep the animals alive. They had lost several of them to wild dogs, despite their care.

Demetrius looked up at the stars that glittered above them. "Do you remember the star lesson?"

"Yes. There's the Little Cup and the Big Cup, and right there is the star that never changes."

"That's right. I will teach you many more when we get to my home."

"It seems impossible for us to be going there."

"It's not. We will be there very soon." He took her hand, and kissed it. "But all things seem slow to lovers."

She reached out and put her hand against his cheek. She could not speak, so full was her heart. She had been this way since they had become engaged, and she said, "I hope I always love you as much as I do now."

"Oh, much more!" He smiled and then took her hand and kissed it again.

———————

Jacob stood before the altar he had built. He was exhausted, but now the trip was over. Everything about it had been hard. Rachel's condition had deteriorated so that Jacob walked in fear.

Now he stood before the altar he had built, and his mind went back to the times when God had spoken to him. This was the same country where God had met him and where he had seen the gate of heaven with angels going up and coming down the stairway. Of all the visits of the Most High, that had been the clearest, when God had been so real. But then during the many years that followed he'd had to struggle to keep himself reminded of the mighty promises he had received.

Jacob stepped forward and poured water over the altar and cried aloud,

"O God, you are my God, and I love you!"

He prayed for a time, then took out a flagon of oil he had brought. As he poured it over the altar, the sun caught the oil and made it look like molten fire. Jacob stepped back and knelt down, putting his face on the ground. "You have kept your promise, O God. I left this land with nothing but a scrap in my hand, but I had your promise to multiply your blessings. And now, Lord, you have been faithful, and I bow before you and ask you for another blessing."

As Jacob knelt there, God spoke to him in a simple, quiet way. He repeated the promise and reminded Jacob that his name was Israel and that out of him a nation would be born and kings would come forth from his loins. He reminded him that the very land that he gave to Abraham and Isaac would be his and his children's.

Finally Jacob arose, and he felt a great joy. As he made his way back to the camp, his mind went forward, and he had something like a dream, although his eyes were wide open. He saw a teeming multitude of people, all his descendants, worshiping the God of Bethel. The God of all the earth—the Strong God. It was more than his mind could take in, that from him all peoples of the earth would be blessed, and as he rode along, he was humbled by the vision he had seen and by the promises of God.

———————

For Rachel every day seemed interminable. They had reached the land of Bethel and had stopped at a place called Ephrath. Things had gone so hard with her, but now she knew her hour had come. She called out, and Jacob was by her side instantly. "The pains are beginning," she panted. "The child is coming."

Jacob instantly began to shout for the midwives.

They came at once, along with Leah and his concubines, and he was thrust out, as was customary, for men were not welcome during a woman's travail. They had been careful to do their best for Rachel during the last few days. They had given her terrible-tasting medicines with a great deal of oil that made her ill. They included swine's fat, fish, herbs, and un-mentionable things. Each night an offering was placed at her head—although they did not mention this to Jacob. They believed that the greedy demons might take it and leave her alone. The bed she lay on was in the center of the tent, and when she began to cry aloud, unable to contain herself, the midwives smeared the sides of the bed with the blood of a freshly slain lamb.

Outside the tent Jacob paced frantically to and fro. Leah, Bilhah, and Zilpah came and went, and each time one came out Jacob would frantically ask her, "How is she?" seeking some encouraging words.

Bilhah wanted to give encouragement, but when Jacob grabbed her and demanded to know how Rachel was, she shook her head. "She's very weak."

Jacob could not be still. He was short-tempered, and even Dinah, who tried to comfort him, knew there was nothing anyone could say to him.

"She can't die. She mustn't die." Jacob groaned this at first inwardly but finally began crying aloud and cared not that others heard it.

His cries mingled with the cries of Rachel. His were strong and agonized, while hers grew more and more feeble.

The anguish was more terrible than anything Rachel had known. Joseph's birth had been hard but nothing like this! She bit her teeth together, but her fortitude did not help her. The pangs came now in great waves, and she knew that this time there would be no joy for her in the birth of this child.

She looked up at Leah, who stood upright and then at the midwives, and she begged for Jacob.

The midwife said, "It's not fitting that a man should come into the tent during the birth."

Rachel pleaded, but the tradition was too strong.

"It's been going on for two days," Jacob whispered. "O God, why do you not have mercy?"

Jacob had not slept or eaten, nor had many others in the camp. They all knew of the terrible birth pangs, and the whispers were, "She is too old to be having a child."

Finally the tent fell silent, and as Jacob became conscious of the change, he saw Bilhah come out. She approached him, her face pale and wet with perspiration.

"The child has come," she said. "It is a son."

"And Rachel?" Jacob demanded. He searched her face for an answer and saw only that which he feared.

"She yet lives. Go quickly," Bilhah whispered.

Jacob entered the tent. Leah was cleaning the child, but Jacob paid the newborn no heed. He went straight to Rachel and fell down beside her. Her eyes were closed, and her mouth was open. His heart suddenly contracted, and then he saw her chest move slightly.

"Rachel," he groaned. "Rachel, my Beloved Wife . . ."

Rachel slowly opened her eyes, and her lips moved, but Jacob could not hear her. He stroked her brow and begged her to speak to him, and then Leah brought the child and put him beside Rachel.

Rachel's eyes were only half open, and Jacob knew that the end was near. He saw her look at the child and then she turned back to him. "He is . . . our son."

"Yes," Jacob groaned. He looked at the infant briefly but then turned back at once to Rachel.

"Call his name . . . Ben-Oni."

The words were so faint that Jacob thought he had misunderstood. Ben-Oni meant "son of my trouble."

"Yes, my Beloved Wife. His name shall be Benjamin, 'son of my right hand.'"

Rachel arched her body then and reached out. She touched his face, and for one moment her eyes opened wide.

"I've always loved you," she said, and her words were clear.

"And I have loved you, my Beloved Wife," Jacob said, weeping.

And then Rachel's eyes slowly closed, but she smiled as she left Jacob alone with his son.

———

"I think my father . . . I think he cannot live," Dinah whispered.

Demetrius stood beside Dinah. They were watching Jacob, who stood over the grave in which he had put his Beloved Wife.

"I never saw a man suffer so. How he loved her," Demetrius said quietly.

Dinah reached out and took Demetrius's hand and said, "He will never be the same again."

"I think you are right."

"He was crippled in his hip after he wrestled with God, or the angel, but this hurt is in his heart. He limps physically now, but his heart will never heal."

The two stood there clinging to each other as the sun went down, and Jacob finally knelt down and pressed himself against the earth, weeping and crying out, "Oh, Rachel . . . my Rachel!"

CHAPTER

38

"Another week and you will be my wife!" Demetrius exclaimed, picking up Dinah and swinging her around. "Then I will have you exactly where I want you!" He put her down, kissed her, and then smiled. "Back in my homeland wives know how to treat their husbands."

Dinah's eyes were dancing. It had been six months since the death of Rachel, and during that time she had given herself to comforting her father as best as she could. Now that she was to be a bride, however, she felt that her joy might overflow.

"And pray, how do wives behave in Minoa?"

"Well, they do everything for their husbands to make them comfortable," Demetrius said with a stern face, but the twinkle in his eyes belied his seriousness. "They cook them all the best food and see that they are fed before they eat a bite. They bathe them so that they are not put to the trouble of it, wash their hair, and make sure that their every wish is granted."

"I can hardly wait!" Dinah exclaimed. Then she burst out laughing. "I hope you don't expect me to do that. And I don't believe women in Minoa do that either."

"Oh, I assure you. Our women know how to treat their men."

The two were walking along in a grove of trees, and the sun filtered down through it. The breeze was cooling, and they spoke of foolish things as lovers will.

"I worry about Father," Dinah said, and for a moment her face lost its gaiety. She shook her head and added, "I don't think he's smiled since Rachel died."

"Only for you a few times."

"I hate to go off and leave him."

Demetrius stopped and turned her around. "Would you rather stay here, my dear?"

"No. We must go to your home. Your parents are grieving. We must let them know that their son is alive."

"We will come back. I promise you."

Dinah drew his head down and kissed him. Then she took his hand and they continued their walk.

Finally Demetrius said with some hesitation, "Has your father said anything to you about—" He broke off and did not seem inclined to continue.

Dinah had learned to know this man very well. "You mean about Bilhah and Reuben?"

"Yes. It must have been terrible for him."

Dinah could not speak for a moment. She had always loved Reuben, who had been kind to her since she was a child. She knew he was a simple man but had not thought he was capable of such a thing as sleeping with his father's concubine. They had been seen, and the matter was reported to Jacob. Of course, a thing like that would be gossiped about by everyone.

"Father only spoke of it one time, but his heart was broken."

"What did he say, Dinah?"

"He said that Reuben had forfeited his birthright."

Demetrius considered this, then shook his head. "That takes out your oldest three brothers. He's always said that Simeon and Levi could never get the birthright because of their murderous acts at Shechem."

Suddenly Demetrius regretted his words. He had promised never to mention Shechem again, but the words had just slipped out. However, when he turned he saw that Dinah had not reacted.

"Poor Reuben! I don't think he realized what he was doing. He's always had an affection for Bilhah, and it just got out of hand."

"Do you think your father meant it?"

"Yes. He always means what he says."

"Reuben, Simeon, and Levi—that leaves Judah as the next in line for the leadership of the family."

"I think it will have to be that way."

The two walked on silently, thinking about what had happened between Jacob's oldest son and Bilhah.

"I can't understand it," Demetrius said finally. "I thought better of Bilhah."

"She's a very simple woman and very lonely. My father's had nothing to do with her since the birth of her sons. That's a long time for a woman to go without a man."

"It came at a terrible time. Jacob lost Rachel—which almost destroyed him. In a sense he's losing his only daughter too. Of course, he's not really losing her, but it must seem so. And now his firstborn, in a sense, lost. Poor Jacob!"

Dinah did not answer for a few moments. She finally turned and said, "We mustn't think of these things. In a week we'll be married. Then we'll be going to your home."

"Yes," Demetrius said. "We'll do what we can to cheer your father in his great grief."

The two turned and headed back toward the camp. Dinah grew more cheerful, and he took her hand as they talked about the upcoming wedding.

The bridal feast took place in the full moon of summer, and Jacob spared no expense. He had invited musicians from all over the country to play and a troop to dance. He had given commands to kill two bullocks and as many sheep as necessary to feed the guests. He had furnished Dinah with a beautiful wardrobe, and in truth the activities of the wedding seemed to have cheered him considerably. He was seen to smile and even to laugh now and then.

The time had come, and Dinah had donned her wedding garment. It was a beautiful garment indeed, the work of many hands and long labor. It was made of the palest blue, woven thin and fine as a breath of air. Over it was an outer gown with brilliant, glittering colors in gold and silver. The colors mingled white, purple, rose, and olive, and even black and white, all in beautifully done designs. Outside the tent the people were rejoicing and laughing as they had been for several days. They had eaten and drunk. The musicians had played on drums, harps, and cymbals, and now Dinah waited. Leah was beside her, fussing over her gown, and then Zilpah stepped inside and smiled as she spoke. "It's time."

Leah said, "Come, daughter, and greet your husband."

Dinah rose and walked out of the tent. She saw her father standing there beside Demetrius, who was clothed in a pure white robe. His hair was carefully oiled and hung down his back, and his eyes seemed to devour her.

Dinah walked slowly toward the pair, and then when she stood before them, Jacob reached out and touched both their foreheads. Then he stepped between them and laid his hands upon them. "Embrace each other," he said, "for you must be man and wife."

This was only the beginning of the ceremonies, which were intricate and ornate. There were young boys with torches who came to sing, and women who performed a dance that was formal yet sensual.

Demetrius spoke his vows to Dinah, and she ardently gave him an answer.

Finally it was all done, and Jacob led the procession toward the wedding tent. Dinah's hand was on the arm of Demetrius, and when her father pulled back the flap of the tent, she stepped inside, and Demetrius followed her.

Dinah and Demetrius stood quietly listening to the songs, and then the voices began to fade as the wedding party moved away.

Demetrius looked around the tent, for neither of them had seen the interior. Leah and Zilpah had decorated it, and now he said, "It's a beautiful place." The two moved over the thin carpet that had been put on the floor, and the bed was dressed with coverlets of pure silk.

Dinah could not speak, for her throat was full. Demetrius came to her then and lifted the veil, dropping it on the floor. He cupped her face in his hands and said simply, "I am your husband, and I love you dearly."

These were words that Dinah needed to hear. She felt inadequate and a little frightened, for though she had heard talk, she did not know how to be a bride. Still, she put her hands on his shoulders and looked up at him, and diamonds were in her eyes. "I love you and pray that I will prove a good wife."

———

Dinah awoke with a start. She was lying on her side, and when she opened her eyes, there was Demetrius's face framed in her vision. She put out her hands for a moment, frightened at having a man in her bed, but then memory came swarming back.

Demetrius laughed quietly and reached out and caught her hands. His lips turned upward in a smile as he said, "Have you forgotten who I am already?"

The two laughed and giggled and talked foolishly and then finally she said, "When will we leave for Minoa?"

"In two weeks," Demetrius said. He winked and added, "I think you'll have me trained to be an obedient husband by then."

"Don't be foolish! How will we get there?"

"I expect we'd better go by ship. It would be a long swim for us."

She laughed again and finally said quietly, "I love you, husband, and I always will."

Demetrius kissed her. "You are a fine wife, and I love you dearly. And I promise to bring you back to this place when we have our first son."

CHAPTER
39

"We've got to do something about Joseph," Simeon said bitterly. He looked around at his brothers. They had met secretly out beyond the camp, and there was a furtive expression across the faces of most of them. "He's nothing but a talebearer and it's got to stop!"

Judah stared at Simeon and said loudly, "If you'd stay out of taverns and away from those Hittite prostitutes, you wouldn't have to worry so much."

"It's none of your business what I do and certainly none of Joseph's!"

"Well, you're the one who called this meeting, and if you ask me, I think you're the one who needs correction, not Joseph."

Simeon had a violent temper and had always refused advice or counsel from anyone. Now he advanced toward Judah, his fists clenched and his eyes blazing. "You can't talk to me like that, Judah! I'm your older brother."

"That doesn't make you right!"

"If you can't do any better than that, then get out of here!" Simeon yelled.

Gad, the oldest son of Zilpah, stepped up. He had dark hair and brown eyes, and he also had a pronounced stutter. He could make anything with his hands but he struggled with words. "Simeon, d-d-d-don't——" But as he labored to get the words out, Naphtali, Bilhah's younger son, came to his aid, as he usually did. Naphtali had a badly scarred face. A fishhook-shaped scar—from a dog bite years ago—twisted his mouth to one side. He was a small, agile, and quick-witted man. "He's trying to say that you're wrong, Judah, and Simeon is right."

Gad tugged at Naphtali. "N-nooo! Judah r-r-right."

The argument raged, and finally Dan said bitterly, "Maybe I'll just give Joseph a good thrashing."

"You won't do that," Naphtali said. He turned then and said, "Reuben, you've got to talk to our father. You're the oldest."

Reuben, who towered by a head above all of his brothers, felt Naphtali's eyes upon him, but he could not speak. He lowered his head, turned around, and walked off almost blindly.

"There's no sense in talking to Reuben," Levi said impatiently. "Ever since he slept with Bilhah, our father's barely spoken to him. What a fool he was—and her too!"

The debate became more heated, and Judah tried for a time to calm his brothers down, some of whom were angry with Joseph. He finally shook his head and walked off, unable to bear the argument anymore.

———————

Jacob was holding Benjamin in his lap. He was smiling, and as Judah entered the tent, he said, "This is a fine boy, Judah. Don't you agree?"

Judah's face was troubled. He came over and put his hand on the baby's head. "He is fine."

"There's something about a baby," Jacob said quietly, "that makes a man think. What will he be when he grows older? What kind of a man will he make?" He shook his head. "I wish I could be sure he'd be as sweet tempered as his mother was."

"He probably will be. He had two good parents," Judah said, smiling. He stood there for a while, and finally Jacob looked up and saw that his son was troubled.

"Is something wrong, Judah?"

Judah hesitated. "I hate to bring this up, but it's something you really ought to know." He paused, trying to find a way to put his words together, and finally said, "Some of your sons are jealous of the attention you pay to Joseph and now to Benjamin."

Jacob looked at Judah. He knew his fourth son was a proud man and emotional, quick to laugh or to weep. He also resembled Jacob greatly, with his chestnut hair, and had Jacob's good singing voice. He was a man with a quick conscience, which was more than Jacob could say for some of his other sons.

"And what about you, my son? Do you resent me?"

"Of course not! It's only natural your heart would go out toward a younger son."

Jacob passed his hand over the soft, silky hair of Benjamin and studied his face. Finally he collected his thoughts and said, "You have been a faithful son, but I am troubled."

"About what?"

"I had always thought that the blessing and the birthright would go to the firstborn, to Reuben, but I cannot do that now that he has defiled my bed."

"Father, he's such a simple man. Can't you forgive him?"

"Of course I can forgive him . . . and I still love him. But he has denied himself the birthright. So have Levi and Simeon. Their murderous attack on Shechem . . ." He shook his head and said, "I cannot overlook that."

Judah nodded but said nothing.

Finally Jacob looked at Judah and said, "So Reuben, Simeon, and Levi cannot have the birthright. That leaves you, Judah."

Judah was startled. "No, that can't be! My older brothers would resent it."

"They have no right to resent anything. Besides, I strongly feel this is the way God would have it."

Judah was disturbed by his father's words. He was not an ambitious man and had been quite content for Reuben to receive the blessing. He argued this for a time with Jacob but soon saw that his efforts were useless. Finally he said, "I must say something else, Father."

"Speak, my son."

"It's about Joseph. I love my younger brother, but the truth is, he is a little self-righteous. And we all know that he brings tales of any wrongdoing to you."

"But never about you, my son," Jacob said quickly.

"That doesn't matter. The others resent him, and it's not a good trait. You must talk with him about this, Father."

"All right. I will speak with him."

———

Joseph had been summoned to his father's tent, and now he sat listening as Jacob spoke about various things. Joseph knew, however, that his father was holding something back and it troubled him. He finally asked, "What is it, Father? You can speak straight out. Have I displeased you?"

Jacob lifted his head and met Joseph's eyes. He had always loved this son the best, and now he freely admitted that. "You have always been my favorite, Joseph. The son of the Beloved Wife. Perhaps this was wrong, but I have not been able to help it. And you have known it also, have you not?"

Joseph swallowed hard. "Yes, you always favored me . . . and Dinah."

"Well, Dinah is a girl, and she's now gone with her husband. But you will always be here and be a part of the family." Jacob hesitated, then said, "I see your mother in you so clearly." Tears came to his eyes and rolled unchecked down his cheeks. "I cannot even speak her name without weeping."

"I loved her too, Father."

"We must always honor her, and I will go to my grave with loneliness, for no woman could take her place."

Joseph watched as his father struggled to regain his composure, and finally Jacob said, "I must give you one warning, Joseph. You must no longer bring me tales of your brothers' wrongdoing."

Joseph dropped his head and did not argue. "Yes, Father," he said.

"You're a good boy in all except that. But you must make peace with your brothers. You must be one, all of you. Nothing except God himself is stronger than the family. Will you try to do this, Joseph?"

And Joseph, beloved son of Rachel, lifted his eyes to his father. "Yes," he whispered, "I will try."

In times of crisis Jacob had learned to go away from people and seek God alone. This meant going out into the wilderness, and now he was surrounded by nothing but the empty land before him and the endless space above. The sun was high in the sky, and all morning he had been praying. Judah's warning had disturbed him, and he had come out to see if God might give him some guidance.

Now as he waited and listened for God's voice, it was an intense struggle not to think of Rachel. He had to deliberately turn his mind away and direct his prayers to his sons. They were the ones who needed his help now.

After several hours he grew weary and was ready to leave. But at that very instant he saw a shimmering column of light, and he fell on his face, knowing that he was in the presence of God himself. He lay there for a time saying nothing. It was enough simply to be in the presence of his Creator.

Finally Jacob began to pray, "O God, please give me guidance! My sons need you as their God, and I need to know who will receive the medallion that I received from my grandfather Abraham. Which one of my sons will pass on the line from which the Redeemer will come?"

The voice came, and it was warm and filled with love. *"I chose your grandfather when he was an idolater, and I promised him that his seed would be as the sands of the sea. I renewed the promise to your father, Isaac, and now I renew it to you. From one of your sons will come the stream that will be as countless as the stars of the sky."*

Jacob could not speak, but he simply waited.

"You know that the world is evil, but I plan to renew it. One will come who will cleanse all sins. He will destroy evil and redeem a chosen people to rule with him forever."

The voice of the Lord went on for some time, and Jacob knew that he was being permitted a glimpse of the future such as no man had ever seen. When it became quiet, he meekly asked, "Is it Joseph to whom I should give the medallion?"

Jacob waited, longing to hear God agree, for he loved this son of his. But God did not answer, and a great sadness came to Jacob. He continued to bow before the light and to wait, not understanding why God did not speak. But finally the voice came.

"I am the God of Gods, Jacob. I promised Adam and Eve that I would send the Redeemer. I promised Noah and Abraham and your own father. Believe in me, Israel my prince, and obey my voice. When the time comes, I will reveal which of your sons will bear the medallion."

The voice faded, and Jacob slowly got to his feet. He turned from the place and stumbled away uncertainly. As he made his way homeward, the faces of his sons came into his mind clearly.

"One of my sons will be chosen of God, and the Redeemer will come through him."

Reaching up, Jacob pulled the medallion by the cord that held it under his clothing. He stopped and stared at it. He did not understand the significance of the lion on one side or the lamb on the reverse, but suddenly a warmth came over him. He had no knowledge of the future except that which God had given him. He knew from God's promises that from his loins would come multitudes. He did not know who would be next in the line that would bring forth the Redeemer, but he stopped and stood and lifted his arms, with tears running down his cheeks, and he cried out with a voice of triumph, "God does all things well!"

EPILOGUE

Metus picked at his food and finally shoved the plate away. He was deep in thought, his brow furrowed.

"Aren't you hungry, Metus?"

Looking over to his wife, Theodora, Metus shook his head. "I don't have much appetite. Nothing's wrong with the food. It's me."

The two sat there silently. The servants moved back and forth, but there was little to be done. Finally Metus said, "What did you do all day, wife?"

"Just the usual things."

"You went to see Thea, didn't you?"

"Yes, I did."

"Are the children all right?"

Theodora nodded. "Yes. They're fine." She twisted her hands nervously and said, "They're all we have now that our boys are gone, Metus. I want us to spend more time with them. They're good children."

"You're right about that. I think that tomorrow—" He broke off suddenly as his steward entered. "What is it, Phillip?"

"Someone to see you, sir."

"Who is it?"

"I'm afraid I don't know, sir, but then I don't know many of your acquaintances."

Phillip was a new servant, and Metus looked toward Theodora. "Are you expecting visitors?"

"Why, no. I can't imagine who it would be."

"Send him in, Phillip."

"Yes, sir, at once."

Metus said irritably, "It's impolite to call without an invitation at this time of the night."

"Perhaps it might be—" But Theodora never finished her sentence, for at that instant a figure appeared in the doorway, and Theodora uttered a sharp cry and jumped to her feet. "Demetrius!"

Metus jumped up as well and turned pale. He could not speak for a moment, and then when his son came forward, he cried out, "My son, you're back from the dead!"

Demetrius opened his arms, and his mother threw herself into his embrace. His father was behind him, his arm around his shoulders, patting him. Demetrius's eyes were misty, and he could not speak, his throat was so tight.

"Here, Mother, sit down." He moved over to the chair, and when his mother sat down, he knelt beside her. She kept running her hand over his face, and she was weeping.

"I . . . I can't believe it," she whispered brokenly. "I just can't believe it."

Metus cleared his throat and turned away for a moment to wipe his eyes, and then he turned back and said, "Well, this is a miracle. I should be angry—but somehow I'm not."

Demetrius kissed his mother's hand but did not rise from his knees. He turned, however, to face his father. "I'm sorry, Father. I wanted to send you news that I was alive and returning finally, but after years of captivity, I knew no one who could do it. Forgive me for giving you such a shock."

"Where have you been, Demetrius?" His mother's voice was still shaky.

"Yes, sit down, boy, and tell us what has happened. We gave you up for dead a long time ago . . . although, in truth, your mother never gave up hope."

"No, I didn't, and now you're home again," Theodora said. She was wiping her tears away, but her eyes were fastened on her son. "Where have you been all this time?"

The two sat spellbound as Demetrius told the story of his shipwreck and of being captured by slavers and then sold.

"I'll make a special offering to the gods," Metus said. "Such an offering as they've never had."

Demetrius smiled but shook his head. "I must tell you one thing. I've become very fond of the one who bought me."

Metus stared at him. "Fond of the villain that owned you? I can't believe it!"

"Was he cruel to you?" Theodora asked, compassion in her voice.

"Early on I was treated somewhat cruelly, but recently my owner has been very kind to me. As a matter of fact, I thought it might be best if you were to meet the one who owns me."

"Owns you!" Metus gasped. "But . . . you must have escaped!"

"Not quite, Father. Would you like to meet my owner?"

"The scoundrel! I'll give him a lashing is what I'll do!" His eyes were burning. "I didn't bring my son up to be a slave."

"Now?" Demetrius asked, his eyes dancing.

"He's outside? Bring the rascal in!"

Demetrius rose at once and left, and Theodora went to her husband. "Be calm, Metus. The important thing is our son is alive and he's home."

"Own my son!" Metus said. He had an aristocratic streak in him, and the thought of Demetrius being owned by a wicked slave owner was more than he could take. "No doubt he humiliated our boy. Well, I'll take care of that!"

The two stood staring at the door, and then Demetrius entered. Both of them were struck dumb at the sight of the beautiful young woman by his side. Her hand was on his arm, and her glossy auburn hair was done up in an unusual way. She was shapely and dressed in a beautiful gown, and her eyes were lustrous, and yet her lips were trembling as if she were afraid.

"This is my former owner, Dinah, daughter of Israel. Dinah, this is my father, Metus, and my mother, Theodora."

"Why, you young fool! What do you mean by all this?" Metus cried out. He could not take his eyes off the young woman, who seemed very timid.

"Be quiet, Metus," Theodora said. She went at once to Dinah and put out her hand. Dinah grasped it instantly, and Theodora said, "Welcome to our home, Dinah, daughter of Israel."

"What's this nonsense about your owning my son?" Metus demanded, though in a softer tone.

Dinah was overwhelmed by the opulence of the home that Demetrius had brought her to. She had fallen more in love with her husband on the long sea voyage, but now to meet his parents was overwhelming. "It's true enough. I did own him, but now——"

"But now I own *her*."

"What do you mean you own her?" Metus demanded.

"I mean she's your daughter-in-law now, and I hope you'll love her as I do."

"Your wife!" Theodora exclaimed. And then she went forward at once and kissed Dinah on the cheek. "Welcome to the family, daughter."

Metus, not to be outdone, blustered as he came forward, "I'm afraid you'll have to give your father-in-law a kiss, my dear." He took the kiss from Dinah, then said, "Now, we've got to hear all about this."

"Come. There's food on the table. You must be starved," Theodora offered.

"One more thing," Demetrius said. He could not contain his smile, and his eyes were lit up. He looked strong and handsome as he stood before them, holding his bride. "Dinah has a gift for you."

"A gift? Why, how sweet," Theodora said. "What is it?"

Dinah suddenly straightened up, and there was pride in her voice and in her demeanor. "I can't give it to you now . . . but in about six months I hope to give you a strong, handsome grandson."

And then Metus and Theodora knew true happiness. They came forward rejoicing and could not make enough over Dinah. Demetrius stood back watching them and saw the happiness that flooded his wife. He knew she had been apprehensive, but now he saw that she would be as much a favorite with his own parents as she was to her father. And he was glad!

"Look," Dinah said, "that silver road. It looks like it's going right up to the moon."

"Yes. It's beautiful, isn't it?" Demetrius said. He was standing with his arm around Dinah. They had come out after the meal for a moment before retiring. "What did you think of my parents?"

"They're so wonderful."

"They love you already. I can tell."

The two stood holding each other, and finally he said, "There's a spot down the coast where I want us to settle. I'll take you to it tomorrow. We'll build a house there and have our children there."

Dinah turned and put her hand on Demetrius's cheek. "You went a long way to find a wife. All the way to Canaan."

"But it was worth the trip." He kissed her then, and a thought came to him. "I found more than a wife in Canaan."

She looked at him in surprise. "What was that?"

"I found the true God."

They stood underneath the moon, the silver light flooding down upon them. They watched the path on the sea as it sparkled and glittered with the movement of the water. Suddenly a star made a silver track as it streaked across the sky, and the sea whispered.

"I had to become a slave to find the true God—and the woman that God had for me," Demetrius said. "But it was worth it."

Dinah laughed with exultation and embraced him. "Yes, and now we belong to each other."

"That's the kind of slavery I like." Demetrius laughed.

He kissed her, and the two stood gazing out at the sea. The night was brilliant with the light of the moon, and as the sea whispered its message, they knew they had come home and that their home was in each other and in God.

Gripping Fiction Based on the Life of Esther

From the pen of award-winning author Tommy Tenney, the age-old story of Esther blossoms into new life in this novel bursting with powerful truths. *Hadassah: One Night With the King* adapts the Esther saga as never before. Both palace thriller and Jewish woman's memoir, here is fiction with more layers of suspense and intrigue than you would ever think possible.

Hadassah: One Night with the King
by Tommy Tenney with
Mark Andrew Olsen

You'll Love This Heroine With a Heart for Justice

Following fast on the beloved SHANNON SAGA, Kit Shannon returns for more dramatic law cases, more romance, and more 1900s Los Angeles history. Engaged to a man who may be more than he appears and faced with some of the toughest cases in her life, Kit now must struggle to preserve her fight for justice against those who would stop her.

A Greater Glory by James Scott Bell
A Higher Justice

FICTION LOVERS WILL TREASURE THESE NOVELS!

⬧ BETHANYHOUSE
The Leader in Christian Fiction!